Praise for the novels of Emilie Richards

"I love settling down with a book by Emilie Richards, knowing I can turn myself over to her for a story that's both infinitely readable and emotionally deep. In *A Family of Strangers*, Emilie seamlessly mixes intrigue, romance and emotional drama as she puts family ties to the test with a protagonist you won't soon forget. You'll root for Ryan Gracey to do the right thing, even as you struggle along with her to determine what that right thing might be. A page-turner to the end!"
—Diane Chamberlain, *New York Times* bestselling author of *The Dream Daughter*

"*A Family of Strangers* is an absolutely riveting, thrilling read. I could not put it down. The suspense starts with the first line and does not let up until the last sentence. Emilie Richards writes electrifying family drama. There are deep emotions and startling secrets on every page. This one will keep you up all night."
—Jayne Ann Krentz, *New York Times* bestselling author

"I emerged at the last page as a better and more thoughtful person."
—Catherine Anderson, *New York Times* bestselling author, on *When We Were Sisters*

"Emilie Richards is at the top of her game in this richly rewarding tale of love and family and the ties that bind us all. *One Mountain Away* is everything I want in a novel and more. A must-buy!"
—Barbara Bretton, *New York Times* bestselling author

"Richards creates a heart-wrenching atmosphere that slowly builds to the final pages, and continues to echo after the book is finished."
—*Publishers Weekly* on *One Mountain Away*

"Emotional, suspenseful drama."
—*Library Journal* on *No River Too Wide*

"Portraying the uncomfortable subject of domestic abuse with unflinching thoroughness and tender understanding...[*No River Too Wide*] offers important insights into a far too prevalent social problem."
—*Booklist*

Also by Emilie Richards

THE SWALLOW'S NEST
WHEN WE WERE SISTERS

The Goddesses Anonymous Novels

THE COLOR OF LIGHT
NO RIVER TOO WIDE
SOMEWHERE BETWEEN LUCK AND TRUST
ONE MOUNTAIN AWAY

The Happiness Key Novels

SUNSET BRIDGE
FORTUNATE HARBOR
HAPPINESS KEY

The Shenandoah Album Novels

SISTER'S CHOICE
TOUCHING STARS
LOVER'S KNOT
ENDLESS CHAIN
WEDDING RING

THE PARTING GLASS
PROSPECT STREET
FOX RIVER
WHISKEY ISLAND
BEAUTIFUL LIES
SOUTHERN GENTLEMEN
"Billy Ray Wainwright"
RISING TIDES
IRON LACE

a family of
strangers

USA TODAY Bestselling Author

EMILIE RICHARDS

Recycling programs for this product may not exist in your area.

ISBN-13: 978-0-7783-0785-3

A Family of Strangers

For questions and comments about the quality of this book, please contact us at CustomerService@Harlequin.com.

BookClubbish.com

Printed in U.S.A.

For my brainstorming friends, Casey Daniels, Shelley Costa Bloomfield and Serena B. Miller. I'm not sure which is more important, our friendship or the ideas we share. I'm grateful for both.

a family of
strangers

CHAPTER ONE

What do alligators dream about?

I was four years old when I asked my sister that question. Wendy was home from college, introducing Bryce Wainwright, her future husband, to our parents. I liked him because Wendy seemed happy whenever he was in the room. The day we talked about alligators she seemed intrigued by my question.

"Fish," she said at last. "They dream about fish. Everything dreams about something smaller and weaker, whatever they don't have to be afraid of. Otherwise they'd never get any sleep."

"Sometimes I dream about alligators." I had lowered my voice in case my mother was lurking nearby. "Scary alligators."

"Then you'll have to grow up to be bigger than one." She lowered her voice, too. "Until you do, sleep with the light on."

Since our no-nonsense mother, Arlie Gracey, had already told me there were no alligators in the house, I knew she was unlikely to cooperate. But that night after Mom left me in darkness, my sister slipped into my room with a new night-light. When she plugged it in, the friendliest possible alligator grinned, and light beamed through a mouth not large enough to nip a finger. I was only four, but I never forgot the way Bryce smiled from the doorway as Wendy tucked the covers around my shoulders.

"See how much bigger you are than a silly old alligator, Ryan Rosie? Now you can dream about fish, too."

Wendy had assumed our mother would never throw away any gift she gave me. And she was right. The gator glowed for years until I was no longer afraid of the dark and dreamed of other things.

I know Wendy remembers that night, because for my last birthday she gave me an alligator clock. The smiling gator, two tones of bright green, clutches a fish—definitely smaller and weaker than he is—while another fish swings back and forth, waiting for his turn to be eaten.

Now, above my desk, the poor doomed fish was lulling me into memories of my sister. I had just consulted the clock—which routinely gains one minute per hour—because ten minutes ago, Wendy had texted me.

Privat call soon. B reddy. No 1 else.

As instructed, I was waiting, even though a party was getting started in the common area behind my shabby little duplex in Delray Beach, Florida. When the text arrived, I'd been enjoying a frosted mug of Cigar City Jai Alai and a plate of Sophie Synecky's grilled pierogies and kielbasa.

Now Sophie came inside to find me.

My duplex is tiny, which is why the crew for *Out in the Cold*, the podcast I'm lucky enough to produce and host, was celebrating outside after fighting for space in my cramped living room for two hours. My office is the smaller bedroom of two. With my desk, a chair, shelves and files, there's hardly room for air, but that never stops Sophie from barging in.

"Crew meeting was adjourned, Ryan. Work's over for the day and tomorrow's Sunday." Sophie is *Out in the Cold*'s administrator, researcher and coproducer. She's three sizes larger than she wants to be, and her long blond hair is turning gray, another attribute she dislikes but chooses not to address. Today she was wearing a voluminous flowered tunic over skintight white leggings. We both thought she looked fabulous.

"I'm expecting a call," I said. "It's personal."

As I spoke, the photo on my computer screen changed. A shot of my sister and me in bathing suits, arms around each other's waists, filled the space. There we were, me, short at five foot four, curling dark hair, squinting into the sun with my dimples in plain view, and Wendy, towering over me at five foot nine, her straight blond hair hanging over one shoulder, a smile lighting her face. Even the sun's glare couldn't stop Wendy from looking her best.

Looking at it now, I remembered the coconut-and-lime scent of our sunscreen, and later that evening, our mojitos. I remembered the sun on my shoulders and the air-conditioned bar where we went to get away from our parents. Wendy and I spent so little time together that those moments are etched in my memory.

Sophie always needs to know more. "Is the call about your father?"

I gave her "the look," which should have stopped her, but didn't. Her eyes lit up. "A man? Somebody I've met?"

I pointed to my office window, more like a porthole, where I could just see a Frisbee sailing back and forth in front of the communal laundry room. "The party's going to fade unless you get out there. You're the only one who can convince them to eat too much."

She made a noise low in her throat. It was the one she made when she conducted preliminary interviews for our podcast, and didn't believe the answers she was being fed.

Of course Sophie had many ways of getting to the truth. Now she pulled out guilt, a tool she manipulated with the precision of a top chef's boning knife. "It's not every week we get nominated for an award."

"Which is another reason you should be outside keeping energy high. That's a naturally suspicious bunch. Pretty soon they're going to come looking."

She gave up, something she never does on phone calls, and after she removed my clock from the wall and reset the time, she left me to wait alone.

The party, originally planned as a casual passing of cheap champagne around my living room, had morphed into a barbecue. This was all good. Something a bit more raucous was fitting for the year's final meeting of the talented crew that had created the first season of *Out in the Cold*.

Our podcast's stated mission was to take one cold case per season, warm it up again and bring it to the attention of the authorities. Apparently we hadn't done badly, which is why the meeting had turned into a celebration. Three days ago we had been nominated for a Webby for best documentary.

As if to remind me what I was missing, I heard shouts in the common area I shared with two other units. Before I came inside, the sound designer and recording engineer, as well as two editors and a fact-checker, had been grilling miscellaneous cuts of meat. The composer of our theme music, along with two production assistants, had been laying out salads and desserts. Several cops, a lawyer, and our personal technology wonk, had promised to stop in later. They had advised us during the countless hours when we'd been so depressed about the show's prospects that we had secretly honed our résumés.

I was itching to join everyone, but I was worried. Our father, Dale Gracey, who'd had bypass surgery six days ago, was due to come home from the hospital that afternoon. While I lived on the east side of the state, Wendy was staying on the west, just a few miles from our parents while her submarine commander husband was submerged—God knows where. It was possible she'd heard something I hadn't.

Wendy always gets the news first. When you grow up in the shadow of a much older sister, you learn not to protest. The flaws of an older child are bleached by time, while a younger's are always in plain view. When the older child is Wendy, who is good at nearly everything, the right daughter to help during a family crisis is obvious. I am either protected or overlooked. That's how we roll.

The one place where I beat Wendy hands down was the written word. Although she's now forty-five, judging from the text, my sister still couldn't spell. Of course it was possible abbreviations and misspellings were one and the same. But how would I know? Wendy started college the year I was born. By the time I was in kindergarten, she was learning to be the perfect navy wife. Wendy turned into a larger-than-life role model who popped in now and then to tell me how big I'd gotten, while proving, by her very existence, that I could never catch up.

At last, my cell phone blasted the opening notes of Carly Simon's "Older Sister."

"Hey." I waited, knowing that if I didn't, my next words would be swallowed.

For once she didn't hop right in. "Listen," she said after a pause, "this is serious. I need your help."

I'm suspicious of emotions, including my own, but I felt an unmistakable surge. Delight I was needed, countered by fear something unthinkable had happened. "Is it Dad?"

She fell silent again, but when she finally spoke she sounded surprised. "No. No, last I heard he was doing okay. I'm not in Florida. Remember?"

It was my turn to be surprised. When our father was catapulted into emergency bypass surgery last week, Wendy had been out of town traveling somewhere in the west for the development company that Dad built one rental property and vacation resort at a time. Wendy is Gracey Group's concierge and tour manager, and the story goes that as Dad was being wheeled into the operating room, he demanded that our mother tell her to continue the trip.

I was almost sure, though, that she had been scheduled to fly back to Seabank before he was released from the hospital today.

The details were a little foggy because I hadn't yet been home. The moment I'd learned about the surgery, I had offered to drive to Seabank, but Mom had insisted I stay put on Florida's Atlantic coast until Dad was ready for a real visit. In the meantime, Mom-of-Steel had continued to care for Wendy's young daughters, Holly and Noelle, while Wendy was away.

Now, even for her, taking care of the girls and a postsurgical patient was going to be impossible. My father was used to telling everyone else what to do. He was bound to be hell on wheels while he recovered.

I hoped I was worrying for nothing. "When do you get back?"

"That's the thing. I'm not coming home. I can't, and I don't know when I'll be able to. I need you to go back to Seabank and take care of the girls until things clear up for me."

"You're kidding." I really thought she might be.

"I don't want to go into detail. Can't you just trust me and do it?"

I paused, with no plan to restart until I made sense of her

request. Finally I said the only thing that occurred to me. "Look, this sounds crazy. You have to tell me more."

"Great. Thanks a lot." For the first time Wendy choked up, as if she was trying not to cry. "I'm in Phoenix. Okay? There was a murder last night, and I'm pretty sure the sheriff will think I'm involved. I need to disappear for a while until it's sorted out. Is that enough to get you moving?"

I tried to rearrange her words into sentences that didn't catapult our family into an unfamiliar dimension. "Murder?"

"Yes. Probably, anyway. Will you help?"

"You're not kidding, are you?"

"You got that right."

Stunned, I fell back on the advice I would have given anybody. "If you run they'll find you, and then you'll look doubly guilty. Talk to a lawyer and get advice on what to say, how and when. Do it right now. I can get you a referral."

"Don't you think I know what a huge mistake that would be? I listen to your podcast, Ryan. I was right there in that awful prison with that poor woman, the one who was sentenced for a crime she didn't commit. That's as close as I want to get to iron bars and a cellmate named Butch."

I wasn't sure which was more startling. That my sister was on the run, or that she listened to my podcast.

My heart was pummeling my chest. "If you see a lawyer, he or she won't turn you in. Attorney-client privilege, remember? They'll help you figure out the best thing to do. You don't have to take their advice. But it could save you a lot of time and hassle."

"Ryan..." She sniffed, and her voice vibrated. "I can't take a chance I'll be arrested. I know if I lay low long enough, the murderer will be found and then I can surface. But I don't know anything that will help, and there's no guarantee these local bozos know their way around a murder investigation.

Cops peg somebody for a murder right off the bat and stop looking. I don't want to be that somebody."

She was talking about a problem called confirmation bias, and she was right. Sometimes cops pegged a murderer early in the investigation, and from that point on they only looked for evidence that would prove they were right. "What do you need—"

But she was way ahead of me. "Drive to Seabank. Call Mom as soon as I hang up and give her some reason I didn't fly home this morning. But not the truth. That would kill Dad. Once you get there, take the girls back to the town house and stay with them until I'm able to come home. Can you do it? You can work in Seabank, can't you? They're in school during the day. And if you're there, you can help Mom if she needs you."

She made the trip sound like a cozy holiday. I pictured our family toasting marshmallows and singing "Now the Day Is Over." I could play cheerful auntie and give comfort to our mother, the same woman who wouldn't grab my hand if she was sinking in quicksand.

The whole idea was crazy. I hardly knew Holly and Noelle. When I was with them, they rarely spoke and always refused my invitations to swim in my parents' pool or collect shells on the beach.

I was such a bad aunt that I was usually relieved when they refused.

I tried once more to change her mind. "Are the authorities looking for you yet?"

"I don't think so."

"Then just come home. Please. Right now." My voice was growing shrill. "Drive to another city if you think you need to, and get a plane home from there. I mean it. It would be a big deal for a sheriff to arrest you in Florida and take you back to Arizona, unless he has an open and shut case. Maybe the navy will give Bryce leave so you can work this out together."

"Are you going to help or not?"

"What if I say no?"

"Then Mom's going to be alone with the girls. And she won't know why I'm not there, because I'm not calling her or anybody else. In five minutes I'm going to disappear." She drew in an audibly ragged breath. "This is the last call I'm making on my cell phone."

"What am I supposed to tell her?"

"You're the journalist. Come up with a story."

"Wendy—"

The line went dead. If I tried calling back, I knew she wouldn't answer. As far as Wendy was concerned, we were finished.

Where had she called from? I'd heard background noise as we spoke, cars passing on what might have been a highway. Last year after Wendy lost a cell phone, I'd helped her place a tracking app on her new one. Now I went through the steps to locate her, but the app had been disabled.

I zipped down to recent calls and hit Wendy's number just to be sure. I waited until I heard her voice again, but as I had predicted, this time the voice was a recording. She told me, in the sweetest, most genuine way, that she was sorry to miss my call, asked me to leave a message and wished me a good day.

Of course nothing about the recording was true. Wendy wasn't sorry to miss my call, and she'd made it clear there was no point in leaving a message.

Worst of all? I was pretty sure I wasn't going to have any good days, not a single one, in the near future.

CHAPTER TWO

I'm only a mediocre liar. Although Wendy graduated from Seabank High, our parents sent me to Catholic schools, my education culminating in an all-girls academy one town away. The nuns and lay teachers were as relentless as my mother, and I quickly learned they could spot any lie unless it had a large dollop of fact mixed in. Since lining up facts and bending them slightly is tedious, most of the time the truth is the easier path.

Unless I'm working.

Now I remembered that lesson as I tried to come up with a story to tell my mother. Mentally I listed facts I could use. Arlie Gracey adored her older daughter. She was sinfully proud of Wendy's accomplishments. Like my father, my mother also hoped that one day Wendy would take over the family business. Finally, she adored her grandchildren and wanted the best for them.

So far so good.

Then I listed facts I couldn't use. Wendy was afraid she was about to be arrested for murder. She wasn't coming home anytime soon because she planned to disappear. While she'd made her phone call to me from Phoenix, I had no idea where she planned to go from there.

Of course the facts I couldn't use were the ones Arlie would most want to hear.

I was still considering my story when my cell phone blasted Rachel Platten's "Fight Song," my tongue-in-cheek ringtone for Mom. I didn't want to answer until I had my story straight, but we had no time to spare.

I held the phone to my ear. "Mom." Just as I had with Wendy, I waited. She usually ran over me, too.

"Ryan Rose, have you heard from your sister?"

I'm named after Mom's mother, Rose Ryan, while Wendy is named after Dad's. Mom flipped my grandmother's names, for which I have always been grateful. Now I tried to form a mental image of the woman who had named me, molded me and driven me crazy far too many times.

Was she at the hospital waiting to bring my father home? Were they home already, in their bedroom, which was large enough for a family of ten? And where were the girls? I couldn't picture my nieces at all.

I cleared my throat. "We just got off the phone."

"What in the world is going on?"

I was digesting the fact that Mom had called *me*, despite knowing I was an unlikely choice. My sister and I only speak every month or two.

"There's a long list of other people I'd expect you to call first," I said, buying time.

She ignored that, which led me to believe she'd probably already called them. "She was supposed to fly home from California hours ago. The girls are at a Saturday field day at their school, but one of the teachers just called. Wendy didn't pick them up, and they're still waiting. I assumed she'd gotten home and headed straight over to watch them compete."

Clearly she was upset, since Wendy had been in Arizona, not California. "Are the girls okay?"

She continued as if I hadn't asked, and each word was louder than the one before. "I know her plane got in on time. I just checked the website. She knows I have to pick up your father today, and she's not answering her cell. The school wants to know what to do with my grandchildren." She paused and then said, loudest of all, "And why *would* she call you?"

I uttered my first lie. "She said she wasn't able to get hold of you."

"Nonsense. I've had the phone with me all afternoon."

"I don't know about that, Mom, but she didn't catch her flight, and she asked me to drive to Seabank and take care of the girls until she can make arrangements to come home."

"She called *you* and asked you to drive all that way, just for the hours it will take her to get another reservation?"

I skirted the truth. "I think there was more to it than she said. Whatever caused her to miss the flight seems complicated. She says she'll let us know more soon. Meantime, I said I'd drive over and stay with the girls until Wendy gets home."

"This isn't like her. Are you telling me everything?"

"She was in too much of a rush to go into detail."

"Do you have any idea how this affects us? Your father needs a quiet house and my complete attention. This morning his doctor told him that from now on he should eat a low-fat vegetarian diet. Preferably vegan. No dairy, no meat. Do you think I know how to prepare that kind of food? He's a steak and potatoes man. He thinks salads are rabbit food."

We both knew that if Dad had been eating rabbit food, he'd probably be out on the tennis courts right now instead of recovering from bypass surgery.

"I know it's major," I said. "That's why I'm happy to fill in for Wendy so you can devote yourself to kale and lima beans."

"You think this is funny?"

"Am I laughing? I know it's going to be hard on him and you. That's why—"

"Yes, I heard you. You're happy to drive here and care for the girls."

Just minutes ago Wendy had insisted I move my entire life across the state of Florida to take care of her daughters. On top of that I was supposed to lie to our parents. I understood my mother was feeling stressed, but so was I.

"I promised Wendy I would help," I said. "Would you prefer to handle it by yourself?"

"Of course not. I need you right this minute. I've never understood why you moved all the way to the other side of the state. You could have found a job near Seabank. And now, when I could use your help, you're four hours away."

"I offered to come and stay last week. You declined."

There was another silence. I was getting tired of them. Mine, hers, Wendy's. So many thoughts unspoken.

"When can you get here?" she asked at last.

"Not in time to pick up the girls, obviously. I have a party going on in my backyard. I have to pack. I have to assemble work to do while I'm there. It's going to be eleven or so before I arrive, and everybody will already be in bed."

"Then come tomorrow. I don't want you disturbing your father tonight."

"Can you manage until then? Can somebody else pick up Holly and Noelle?"

"You think schools today let just anybody make off with students? No. I'll have to go and keep your father waiting, because I don't have a choice. But he needs rest and quiet tonight. I don't see how I can make sure of it."

This kind of confession, and the slight tremor in her voice, were unheard-of, and I unbent a little. "I'm sorry, Mom. I really am. I wish I could sprout wings and fly, but since I can't, I'll just get there as fast as I can."

"I don't know why your sister called you."

"Maybe because I've had so much practice disappointing you." I hung up and went outside to find Sophie.

The party ended just before dark when clouds moved in, rain threatened, and my neighbors began to come home. The air felt unbearably heavy, and what breeze there was smelled of ozone. The crew straggled off a few at a time, and everyone except Sophie was gone by the time lightning split the sky and the downpour began.

As I packed, Sophie lounged on my bed, her laptop positioned so she could use the keyboard. At her feet was a growing mountain of jeans and T-shirts.

Nobody sets out to be a journalist for the money. My Honda Civic is old enough that no one would guess it's a distant cousin to newer models. My duplex is a rental. The last paint job faded before the brushstrokes dried; the windows don't seal, and my next door neighbor comes and goes on his Harley at all hours of the night. Still, I could never pay what it's worth.

Delray Beach is an expensive community, and this location is ideal. I can ride my bike along A1A or over to Atlantic Dunes Park where I can lie in the sand and listen to seagulls. Finding it wasn't luck. When he saw my first apartment, my father bought the three duplexes on this property, claiming they were a great investment, and immediately moved me into this one. I earn most of my rent by managing the others.

The wardrobe on my bed reflected the state of my finances. Earlier I found a dress at the back of the closet. Since it didn't look familiar, I guessed that my mother or Wendy had given it to me hoping I wouldn't embarrass them at some event. Now it was draped over a chair to add to the growing stack.

Several years ago Wendy had given me a peach-colored leather tote with myriad interior pockets, but now after a search, I located it on a closet shelf, speckled with mildew, the result of a particularly steamy summer and a faulty air conditioner. I settled for canvas bags a PR firm had created to advertise *Out in the Cold*'s first season. One set, the more popular, read, *You Can Run, But You Can't Hide* with the show's name beneath it. The other claimed, *There's Nothing Colder Than A Corpse*. We still have lots of that one stored away. I guess women don't want to be seen in public with "Corpse" stenciled on their shopping bags.

Now I opened one of the corpse bags and began to toss. "I need enough clothes to last a week." I was talking to myself and to Sophie if she wanted to listen.

Sophie looked up from her laptop. "You think you'll only be gone a week?"

"Wendy's town house has its own washer and dryer. Hopefully I won't be there long enough to fall in love with them."

"You're sure she said Phoenix?"

After the rest of the crew had gone, I'd filled Sophie in on the phone call with my sister. Being Sophie, she hadn't tried to sympathize or comfort me, knowing how much I would hate either. Instead she'd immediately begun to scour the internet.

The world might look at Soph and see a part-time grocery store cashier who likes to eat as much as she likes to cook. She favors the brightest colors and anything that sparkles, and she invites her ex-husband, Wayne, back into her life and kicks him out again on a regular schedule. All of that's true, but I look at her and see a good friend who happens to be an insomniac with an exceptional intellect who entertains herself by uncovering secrets.

Sophie is completely trustworthy. I never have to tell her how important it is not to share what she finds. This time I didn't have to tell her much at all. She knew immediately how best to help.

"She said Phoenix," I told her, "but my mother thought she was flying back from California. Maybe she was there first or planned to be later, or maybe Mom isn't thinking straight. Anyway, I'm assuming Wendy meant somewhere in the area. Greater Phoenix?"

"That could mean Mesa and Scottsdale. They call it the Valley of the Sun. So far nothing's turning up. Unless she was involved in a fight with the WetBack Power Gang. Two gang members' bodies were found last night in Chandler. Or maybe she was dressed as a red-haired man in a pickup truck and just kept going after she killed a pedestrian."

"Would everything that happened last night be online already?"

"Not for normal people." She looked up. "Tell me more about your sister."

Wendy was easy to describe. "She's beautiful, one of those classic blue-eyed blondes, like Grace Kelly or Margot Robbie. Tall, willowy, thin enough but never skinny. She wears expensive jewelry, expensive scent. She can talk to anybody about anything. She has all the social graces I forgot to learn."

"There's nothing wrong with your social graces."

We'd had the same mother, Wendy and me, although my version had been older and less focused. Still, Arlie Gracey couldn't be faulted. I had just preferred not to be in situations where I always had to be on my best behavior.

As I began to load sandals and athletic shoes into another bag, I realized how little I'd told Sophie about my sister, probably because Wendy had so often overshadowed me. "She was one of Seabank High's golden girls. You know, homecoming princess, member of the national Honor Society, a star in the drama department. She planned to act professionally, but she met Bryce in her second year of college and married him in her third. When she got around to finishing her education, she changed to marketing."

"If she has all those attributes, she was probably a whiz."

"I don't know. She didn't work much at first. Bryce is a fast-track submarine commander, and they traveled a lot."

"Kids?"

Obviously I'd been remiss in mentioning my nieces, too. "Two girls, Holly and Noelle, eight and six. Guess what month they were born?"

"Somebody climbed out of his sub and swam to shore around March?" I smiled. "Christmas babies, but not until Wendy was in her late thirties. I don't know if she and Bryce had trouble conceiving—my mother did. More likely she was just waiting until they could settle down. Wendy looks like Mom, and Noelle looks like Wendy. I favor my father's family, dark hair, brown eyes, shorter and wiry. Holly looks a little like me and a whole lot like her dad."

"You know I have two girls. They're out of the house now, but when they were young I would never have disappeared and left them, not unless I had one hell of a reason."

"Judging from our call, she thinks she has one."

Sophie kept her cashier's job at least partly so she could hob-nob with strangers and sharpen her investigative skills. Now she used her expertise. "If I'd asked you yesterday if your sister was the kind of person who might run away and leave a mess for someone else to clean up, would you have said 'of course'?"

"The thing is, I don't think Wendy's ever made a mess. She set the standards in our family, and they were high. Sky high."

"That's a hard act to follow."

I clutched a flip-flop to my chest. "Growing up I realized I would never be anywhere near as perfect as she was. I remember feeling so relieved, so I stopped trying and just lived my life." The flip-flop went into a bag, and I examined my collection of running shoes. "It worked out. I'm happy."

"Is she?"

That stumped me. Wendy and I never talked about feelings, except the most superficial. We might admit we were afraid Dad's surgery wouldn't go well, but we would never discuss the way we felt about him.

"While you're home mull that over," Sophie said. "If she was trying to change her life, it might have prompted this situation. Maybe she was somewhere she shouldn't have been, doing something with someone she shouldn't have been with, for instance."

That felt wrong, but having a friend who wasn't involved was helpful, and I didn't want to stop her. "I hope I won't have time to mull. I hope she'll figure this out and come home before I have to tell my mother the truth."

"Maybe she'll change her mind and tell your mother herself before you even get there. Any chance?"

To save face Wendy could dance around details, but lying outright would be new—although next to being accused of murder, lying seemed incidental.

"I don't think she'll tell her," I said. "Not until she can tell her the whole truth."

"But she doesn't mind if you lie?"

I shrugged. "I doubt she's thinking straight right now. She's going on instinct."

"I know you want this to go away fast, Ryan, but wouldn't Wendy just ask your mom to soldier on a bit longer if she thought that was a possibility?"

I tried to think like my sister. "She knows Mom's going to be busy with Dad. She's probably trying to spare her right away."

"Does she ask for your help very often?"

"A couple of times at my parents' house she's asked me to keep an eye on the girls. But my nieces are well-behaved. It's not like they were going to fall in my parents' pool or run into the street. They watch TV or color. That's about it."

"But what she's asking now *is* a big deal." Sophie closed the laptop.

I knew she wasn't done helping me, but I had to be sure. "You'll keep searching for a murder that fits? I know it's a lot to ask, but I'd be grateful."

She looked offended. "You couldn't stop me."

"If nothing turns up, maybe you should branch out to the rest of Arizona."

"Don't worry. I'll widen the circle a little at a time. What work are you taking with you?"

Out in the Cold's next season had to be a priority. Sophie and I were gathering and reading information on promising cold cases, looking for the right one to feature next. We'd screened out almost a hundred so far, and more recently we'd rejected two dozen or so suggested by crew, consultants and saddest of all, families still hoping to discover the truth about a loved one's death. It was time to zero in.

I listed what I planned to bring along, finishing quickly. "Most of what I need is on my laptop, but I'll bring the files I haven't had time to look at yet. You and I can send info back and forth, like we always do."

"Do you have meetings you'll miss? Do you need me to take them for you?"

"I think I can do all of them by phone, unless Sebastian wants a sit-down." Sebastian Freiman is the podcast's executive producer, which means he forks over whatever money we need to stay on the air, and most of the time leaves us alone. But soon it would be time for a meeting to discuss whatever idea Sophie and I settled on.

"You'll have to come back and take that one." Sophie wasn't intimidated by Sebastian, as much as she was mystified. She'd grown up in poverty, while Sebastian was rich enough that

Out in the Cold was nothing more than a hobby, like his collections of antique cars or his forty-foot yacht.

"I can come back for a day if I need to," I said. "My mother can manage the girls short-term. She can hire help if she has advance notice."

"No matter what, it's going to be hard. Your mom's no spring chicken."

Wendy had been born when Mom was almost thirty, and I had been born when she was forty-five, the proverbial change of life baby. Now she was seventy-three.

"Yeah, she deserves better." I slapped one final running shoe into the bag. "Then there's Dad. I don't know what this thing with Wendy will do to him. So I need to keep this to myself as long as I can."

"Which won't be long." Sophie stood and stretched. "You know I'll do whatever I can on this end. If you need more, just holler."

I wished I didn't need her, that I had friends at the ready in the town where I grew up. But that wasn't true. Unlike my popular sister, as a girl I'd had only a few close friends, none of whom had stayed in Seabank. A colleague or two from my internship at the *Seabank Free Press* might still be around, but I hoped to avoid them.

The face of the one friend who'd remained in town flashed through my mind. Just as quickly, I shoved away the image of Teo Santiago, the man whose life I had changed forever, and not for the better.

I walked Sophie to the door, and she gave me a quick hug. The sun had just gone down and what clouds remained billowed along the plum-streaked horizon.

The storm had passed quickly, as coastal storms often do. I wondered what storms I could expect in the future.

CHAPTER THREE

After I left for college, my parents sold the house where I had been raised and moved to an exclusive gated community. Gulf Sands borders the Gulf of Mexico, although almost every grain of sand is covered by thick mats of grass and blooming shrubs. My parents' house sits back from the water, elevated to avoid floods and protected by a blue tile retaining wall. Just below, a patio bordered by St. Augustine grass leads out to the seawall and dock. The house itself is two story, with acres of glass on the first floor looking over the infinity pool and a lanai furnished with tasteful all-weather wicker.

The property is too valuable to be truly private, but my parents' home sits at a point, so views of neighbors are limited. Inside, travertine floors gleam, and Tommy Bahama furnishings adorn the great room, which borders a kitchen with golden granite countertops and natural maple cabinetry. While my mother and I share few interests, we both like to cook. This kitchen is twice the size of the one in Sea Palms, but I doubt Mom uses it half as much.

The upstairs bedroom suites have views of the gulf, but

luckily for my father, the master suite is downstairs. While the master doesn't look over the water, French doors open to a shady walled courtyard, complete with tubs of flowers and a fountain. I hoped that Dad would feel well enough soon that he could enjoy the beautiful November weather there.

About noon I parked my Civic in the circular driveway, unlocked the front door and let myself inside. I listened for voices. If children were present, they were silent children, which perfectly described my nieces. I found my mother closing the master suite door behind her, and I didn't speak, not wanting to disturb my father.

When she saw me, Mom frowned and motioned for me to follow her through the great room and outside to one of several tables on their expansive lanai. Our entire family can be outside at the same time and never have to talk to each other.

My mother looked exhausted. She is still blond, although her hairdresser has worked that particular magic on her layered bob for decades now. She's never weighed more than a pound she shouldn't, never gone out into the sun without protection, never attended fewer than three exercise classes a week. She uses makeup skillfully and daily, favors classic sporty attire and believes that diamonds are everyday wear. Today a wire bracelet set with several sparkled at her wrist, and one-carat studs sparkled in her earlobes. In contrast her eyes had no sparkle at all.

"Where are Holly and Noelle?" I wondered if I'd missed a call and my sister had come back to get them.

"The Millers have a niece who babysits. She took them to the dog park."

I waited for an explanation. When none arrived, I shrugged. "Did Wendy acquire a dog and you're taking care of that, too?"

"No, the niece has a dog. The girls lit up when Tina brought Oodles to meet them. They were so excited."

I had never witnessed excitement from either of my nieces, so I was sorry I'd missed it. "How are they doing? More important, how's Dad?"

"He's wondering where your sister is. What have you heard?"

Mom hadn't wasted time getting to Wendy, but I couldn't blame her. "Nothing more than I've told you."

"You didn't tell me enough."

"I told you all I could. And before you ask, of course I've tried calling her. But even her voice mail is down." Down as in "disconnected," something I didn't add.

"And all she told you was that the problem was complicated, and she would get back to you?"

I didn't answer directly. "I realize that's not much. I'm sorry. I wish she'd walk in and tell us what happened. But she made it sound like that might not happen for a while."

"None of this is like her."

"So tell me how Dad is."

"He has the same heart condition as Bill Clinton. You remember him?"

I didn't laugh, although the fact she'd asked struck me as funny. "Not personally, no. But I did graduate from college, and I voted for Hillary."

"Unless your father changes his lifestyle, everything will clog up again. When he said he had no intention of becoming a vegetarian, his cardiologist asked him if he had a will, and offered to call a lawyer."

I whistled softly. "Hardball. What else?"

"Exercise. An absence of stress."

I couldn't imagine how we could pull off that last one until Wendy was home again and taking more responsibility for Gracey Group. I got to my feet. "It's lunchtime. Will you let me fix you a sandwich? You can rest while I do."

"It's been so nice having Wendy nearby. I've been counting on her help with your father. I hope she resolves whatever the problem is quickly."

I felt like something Mom had reluctantly fished out of the recycling bin, but I repeated my question.

"No, I'll come with you, and we can get lunch ready for the girls, too. You'll want to feed them before you take them back to the town house. You'll be comfortable there. Wendy's enjoyed it."

When Wendy moved to Seabank from Connecticut, where she and Bryce own a showy Colonial, I wondered why. At the time neither of my parents were ill, so they didn't need help. In fact, Wendy had claimed that with Bryce at sea, she was the one who needed it. Since she was traveling more for Gracey Group, she'd wanted my parents to keep the girls while she was away.

Instead of moving into their home in Gulf Sands, Wendy had asked if she and the girls could move into a roomy town house on the other side of Seabank that Dad owned as one of many investments. The town house, which commands a steep rent, was between tenants, so Dad had agreed.

Since my father owns my duplex, I certainly couldn't question his generosity to my sister, and now there was a hidden bonus. While I was serving out my time as my nieces' babysitter, I wouldn't have Mom looking over my shoulder.

In the kitchen I took bread, sliced turkey, cheese from the refrigerator. "What do the girls like for lunch?" I poked my head around the door, hands full. "Peanut butter? Soup?"

"Grilled cheese. Plain. American cheese. White bread."

I made a face. "Can they be trained?"

"I hope you won't have enough time to try."

Those were my sentiments exactly. I set food on the counter and dove back in for my mother and me, coming up with ham and mustard. "Has Dad eaten?"

"Last night for dinner I made whole wheat pasta with chopped tomatoes and basil. He ate three bites and said he wasn't hungry. I served it again today for lunch. He didn't like it any better."

My mother has always been determined to plow straight through the worst life has to offer. Even her recreational choices reflect that. She raises money for foster children, serves on a county committee studying homelessness, and participates in local pro-life marches. Still, since I knew her so well, today I heard the mixture of concern and annoyance in her voice.

"I bet you'd like some help with meal prep," I said. "I'll find some vegan recipes and see what I can do. Maybe the girls like to cook, too."

She was silent so long I thought she'd blown me off, but she finally sighed, a sound I rarely heard. "Holly and Noelle don't seem to like much, Ryan. Maybe they feel strange with us since we've never lived in the same town. But I remember you and your sister at their ages. Wendy was busy making friends. You were always outside doing something. Trying to build a fort. Kicking a soccer ball. In the pool. You loved books. I was at the library practically every other day to keep you supplied. By the time you were Holly's age, you'd already cooked your first meal. All by yourself."

I was surprised by the recital, and more surprised she remembered the meal. "Macaroni and cheese and sliced tomatoes. And it wasn't quite by myself. You insisted on draining the macaroni. I was furious."

"And I'd do it again." She almost smiled. "You made ice cream sandwiches for dessert."

"Chocolate ice cream between oatmeal cookies."

"I don't think the girls would do any of those things. Don't be disappointed. They're good children." She paused. "But they aren't fun to have around."

I didn't know what to say.

Mom looked up and saw my expression. "I may be their grandmother, but I'm not blind to who they are. Wendy's absence is going to weigh on them, especially Noelle. She's at that age where she worships her mother. You'll have to keep things running smoothly while your sister's gone. They'll need nutritious meals, a schedule they can count on, assistance with their homework, early bedtimes. Their booster seats are in my car, and you'll have to move them to yours. But they can get themselves in and out and use the seat belts."

My warm feelings had evaporated. "I realize I don't have children, but I think I can figure out how to take care of Wendy's."

"You might be surprised how hard it is to take care of anybody's children. Even your own."

"I'll probably never find out."

"No man on the horizon?"

The question came out of nowhere, more surprising since she had so many other things on her mind. "I work closely with several," I said. "One's gay, one's married, one's going through a breakup and doesn't like women at the moment and won't for a while."

"Don't women your age hang out in bars looking for Mr. Right?"

"Women my age also sleep with strangers they pick up on the street, but that doesn't mean I find the idea attractive."

"I raised you right."

"Are you kidding? As far as men go, you didn't raise me at all. Wendy had to tell me about sex. I thought it was a joke."

"She thought you were ready, and I didn't. I would have done it better, if I'd had the chance."

"Her version worked wonders. I wouldn't let a guy near me for years." I laughed. "Of course that wore off."

"I don't want to hear this part."

"No chance you will." The front door opened, and we both heard the clatter of feet followed by a sharp, high bark.

"Just remember," my mother said, "first Holly and Noelle lost their father, and now they've lost their mother. At that age, temporary feels like forever. Be kind to them."

"I'll do my best."

My mother's expression said it all. She wasn't a bit sure that my best was going to be good enough. Sadly, neither was I.

CHAPTER FOUR

"They have so many flavors. Peanut butter chocolate chunk. Raspberry coconut swirl. Lemon meringue."

I finished reading the list off the signboard and glanced down at the two little statues beside me. I was sure eight-year-old Holly could read. And while six-year-old Noelle probably couldn't read well, she could certainly listen to the flavors available at Creamworks, an ice cream shop halfway between my parents' house and the town house.

Although the name was new, along with the more unusual flavors, the pleasantly rundown shop was much the same as it had been when I was little. As I'd read, I had skipped the oddest possibilities. I didn't think my nieces were in the market for Gotcha Sriracha or Faking Bacon.

"So what will it be?" I asked. When they didn't answer, I gave an example. "I'm going to try pumpkin praline." Thanksgiving, that land mine for both normal and dysfunctional families, was safely behind us, but clearly Creamworks hadn't run out of the holiday's prime flavors.

"I don't like pumpkin." Noelle, a miniature Wendy with

blond hair halfway down her back and a winning smile, wasn't smiling now. She stamped one rhinestone-encrusted flip-flop on the ground, and folded her little arms in front of the ruffled pink shirt that matched her polka-dot capris.

I wondered if the girls would feel more comfortable with me if I had visited more since their move to Seabank. Maybe if I had, I would have sensed a problem with Wendy, too, something in her life she needed to talk about. Unfortunately, the only thing I could do for my sister now was buy ice cream for her daughters.

"You don't have to have pumpkin, Noelle." I pointed at the sign. "They have more than a dozen flavors you can choose from. I just read them to you. Did you hear anything you might like?"

"She eats vanilla," Holly said.

Holly was a head taller than her sister, with long brown hair and eyes as dark as my own, along with her father's widow's peak. I had never seen a winning smile on my niece's face. Holly was perpetually solemn, with lips that sagged between a pout and a grimace. Apparently that had never stopped Wendy from buying her expensive girly clothing. Holly's outfit matched Noelle's, only in yellow.

"Vanilla, then," I said, sorry that I'd thought bringing them to Creamworks was a good way to get to know them. "How about you?"

She shrugged. "I don't care."

"Do you like peanut butter?"

"No."

"Lemonade?"

"No."

"Vanilla?"

She shrugged again. I ordered vanilla cones for both girls, along with my more exotic choice.

When the cones arrived, Noelle carefully wrapped two napkins around hers. Holly, more daring, wrapped one. I grabbed a napkin for mine, just in case, and led them outside to an iron bistro table, packed tightly among half a dozen like it.

"Vanilla doesn't stain," Noelle said before she began to rotate the cone and carefully lick away any drip that might make it past the bundled napkins.

Wendy's voice emerging from a six-year-old was disquieting. I wondered if Noelle was parroting a dictate, thus the root of the vanilla fetish. Since I wasn't their mother, I couldn't criticize my sister. For all I knew, the ice cream mandate had come about after an entire wardrobe of little girl clothes had been ruined by Persimmon Cinnamon and Banana Manna stains.

"This is so good." I held up my cone in demonstration. "How's yours?"

Noelle was too busy battling drips to answer. Holly shrugged again.

I tried a different topic. "So how's school, Holly? Do you like your teacher?"

I was treated to shrug number three. I tried a question she had to answer with actual words. "What's your teacher's name?"

This precipitated a world-weary sigh. "Mrs. English."

"How about you, Noelle? What's your teacher's name?"

"Her name is Mrs. English, too," Holly said.

"How unlikely is that?" I smiled. "Are they sisters?" I winced as I realized I'd asked another shruggable question and immediately got my comeuppance. "You don't know?" I winced again because, let's face it, I wasn't catching on very quickly.

I tried once more, thinking carefully first. "So two Mrs. Englishes. Noelle, what color hair does your Mrs. English have?" I held up a finger as Holly began to answer. "This question is for Noelle."

"Blue," Noelle said between careful licks.

"Really?"

Noelle blinked, as if she couldn't believe I had doubts.

"Is it blue?" I asked Holly.

She shrugged.

"Let's talk about your mom."

"Why?" Holly said.

Surprised, I searched her face, only to find her expression hadn't changed. "Well, because you're probably worried, right? I just wanted you to know that I talked to her yesterday, and she sounded fine. She's anxious to come back as soon as she can."

Holly took two bites of her cone before she spoke. "Gram can take care of us."

"No, she can't. Not right now. She's taking care of Grandpa. That's why I'm here."

"Does Daddy know?"

I made an educated guess. "I don't think your mommy wants to bother him while he's on his submarine."

Nothing else was forthcoming. I knew they must have questions, but if so, they weren't going to ask me.

"Your mommy told me to take good care of you." It wasn't quite true, but I was sure that Wendy would have remembered if she hadn't been in the middle of Arizona trying to escape the police. Or California. Or...somewhere.

"Can you braid my hair?" Noelle suddenly looked more interested in me. "Mommy can."

At the moment my hair curled just past my collar, as long as it had ever been. I tried to sound optimistic. "I bet I can learn."

Nobody seemed impressed.

We finished in silence. When their cones were a memory,

both girls were as clean as they'd been before their first lick. I, on the other hand, had ice cream puddling between my fingers. I snatched more napkins inside and scrubbed my hands on the way to the car.

I wondered about groceries. Had Wendy left anything in the refrigerator that was still good to eat? One stop with my nieces had convinced me we didn't need another. I wanted to get them home and turn them loose. I wondered what they did when they were alone with Wendy, and I hoped there were plenty of toys and art supplies. If I was lucky, they could escape to hiding places I would never find.

The town house sat in an ungated community of probably sixty like it called Tropicana. The architect had possessed the good sense not to design exact look-alikes, which cut down substantially, I was sure, on residents trying to enter strange homes after socializing at the local happy hour. Each group of six was a different earth tone, and while the footprint was the same, with garages fronting the street and living quarters behind, the setback created privacy. Tropicana's landscaping was mature and individual, with live oaks nestled by walkways, and palms and brightly colored croton adding visual interest.

I followed my mother's directions and parked in front of an end unit. I could see why my father had purchased this property. The community was well kept and blooming with carefully tended perennials and shrubs. The area behind the houses was wooded and undeveloped. The end unit was surprisingly private, with a wide lawn on the side ending in more woods. The town house would be in high demand as a rental, especially in the winter when snowbirds flew down from the frozen north to soak up Florida sunshine.

Since Wendy's car was parked at the airport, her garage was probably empty. At the moment I didn't plan to retrieve her car, even if I found an extra key, because I was still optimistic that she'd need it soon. In the driveway I got out of my Civic to punch in the garage door code my mother had given me. Undoubtedly the remote was waiting for my sister at the airport, too.

Inside the garage I began to unload my canvas bags on the passenger side. "Girls, get whatever you took to Gram's and put it back in your room."

I expected grumbling, but they were silent. I watched as they each took one small thing and started toward the door.

"You can carry more than that, right?" I had three bags under one arm and two under the other. I looked behind me and saw they were making faces at each other. I was encouraged. It was the most normal thing I'd ever seen them do.

I made a face, too, but not so they could see. "Each of you bring in one more thing. You're strong. Like Wonder Woman."

The door opened into a narrow mudroom leading into the kitchen, with a half bath tucked to one side. The kitchen was medium-size and standard issue, with a greige tile floor and plenty of white cabinets over gray laminate counters, along with a small jutting peninsula furnished with two black metal stools. A louvered door hinted at a pantry, while the farthest counter fronted on a small dining area. Beyond that a screened porch looked over a wide yard and the woods behind.

"Hey, this is nice." The town house was more upscale than my duplex in Delray, even though mine had midnight sound effects by Harley-Davidson. I was guessing that most of the residents in this development had given up their motorcycles for golf carts.

Neither girl responded, something I was fast getting used to.

On my second trip inside, with the two girls trailing with more bags, I took a better look through the downstairs. The house looked clean enough, but cluttered. Papers were piled on counters, as well as end tables in the great room. That room itself was large and open, with a vaulted ceiling sporting dual skylights. The laminate floor was home to two sea-grass rugs dotted with sofas and chairs and a square glass coffee table, also covered with papers. I didn't see anything that would indicate children lived here except, possibly, a large screen television with a basket of remotes beside it. I wasn't worried. Judging from at least one of the bags they'd reluctantly brought inside, they'd taken games and stuffed animals with them to my parents' house.

"Do you girls usually play in your room?"

Neither answered. I was catching on. In the future I would have to single out one of them by name.

"Run upstairs and put your things away," I said. "I'll be up in a minute."

As I watched them trudging up the staircase, I tried to dredge up Mom's lecture on my childcare duties. I was to make sure Holly and Noelle had nutritious meals, schedules, and early bedtimes. That was easy, since it sounded like a replay of my own childhood. I wondered if multiple charts were required here, too.

In the kitchen I opened the refrigerator to see that the shelves were almost empty except for condiments, a tub of cheap margarine—hadn't Wendy gotten the memo about the dangers of hydrogenated fat?—half a carton of eggs and most of a loaf of white sandwich bread that would probably look fresh and perky until Doomsday.

What I'd guessed was a pantry was actually the home of the stacked washer and dryer. The cupboards yielded little. I found a few basics, like sugar and salt, canned tomatoes, tuna and green beans. Wendy either cooked and planned so diligently she'd used up everything before her trip, or Wendy never cooked.

A peek inside a drawer by the stove answered that question.

A stack of menus took up the valuable real estate where spatulas and whisks should have resided. Since this wasn't the take-out mecca of Manhattan, most of these menus featured pizza.

I leaned against the refrigerator. "I guess I know what we're having for dinner."

The girls only liked cheese pizza with nothing added, which was no surprise. Nor was I surprised at their lack of enthusiasm for cleaning up afterward.

Now, though, my nieces were freshly showered, dressed in frilly white nightgowns from a drawer filled with more frilly nightgowns in cotton-candy colors, and ready to be tucked into bed.

Tucking in was a mystery of sorts. I thought back to my parents' bedtime rituals. After extensive prayers at my bedside, Mom would read a short book, or when I was older, one chapter of a longer one. The lives of saints were her favorites, complete with carefully muted details about the horrifying ways they had died. It's not easy being saintly.

Bedtime with Dad was very different. If he happened to be home early, he always tossed me into bed and mumbled prayers at lightning speed. Then he sat on the edge and told me stories about a little girl—coincidentally named Ryan—who took spectacular journeys to faraway places on a magic carpet.

Holly and Noelle's room was small, with beds against opposite walls. Tonight I sat on Noelle's and scooted to the bottom, so I could see them both. I had given up bedtime prayers years ago and doubted that Wendy, an Easter-and-Christmas Christian, engaged in this ritual. But I knew I'd better ask.

"Would you like to say your prayers together? And this is a yes or no question." I cocked my head and waited.

Holly turned away from me, answer enough. "Noelle?" I asked.

"You do it."

An answer of any kind was a surprise. Three whole words were a miracle. Of course now I was in trouble. I cleared my throat and knew enough to keep it short.

"Let's close our eyes." I considered what must be troubling them the most and began. "Dear Lord, we thank You for all the blessings in our lives, and tonight we ask that You watch over us and those we love, especially Dale Gracey, who is recovering from surgery, and Wendy and Bryce Wainwright, who are far away and missing their daughters."

I didn't know what else to say. My problems with prayer had just surfaced. Prayers aren't always answered the way we want them to be. These little girls were a bit young for theological explanations, so I didn't want to promise something that might not come true. Dad's future health was in question. Bryce was at sea in a nuclear sub, and Wendy was running from the sheriff. Keeping them all safe under those circumstances was a tough job.

I did my best. "We know that You see everything we can't, and so we trust in Your loving care." I ended by crossing myself and repeating the standard words. "In the name of the Father…"

Noelle was staring at me when I opened my eyes. "Will that work?"

Holly turned over. "Noelle, be quiet."

I ignored Holly and remembered how a nun from my childhood had answered every question we ever put to her. "We can only ask. The rest is up to God."

"We want to go to sleep," Holly said.

The girls were talking to me. It wasn't a prize-winning conversation, or even a friendly one, but they were proving they had a vocabulary.

"I could read you a story. Or tell you one. Would you like that?"

As if they'd choreographed their movements, both girls turned on their sides. I took that as a no and wished them good-night, but I didn't kiss them. I wasn't sure it was safe.

I turned off the light and immediately a night-light by the door, a fairy with gossamer wings, clicked on to keep them company. It was no alligator, but it would do.

When I'd come upstairs to carry my own things into Wendy's bedroom, I had discovered the play area. At the head of the stairs, a wide loft bordered the bedrooms and the girls' bathroom. Shelves with colored cloth bins lined one wall, and games and toys peeked out of several. A tall dollhouse with furniture—and grinning fifties-era white people—occupied one corner. A child-size table adorned the other, and a small bookshelf with maybe a dozen children's books stood outside the bathroom. Everything seemed to be exactly where it should be.

Since I hadn't found another set of sheets in the linen closet, I stopped by the master bedroom and stripped off the ones on Wendy's bed. The master bedroom was larger than the one that the girls shared, and unlike the downstairs, orderly, except for a corner desk piled with more papers.

As the sheets washed, I did a final check to be sure everything was locked up for the night. The house was in good condition, but it needed minor maintenance. A light switch cover hung from one screw. Several bulbs were burned out in the great room ceiling. Hinges on one kitchen cabinet needed to be adjusted. And when I got to the front door, I noticed it didn't close properly. I shoved it hard with my hip and held it in place, but even then, neither the knob lock or the dead bolt would turn. Someone had rigged up a cheap hook latch instead, but one good kick to the door would unseat it.

Tropicana was surrounded by other middle range develop-ments, and most likely the local crime rate was low. Still, snowbirds hadn't begun to return, and many neighboring houses would be empty until after Christmas. I was surprised Wendy was so relaxed about security.

As a child, I had loved being Dad's assistant when repairs were needed. Consequently, I wasn't too bad at simple car-pentry and plumbing. I'd noticed a toolbox in the garage, so now I went to find a screwdriver.

Fifteen minutes later I made a note to call my mother about a new knob and dead bolt, because these were beyond redemp-tion. Gracey Group probably had a list of service providers. I wedged a chair under the doorknob, turned on the security alarm and went back to the garage to finish emptying the car and retrieve my laptop.

The girls had taken up my time, but not my thoughts. All afternoon I'd made mental notes about finding my sister. So-phie was looking, and she could find almost anything. At the same time I had to check for myself, in case something un-usual jumped out at me.

I logged on and did a quick search of general news sites for crimes in Arizona. Then I searched for the names of all the major newspapers in the state and methodically visited those that had websites I could access. Two hours later I hadn't found anything promising.

Because of our age difference, Wendy and I had never shared friends, so there was no one I could call to question. Besides, I doubted my sister was calling old pals and giving away her location. The same with our few living relatives, who were all as distant on the family tree as they were in miles.

I started a file for a list of things I could do next. Searching the town house was a long shot, since whatever had happened, wherever it had happened, probably had nothing to do with anything Wendy had left behind. Still, a search had to be made. I was sure I wouldn't find my sister's laptop, because she traveled with it, but I could look through the stacks of papers littering the downstairs and Wendy's desk, even though a quick shuffle had turned up nothing more than household bills, high-end fashion catalogs and Gracey Group memos. Again I suspected anything relevant—if such a thing existed—was in Wendy's possession.

Six items later I called Sophie. She answered immediately.

We were used to dispensing with preliminaries. "Any luck?" I asked.

"Nothing. Nada. Is it possible that the body hasn't been found yet?"

This was the type of conversation we often had, only usually, we had it about murders that were committed years ago.

"Anything's possible," I said. "She told me so little."

"I searched for missing persons, too, but you know how that goes. Maybe whoever it is hasn't been reported missing. Or they have been, but the authorities are waiting some number of days or hours before they fill out a report. Can you ask your mother for more information about your sister's trip?"

"I'm going to try."

"You know, you're going to have to tell her something more concrete soon. If Wendy really is a murder suspect, the sheriff or the police, whoever has jurisdiction where it was committed, may well be calling your parents."

I got up and walked to the door looking over the porch, and stared into the night. "I can't imagine what I'll say."

"Yeah, me either. I'll give it some thought."

"Maybe we'd better widen the search to the whole state. And then move over to California. That's where Mom thought Wendy was, unless she's just so rattled she doesn't know one state from the other."

"How easily does she rattle?"

"How often does she almost lose her husband and then her daughter?"

"I'll widen."

We hung up. I moved the sheets into the dryer and hoped that soon, Wendy would be standing in the kitchen washing and drying them all over again so she could move back into her bedroom.

I remembered my prayer. I hoped somebody upstairs had been listening.

CHAPTER FIVE

The girls' school was only two blocks from the town house. My mother had jotted instructions and directions, covering everything I needed to get them to their classes by eight-thirty the next morning.

Despite that, my cell phone jolted me awake at seven. Mom wanted to be sure the girls were up, that I had picked out their clothes and helped them dress. The list went on. Was I cooking a healthy breakfast—with what Wendy had in her kitchen?—and had I made lunches—same question. I should make sure their homework was still in their backpacks. Once they were safely in school, I was to stop by the office to sign papers making me the official contact while Wendy was away. Mom would call to assure the school I was legit.

"Any questions?" she asked once the to-do list was complete.

I was surprised she hadn't told me to time the girls with my stopwatch as they brushed their teeth. "How's Dad this morning?"

"I made him a banana–almond milk smoothie for breakfast."

"In other words, not good."

"He will adjust."

I felt even sorrier for Dad than I had before the phone call.

Since I was awake I went into the girls' room. Why should they sleep when I couldn't? They both sat up, groggy-eyed, long hair tangled from what must have been a restless night.

I put on my brightest smile, the one that turned normal dimples into canyons. "Time to get up, sleepyheads. Do you need help picking out your clothes?"

They both stared at me. Either they thought I was crazy to assume they couldn't pick out their own, or crazy to assume they could. Since I couldn't tell, I smiled again. "See you in the kitchen in a few minutes."

I dressed quickly, then padded barefoot downstairs, turning over breakfast possibilities as I went. I had bread, I had eggs, and while there was no milk or syrup, I'd found honey with the other basics. So I melted margarine, asking forgiveness from the nutrition gods, and made French toast using eggs and water, finishing with diluted honey as a topping. While the toast cooked, I assembled two bagged lunches.

By the time breakfast was ready, the girls still weren't downstairs, so I trooped back and found them sitting exactly where I had left them.

"Up, and dressed." I clapped my hands, so reminiscent of my mother that I flinched. "What do you want to wear?"

Holly slung herself to the floor, and shrugged.

"Your bathrobe? A bathing suit?"

Noelle actually giggled. Holly stared at her through narrowed eyelids. "I don't care."

"Pick something." I turned to Noelle. "Want some help?"

At the dresser closer to her bed, I opened a drawer and held up a pink shirt with purple hearts. Pink was no surprise. "Like this?"

"Can I wear my red shorts?"

Since red, pink, and purple are kissing cousins, I dug for the red shorts and held them up. "These?"

"She can't wear red shorts with that shirt," Holly said. "It's ugly."

"What are you wearing?" I glanced at her. She hadn't moved since I'd challenged her. "Oh, goody. I get to pick out something and dress you myself." I wiggled my eyebrows. "Where's your Halloween costume?"

The hair took even longer. Holly, finally clad in denim capris and a green shirt, managed to unsnag her own after I told her she was welcome to go to school without combing it. Amid squirms and moans I did Noelle's. I couldn't imagine my sister loved going through this torture every morning. Was Wendy such a whiz at braids and pigtails that she needed a showcase?

When the tangles were finally tamed, I found twin gold barrettes and snapped them into place to keep Noelle's hair out of her eyes.

Downstairs the French toast was not a hit.

With no other choices, I'd made less-than-healthy butter and honey sandwiches to take for their lunch, scrounging for raisins to go with them. I knew better than to exhibit what I'd packed ahead of time. After what passed for breakfast, they retrieved their backpacks, and I stuck the lunches inside. "The lunches will be a surprise." I beamed as if this was a special treat.

"We buy lunch," Holly said.

"That's not what your grandmother told me."

Somehow I got them out the door, and we started down the street with much dragging of feet, passing one of the few residents I'd noticed. The woman, who looked to be ninety, was hauling a small mixed breed dog along the sidewalk. She nodded, and the dog yapped, showing its remarkable lung power and vocal range until we were half a block away. So much for social life in Tropicana.

Even with a shortcut through a tar pit, we would have gotten there faster. Luckily, by the time we stood in front of the school, the bell still hadn't rung.

The building was defined by buckling wood panels and outdated windows. At the end of the sidewalk two women waited to welcome students. I dragged the girls, one on each arm, toward them, more than ready to turn them over to a willing adult—or even an unwilling one.

"Holly," the woman on the right said, "good morning. Is this your mother?"

This was probably one of the two Mrs. Englishes. She was in her midthirties, rosy-cheeked and wholesome, and dressed casually in a striped tunic and leggings.

Since Wendy and I look nothing alike, I was surprised she had confused us. I held out my hand. "I'm Holly and Noelle's aunt, Ryan Gracey. The girls' mother is my sister, and I'm filling in while she's out of town."

"Gretchen English, Holly's teacher," she said, shaking my hand with vigor. "I was told they were staying with your mother."

"Not anymore."

"I see." She turned to the girls. "You run inside now. School's about to start."

Neither girl said goodbye or gave a backward glance, which probably surprised the teachers but not me.

I smiled at Mrs. English to show I was really a nice person, no matter what the girls believed. "My mother says I'll need to complete some paperwork so I can pick them up and be the official contact until my sister comes home."

She inclined her head to one side, as if she wanted us to

have a little privacy. We sidestepped a bit so we wouldn't be easily overheard.

She didn't waste time. "I'm worried about Holly."

I couldn't add that I was, too, because as far as I knew, my niece's behavior was perfectly normal for her.

She didn't wait for an answer. "A lot of mornings she seems tired. Exhausted, actually. She's fallen asleep at her desk more than once. I need to have a conference with her mother."

I could relate because I needed one, too. "I'm not sure when Wendy's coming home. But I'll certainly mention it when she does. Did you tell my mother this?"

"No. I haven't met your mother. This is my first week on morning duty. And I thought it would be better to talk to Holly's parents about giving her an earlier bedtime. But her father's away in the navy, right? And since her mother's absence seems ongoing…"

"I'll be absolutely sure she gets to bed early enough for a good night's sleep. You can count on that."

"Sleep is so important." She paused. "Along with an absence of stress."

I thought about all the stress in the girls' lives. "I'll keep things as calm as I can." I gave a firm nod.

"You will tell their mother to get in touch with me?"

I planned to add that request to my long list of things to tell, ask and insist on with Wendy.

Inside the school I talked to the administrator, who gave me a form to fill out and one for my mother to sign. He told me to bring them back that afternoon. Since Mom had been designated "temporary guardian," he seemed to feel the forms would cover it.

I walked back to the town house at an even slower pace. The first part of my day hadn't been a trip to the amusement park. The next part was going to be less so.

What little gift do you bring a heart patient on a heavily restricted diet? I wasn't sure Dad was allowed to drink coffee, so even with soy milk, Starbucks was out. Certainly chocolate and baked goods were no-nos. Dad had never been much of a reader, but I stopped for half a dozen bestselling thrillers at the mystery bookstore closest to Gulf Sands and slipped them into a gift bag.

Unlike ungated Tropicana, Gulf Sands has a suspicious set of guards. The guard of the day didn't recognize me, and gave me the third degree before he allowed me to pass. Since one of the cold case murders Sophie and I were considering took place in a gated community like this one, I wasn't offended.

Researching a show like *Out in the Cold* lends itself to paranoia, but I think my interest in crime began earlier when Mom read me all those gruesome bedtime stories. My education added a layer, too. As an undergraduate, I was a criminal justice major, and afterward I pursued a graduate degree in journalism. These days I dig deeply into the hearts and minds of bad guys, and report the salacious details to my listeners. So it's no surprise I'm inclined to be cautious.

What most people don't know is that I keep a Smith & Wesson revolver locked securely in my glove compartment. Nor would they guess that the handgun is the result of an armed assault I barely survived when I was twenty-four.

When I finally pulled up to the house, the sun was peeking out behind billowing cumulus clouds. I got out and stretched before I navigated the curving walkway to the front door. As always, I wondered why my parents had built such a large house after both daughters left home. Dad travels a lot, and while Mom sometimes travels with him, most of the time she's rattling around here alone. When they're both home, can they find each other? I hoped these next weeks and months while

Dad recovered right under Mom's nose wouldn't present an impossible challenge to their marriage.

I let myself in and made my way to the master suite. The door was closed again, so I left the gift bag just in front of it and went to look for Mom.

My parents have so much money they could throw wads of bills into their fireplace every night and still die rich. Mom employs a cleaning lady twice a week, and crews arrive quarterly to wash windows, steam rugs and scrub the travertine floors with a toothbrush—if needed. Despite that, she cleans constantly. Clutter offends her, and dirt is her archenemy.

I wasn't surprised to find her upstairs in the room where the girls had slept. She was down on her hands and knees with a lamb's wool duster, vigorously swishing it under the bed.

I lounged in the doorway and cleared my throat. "Don't you still have a cleaning lady?" I didn't know the latest martyr's name, since Mom's standards were so high nobody lasted for more than a few months. She'd immediately run through Gracey Group's official cleaning staff, and was now working her way through the general population.

She slid backward and rose up on her knees. "I wanted to be sure there was nothing under here to attract bugs."

"You should have started your own franchise. You'd have been more successful than Dad."

She wasn't in the mood for backhanded compliments. "Have you heard from your sister?"

"No. I got the girls off to school, though, and I brought a form for you to sign." I produced it, along with a pen, and she did just that.

"Be prepared," she said when she had finished. "The girls will be bringing home paperwork to sign almost every day."

"Thanks. I'm not prepared for a lot of things, like making

lunches. There wasn't much in the house, and Holly swears they always buy lunch at school. Did you know that?"

"The lunches I packed last week were healthier."

I made a mental note to call the school about lunch tickets. "I even met Holly's teacher. She was out front welcoming students." I didn't tell her about our conversation.

"I'll get your father up before you leave. He's supposed to stay awake as much as possible."

"What else can he look forward to?"

"He starts cardiac rehabilitation on Wednesday. At first he'll go three times a week. They work on exercises and monitor him while he's doing them. That goes on for a while."

"When can he go back to work?"

"No sooner than six weeks. Longer if I have my way." Mom got to her feet, using the bed to help herself stand. I felt a pang. This was a woman who never wanted to show even minor weakness. My parents were aging and needed a stress-free environment. Instead they had a daughter on the run.

Since Wendy was near the top of my list of reasons to be here, I suggested we go downstairs and make a cup of tea. She followed without argument. In the kitchen I put water in the kettle and got the tea caddy so we could choose. When I had everything, including cookies that I found in the cupboard, I brought the cups to the table and sat across from her.

"What can I do to help, other than watch the girls?" I asked, knowing what her answer would be.

"Bring your sister home."

"I wish I could." I reached across the table and put my hand on hers for a moment. Mom and I are short-term touchers.

She looked tired. "I've tried calling, but she doesn't pick up. I guess she's trying to work out whatever it is and spare us. I can't believe the problems with airlines these days. Every time I open the paper there's another horror story."

I'd been working out what to say, and now I had no choice but to launch right in.

"It's not the airline's fault, Mom. It's not a simple question of scheduling. Wendy ran into a problem while she was away, and she has to stay in…California until she can resolve it. Except for childcare, she doesn't want help. She needs to work out whatever this is on her own, and she'll let us know when she has. In the meantime, she doesn't want to talk to anybody."

She digested that. "That's not what you said before."

"I told you the situation was complicated, and that's still true. But she's not trying to reschedule a flight and running into delays. There's more going on, which is why she called me. It's doubtful she'll resolve it right away."

"Resolve *what*? What's going on?"

I held up my hands. "She was in a hurry, and she didn't want to answer questions. But she did say she won't be using her phone anymore, so we won't have any luck reaching her. You can stop trying."

Her expression was a storm about to break. "Why wouldn't she want to use her phone?"

"Like I said, she wants to do this alone. I'm sure she'll explain the whole thing once she's back."

"You should have gotten more details!"

"Remember this came out of the blue. I tried."

"Your sister does not behave this way. The whole thing is hard to believe."

"For me, too."

"This is so bad for your father. He counts on Wendy here and at work. You need to invent a story he'll believe."

Throughout our exchange, she had stared at the table as if the wood grain spelled answers. Now she looked up. "The girls will need an explanation, too. Later we can explain to your father that not telling him the whole truth was for his own good."

When the time was right, I would have to explain the same thing to her. I felt a stab of resentment that my sister was putting all of us in this position.

I struggled to lighten the mood. "You're asking me to make up a story out of thin air? To lie? Arlie Gracey, champion of the truth?"

"Ryan Rose." She narrowed her eyes.

Wendy had told me to invent a story, too. The problem is that while I'm a writer, I don't invent facts. I report them. Accurately. I certainly couldn't report these.

I looked down at my unpolished toenails and thought out loud. "Dad's not going to believe she's staying away for a break. Not when she knows he's had major surgery. He's not going to believe the absence is work related. All he has to do is pick up a phone and check." I looked up. "I can tell him she's on a religious retreat, that while she was traveling she had a spiritual awakening."

Mom looked skeptical. "She's a Catholic. We're awakened enough."

"A friend's in trouble? Someone from college? She's afraid to leave because her friend has nobody else right now. She's going to wait until things improve?"

"Too sketchy." She sighed, as if our conversation was too grueling to endure. "Who's the friend?"

"Somebody named...Chloe. They pledged the same sorority. Chloe helped Wendy out of a jam during their first year in college. Now she feels like she owes it to her to lend a hand."

"There was nobody named Chloe in her sorority."

I couldn't believe Mom remembered the names of Wendy's sorority sisters, or that she was nitpicking. "Choose any name you want."

"Your sister didn't get into jams in college."

"If she did, she certainly wouldn't have told you."

Mom thought a moment. "And she's not calling why? She's just *disappeared* with this girl?"

I tried not to wince at the "D" word. Because *disappeared* exactly described the situation. "Chloe lives in the Arizona desert. Off the grid. No cell towers."

"California, not Arizona."

I remembered Sophie had encouraged me to find out if Mom knew anything else about Wendy's trip. "You seem certain."

"Don't you think I know where my daughter is?"

The sentence hung in the air, because, of course, nobody knew where her daughter was.

She finally looked away. I finished quickly. "Can you tell me what you know about Wendy's schedule? Exactly where she was going and maybe why? Was she traveling from place to place? Do you know who she was meeting?"

"Your father would be the one to answer, but I'm certainly not going to ask him for details. He'll know something's up."

"Of course."

"Your story will work for a day or two, maybe a few more."

"Hopefully that's all we'll need."

Mom sat back and stared out at the water beyond the kitchen windows. "Please don't think I like lying. I'm angry your sister hasn't called to hash it out."

I added the last thing I'd decided to tell her. "While we're waiting to hear, let's not tell anybody outside the family what's going on. When the subject comes up, which it will when Gracey Group's staff starts asking questions, just say it's a normal business trip that got extended."

"Suddenly you're in charge."

"I don't have to be. But don't you think you have your hands full right now?"

She gave a curt nod. "And we're lucky you're here. I know. Thank you." She checked her watch, then got to her feet. "Let me wake up your father. He'll want to see you. I told him you'd come by this morning."

"I'm going shopping for groceries. Any ideas what the girls eat?"

"I made macaroni and cheese one night, and they asked for seconds."

"White flour. Cheese. It's a pattern."

"Some children are born picky. Wendy was. You weren't."

We headed for the master suite, and I told her about the problems with the front door and asked her to suggest a locksmith.

"We have a handyman who takes care of all property repairs. He can install a new lock and take care of anything else you've noticed. I imagine Wendy just didn't want to bother us."

I did not roll my eyes, but they nearly crossed from the effort. "I'd appreciate that. It's not safe the way it is."

"We have groups who travel through about this time of year and leave town with more than they came with. Especially in places like Tropicana where so many snowbirds aren't back yet. I'll try to get him there this afternoon."

We chatted until we got to the door. I waited outside until Dad was awake and propped up in bed. Then I scooped up the gift bag and went in to see him.

"Look who's up." I perched at his side and leaned over to kiss his cheek. Dale Gracey was a handsome man, with a full head of silver hair, tanned cheeks from hours at the golf course with clients, and eyes as dark as my own. Today, though, he looked pale and tired, with circles under his eyes and a new worry line in his forehead. I tried to remember how many times I'd seen him in pajamas. He had always been up and ready to start his day before six.

He seemed pleased to see me. "It's great to see you, doodle-bug."

I took and squeezed his hand. "I hope you call me that until I'm ninety."

"If I'm around when you're ninety, I'll be a medical miracle."

I showed him the books, and as he rifled through them, he pretended interest. "I can't wait to read these."

"Until your heart is stronger, start with the least terrifying."

He asked about *Out in the Cold.* I asked about his surgery, how he felt this morning and whether I could do anything for him other than visit every day.

We chatted some more, but he finally graduated to what was obviously most important. "I hear you've got the girls with you."

My smile felt forced. "I took them to school this morning and met their teacher. They're doing well."

"When is Wendy coming back?"

I glanced up at Mom, who gave a nearly imperceptible shake of her head. "I'll let Mom tell you the whole story. But I've talked to her. She's fine, just busy. She'll get here when she can. Meanwhile I get to spend some time with my nieces."

He looked too tired to question me further. He nodded, and I knew that was my signal to leave. After another quick kiss I left them together and headed for my car.

I'd bought myself a few days with my latest escalation of the Wendy story, but I knew that soon, I'd have to tell my mother the truth. If Wendy truly was a suspect in a murder case, then the authorities would, at the least, be calling my parents, if not showing up at their door. And what would they say?

I had very little time to figure out what was really going on. It was time to step up my game.

CHAPTER SIX

The grocery store closest to Wendy's was huge, and by the time I'd filled my shopping cart, I was so hungry, I stopped in their café for a fast-food breakfast sandwich. I ate by a window, making lists on my smartphone of what to do next.

While my thumbs were flying I received a text from Sophie. Arizona's a wash. Working on California. I rewarded her with a thumbs-up emoji, the adult version of smiling bunny stickers.

At the town house, putting groceries away was simple, since there was nothing to rearrange. I slid my purchases onto empty shelves, leaving chicken breasts at the front of the refrigerator, along with a bag of fresh green beans. Those belonged to tonight's dinner, along with roasted new potatoes I'd stowed in the cupboard. No fool, I'd also bought bread and sliced cheese, in case of a munchkin riot.

With a mug of hot jasmine tea in hand, I started The Big Snoop in the great room. I'd already done a search for Wendy's laptop last night, but the consolation prize would be a tablet or other device that synced calendar and contacts. I lifted cushions and slipped my hand into crevices hoping something might have ended up there.

When that proved futile, I collected all the papers piled throughout the downstairs and settled on one of the sofas. Since I'd already leafed through them, I wasn't optimistic. Still, I took a closer look at each page, stacking the few utility and household bills in one pile, incidentals and clothing for Wendy and the girls in another. There might be little food in the cupboards, but there was obviously a fortune in clothing in their drawers and closets. Gracey Group paperwork went into a third pile, and I carefully went over each page for hints about Wendy's western trip. As expected, if there'd been any related paperwork, she'd taken it with her.

The piles grew and multiplied. In the end I had half a dozen neat stacks and nothing to show for my time except a talent for organization. I placed them in an empty drawer in a desk in the corner, and while I was at it, searched the rest of the drawers. Next I went through the downstairs, fruitlessly searching the coat closet and the pockets of the jackets, checking behind and beside the television set, lifting everything I could. I was glad nobody was watching. The likelihood that anything related to Wendy's trip would be hidden behind the television cable box was ludicrous.

Still, I checked.

After I'd searched every cabinet and drawer in the kitchen, I made a turkey sandwich and took it out to the screened porch. For entertainment, a mockingbird serenaded me, practicing trills and the calls of other birds while I munched. I wondered if mockingbirds had calls of their own. Would anybody notice if they slipped in an original phrase?

The concert was solo, uninterrupted by human voices or even the hum of cars. While I wasn't expecting a parade, I wondered how many people were actually in residence now.

I decided to take a closer look. With half my lunch still un-eaten, I dusted the crumbs from my hands and changed my shoes, locking the doors leading outside before I started my jog down the road.

Forty minutes later, after a healthy dose of Florida humid-ity, I still wasn't sure. Even though many houses showed no obvious signs of life, cars might be in garages and shades or curtains drawn against the harsh sunlight. Using flowering potted plants, display flags and proliferating Christmas dec-orations as evidence, I estimated that no more than half the population of Tropicana was here at the moment. I wondered if my extroverted sister had felt lonely.

Inside the town house, the rest of my lunch and a shower re-vived me for the second phase of my snoopfest. The next place to search was Wendy's room, temporarily my own. I'd saved it, hoping that by now I'd be ready for the more intimate de-tails of her life. Unfortunately, electric bills and Holly's spelling tests hadn't prepared me.

The master bedroom had a small sundeck looking over the street and shading the front entrance below it. I saw no point in searching there. I piled my canvas bags in the middle of the bed so they would be out of the way, then I started with the nightstand, which had one drawer and a small cabinet with shelves below it. Nothing of interest graced the top. A land-line, a small lamp, a pair of reading glasses in a green leather case. The drawer held nothing of interest except an unopened box of condoms, in preparation, I supposed, for when Bryce surfaced and came to Florida to see his family. I hoped one box would be enough.

Of course Wendy would have to come home for the con-dom supply to matter.

The cabinet held more tissues, a bottle of floral-scented hand cream and a few paperbacks that still looked new. Wendy was probably too exhausted by the time she got in bed to read. Did anything I'd seen so far have anything to do with her disappearance? I profoundly doubted it.

The desk could have been a treasure trove, but it wasn't. I did find a note from Holly's teacher asking Wendy to come for a conference, and she'd probably planned to arrange that when she returned. At least she'd been informed.

I moved on to the closet. Wendy was neater in the confines of that small space than she was anywhere else in the house. In fact she was over the top. Her clothes were sorted by color. Black, navy and gray—formal and informal—were at the back, leading toward brighter colors in the middle and pastels nearest the folding closet door. I wondered if organizing so thoroughly made it easier to face each morning.

How much of Wendy's life in this house was a reflection of that reality? The empty cupboards? The piled papers? The pizza menus? I'd never really given much thought to how difficult each day must be with Bryce away so much. I'd shrugged off her desire to move closer to our parents as a form of mooching. But having spent less than twenty-four hours with my nieces, I understood much better.

Guilt joined hands with worry. What had stopped me from offering to help if she needed me? Wendy had always seemed so competent, and confidence is a hard barrier to breach. Still, I should have seen past it. Now I wanted her to come back for any number of reasons, including a need to tell her so.

I searched every item in the closet, and even the purses were a dead end. Wendy had thoroughly emptied each one before relegating it to a shelf. Not even a breath mint or receipt remained. Afterward I got on my hands and knees and searched under the bed. As I got up again, the dresser mirror showed a woman in her late twenties, uncontrollable dark curls springing every which way and a face scrunched in distaste. Although normally I'm not unpleasant to look at, this was not a pretty sight.

I had planned to start with the substantial jewelry box, the only item on top of the dresser, but not surprisingly the box was locked, most likely against little fingers, since any thief worth his salt would simply carry it away. I hoped the key was inside one of the drawers.

Predictably, the top one held lingerie. My own holds the same, so it's possible our mother passed on this tried-and-true feminine organizing tip. The similarity ended there. While I'm fond of cotton briefs and sports bras, my sister is apparently fond of skimpy. Skimpy bras, skimpy thongs, crotchless panties—no need to repeat skimpy there. Theoretically Wendy had twice as many bras and panties as I did, but they took up less than one-third the room. I wondered if the more utilitarian variety had traveled out west with her. Maybe this was the Bryce-Is-Home drawer. Or maybe Wendy just needed the reminder she was still feminine and sexy, even if her husband was at sea.

I thrust my hand down among the fluff and fancy, and separated items to see if anything was hidden there. No luck.

The second drawer held less exotic lingerie. The third was filled with T-shirts and yoga pants, shorts and bathing suits. The fourth contained a collection of beautiful filmy shawls in a variety of colors. Whenever she went out, Wendy battled air-conditioning with a shawl, so a new one was always a safe birthday gift from me.

I hit pay dirt behind the ones stacked on the right side and pulled out a cardboard box, which had probably held a necklace or earrings. Inside I found a key.

I skipped the bottom drawer in favor of the jewelry box and unlocked it. It was suede and carved wood, probably as expensive as some of the jewelry inside. Once opened I saw a mirrored lid, and a top shelf divided into segments, half with holes for earrings. Every segment was crowded with an assortment of silver jewelry, and every hole was filled.

Below the top were three drawers. Some compartments held gold pins or brooches, some gold bracelets. A door on each side had hooks for hanging necklaces with an elastic pocket below where they could pool.

Nothing I held to the light was fake or cheap. Wendy had always liked and collected jewelry, favoring expensive and classy over fun and funky. I wasn't surprised at the amount she had brought to Florida. Like our mother, she wore jewelry every day. She was never embarrassed to be seen putting gas in her car wearing pearls or her birth stone sapphires.

Since I rarely bother with jewelry, I'm no expert. But I guessed that some of this was worth a great deal of money.

I closed and locked the box, and replaced the key where I'd found it. By now one thing seemed clear. My sister had planned to return. Disappearing for good had never been in the cards. If she'd planned to stay away, she would have taken her pearls, the diamond studs Bryce had given her on their tenth anniversary, the necklace with the emerald-cut amethyst surrounded by tiny sapphires and diamonds.

As I put everything back and prepared to leave, I realized I'd forgotten to check the bottom drawer. I pulled it out, expecting to find more clothing. Instead I found my sister staring back at me.

I didn't have time to search the girls' room, which wasn't urgent anyway. After I finished searching Wendy's, the handyman called to say he was on the way.

Dave was a little guy, several inches shorter than my five foot four but as solid as a retaining wall. Since he clearly knew his stuff, I gave him my list and made a few advance dinner preparations while he ran through the little jobs. After he took a good look at the front door, he called me out of the kitchen to consult.

"The doorknob is inoperable, and the dead bolt can't be fixed."

I dried my hands on a dish towel. "That's what I told my mother."

"I'll replace them both, but while I'm at it, I can do the door out to the garage, too. It's not in great shape, either. Same keys. That'll make it easy for anybody living here."

I figured we ought to go for broke. "Can you put a better lock on the glass door leading out to the screened porch?"

"That lock's fine, but I can rekey it to match."

This time while he worked, I trooped upstairs to avoid the grinding and banging. I had my sister to keep me company. The bottom drawer of Wendy's dresser held two bulging scrapbooks filled with the minutiae of her life.

In the first, every school photo had been carefully preserved, along with candid photos of Wendy with friends, and one of her holding me. In that one, like the others, she was smiling, but she didn't look happy. Who wants a living reminder that your parents are still having sex when you're already starting college?

The array of photos showed a beautiful child growing into a radiant young woman. If she'd ever gone through an awkward or homely stage, pimples or buckteeth, the bad news had not been recorded. From page one until the end, Wendy was a poster child for good genes and parenting.

The second scrapbook contained every award, every newspaper article where her name had been mentioned, every recital program—be it dance, piano, or the middle school concert band where she'd played second chair flute. There were art projects, letters she'd written from summer camp and report cards. I expected to see baby teeth and fingernail clippings.

My mother had lovingly compiled every achievement of Wendy's childhood and adolescence, a historical record of supremely happy and successful decades of my sister's life.

As I closed the second book, I wondered if Mom, who had clearly reveled in Wendy's popularity and accomplishments, had stood over a copy machine and replicated each of these pages for herself.

My second thought? Had she compiled even one scrapbook for me?

My childhood wasn't exactly normal. By the time I came along, my parents should have been saying a fond goodbye to child rearing. The evidence in my lap concluded they'd done that first stint well, and it should have been enough. Wendy, the living proof, had exceeded all expectations. Then along had come Ryan Rose, whose premature birth in a foreign country had been such a trauma that I had started life with the wrong foot forward.

None of this was to say I had been unhappy, or that Mom and Dad had seemed unhappy to start all over again. What had been true? The majority of their parenting energy had gone into daughter number one, and daughter number two, the universe's big surprise, had received the leftovers.

At times in my life I've considered being a leftover a bonus, but now, with Wendy's senior photo smiling up at me from the cover of the thickest scrapbook, I wondered what it would have felt like to have this kind of attention showered on me. I really didn't know.

Dave yelled up to tell me he was finished, and I saw it was almost time to walk over to the school with the form so I could pick up the girls. I replaced the memorabilia in the bottom drawer, thanked Dave who handed me keys and locked up after both of us.

The afternoon had progressed from warm to hot, and by the time I got there I wasn't sorry to enter the hallowed halls and head straight for the office. Everyone was on the phone, so I took a seat, enveloped in nostalgia. I'd spent hours of my school days in an office much like this one, waiting for a reprimand. The nuns had liked me, but I had tried their patience.

When the administrator finally finished his phone call, he looked over the form and promised we were all set. "Would you like to peek into the first grade room while you wait? You can watch your niece. Noelle, right? That would be Mrs. English's room, number six on the left."

I started down the hall. The door to six was open, and when the teacher saw me, she motioned me inside. Noelle had been right about the hair as well as the name. This Mrs. English was an older woman, with lovely gray hair that shone with just the faintest tinge of blue. The children were sitting on a rug at her feet as she read a story about a cat named Ringtail who wanted to be a raccoon. I lounged beside the door and watched. Some of the children had turned as I entered, but not my niece. Her attention was riveted on the pictures in the book and the story.

To my surprise Noelle raised her hand, and the teacher recognized her. "That picture shows Ringtail chasing a butterfly. There's no butterfly in the story."

"Not yet."

"The picture can tell the story before the words do?"

"It can," Mrs. English said.

"Can somebody tell a story with pictures and no words? That would be okay?"

They continued the conversation as the other children started to move and whisper to each other, but Noelle was so focused she didn't notice. It was the most I'd ever heard her speak.

"I think you should try one yourself," Mrs. English said, just as a bell rang.

As the children filed out of the room, she came over to speak to me, although Noelle didn't, even though she'd finally noticed I was there.

I introduced myself, and Mrs. English nodded pleasantly. "My daughter-in-law said she met you this morning." The mystery of the identical names was solved.

"Noelle seemed..." I couldn't think of the right word.

"Involved," she supplied. "Yes, she's such a bright little girl, and her artwork is unusually advanced. Plus she's so much fun to talk to, I sometimes forget the other children need attention, too. I have no doubt that tomorrow she'll sit at her table and tell a story with drawings. And it will be wonderful."

"I don't know this little girl. She's nothing like this at home."

"Have you spent much time with her?"

I had to say no.

"Well, you'll get to know her now, as well as her sister. My daughter-in-law tells me Holly is smart as a whip, too." Her smile faltered, as if she was trying to think of a way to broach the bad news I'd already heard.

"But tired too often," I supplied. "There's been a lot going on in their lives, but I'll be sure they get to bed early."

"Good, because Noelle seems tired in the mornings, too."

"I guess I have a lot to learn about children."

She clapped a hand on my arm. "I wouldn't worry. They'll make sure you learn whatever you need to. You can always count on that."

CHAPTER SEVEN

At the grocery store I'd stocked up on after-school snacks my nieces might like. String cheese. Whole grain crackers. Fruit. Yogurt.

Now, with their backpacks stowed and hands washed, I set an assortment on the counter. "I bet you're hungry." I got apple juice out of the refrigerator, and when I turned around to show them, they were gone. The snacks lay exactly where I'd left them.

I found both girls in front of the television set in the great room, watching something that passed for a cartoon, but only because it was animated. This definitely wasn't Looney Tunes. The little debutantes, in sherbet colored party dresses, were prancing back and forth reciting insipid moral lectures. Was I lucky my nieces hardly spoke? Would I be forced to listen to constant discourse on the importance of being a good friend, or not copying homework if they did?

I stood in front of the screen and waved my hands. "Nobody's hungry?"

Holly was galvanized enough to speak. "We always watch this show."

"Not today." I flipped off the set and folded my arms. "Come in the kitchen and tell me about school. There's apple juice if you're thirsty."

I went in the kitchen and poured juice, whether they wanted it or not.

When I turned around they were in the doorway, staring at me as if I were a chimpanzee at the zoo. "Mommy lets us watch TV," Noelle said.

Since Wendy wasn't there to defend herself, I held out the juice. "What else do you do when you come home?"

They took the glasses, but not with enthusiasm.

When they didn't answer, I supplied possibilities. "Stand on your heads? Cut the grass? Make long-distance phone calls to Australia?"

Nobody cracked a smile.

"Or maybe you go upstairs and play, before you come back down to do homework?"

Noelle looked down at her feet. "We're tired."

"Do you need naps?"

Holly, who was still staring at me, narrowed her eyes in answer.

"Would you like to go down to the playground?" On my jog I'd discovered a small one beside the community pool. "Or would you like to go for a swim?"

"TV." Noelle came over and set her glass on the counter, but while she was there she took a sleeve of string cheese.

Encouraged, I compromised, which meant I hadn't been completely brainwashed by the Arlie Gracey School of Parenting. "Tell you what. While I'm taking care of you, you can watch a half hour of TV after school, but you have to agree on what you'll watch or take turns choosing. And just half an hour."

The girls looked at each other. I'd already noticed they practiced the art of silent communication with skill and cunning. When Holly named another show I'd never heard of, Noelle nodded, as if it was her idea, too.

I was beginning to see how my sister had been able to work at home in the afternoons. "How was school? I know Noelle heard a story about a cat who wants to be a raccoon."

Silence.

"What did you do, Holly?"

"Who cares?"

"I do if you want to tell me."

"I don't."

"Why don't you finish your drinks down here, and then go upstairs and play until your show comes on? You can take snacks up with you if you're careful."

"Did you buy cookies?" Noelle sounded hopeful.

"Didn't think of it." A more precise reply would have been: didn't think of it because I didn't want you to have them.

"Or potato chips?"

"We'll be eating early, so you won't starve. You can do homework after your show."

Holly set her full glass of juice on the counter and left, muttering under her breath. Noelle waited until her sister was out of sight, then grabbed some crackers and followed in her wake.

The afternoon dragged. There was half an hour in front of the television. Another half hour when they sat and stared at the blank screen in protest. Eventually, homework. I scraped carrots and cut up red peppers for all of us to snack on while I made dinner. I snacked alone.

Dinner itself was a wash. Each girl ate just enough to keep

from passing out. Before they left the table, I got a pad and pen and sat down again.

"Tell me what you'd like for dinner."

Nobody spoke.

I prompted. "I hear you like macaroni and cheese."

Noelle gave a tiny nod. Holly glared as I put that on my list.

I pointed at her. "Holly, your turn, and don't shrug. We're staying here until I hear your ideas."

She looked mutinous and didn't reply.

Noelle looked at me, then at her sister. "She likes hot dogs."

"Be quiet," Holly snapped.

"Thanks." I wrote down hot dogs and hoped I could find healthy ones. "How about hamburgers, Holly?"

She didn't answer.

"Whale? Groundhog? Tasmanian Devil stew?"

No response.

"Maybe you're vegetarians. I make a mean salad out of leaves and twigs."

Noelle actually giggled.

In a quick preview of her adolescence, Holly rolled her eyes. "Can we go now?"

I pretended to think it over. "Well, if you do, you're leaving the menu up to me. And you'll have to eat every bite of whatever I choose."

"Fish and chips," she said, as if I'd dragged the words out of her with a real fishing rod.

I knew better than to push. "Great. We're done for now. Want baths or showers tonight?"

I was so tired by seven-thirty—the time my internet parenting research insisted I should tuck them in—that I thought about crawling in with them. Safely in bed, though, neither girl looked sleepy.

I widened my own eyes to keep them open. "Would one of you like to say the prayer tonight?"

Of course neither volunteered. I repeated a version of the previous night's, and asked if they wanted a story. Again, no response.

I pulled Holly's *Frozen* sheet over her shoulders. No surprise her back was to me. I expected the same treatment from Noelle, but when I made it to her bedside, she was watching me intently.

"Why didn't Mommy come home?"

The question had taken so long to emerge that whatever story I'd concocted yesterday disappeared. Luckily, Holly gave me time to rethink it.

"Shut up, Noelle!"

"'Shut up' is something we don't say," I told her. "Everybody has the right to ask questions."

"Noelle..." Holly's tone was still threatening.

By then I'd recovered my poise. "Like your gram said, your mom found out she had other commitments and couldn't leave when she planned to. She has a friend who needs her help."

"Why didn't she tell us?" Noelle asked.

Noelle had said this as if Wendy communicated with her daughters directly. There were several ways to read her question, but I wasn't taking chances.

"How would she tell you?" I asked.

"Holly's phone."

Holly sat up. "I'm trying to go to sleep."

So far out of the parenting groove was I, that an eight-year-old with her own phone stunned me. "Does she text you, Holly? Or does she talk to you?"

Holly just glared at me.

"She puts words on the screen," Noelle said.

"Holly, has your mom texted you in the last few days?" Holly stared blankly at me.

I waited, but an answer had been too much to expect. "If you do hear from her, will you let me know?"

She lay back down and presented her back once more.

Holly hadn't denied having a phone, or receiving texts. During my search I hadn't gotten as far as their bedroom, so of course I hadn't found it. On the other hand, my suspicious little niece probably took the phone with her everywhere and hid it inside a pocket of her backpack while she was at school. The same school that had required two forms so I could pick them up in the afternoons probably did not encourage cell phones on desks.

I tucked in Noelle and turned off the overhead light. The reassuring fairy night-light came on. I wondered how long it would take the girls to fall asleep, and how soundly they would sleep once they did. Because with the help of the little fairy beaming light into their room, I was going to find Holly's phone and see what was on it.

By ten o'clock I was still waiting for Holly to fall asleep so I could check her backpack. The little girl's morning exhaustion might not be a mystery. If tonight was any example, once she was in bed my niece was routinely lying awake for hours. I wondered if she was worried about all the changes in her young life. There had been months in my own when every time I closed my eyes, I sank immediately into nightmares.

As I waited, I worked on the files I'd brought with me, gathering a list of questions for a call to Sophie about the cold cases they referenced. Of course the more important question was what we should do next about tracking my sister. If Sophie had found anything important, she would have called, but it was time to coordinate our strategies.

By now I was working from Wendy's bedroom to keep better track of Holly's tossing and turning. I reached for my cell phone and realized I'd left it on the kitchen counter. Since Wendy has a landline extension right beside the bed, I lifted the receiver and heard a series of beeps. I gave up my landline years ago, but I knew what that meant. Wendy had voice mail. And didn't I wish I could log in and listen?

I punched in Sophie's number and waited. She spoke the moment she picked up. "I was just getting ready to call you."

"How'd you know it was me?"

"I made a note of your sister's telephone number from the web."

"Why?"

"To get a record of calls she made before she left."

"Why didn't I think of that?" I didn't bother to slap my forehead. I'd be black-and-blue if I slapped myself every time Sophie thought of some stone I'd left unturned.

"Don't get excited. Dead end. I could check the carrier's website or call and ask for a list, but I'd have to have her password. Have you checked the town house phone menu to see if there's a record of recent calls?"

"Another thing I didn't think about."

"Do it after we hang up, so you don't disconnect me. Does it look like an old model?"

I held the phone away, and then put it back to my ear. "It looks familiar. Like maybe I grew up with it. My mother refuses to throw out anything that's still working. That's why she and Dad are so rich. She probably brought it over when Wendy moved in."

"Earlier models were bare bones basic. Check, but you're probably out of luck, unless you found a record of your sister's passwords somewhere. Did you?"

"Nothing at all in her paperwork. She probably keeps everything important on her laptop or phone."

"What about phone bills?"

"I did a heavy-duty search. She gets statements from the electric company, but I didn't come across phone bills."

"She probably pays basic bills online."

"And we'd need a password to get them." I told her about the voice mail messages waiting to be picked up.

"You know she can access them remotely and probably will the minute she thinks of it?"

"From wherever she is."

"So it would be good to get those messages before they disappear. As soon as they come in, but—"

"I'd need a password," I finished for her.

"Usually you dial your home number with area code and put in anywhere from a four- to a six-digit code. You could try her birth date, the girls' birth dates, the year she was born."

"What fun that will be."

"I live for those moments."

Most of the research I'd done in my career had been for cases that had gone down before the technology explosion. No one carried phones in those days or used voice mail, and before the mid-1980s, answering machines weren't even in use. I knew this particular tidbit because I'd just looked into a cold case that hinged on a degraded tape in one of the first analog models. But most of the time, Sophie researched and I interrogated.

I went to the heart of the discussion. "Where are we on Wendy? Since her phone calls seem to be a dead end." I reconsidered, got up and closed the bedroom door and told her about Holly's phone.

"Let me know what you find. I'm sending links to two cases in California for you to look over. But honestly? Neither one is the least bit promising. Coverage on the first indicates the cops are already close to solving it. So if your sister is involved, law enforcement will either be calling in the next few hours, or she'll be on the next flight home."

I clutched the phone to my ear. "The second?"

"It looks like something to do with the Russians. Maybe espionage?"

"I can't see Wendy in a trench coat."

"The possibility stayed with me because her husband commands a nuclear sub. He might have secrets they want."

I pondered but dismissed it. "Bryce wouldn't share secrets with Wendy or anybody else. He's Commander Straight Arrow. And Wendy told me once that he doesn't bring paperwork home, that he does all his work in the office to keep everything confidential."

"Did that bother her?"

"*Au contraire.* She sounded delighted. The sub stuff doesn't interest her. She likes the officers' spouses' club and climbing the social ladder. She likes the prestige, but that's it. Sub talk bores her."

"Okay, but even if this doesn't pan out, and I doubt it will, her husband's job is an angle to keep in mind. So that's where I am. The mostly solved murder was in LA, but the second was out in the boondocks."

"They have boondocks in California?"

"Boondocks are universal. So what do we do next?"

If Wendy had been involved in a murder in either Arizona or California, wouldn't we know by now? The body either hadn't yet been found—an image I didn't want in my head—or she'd lied to me and possibly to our parents about her destination, or at least the tail end of the trip.

I gave in to the inevitable. "I guess we open this up a state at a time. It would help if I could get Wendy's travel schedule from someone at Gracey Group. But that's too suspicious now that she's been *delayed*."

"I'll keep nosing around."

We talked about the cold cases I'd looked into since arriving in Seabank. We did our usual give and take on questions, and hung up with three possible cases to concentrate on for the next week, with hopes of making a decision soon.

As soon as I disconnected, I checked the phone for a call log, but thanks to my mother's frugality, there wasn't one. Then I opened my computer, and when Sophie's links to the two murders came through, I looked them over. But she was right. They weren't promising.

On a whim I called my favorite technology wonk, a young man in his final year of high school, who would rather answer questions than eat or breathe. He'd been a big help on *Out in the Cold*'s first season, and he'd promised to help us next time in return for having his name in the credits again. Sophie and I specialized in getting first-class advice at bargain basement prices.

Ten minutes later I hung up after a lecture I only partially understood. My question had been whether Wendy's cell phone call to me could still be traced. Just knowing where she'd been when she made it would be a starting point. Now I knew that the authorities could get a reasonable approximation on the location of the call using cell phone towers, but unfortunately I could not. Of course if there really had been a murder, the authorities already knew where it had happened, so I certainly wasn't going to give them proof my sister had been anywhere in the vicinity.

Dead end.

When I noticed the time was after midnight, I closed down my computer, hoping that Holly might be asleep by now. I peeked in her room and saw she was tossing from side to side.

One shower later, dressed in boxers and a tank top, I checked for what I hoped would be the last time. Gentle snuffly snores came from Holly's side of the room.

"Bingo." I tiptoed in and carefully lifted the pink butterfly-adorned backpack off the floor at the foot of her bed, surprised how heavy it was. I took it to Wendy's room and sat cross-legged on the bed to go through the main compartment one item at a time.

I removed a math textbook and the workbook that accompanied it. Next out was a plastic binder with her homework neatly tucked in the front pocket, followed by a plastic case with pencils, pens and erasers. She was a neatnik, our Holly. If I'd carried a backpack at that age, the inside had probably looked like a barn floor.

The only item out of place was a plastic bag with the uneaten sandwich I'd packed for her that morning. Now it looked like a school bus had run over it. I debated whether to throw the bag and contents away, but if Holly noticed they were gone, my snooping would be revealed. I wondered how long the squashed sandwich would remain there. I wished somebody was around to make a bet with me.

The zip pocket on the back yielded a library book, another workbook and nothing else. I was reminded of my morning's futile search. I checked the back pocket's pocket—every pocket had bred another. I gave up and started to replace everything in the main compartment when I felt something hard against my fingertips. I realized I'd missed a zipper.

I pulled out Holly's phone.

I'm not the digital genius Sophie and other staff members are, but I recognized that this one was bare bones, and well suited to a child. The phone looked sturdy, the numbers were large and slightly raised to make tapping simpler, and each tap produced an audible click. I played around and found that the phone had no internet capabilities—perfect for a child not old enough to use them safely—but I found the caller list immediately.

Holly had received no calls in the past week.

Disappointed, I fiddled for another minute and found text messaging. The last text she had received from my sister had been weeks before, and had to do with where to wait at the local library until Wendy could pick her up.

So Holly's mother hadn't called since leaving on her trip, not even before things fell apart. And she hadn't texted. But there was good news, too.

Holly's father had.

CHAPTER EIGHT

Finding a way to text Bryce and actually doing it were two different things. What would I say to him? "Hey Bryce, don't worry about your girls? Wendy might be running from the law, but I've got things covered?" Or maybe, improvising on the case Sophie had turned up, I could casually ask if Russian spies were in the market for any of his secrets. Just in case.

I went to bed wondering what to do about Bryce, and woke up the next morning having decided not to do anything. His contact information was a piece of good luck, and I'd added it to my own phone. If the time came when I needed to get in touch with him, I knew how—at least I did if he was somewhere he could receive messages. I didn't know exactly how that worked on a sub, but at the moment, I didn't need to. Once I did, my mother could probably tell me. In the meantime, the less concerned I seemed and the fewer questions I asked her, the better.

I managed to get the girls off to school with multigrain waffles in their little tummies. Poor Holly drooped her way out the door, as if the sandman had held her hostage all night.

At most, she'd had seven hours of fitful sleep. If that didn't change in the next few days, I had to consult a doctor, and I hoped my mother had the necessary permissions.

After I dropped them off, I didn't go back to the town house. I had dressed for a run through the country, so I hopped on the interstate, and eventually took an exit not far from the county line. Southwest Florida was not all sand, gulf and palm trees. Away from the water, this little corner of heaven still had centuries-old oaks, which no developer had yet destroyed, along with scruffy fields dotted with Hereford cattle and clumps of saw palmetto. Pastel concrete block farmhouses stood in the shade of chinaberry and silver buttonwood. Pools graced front yards, and substantial vegetable gardens were finishing one growing season and greening up with the next.

I parked where I usually did when I took this particular turn, off the feeder road about six miles from the interstate on a smaller dirt road. The signs at the crossroads that pointed in the direction I planned to run read Buttonwood Nursery, 1.5 miles, and Marvin's Masterpieces, 3 miles. That particular sign claimed that Marvin, a taxidermist, specialized in "odd beasts and rare." I always pictured a stuffed unicorn waiting in his yard to greet customers. Someday I planned to run that far and find out.

The biggest sign, Confidence K-9s, 2 miles, was the only one that was freshly painted and positioned in the best place for travelers to see. Mateo Santiago, who owned the kennel and training facility, was meticulous and smart. Teo rarely did anything without thinking carefully about the best way to proceed and then barreling full speed ahead.

I limbered up a little, although I would do the bulk of my stretching afterward. Temperatures had dropped into the low fifties overnight, and so far had only climbed into the sixties. I wore running capris patterned with a beach scene and a long-sleeved crop top shirt. Apparently it was important to protect my arms from the cold, but the designer had declared open season on my midriff.

For Christmas last year Wendy had presented me with this outfit and three other running ensembles, along with bright purple headphones. That much glamour is definitely out of place in my wardrobe. Most of my clothing looks like I picked it up on sale at Dollar General, but when I run, I'm the bomb. In exchange I gave her an embroidered Mexican shawl I'd found in a vintage clothing shop and a hand-thrown mug that read: "You and I are sisters. Always remember that if you fall I will pick you up..." And then on the other side: "...after I stop laughing."

Sadly, I'm not laughing.

I started my jog slowly, keeping to the middle of the road since the ground was harder, and traffic was light to none. The route was nothing short of an obsession, and every time I ran, I told myself I could turn around before I reached Confidence K-9s. I never did. Seeing what Teo's life had become was like picking the scab off a sore. Not that Confidence K-9s was anything to be ashamed of. In addition to boarding and obedience training, Confidence raised dogs for personal protection and security. Last month when I whizzed past, I'd seen a foundation for a new building behind an extra parking area. At home I tried not to call up Teo's website, but I was sure he was doing well. It's just that he wasn't doing what he'd trained to do, the job he'd loved as much as he'd loved breathing. Teo was no longer a K9 officer, and I was the reason.

A light breeze kept me cool, along with shade trees bordering the roadside. At one point an ancient Jack Russell popped out of the bushes to run with me, yapping as we went, but he tired well before I did and left after he'd done his shift as watchdog. Plenty of people ran here; the road was more or less an open secret on the runners underground.

By the time I was only about a city block from Confidence, I slowed, knowing it was time to turn around. I glanced at my fitness tracker to see how many miles I'd gone already. If I wanted to talk to Teo, to find some kind of closure and satisfy myself he was all right, I needed to show up at his front door one day and see if he was willing to have a conversation. Despite that, I didn't turn around. I kept going, and when I got to the property line I sped up again.

The kennel acreage was divided between rows of concrete block kennels with attached runs, play and training yards, and another low-slung building that probably served as an office. The grounds were still well-tended, and the foundation I'd noticed had grown into an unassuming metal storage unit. What I had failed to notice was a brick ranch sitting at the edge of the property. Teo probably lived there, maybe with a girlfriend or even a wife, although I probably would have heard if he'd married. Some member of the Seabank Sheriff's Department would have made sure to let me know that Teo was happier without me.

Usually when I ran past Confidence, I saw activity on the grounds behind the high chain link fences where dogs were trained. Today was no different. In the largest of the enclosed yards, I glimpsed a woman with blond hair guiding a dog tethered on a long leash between boxes in a field. They were too far away for me to tell more, but they were both running, and I slowed to see if I could tell what the dog was supposed to do.

I caught more movement out of the corner of my eye, and saw a man coming toward her from across the field. Even now, all these years later, I easily recognized Teo, although the last time I'd seen him, his gait had been much different. Then he'd been recovering from a gunshot and learning to walk with both a brace and pain so fierce that more often than not, he couldn't put weight on his injured leg.

I wasn't worried I might be seen. The sun was shining through the trees to my left, and the distance and glare would easily hide my identity. I sped up anyway, making a wide circle and heading back the way I'd come. But not before I saw the woman stop what she was doing, and throw her arms around Teo's shoulders for a hug.

Back at the town house the doorbell rang as I was drying off after a long shower. By the time I dressed and went downstairs to answer it, no one was there, but a package the size of a paperback novel had been shoved nearly out of sight under the tall podocarpus trees beside the front door.

Inside, I scanned the label, assuming it was something for my sister, but the package was for me. Far odder was the return address, which was the town house itself. Since I wasn't in the habit of sending myself mail, and since I'm eternally suspicious, I noted the postmark, Cross City, Florida, and went to my computer. A minute later I'd learned that Cross City was a town west of Gainesville, with fewer than two thousand residents. Most likely nobody I knew lived there, and certainly nobody who knew Wendy's address. I'd found information on where to eat and go to church, but not much else.

By now I was almost sure who the package was from. I picked it up once more and lifted it to my ear. Bombs today aren't the Wile E. Coyote variety with dynamite wired to a ticking alarm clock, but cartoon habits die hard. The package was silent, and I was left with two options. Since I didn't want to plunge the box into a bathtub filled with water, I unwrapped it carefully and pulled out a burner phone.

I breathed my sister's name. "Wendy."

A note was attached to the box in unfamiliar handwriting. I read it out loud. "'Don't call me, I'll call you.'"

Was Wendy back in Florida? The handwriting wasn't hers. Wendy's handwriting is neat and precise, like pared-down calligraphy. This was perfectly readable, but the letters were sprawling and uneven. Wendy's worst scrawl was more accomplished than this.

Had she enlisted a friend to mail the package? And what about the note?

I went back to the computer, and this time I searched for local businesses in Cross City and found one called Risk-Free Remailer.

"Gotcha."

Remailing services exist to keep secrets. After ditching her cell phone, Wendy had probably purchased a prepaid phone, a burner, something she could do almost anywhere. If she paid for the phone with cash, no record of the purchase would be linked to her, since no identification would have been needed.

But overachiever that she was, my sister hadn't bought just one, she'd bought two. Whether it was necessary or not, she'd been trying to think like law enforcement. If the authorities got around to checking my cell phone, so they could look for calls from my sister, they might find repeated calls from a cloaked number I couldn't explain. Now, instead, those calls would be on the burner in my hand, the burner no one would know about, the one Wendy had probably expressed to the remailing service to be sent to me.

My sister was thinking like a criminal.

I set the burner down, unhappy to own it, but glad that at least she planned to communicate. Of course the note was clearly a joke. Because how could I call her? I didn't have her number and probably never would.

Contacting Risk-Free Remailer was certain to be a dead

end, but I tried anyway. When I hung up a few minutes later, my hunch had been confirmed. Risk-Free meant exactly that. A remailing service provided everything a client needed to keep identity and location secret, handwritten letters, trips to a variety of post offices for different postmarks, delayed mailing and much more. Paperwork that had to do with any transaction was shredded immediately. Even if Risk-Free had wanted to help me—which, of course, they hadn't—they no longer had records.

I shoved the phone into the pocket of the shorts I'd changed into and went upstairs to search the girls' room.

After batting zero in the closet filled with pretty little dresses and too many matching shoes, I was backing out when my pocket vibrated.

I had the phone to my ear in seconds. The caller's name was blocked, but who else could it be?

"Wendy, what the hell?"

"Don't lecture, please. I see you got the phone."

"Exactly what I've always wanted. Are you okay?"

Her sigh sounded like a gust of wind. "Okay? How can I be okay?"

"For a start, come home. We can work this out."

"No, we can't. I have to be here to do that. I'm sorry, but I'm stuck for now." She sounded like she was about to burst into tears.

I plopped down on the nearest bed, trying to stay calm. "Are you safe where you are? Is someone trying to hurt you?"

"I'm safe."

"You're safe *where*?"

"Ryan, it's just better you don't know, okay? In case the cops show up."

Frustrated, my voice grew louder. "Are they going to show up?"

"I honestly don't know what they know. I don't know what they think."

"You weren't calling from Phoenix, were you? Before, I mean. There's not one murder on record there you could have been involved in."

"Look, I can only tell you one thing today, okay? And please don't say no. It's important, and it's something you can do. There's a man involved in this. I won't say how, but his name is Milton Kerns." Her voice broke on the last word, as if it had taken everything to say that out loud.

"Who is he and how is he involved?"

"I think he may have had something to do with what happened. He grew up in Costa Rica. I know that much. But I need you to see what you can find out about him because you have better resources for that kind of thing. Because of the podcast, I mean. I can't tell you what to look for, because I don't know. Whatever you can find. Can you do that?"

"You have a name and the place he grew up but nothing else?"

"I'm sorry, but that's it for now. I'm trying to keep everybody safe."

For a moment I was touched that my goddess sister was turning to me for help, and everything else fell away. I had never believed the balance of power in our relationship could change this drastically. We were so far apart in age and experience that I had never expected to have an impact on Wendy's life, and now she was turning to me for help.

Then the still, small voice of a journalist made itself heard. No matter what I felt, if I was really going to have an impact, I had to dig for more. Starting with a confrontation, whether Wendy liked it or not.

"You told me you were in Phoenix. But I don't think you

were even in Arizona, and I'm guessing you weren't in California, either, which is what you told Mom."

"Just do this for me, please? I'm still hoping I won't be implicated, and the whole thing will blow over. If it does, there's no reason for anyone in the family to know details."

Was she worried about us, or was she worried about her reputation? What could she have done that she didn't want us to know about?

I tried again. "Are you afraid we'll report you to the authorities because we think that's best for you? We aren't going to do that, Wendy, but I still think you aren't giving the cops enough credit. Why would they pin this on you if you had nothing to do with it?"

"You know if the police think I might be guilty of murder, they'll find a way to pin it on me. And I'm not guilty of anything, Ryan, nothing, except being in the wrong place at the wrong time."

"Mom and Dad aren't going to be content with a made-up story, not for much longer."

"Don't tell them anything, and for sure, don't tell Bryce. I don't want to worry him with everything already on his shoulders. I'll call again when I can. Keep the phone handy."

There was an audible click, three beeps, and our call was over. I checked the phone's menu, but, of course, Wendy's number was blocked. There might be an app or a service to unblock it, one that would help me call her back. But having her number wouldn't tell me where she was. If she didn't want to say more, she wouldn't. I could prod until her girls were writing essays for their college applications, and Wendy wouldn't budge.

Her girls. Holly and Noelle had made their way into my head for a good reason. Wendy hadn't asked about them. She hadn't asked how they were, what I had told them about her absence, or if they were eating and sleeping or doing well in school. During our phone call, the girls had apparently been far from my sister's thoughts.

I tried to put myself in Wendy's place, which was impossible because I still knew so little. But when I tried to guess how I would feel as a mother separated from her young children, I was pretty sure I would be begging for information and reassurance.

Of course Wendy knew the girls were safe and well cared for, and that whatever I couldn't manage would be handled by our mother. We were her family, and we would never let anything happen to Holly and Noelle.

So far she was right. The girls were okay, even if Holly's lack of sleep was worrisome. Still, how did Wendy know for sure? I could only imagine the stress my sister must have been feeling not to have asked about her daughters.

CHAPTER NINE

I was not oblivious to the most important revelation from my sister's telephone call. I had been transformed from a journalist who meticulously investigated details to a clueless civilian. I was supposed to dig up information on a stranger, but Wendy wouldn't tell me why. I wasn't allowed to know who had died or where, or what she or this Milton Kerns had to do with it.

When looked at that way, my real job and this new one had blind alleyways and locked doors in common. Only this time I was starting with almost no information. If the call had been from anyone else, I would have turned over the burner to the police and given a statement to go with it.

I set that aside and concentrated on searching the girls' bedroom. I looked under beds and among the few neatly displayed dolls on a low shelf. None of them looked as if they'd been played with. No comb had ever been yanked through their gleaming hair, no dress had been stripped off repeatedly to fray at the edges. I remembered my dolls, a ragtag, half-naked assortment with dirty faces and limbs askew. They had been beside me in bathtubs and sandboxes, my companions and confessors until I was old enough to range farther afield.

In newer condition, they'd been my best friends during the heart surgeries that had characterized the first years of my life. Decades later, when my mother had suggested we trash them because my own daughters would never want anything so vile, I'd balked. Today my dolls are carefully packed away under my bed in Delray Beach. I'm not particularly sentimental, but I am loyal to a fault.

Which made me think about Teo again.

When I heard the theme from *Murder She Wrote*, I grabbed the burner before I realized the song was coming from the master bedroom. I crossed the hall and found my cell phone, answering just in time to catch Sophie.

"Checking in," she said. "Anything new?"

I debated silently, but in the end I told her about the new phone and Wendy's call.

"She sounds like she's in this for the long haul," Sophie said. "You see that, too?"

She was right. I did see it, and it worried me.

She didn't wait for an answer. "You're going to be there awhile. I can drive over. Make a list of whatever you need that you didn't pack."

"This could all blow over."

"So give me the guy's name. Did she spell it for you?"

"Milton Kerns." I stopped. Had Wendy said Kerns or Kern? And did it have a silent *a* in the middle? "I think that's what she said."

"Hopefully it's spelled the way it sounded to you." Sophie quizzed me about the rest of the call, and finished with the question I was asking myself. "Think this is busywork?"

"You mean if I spend my time looking for someone who doesn't exist, I can't look for her? I don't know, but she's a mother. She must know I'm already immersed in busywork. Showers, meals, homework. And a child who isn't sleeping."

"This has to be hard on your nieces. What have you told them about their mom?"

"Not much. They aren't asking a lot of questions."

"That seems odd."

"Everything seems odd. It is odd. Supremely odd."

"I'll see what I can find on your sister's guy."

"I doubt he's her guy. I don't know what his connection is."

"Start making a list of things you need, and text me." She hung up.

Back in the girls' room, I started on the dresser that belonged to Holly. Clothes were folded and stacked, although they showed signs of rummaging. I wondered if Wendy did everyone's laundry or if her cleaning lady, due to come Thursday, did it for them. I was really hoping for the latter.

I found the usual. After a cursory examination of the third drawer, I was about to move on, but the bottom pair of cargo shorts looked oddly lumpy. I found a small treasure trove inside the pockets.

I emptied them on Holly's bed. My niece doesn't show much emotion, except anger, of course, but as I removed objects, everything she repressed was laid out on the bedspread—a Bryce Wainwright museum. There was a worn leather key chain inscribed with *BW*, and an expired Connecticut driver's license with a smiling photo of her father. Bryce had brown hair and eyes like Holly's, remarkably even features under a widow's peak, and the physique of a man who knew he had to stay in shape, even under the ocean. There were also carefully folded and creased birthday cards he'd sent his daughter.

Holly might not be asking questions about her mother, at least not yet, but here was the evidence that she missed her dad.

Carefully I put everything back into the correct pockets,

refolded the shorts and replaced them in the drawer. Nothing else turned up.

I conducted the same search in Noelle's dresser. Nothing was hidden in clothing, but under a stack of sweaters in the bottom drawer—sweaters that wouldn't get much wear in Seabank—I found a carved wooden box, inlaid with chipped mother-of-pearl, most likely a rescue from the trash. If Holly's pocket stash was a testament to how much she loved and missed her father, this was the same. Only the target of affection was my sister.

On Noelle's bed I carefully removed items, starting with a perfume bottle labeled Coach, the size a woman might travel with or buy as a trial. I removed the top and recognized the scent. The last time I'd seen my sister we had lounged by my parents' pool, Wendy in a bikini, me in the one-piece that covered the scars on my chest. I'd refused to tell her how fabulous she smelled, for fear I would receive the entire collection of whatever it was on the next holiday.

The pile included some outdated costume jewelry. The turquoise-and-coral necklace had a broken clasp. One sparkly earring was missing a post. I found half a silver heart on a tarnished chain, along with a metal cuff bracelet that was dented and bent out of shape.

Along with everything else, I was surprised to find cards from Bryce to Wendy, cards with sappy, romantic messages that many women would keep forever. Had Noelle retrieved them from the trash? From Wendy's own collection of keepsakes? I hadn't seen much sentiment on display here, but it was possible all the real mementoes of Wendy's marriage were still in their house in Connecticut.

As I put everything back the way I'd found it, I wondered why my younger niece, who was living right here in the town house with her mother, needed reminders. Were these play items she incorporated into an imaginary world? Or was Wendy so often away that Noelle needed tangible evidence her mother was real?

I thought about all the things I'd found. Neither girl was communicating in a meaningful way. I'd fed them food they didn't want to eat, bought them ice cream, tucked them in and tried to establish a bedtime ritual. But I'd hardly scratched the surface of what they really needed.

Obviously both were suffering from their parents' absences. I'd spent too much time wishing I were somewhere else and hoping things would resolve quickly. Wendy was thinking ahead, in case her absence dragged on. Now it was my turn. At the moment I was the lone caretaker here, and it was my job to help them express themselves at what was clearly a difficult time.

I just had to figure out how.

The afternoon was warm, but a cool wind tickled the hair on my arms and sent my curls flopping against my cheeks. After I sent Sophie a list of the few things I needed from home, I walked to the school to pick up the girls, figuring the wind wouldn't hurt any of us. Halfway back I described the rest of the afternoon. "When we get home, we're baking cookies for Grandpa. Do you like baking?"

Neither girl answered.

"Holly?" I asked directly.

"We're not allowed to use the stove."

I felt encouraged by the sheer number of words. "Good rule, but if I'm right there, it'll be fine. And we're just putting cookies in the oven."

"Why?" Noelle asked. "They have cookies at the store."

"Grandpa's on a special diet. Remember how he went to

the hospital and had surgery? Well, they want him to eat certain foods that are good for him."

"Mommy goes on diets."

"Be quiet, Noelle." Holly walked a little faster.

"It's okay for Noelle to talk." I looked down at the top of my younger niece's blond head and resolved to find a video on YouTube about braiding hair. No matter how carefully I untangled every strand in the morning, by the time I picked her up, her hair was a disaster.

Noelle stuck out her tongue at her sister's back. "Mommy said we have to be careful not to get fat."

I wondered if my sister understood the roots of eating disorders. "You aren't fat, and neither is Holly. You can eat plenty of good food and not worry one bit."

Holly surprised me by tossing words over her shoulder. "Cookies aren't good food."

"The ones we're making are. They have bananas and oats and maple syrup. All kinds of good stuff." I knew because I'd spent time on the internet coming up with recipes that were both low-fat and vegan. Edible remained to be seen.

Now Noelle sounded interested. "Do they have chocolate chips?"

"I found other recipes that do. We'll try those next time."

At the town house I sent them to wash their hands, and while they were gone I took out fruit I'd cut up. When they came into the kitchen, I motioned to the counter where I'd laid out everything, including juice boxes and a bowl of pretzels.

"I always get hungry when I cook. You guys ready to help? Grandpa will be so glad to get something we made."

"I'm tired," Holly said. "I want to watch TV."

"You had trouble falling asleep last night, didn't you?"

She glared at me, but I ignored it. "No TV this afternoon. We're going to finish these and take them right over to Grandpa. Who wants to grind up the flax seeds?" I'd found a little dome-shaped coffee grinder in a cupboard. We had to grind the seeds to make an egg substitute. I was learning things I didn't want to know.

Noelle volunteered and shrieked after she pushed start and it whirred loudly. I interpreted that as "I'm having fun."

"Push it again, and this time hold it down. It won't hurt you."

Despite pouts and folded arms, Holly couldn't seem to help herself. She came closer to peer through the top. The whole process took just seconds, and when the grinding stopped, I nodded to her.

"Now we mix this with water. Holly, would you get me that little glass bowl? Then you can measure the water and mix. I'll get the tablespoon."

I smiled and walked away, as if I had no doubts she'd do just that. When I came back with the spoon, the bowl was right where I wanted it. I didn't run circles around the kitchen pumping my arm in victory. I dumped the ground flax seeds inside and thrust the measuring spoon toward her.

"Two of these filled with water, okay?"

"In the bowl?"

"Yeah, and it's supposed to swell up and act like an egg."

Holly met my gaze. There was a long hesitation, as if she was fighting herself. Then a shrug, but not the usual kind. A slight one, almost comical. "How does an egg act?"

If I hadn't known better, I would have thought my niece actually had a sense of humor. "Like a chicken in training?" I made a goofy face, curled up as much as I could while standing and flapped my arms.

She actually giggled. I had to resist undoing all my good work. I didn't hug her, but it was close.

★ ★ ★

In Gulf Sands I left my father in his courtyard with a little girl perched on each side. While the cookies weren't going to win prizes at the county fair, my mother had judged them acceptable if Dad didn't eat too many. So now he and each girl had a plate with two cookies, along with a tattered copy of *The Velveteen Rabbit* that had been Wendy's, then mine. My mother had kept it all these years.

We left them alone to read and went into the kitchen for tea.

"How's he doing?" I asked.

"I have to remind him hourly that eating right and exercising are a lot better than the alternative."

I spoke without thinking. "Boy, I bet he loves that."

She didn't glare exactly, but I felt the chill in her stare.

"Sorry." I sat at the table and reached for a cookie while she poured the iced tea. She knew how I liked it and added the sugar and lemon before she set it in front of me.

"Your father was always your favorite."

I nearly choked. I swallowed and grabbed my tea for a big slug.

"Well, he was," she said.

"You're obviously exhausted."

"Because I'm telling the truth?"

"Because you're talking about feelings. That's not like you."

"This is getting worse by the moment."

I touched her hand, which had stalled on the way to the cookies. "Isn't the absent parent usually something of a favorite because he's not there to be the disciplinarian? That probably happens with Bryce and Wendy. She does the majority of childcare, and he waltzes in with gifts from faraway ports."

I lifted my hand, since I'd probably gone past our touching limit. "The girls miss Bryce. And Dad was away so much I missed him, too. But I could always count on you to be right here when I needed you."

"You think I'm controlling."

"You aren't?"

She blew out a breath. "You did not receive the gift of diplomacy."

"Wendy got enough for both of us. I'm compelled to tell it like it is. Where did I get that, do you think?"

I thought she was trying not to smile. "I just try to make sure things go the way they're supposed to."

Maybe I'm not particularly diplomatic—after all, I'm a journalist—but I don't say *everything* I think. A discussion of "supposed to" would have been fruitless. I settled on another piece of the truth.

"Mom, you never have to worry about how invaluable you are."

"If I was invaluable, Wendy would have called me. Have you heard from her since we spoke?"

I didn't mention the burner phone. "She called this morning. But she's still refusing to say exactly what happened. And there's no talk of a homecoming."

"That's it? That's all she said? You didn't try hard enough. If you had, we'd know more!"

I drank more tea, trying hard to tamp down my anger. I finally set my glass on the table. "I know you think I don't try hard enough, or that I don't measure up to my sister, who always did, but this time you're going to have to trust me. I'm taking good care of Wendy's kids, and I'm doing absolutely everything I can to get her back home."

"I've never told you that you don't measure up. I just wanted you to do your best. In school. In men. In sports. You never tried to win." She'd cleverly sandwiched men in the middle.

"Unlike you and my sister, I don't aim for impossible standards. I don't want to be the best at anything. I just want to be happy."

She grabbed my empty glass and her nearly full one, and took them to the counter. Then she rested against it.

"Are you happy?"

The entire conversation was astounding, but this, most of all. I couldn't remember either of my parents ever asking so directly.

"Sometimes." It was the best I could do.

"Your podcast certainly measures up."

"I have good people to work with." I hesitated. "No, I chose good people. Partly because I'm not doing it for the glory. I'm just trying to tell a story. We all are."

"And your personal life?" When I didn't jump right in, she added, "Now that you're living here, are you going to see Mateo?"

"I don't know."

"I'd tell you that you need to, but I'm already too controlling."

I looked up to see she was smiling, just a little. "Holly takes after you," I said. "She has your sly sense of humor."

"If she does, she's lucky. It seems to stand up under pressure." She began to fuss, stacking our glasses in the dishwasher, wiping the counter. "You'll tell me if you hear anything I should know from your sister?"

"I will."

"Thank you."

I was pretty sure she meant it.

CHAPTER TEN

For dinner I threw caution and nutrition to our local wind gusts and took the girls to Seabank Seafood, my favorite hometown restaurant. Holly had asked for fish and chips, and I wasn't going to settle for fish sticks and frozen French fries. I negotiated seats at an outdoor table protected by a high wall. We were just far enough away from the Jimmy Buffett cover band that I could hear the girls' soft voices if they decided to use them. Plus if I craned my neck, I could glimpse the choppy waves of Little Mangrove Bay, which opened to the gulf.

Our grandmotherly server arrived with crayons, place mats to color and children's menus on the other side. "You girls like hush puppies?"

She'd gone straight to the important people at the table. I watched Noelle look first at Holly, then at me. She gave a cute little nod. For once Holly didn't correct her.

"I'll bring a basket to start you off." The woman finally glanced at me. "You've been here before?"

"My dad used to sneak me in when my mother wasn't looking. I grew up on your fried shrimp."

She winked. "We never fry anything at Seabank Seafood."

After she left I turned the place mats to the menu side. "Noelle, if you can't read yours, Holly will read it to you. Right?" I looked at Holly for confirmation.

She complied, after a ritual eye roll.

"Fish and chips?" I asked when she finished.

She shrugged, but she looked pleased I'd remembered. Noelle asked for shrimp.

They flipped their place mats and began to color an ocean scene. Noelle was determined to turn the fish a fierce purple, but Holly corrected her. "There are no purple fish, Noelle."

She looked crushed, and I pushed her hair behind her ears. "Holly has never heard of the Purple Panama Perch, sweetie. It's my favorite fish. And let's not forget the Lavender Lionfish."

"You're making that up," Holly said.

"And I forgot the Violet Vampire fish. But guess what?" I leaned forward, like I was telling them a secret. "That's a piece of paper and those aren't real fish. They can't even swim. So you girls can color them any color you want."

Noelle looked pleased; Holly looked suspicious. But they went back to work, and I noticed that Holly used a blue crayon on the seaweed.

As the art project wound down, the hush puppies arrived, and our server was effusively complimentary. While we munched I asked about school. Noelle told me she'd moved into a different reading group. Holly didn't volunteer anything, but when I asked what she'd liked most of all that day, she said she liked learning about Florida Indian tribes.

"They are indignant people," she added.

I was pretty sure she meant indigenous, but I could have been wrong.

Our dinners came, and despite the hush puppies and cookies, we did a credible job of cleaning our plates.

On the way home the girls were subdued, but both of them seemed contented. We'd taken baby steps today, but we were moving in the right direction. We were establishing a relationship, and that was not to be taken lightly. Of course if I continued down this path, I was making a commitment, and there was no evidence I did that well. On the other hand, in the past I hadn't seen anything I could give them they couldn't get more of from their mom. Now I did.

Me.

We pulled into the driveway, and something at the side of the house caught my eye. I stopped and opened my door. "Stay here. I need to check something." When I turned to make sure they'd heard, I saw they were both falling asleep. I clapped my hands, Arlie Gracey style. "Wait until we get inside for that, okay? You'll sleep better in your own beds."

I walked to the side of the house where the great room was located. Two windows allowed light inside, both more than halfway up the wall, so as not to be a problem for furniture placement. They were too high for a view, as well as difficult to open and close, but the builder had included screens.

The latter was the culprit. While I was fairly sure the screen closer to the road hadn't been hanging from one corner before we left, now the wind had knocked it loose, and it banged against the house with each gust. I doubted my parents' handyman would come back for such a small job.

I couldn't address the problem without a ladder, but I was able to shove the screen back into place, and hoped it would hold until later. Then I got my sleepy little nieces inside.

Fried seafood coma had set in, and without argument I maneuvered them into the bathroom for sponge baths and next into their bedroom for nightgowns. I said an abbreviated bed-time prayer, then tucked Noelle in first.

"I guess I don't have to offer a story," I told her. "Grandpa read you one already."

She reached up and put her arms around my neck when I kissed her cheek. I smiled at her, and she smiled back. It was the single best moment of my day.

Since Holly had sleep to make up for, I'd hoped she might already be working on it, but I found her on her back staring wide-eyed at the ceiling.

Emboldened by my success with her sister, I perched on the bedside as I pulled up her covers. "You've had a long day. You'll sleep well tonight."

"I have allergies. Mommy always gives me medicine."

My mother hadn't said anything about allergies, and I hadn't noticed sneezing or sniffling. Still, it was possible the wind might have stirred up pollen. I thought I remembered some-thing about children with allergies and sleep problems. Also something about them being especially cranky. Of course I might have been making that up since it fit the situation.

I pushed her hair back from her forehead, and lay my hand across it to be sure she wasn't feverish. She didn't wince. "You often have problems with allergies? Hard to breathe?" I tried to think. "Itching? Problems hearing?"

She shook her head.

"Do you know what your mother gives you?"

She shook her head again, making a rut in her pillow. "She keeps it in the medicine cabinet."

"Your eyes look fine. Your nose seems clear. But if you start having symptoms, I'll find out what to do."

She forced a sneeze. I laughed and ruffled her hair. "You'll feel fine in the morning. I promise."

She was staring at me now instead of the ceiling. I might

not be good at this parenting thing, but I knew that look. She wanted to say something.

"Do you want to talk about what's worrying you? Because I think something has to be, or you'd be sleeping better."

She didn't respond.

I probed a little more. "I know you must miss your mom. And I think you're a little worried about her being gone."

The words spilled out, as if Holly could no longer contain them.

"Can you find Daddy and make him come home?"

I hadn't been prepared for that. I fiddled with her covers, but I couldn't delay for long. "I don't know how to do that. His job is pretty important, and it's not easy to reach him. Your mommy will have to do that when she gets home."

I leaned over to kiss her cheek, and at least she didn't turn away. I was sure something more needed to be said. "I promise, your daddy is just fine. He's out in the water somewhere protecting all of us. You don't have to worry about him. He doesn't want you to worry. I know that for sure."

"Nobody knows anything for sure." She turned on her side. There was nothing else I could say.

Downstairs I considered what to do about the screen. I preferred waiting until both girls were asleep before I went outside, but judging from my conversation with Holly, I didn't think she would be asleep anytime soon. Before long it would be too dark to see.

In the garage I removed a lightweight stepladder from its home against a wall and found a screwdriver. Outside the screen was already flapping in the wind. Once I was level with it, I saw two screws were missing.

I removed the other two and pocketed them. Then I carried everything back into the garage. At some point I would buy new screws and fix the screen for real, but for now, at least it wouldn't be banging against the siding.

Inside I locked up and turned on the security alarm for the first time since the dead bolts had been repaired. Something about being outside had set my teeth on edge. We were isolated here, with no neighbors in residence yet and woods behind the house. Caution was always the best choice.

I checked on Holly, who was staring fixedly at the ceiling. I left her to stare, afraid if I spoke to her she might stay awake even longer. In the master bedroom I pulled out my computer and researched childhood insomnia. As I'd thought, stress was often a cause. Insomnia could also result from too much caffeine, conditions in the bedroom like noise, an overabundance of light, and most interesting of all to me, a stuffy nose from allergies.

"Bingo." I got up to search the girls' medicine cabinet and found cotton balls, but nothing they could swallow. My sister was a diligent, protective mother.

Wendy was even more protective in the master bathroom, where I discovered a locked medicine cabinet and no key, although several nearly empty prescription bottles, one for high blood pressure, another for heartburn, sat on the sink. Since the cabinet didn't match the vanity, I theorized it was an addition. Whether Wendy or another renter had added it, medication was safe in this house, which in today's world of accidental overdoses was a bonus.

Since I had no way of knowing what medication Wendy used for Holly's allergies, I had to let go of that idea. The website had advised allowing children to read in a low light environment to help them relax. I would try that if Holly stayed awake.

While I waited, I changed my search to Milton Kerns and began to scan multiple varieties of the name. Nothing promising turned up, and many of my hits were obituaries. I found one M. Kernston who was starring in an amateur theater production of *The Sound of Music*. Somehow, I couldn't envision Wendy's "Milton" performing the role of Captain Georg von Trapp one night and committing murder the next.

I was typing in "Milton" and "murder" when my cell phone rang.

"Long day?" Sophie asked.

I got up to close the bedroom door. "Things went better."

"Glad to hear it. I—"

I interrupted. "This is always about me. First, how are you? Anything up there?"

"Wayne's moved to Texas to get a job on an oil rig."

Sophie's ex-husband was more of a hobby than a relationship. He came and went as regularly as the meter reader, and she regarded him with the same lack of wonder. "You okay with that?"

"I met a new guy in a singles chat room. He's legit. We're meeting for coffee tomorrow."

I didn't have to warn her. By now Sophie probably knew everything about the new guy, including his blood type and the relative length of his toes. "Is his photo for real?"

"Come on, that only happened once. And that photo was legit, only the guy was a little younger when it was taken."

"Twenty years."

"I could still recognize him."

I grinned. "Wishing you luck. Glad it's coffee, not a bar. Get a go-cup and keep the lid on. Just in case."

"So, I found a murder. The thing that drew my attention? It happened at a resort on Friday night, maybe sixteen hours or so before your sister first called you. Not one of Gracey Group's resorts, either." She said the last in a hurry, knowing that would be my first question. "But I think it's the kind of place your father might be interested in."

"It's for sale?"

"I'm still working on that. Anyhow, the resort's in New Mexico, not Arizona or California, but not ridiculously far from Phoenix. She could have driven there afterward, so maybe she was telling the truth when she told you where she was calling from."

I couldn't figure out why that made me feel better, but it did.

"The murder happened at the Golden Aspen Resort and Spa outside Santa Fe. The property's not huge, but apparently they have fabulous mountain views. The resort specializes in small- to medium-size conferences and events, and they house their guests in casitas—small cabins—nestled all over the grounds. They have the usual meeting rooms, the spa itself, recreation facilities. You could be happy there for eternity."

"Sounds like a scenic place for a murder."

"Apparently somebody thought so."

I had already keyed in Golden Aspen Resort and Spa so I could look while we talked, but the website was taking a long time to load.

Sophie continued. "A doctor was killed, a surgeon of some kind, and the sheriff is looking for several persons of interest."

I could tell from her brief description that she had just discovered the murder, because otherwise I would be swimming in details. "That's all you have so far?"

"They're keeping the whole thing quiet. The resort is probably doing everything they can to keep a guest's murder out of the news, and the sheriff's office isn't releasing details."

We knew so little, how could we tell if this was the murder haunting my sister? On the other hand, it wasn't connected to an urban gang. It wasn't a hit and run with someone who didn't fit Wendy's description at the wheel. It wasn't any of the other possibilities we'd all but discarded.

This murder had taken place at a classy resort, like the ones my father owned. A doctor, not a barfly, was the victim, and the sheriff was looking for several persons of interest.

Sophie moved on to questions. "Can you introduce the subject of resorts in New Mexico next time you speak to your father? In case Gracey Group does have some connection to the property?"

"I'll try. What else can I do?"

"I'd love to know if your sister was a registered guest on Saturday or before. But they'll keep that information private. They won't tell either of us."

When I investigated for *Out in the Cold*, I knew how to get information, which strings to pull, which ears to bend. I could cite my credentials as a journalist and podcaster before I asked for help. But this was different. I didn't want anybody to connect Wendy to what had happened. If anyone was suspicious of her part in this, they hadn't yet traced her to Seabank.

"Do you have any connections you can use?" I asked.

"I'll try to think of some. But at this moment, no."

"Thanks, Soph. This…could be it." I'd almost said "This is promising." But what was promising about a murder? Ever?

We said goodbye, and I went to check on Holly. She was finally sleeping, although fitfully. The long-term solution to her insomnia might well be hush puppies. Somewhere a medical journal was just waiting to hear from me.

When I returned to my computer, Golden Aspen's website had finally loaded, but the information was basic. The resort relied on gorgeous landscape photos to entice new guests. Of course there was nothing about a murder anywhere on the site.

I gave up and got ready for bed. As I slipped between the covers, I wondered where my sister was tonight. I was sleeping in her bed, living her life, taking care of her children. Where was she and why?

I was back to saying prayers now that I was in charge of my nieces. Tonight, though, I said a silent one for Wendy. If we'd found the murder she was fleeing, how much evidence pointed to her and why? I prayed that whoever had really committed the crime would be caught and charged so my sister could come home.

Somehow tonight, prayer seemed like another long shot.

CHAPTER ELEVEN

Holly wasn't exactly bright-eyed the next morning, but she was moving. I put Noelle's hair in pigtails and found their raincoats for the drive to school. Yesterday's wind had heralded a storm, and heavy rain was falling, an unpleasant addition to cooler temperatures.

As we were leaving, I told both girls to bring their raincoats and backpacks. They'd need raincoats for the trip up the sidewalk from the drop-off point. Since I hadn't been the aunt-in-residence long, I hadn't learned that telling a little girl to do something doesn't always bear fruit. When we arrived and pulled into the line of parents dropping off their children, Holly told me she'd forgotten both raincoat and backpack.

"And your head?" I asked. "Firmly in place?"

"We can go back."

Nosing my way into the line had taken minutes. I wasn't about to nose my way back out. "Take this." The rain wasn't letting up, so I stripped off my windbreaker, wiggling my way out without removing the seat belt. "This will keep you dry for the trip inside. I'll get your backpack and drop it off as soon as I can."

"But my homework and lunch ticket are inside."

I admired her whining, which was a step up from sullen silence. "I'm sure you're sorry you forgot them. But hopefully I'll be back before lunch." I intended to come back the moment I was sure the line at the curb had disappeared. But why let her off the hook so easily?

"I don't know why we can't go back now."

"Because Noelle would be late for no good reason. And that wouldn't be fair."

"She's only in first grade!"

"And aren't we proud of her for being right on time today?"

We'd arrived at the drop-off point. I pivoted in my seat and made shooing motions. "I'll be back. You two have a good day."

Holly threw the door open. At least she slipped my windbreaker around her shoulders. I watched them both disappear up the walkway.

My plan for the morning included a trip to visit my parents. I wanted to casually mention New Mexico to my father, and I had the perfect excuse to visit. I had promised my mother I'd check a nearby natural foods store to see if it carried vegan-friendly items she hadn't been able to find. But first I made a detour back to the town house.

When I arrived, a pickup truck was parked on the street several houses away. Someone was probably getting repairs made before the season, which meant with luck, we'd soon have neighbors. Since I had to get out of the car anyway to punch in the garage door code, I parked in the driveway and skidded through puddles to the front door, which was protected by the master bedroom sundeck.

I stopped to get my key and was just taking in the fact that something was different about the door, when I heard a rustling from the podocarpus trees looming beside the porch. I turned as a figure in jeans and a dark hoodie launched itself in my direction. I didn't have time to scream. I threw up my hands and threw myself forward to keep from being knocked over. As I did I registered two things. One, that even though the person was tall and slim, the build was too heavy and broad-shouldered to be a woman. And two, that the "something different" were pry marks along the seam where the double doors met.

The man swiped my hands away and shoved me hard, grabbing for my keys as I fell backward. Once I landed on my butt, I clamped my fingers around them and lifted my feet, kicking hard in his direction and aiming for the spot where a kick would do the most good. He swiveled to one side and then, enraged, threw a punch toward my shoulder. The air moved as his fist grazed my shirt, but the punch missed because I had already rolled away. Now I dove for the front door. He tried to grab my feet, but I kicked out at him again, and then one more time when he dropped the only one he'd managed to get a grip on.

I was too scared to think. If I had, I wouldn't have tried to get inside the house, because the chances were 100 percent this nutcase would follow for tea and a chat. But I scrambled to my knees and grabbed the doorknob. I'm not sure what would have happened next if a dog hadn't barked on the road in front of the house, a high yapping sound guaranteed to frighten a canary.

Yap or not, the sound startled the intruder. In a neighborhood like this one, dogs are always on leash attached to an owner. And this guy probably didn't want witnesses. Before I could scream, he turned and fled around the side of the town house and disappeared.

I was so stunned I could only pull myself to my feet and struggle to insert the key. My hand was shaking so badly that getting it in the slot took three tries, but once I succeeded I pushed the door open, looked behind me to be sure the intruder hadn't returned, and then slipped inside, slamming and locking the door behind me.

Was this maniac going to try to enter another way? He'd been determined to get inside. Against every warning my pounding heart was struggling to send, I went through the great room to make sure he wasn't trying to break in through the glass doors. The screen door to the outside stood open, but nobody was in sight, and the doors into the house were still locked and undamaged. I pulled out my cell phone and called 911. Then I collapsed to the sofa, where I could continue to watch the back of the house.

"There was a pickup parked a couple of houses down the street." The deputy and I had decided to hold our rendezvous by the front door. I pointed to the left, and my surly protector, somewhere in his thirties and not quite bald enough to shave his head, duly noted what I'd said in his spiral notebook.

He glanced up. "No truck was there when I arrived."

"If it belonged to him, he'd have left in a hurry."

"It could have been anybody."

I tried to remember details, but I hadn't registered many. "I think it could have been a workman's truck." I thought harder. "I guess I just assumed. You could ask the woman walking her dog. She lives somewhere around here."

"Color? Make? Identifying features?"

He wasn't asking about the dog. I tried to picture the pickup. What had I seen? Why hadn't I seen more? I'm a journalist, and now that observations mattered personally, I only had a few. "Dark, maybe blue or even black. You know,

I think there was lettering on the door. Maybe that's why I assumed a workman was doing something on the house where it was parked."

"What did the letters say?"

"Sorry, if I'd known what was about to happen, I would have taken notes and photos."

"Anything else about the man?"

I'd already given him all the details I remembered, a guess about his height and weight, his jeans, and the dark hoodie that had been drawn so tightly around his face I hadn't seen his hair. I thought I remembered a long nose and the beginning of a beard or stylish stubble, but that was all I could dredge up. Even the intruder's race was a mystery. His skin was light brown, but this was Florida. He was either tanned or he'd been born that particular hue. I couldn't guess which.

"I can't figure out why this guy tried to break into a house with an obvious security system." I pointed to the sign in front of the house that said we were protected.

"Half those signs are fake. People pay for security for a couple of months, then decide it's not worth it, so they cancel, but the sign stays up. Nobody takes signs seriously. Did you have the alarm set this morning?"

I shook my head.

"You and nobody else. And even if he'd set it off? Probably not many people living around here to hear it. Then it takes the alarm company time to respond, call the phone numbers they have on file and finally call us. He could be in and out—with small stuff like jewelry, drugs, cash—in ten minutes. He probably figured law enforcement wouldn't get here for at least half an hour."

His guess on timing was correct, because it had taken the deputy at least that long to show up and take my statement.

On a roll, he continued. "We have groups coming through

here this time of year and late in the spring. They travel back and forth from somewhere up north and break into houses along the way."

My mother had warned me. Apparently even bad guys needed a change of scenery in the winter. "I think he was alone."

"Doesn't matter. They work all kinds of ways. We've had three daylight break-ins the past week. Have you noticed strange cars?"

"It's really quiet here," I said. "The dog walker is about it."

"Nobody's come to the door to ask where a neighbor lives, or whether they can do odd jobs? Because the people I'm telling you about will do that, strictly to see if the house is occupied."

I shook my head. "Spooky quiet." Then I thought about the screen. "You know, we got home last night after dinner out—"

"We?"

"My nieces. Six and eight. I'm taking care of them while their mom's away on business. My parents own the house."

"So..." He waited for me to finish.

"There was a screen loose on the side of the house. Two of the screws were gone. Maybe somebody was trying to get in that way. The windows are pretty well hidden from the street."

"Probably not. He'd try the doors first."

"Maybe he did. Maybe today was his second try. And I'm pretty sure he did get into the screened porch. The door leading outside was open."

He slipped his notebook back in the shirt pocket of a dark green uniform. "He won't be back. If somebody is really staking out this neighborhood, empty houses are better bets. Now that it's clear this house is occupied, he'll leave you alone."

I wasn't happy he was so offhanded about my safety. "Why don't I feel more secure?"

"Some people leave a chain with a collar staked outside, or put a water bowl and a few dog toys on the porch. Anything to make it look like they have a vicious canine protecting them. You could give that a try, or get a real dog. If this is a group from somewhere up north, they'll move on in a few weeks."

"Great, they skip town and I still own a dog."

"You don't like dogs?"

"Who doesn't like dogs? I just think you get a dog because you want one, not because—" I stopped myself. I was babbling, residual of the attack.

"You're not hurt. You're sure? You could go to urgent care and be checked over, just in case."

"I'm shook up. That's it." That and a bruise that was going to make sitting down a challenge for a while. I thought about Holly and hoped she wasn't in trouble because I hadn't returned with her backpack. Then I realized what might have happened if I'd brought the girls back home with me, the way that Holly had wanted me to. I shuddered.

"I think we're done here. You let us know if you remember anything else. Feel free to call if anything comes up."

He paused before he let himself out. "I just realized why you look familiar."

"Oh?"

"You know Mateo Santiago? He used to be a K9 officer with the sheriff's department."

A chill snaked down my spine. "I know Teo."

He looked substantially less friendly. "I thought maybe you did. Too bad he and his dog aren't on our K9 unit anymore, isn't it? I'm sure he would have been happy to help you now."

Then he was gone.

With the remote possibility that the intruder was still hanging around the neighborhood, I checked and rechecked the town house locks and turned on the security alarm before I dropped off Holly's backpack and raincoat. Instead of heading to the natural foods store, I went home again, and after a careful check, got out and opened the garage and parked inside, closing the door quickly behind me.

Something liquid was called for to help calm me down before I faced my parents. Since by anybody's standards it was too early for alcohol, I settled on green tea and took it to the great room, where I could watch the rain through the doors to the screened porch.

I wasn't surprised that the deputy who'd interviewed me knew my connection to Teo, or remembered the events of four years ago that had made today's attack seem like dinner with an old friend.

I had met Teo Santiago on a gray, rainy day, like this one, although the month had been June, not December, and despite having been raised in Seabank, between the heat and humidity I'd felt trapped in a Tennessee Williams novel.

After high school I'd abandoned Florida for college and my first job, but that summer I'd returned to do an internship at the *Seabank Free Press* for my master's degree in investigative journalism.

I had already earned an undergraduate degree in criminal justice, hoping to become a cop. After my cardiologist refused to certify me to lift more than half my body weight, I'd worked as a fraud investigator for a full-service risk mitigation company. For the most part I'd done background checks, and a limited amount of skip tracing, but I'd learned a lot. Most important, now I knew I thrived when digging up facts that other people found unimportant or useless. I particularly liked putting them together to form pictures of my subjects' lives.

Of course neither my talent nor interest in digging deeper

had been particularly appreciated in my job. Still, that time had been invaluable. I'd realized I was a journalist at heart.

At the end of my course work, I had hoped for an internship at a big city paper and had received a few nods of interest, but when I learned my mother was going into the hospital for knee surgery, I'd queried the *Free Press*, so I could be in town to help while she recovered.

Even then newspapers had a host of problems, and a paper in a small Florida city with an economy fueled by winter residents had more than most. The *Free Press* had a tight budget, and the only reason they agreed to take me on was because they were planning a series of articles about a murder that had happened in Seabank when I was still in high school.

During my interview, I brought up the case and volunteered to help conduct research, pointing out that as a Seabank native and the daughter of Dale Gracey, who had been on the city council at the time, I had contacts that might be invaluable.

In a quiet well-heeled community like ours, the murder had been high profile. A tax accountant named Becky Drake had been murdered after leaving a local charity fund-raiser. At the event she'd been seen arguing with her longtime boyfriend, John Quayle, and the prosecutor claimed that he had followed and killed her later that night. Quayle had been found guilty.

Then two months before I needed an internship, in a stunning turnaround, Quayle had been released. The prosecution's star witness, another fund-raiser guest who had overheard the quarrel, had recanted, claiming the police had threatened to arrest her unless she told her story their way. Then a friend of Quayle's had stepped forward to claim that Quayle had spent the night in his apartment, but his statement had never been admitted into evidence. Quayle's court-appointed attorney had discounted the alibi because the friend had a criminal record and was probably lying.

Based on that and more, Quayle's new attorney won an appeal, and the appellate court ordered a second trial. In a decision that surprised everyone, the state of Florida had decided not to retry him, and Quayle was now a free man.

That summer Quayle had moved back to the county to live with his mother. The *Free Press* wanted to do a series about the murder and include interviews with Quayle and others involved in the case who were still living in town. Their own staff was taking advantage of the summer slowdown to use up vacation time, and the managing editor was afraid that vital information and persons of interest might disappear if the paper waited until fall, when everyone assembled again.

Maybe my hometown paper wasn't the *Washington Post* or the *New York Times*, but I'd been thrilled. The Drake case had seared itself into the brain of a receptive high school junior.

The *Free Press* newsroom was a sprawling affair with artificial light overhead and industrial carpeting underfoot. Cubicles that were defined by dark oak laminate cabinets lined the walls, and tables with multiple computers filled the middle. The building stood beside a city park thick with moss-draped oaks and magnolias, and their shade made the walk from the parking lot tolerable.

The crime and investigation editor, Grant Telford, was a man in his fifties, and the fire in his belly had been extinguished years before. My enthusiasm puzzled him, but he took advantage of it, giving me lists of names and questions to ask. I was to do the initial footwork, then hand my notes to a staff reporter in the fall before I left.

After Becky Drake's body was found in a pond near the Quayle family home, John Quayle had become an immediate suspect. When the police had tried to question him, they had noticed a woman's scarf on the floor of his car, similar to the description of one Drake had worn at the fund-raiser.

When confronted, Quayle had disappeared into the night. A K9 deputy, Mateo Santiago, and his German shepherd, Bismarck, had tracked him to a tree stand in the woods behind his house, and after Deputy Santiago scrambled up the tree to confront him, Quayle had surrendered for questioning.

Mateo, known as Teo, was on my contact list. During the murder trial, he'd testified that on the ride back to the sheriff's office, Quayle had told him he was going to be found guilty.

"Everything is my fault," Quayle had said at the time. "I don't make these kinds of mistakes."

I found Teo's photo on the sheriff department's website, but not his dog's. The man was young, with a cocky, lopsided smile and a military haircut. By the time I called to set up an interview, I had already spoken to Drake's grandmother and her stepfather, who had been a suspect early in the case. On the phone Teo sounded a shade too confident. He corrected my pronunciation of his name, from *tee-o* to *tay-o*, and told me since *tio* meant uncle, only his nieces called him that.

"Tio Teo?" I asked. "Catchy."

"Try saying it fifty times."

He invited me to a K9 demonstration that his unit was doing for a local women's club, and promised we could talk afterward.

The demo was at a local soccer field, fenced and sprawling. Rain had fallen as I parked, and I wondered if the demonstration would go on. But as we waited in line, the clouds dispersed and feeble rays of sunlight appeared. I explained who I was to the woman ushering people into the bleachers, and she motioned me inside. Three deputies, in the same green-shirted uniform as the deputy I'd spoken to today, were on the grass with their dogs, all German shepherds.

Judging from what I remembered of his voice, I tried to guess which of the men was Teo. All were about the same age, and since I was too high in the bleachers to see faces, I made a guess that he was the beefiest, a guy with a weight lifter's body, who moved with an obvious swagger and seemed to think he was in charge. That man's dog was slightly lighter in color than a similarly colored dog at the end of the line, and he held his tightly against him, as if to prove how tough he was to be able to control such a powerful animal. From my perch, the third dog looked to be coal black, although I learned later he was a bicolor, because he had a few small patches of brown. His handler seemed the most relaxed, as if he and the dog were so deeply in tune, they were chilling together until it was time to work.

As it turned out, I had guessed incorrectly. The announcer introduced the men, and Teo was the laid-back handler with the beautiful black dog. I was glad.

In the next minutes the deputies put all the dogs through basics using equipment set up on the field. They ran them through long pipes, up ladders, across what looked like balance beams, and over hurdles the dogs hardly seemed to notice. Then the fun began. Another deputy in a padded suit came out on the field, and one by one the K9 team issued commands to their dogs to take the guy down. I was entranced at how perfectly each dog obeyed, but I was most entranced by Teo and Bismarck, who worked as a perfect team. When signaled, Bismarck stopped just feet from his prey and waited for Teo's command. They clearly trusted each other and worked with efficient grace.

The dogs leaped for arms and hung from the suit, their teeth clamped there like bizarre Christmas ornaments. I watched the dogs take the suited man to the ground when he tried to run. By the end of the half hour, I was sure I never wanted to do anything that would lead to being singled out by any of the three teams.

Afterward I waited until most of the crowd was heading back to their cars before I went down on the field to talk to Teo. His dog was romping with another, chasing tennis balls one of the other deputies tossed for them. Up close Teo did resemble his photo, but he was one of those men photos would never accurately capture. His hair was dark, and his eyes were darker. I thought his family might have come to the US from Cuba, although later I learned his great-grandparents on both sides had been born in Puerto Rico. The grin I'd rated as cocky was more accurately defined as captivating, a point somewhere between warm and seductive.

It also seemed possible that the seductive part wasn't something he turned on for just anybody.

"You look the way you sound," he said, holding out his hand after I introduced myself.

"How's that?"

He smiled. "Tio Teo. Catchy."

Not only had he nailed my voice perfectly, he'd remembered exactly what I'd said. My cheeks warmed. "I bet you do whole routines."

"Your voice is memorable. Low, musical." He paused. "Sensual."

We shook. His hand swallowed mine, although he wasn't a large man, like his show-off colleague. Teo was taller than average, broad-shouldered and long-limbed but trim, like a runner. I knew he had to be strong to do what he did, but I knew he would also be fast.

"The dimples are a great addition to the voice," he said as he dropped my hand.

I tried not to melt. "You have time to be interviewed now?"

Bismarck was circling toward us, and the tennis balls were back in the other deputy's pocket, his dog on a leash now. Teo said something that sounded like it was in German, and Bismarck trotted to his side and sat.

I had done a little research before my arrival, so even if I hadn't witnessed the demonstration, I knew how well-trained these dogs had to be. Still, this was nobody's cocker spaniel. Never having owned any dog, I didn't know what to do.

"You can pet him," Teo said.

"He won't eat my hand? A little evening snack?"

"Only if I tell him to."

I leaned over and held my hand out for Bismarck to sniff before I carefully reached over his head and scratched behind his ears. "He's beautiful."

"My best friend."

I wondered if that meant there was no woman in his life. "My mom's not a fan of dogs, so I'm a dog novice."

"You don't have one now? I bet you don't live at home anymore."

"Actually I do, but just for the summer. While I'm here interning at the paper." I looked up and flashed my admirable dimples. "And the paper's the reason I'm standing here. I'd love that interview."

His gaze held mine. "I'd love to give it to you. But I just found out I'm working this evening."

"Can we set up another time then?"

"We could do it over dinner tomorrow."

There were many times and places for a quick interview. I knew that. He knew that. But I didn't hesitate. Because the idea of sitting across the table from the deputy who had found John Quayle in a tree stand was promising.

Even more so? Finding out about Mateo Santiago was irresistible.

CHAPTER TWELVE

My tea was cold, and apparently so was I, because I was shivering. I was just wrapping a chenille afghan around my shoulders when the doorbell rang. I wondered if a miracle had occurred, and the cops had arrested my attacker and were now at my front door to gloat. I knew better, of course, since at best I'd probably be called down to the local sheriff's office to identify the guy in some kind of lineup. But hope is like a worm peeking out of its hole in the spring when hungry robins are everywhere.

A quick peek through my own peephole brought the second surprise of the day.

"Sophie?" I flung open the door and grabbed one of the two cloth bags loaded into Sophie's arms before I gave her a quick hug. "I told you none of this stuff was necessary." The bag in my arms held folders about potential cold cases. I hadn't expected to need them because I'd foolishly assumed, or hoped, my stay would be short.

"You know the coffee date I told you about?" Sophie stepped over the threshold and let me lock the door behind her.

"Isn't that today?"

"In about an hour. Here. Or almost. Just down the road."

"You drove four hours to have coffee with a stranger?"

Sophie was sparkling more than usual, enough that I had to blink. I hoped the guy liked rhinestones and sequins. Her billowing chiffon blouse, worn low over her shoulders, was crusted with them. To tone it down, she wore plain skintight jeans. Her hair was pulled back with multiple butterfly clips, which exposed hoop earrings wide enough to play ring toss.

"I'm being careful," she said. "I didn't want to tell him where I live."

"And you needed an excuse to check up on me."

"Of course not. Why would you think so?" She began to wander, examining the downstairs.

"You didn't happen to notice anybody hanging around outside, did you?"

Alert, as always, she stopped. "Why?"

"Finish your fact-finding mission, then I'll tell you."

Minutes later we were on the screened porch, rocking back and forth on the cushioned glider. I told her about my morning.

Sophie waits and then she pounces. "I assume you didn't tell the deputy about Wendy's little problem?"

"Of course not."

"Because you don't think the guy who came after you is related? Or because you're protecting her?"

"Both."

She looked pained. "Did the deputy have any advice?"

"He told me to get a dog."

"Do you know how many people get dogs and then abandon them because they don't really think it through?" Sophie volunteers at our local animal shelter. She fosters rescued chihuahuas until they find new and better homes.

"Maybe I could borrow Kiwi." Kiwi is Sophie's permanent

chihuahua, old, overweight and only up for attacking a toe if absolutely required.

"You have better possibilities." Sophie was a student of my past.

She waited, but when I didn't take the bait, she moved on. "Your sister is absent because she's afraid she's going to be arrested for a murder she didn't commit. A man tries to break into her home." She let her words squirm uncomfortably between us.

"The deputy said he's had several break-ins this week. He thinks it's a group that travels through on a regular basis."

"Could be." She pushed the glider harder, and it squeaked in protest.

I asked the obvious question. "Wendy's out west somewhere running from everybody. What could this guy have to do with that?"

"I have no idea. But coincidence is the catalyst of investigations."

"And sometimes coincidence itself is the enemy because it's thought to be more than it really is. Sometimes a cigar is just a cigar."

"You're planning to be extra careful?"

I didn't tell her I'd already toyed with bringing my Smith & Wesson inside. Unfortunately, there were two small children in the house and no gun safe. And what would I have done with my gun today, anyway, had it been handy? Pulled it from my purse while the guy was rolling over me, and then aimed it at his chest? Florida is a "stand your ground" state, so I probably would have been within my rights to shoot him. Unfortunately, then I would have spent the rest of my life wondering if he'd only knocked me over so he could get away. And he would no longer be alive to clear up our misunderstanding.

Sophie was waiting for an answer. "I'm mulling my possibilities," I said. "But I'll come up with something."

"I don't have time to goad you. I want to tell you what else I've learned about the murder in Santa Fe. Then I have to scoot."

"You could come back and meet my nieces after your date. Stay for dinner."

"I have to head right back to Delray after coffee. I'm subbing for another cashier, and she can't leave until I get there."

"So fill me in."

"I'll start with the victim. His name is Vítor Calvo, *Dr.* Vítor Calvo from Rio de Janeiro. He is…was a plastic surgeon, well-known, apparently. His website touts him as plastic surgeon to the stars. If the online rumors are true, lots of celebrities go to his clinic in Rio to have work done, probably on the sly. What I know for sure is that he regularly scheduled seminars for potential patients at a variety of glitzy resorts with golf courses and five star restaurants. He scheduled half a dozen this year in the US alone. He had one scheduled at the Golden Aspen, and he was there relaxing and preparing."

I digested this as she went. "Is there a theory about why he was murdered?"

"In a brief statement the sheriff said he believed robbery was the motive, because Calvo's wallet and a valuable watch were gone, and the room had been ransacked. That's the kind of thing he wouldn't say out loud if he could avoid it. So it's likely they actually think that's true."

While I couldn't imagine my sister killing, even hurting, anybody, I especially couldn't believe she'd do either for money. Bryce made a substantial income, and when our father died, Wendy would probably take over Gracey Group. As CEO she could pay herself a small fortune. For all I knew, my father had beat her to the punch and she was already filthy rich.

I felt relief, although that surprised me. Even relief felt disloyal. "Any evidence linking someone to the crime?"

"Real information is still sketchy. But we have partners in that area. And one of them knows people in the sheriff's office."

"Partners" were Sophie's idea. In the planning stages of *Out in the Cold*, Sophie had patiently explained that some people wanted more than talk from a podcast like ours. They wanted to see photos, converse with other listeners, investigate on their own and draw up new theories. They wanted to share their results, discuss motives, means and opportunity. They wanted to help solve our crimes. So we had two choices. We could let them do this on their own, with no oversight, or we could create a club of sorts, *Partners in Crime*, and keep them more or less in line.

In my opinion "less" was winning, because the partners are a feisty bunch. But I was still glad that Sophie had ignored my skepticism. She'd organized groups by region, set up online bulletin boards and corralled a graduate student into taking on the job of involving our listeners in myriad acceptable ways. In the meantime, I had paid a designer to set up a website.

In addition to creating an almost fanatical interest in our show, our partners had come through for us almost immediately. In our first season, one of them had uncovered documents the state's attorney had carefully misplaced. The case had concerned a woman convicted of her husband's murder back in the 1990s. Three years ago DNA had exonerated her and she had been released, but both the police department in her little town and the state's attorney's office had refused to follow new leads. The documents were used to prove incompetence and malfeasance. We'd had to rewrite entire segments to include the new information, but our efforts had been invaluable. Interest in the case, kindled by *Out in the Cold*, had

led to a hunt for new suspects, and the end of the state's attorney's career.

"So you contacted this partner?" I asked. "You knew somehow that she..."

"She," she affirmed.

"That *she* had contacts who might have more information?"

"It wasn't hard to sort locations and zero in on the three
partners in that general area."

"You know, you could sell your talents and stop bagging
groceries."

"I like my life. I like *Out in the Cold.* I like being beholden
only to me." It was true. Sophie was a free spirit, and she
would hate being nosy for profit in any kind of corporation
or institution.

"So what did this partner turn up?"

"It's not verified, okay? But she says the maid who discovered the body quit her job and left town, and Calvo's driver
refuses to speak to the police and hired a lawyer. Both are considered persons of interest, but investigators are also looking
for several guests who left the resort between the time Calvo
was murdered and his body was found."

"So that's another reason why you thought this murder
was promising. Maybe Wendy was there and got spooked."

"I'm imagining that could have happened, based on what
we actually know."

"We need that list of hotel guests."

"I can't ask anybody to steal them, even if we could figure out a way."

If we had the list, we might not be able to use it for any
reason other than to verify Wendy's presence at the resort
anyway. Of course I could also just ask her outright and hope
she was honest.

If she called again.

"So how long has your sister lived here?" Sophie asked.

"Months. She moved in this past summer."

"The whole place feels very standard-issue. Like everything here came with it, even the dish towels."

"I don't think she brought much with her when she drove down. And my mother probably stocked it with supplies Gracey Group uses for their vacation rentals on the beach."

"Let's say Wendy's been here six months. That's plenty of time to surround herself with things she likes better. Little things."

I wasn't sure where Sophie was going with this. "Wendy's not overly sentimental. She did a lot of entertaining in Connecticut, but I'm pretty sure she turned the decorating over to an interior designer." I'd been to Wendy and Bryce's home several times. My nieces' rooms were both Disney Princess themed and pristine. The rest of the house looked like a spread in *House Beautiful*.

Sophie was clearly not convinced. "I'm always buying little things I like for my condo."

She wasn't kidding. Getting in and out the door of Sophie's condo was challenging.

"Wendy is essentially a single mom," I said, "and she has a job. I don't think there's a lot of time for shopping."

"Especially if she doesn't plan to stay."

"I'm pretty sure the plan is for her to move back to Connecticut when it makes sense again."

"When would it make sense?"

"When Bryce has a longer stint on shore? When the girls are older?"

"I think what I notice most is the lack of photos. When I'm out of town, I even put photos of my girls on motel dressers. Are the family photos all upstairs?"

"Her house up north has family portraits galore." I thought

of the lovingly compiled scrapbooks upstairs, with photos of Wendy at every phase of her life. I wondered if she was doing the same for her girls.

Sophie looked at her watch, a big, jeweled affair with numbers large enough to read from across the room. "Single parenting's not easy, and I never traveled the way your sister does. I can see why she's here where your parents can help. What did she do for help before?"

I couldn't recall, which was another sign I'd never given Wendy's life much thought. "I don't know what she did. I love Wendy, but she and Mom have always been the team, and I kind of dragged along behind. Honestly, I never thought much about it."

"You're sure thinking about it now."

I stood because Sophie got to her feet. "I won't mind when I can go back to blissful ignorance." Except that I was fairly sure I never would. When Wendy returned and this mess was cleared up, things in both our lives would be different.

We went back through the house and stopped at the front door. I restrained Sophie before she opened the door. "I'll go out first and take a peek to be sure Hoodie Guy isn't waiting to get in."

"You could move in with your parents until you feel safer."

"I feel safer here. At least Hoodie Guy won't ask a million questions I can't answer."

"You don't have to go first, I have Mace."

I didn't ask why. Sophie had been on the dating circuit several times in between reconciliations with her ex. "We'll go out together. You punch and I'll kick."

"Next time I'll come when I can meet the girls."

"If you and Mr. Coffee hit it off, maybe next time will be a sure thing."

I hugged her and watched her head out to a street empty

of both cars and trucks. I was sorry to see her go. I really did hope the date was a roaring success.

I only rarely think of myself as lonely. I have a job I love, and a crew who hang out with me when I need company. My little condo complex has an older couple who show up at my door on a regular basis with home-baked bread and yoga DVDs. There's a bar not far away where I can watch the sunset and talk to any number of tourists and regulars. I just make sure none of them follow me home.

Sophie's visit, though, reminded me just how much I depended on her for companionship. In Seabank I had my parents and my nieces, but I couldn't share thoughts or feelings. I was probably suffering an odd kind of homesickness, even though I was actually living in my hometown. Or maybe it was something more.

Being in close proximity to Mateo Santiago was a stark reminder that just a few years ago, I'd had the companionship, even the love I'd never expected to find. And from what I can tell, finding love, then losing it, is like conquering a drug addiction. You never really stop wanting it; you only learn how not to give in to the craving. And sometimes you're tested almost beyond endurance.

Leaving the house for a while seemed like a good idea, so I decided to visit my parents before I picked up my nieces. I wanted to find out about the resort in New Mexico, and I had another question, one I would have to edge into. Finally, as much as I hated to do it, since my parents owned the town house, I had to let them know there'd been an attempted break-in. Since they didn't own me, though, I could fudge a little on my unintended involvement.

I stopped at the natural food store for bribes before I headed toward Gulf Sands. As I waited in a long line of traffic stalled by roadwork on the busiest stretch of the trip, I was still think-ing about lost love. I remembered another trip to my par-ents' house, with Teo in tow. Our relationship had blossomed quickly, from our first dinner together, to a day at the beach, to dinner at his little apartment in a blue collar suburb, and finally to spending every waking minute we could together, often in his magnificent king bed. I liked everything about him, even Bismarck, who was his constant companion. The only times we weren't compatible were when John Quayle entered the conversation.

From the beginning Teo had made it absolutely clear he believed Quayle was guilty, and that the only reason he hadn't remained in prison was legal manipulation. The state's attor-ney had wanted so badly to get a conviction, he'd played fast and loose with the evidence. And now his failures had come back to haunt everyone.

I was less sure. I'd spoken to people who knew Quayle well and were sure he'd been railroaded. I'd talked to people who had testified in his trial who were now less sure about what they'd seen or heard. Of course years had gone by, and some hesitation was to be expected. But as yet, I hadn't heard a thing to convince me he should have been arrested in the first place.

So Teo and I had agreed to disagree, and we'd left it at that. In no way had it affected our deepening interest in each other.

I knew that my mother suspected I'd found a guy. She'd nosed around a little, but the Graceys were devoted to the concept of personal space. If we had a family coat of arms, it probably featured a blindfolded woman in the center with one finger over her lips. When I didn't volunteer informa-tion, neither of my parents pursued it.

After a month I finally asked Teo if he would let me intro-duce him to my parents at dinner. I knew the time had come. "Mom invited us, so I have to ask. I wouldn't do this," I'd promised, lounging on his bed, a sheet more or less draped over me after an afternoon of extraordinary lovemaking. I was watching him dress, before I got up to shower. "But they're right here in town, and eventually they'll get around to the third degree."

"So this means you're not ashamed of me after all?"

I wondered if he was kidding. "Well, you know, in my parents' eyes, nobody's good enough for their daughters, unless they've already made their first million or their ancestors came over on the *Mayflower*. Preferably both. My sister's husband had to pull out genealogy charts and bank statements before they even let him in the house."

"My paternal great-grandparents left Puerto Rico for a New York tenement where they lived with two other families. *Abuelo*, my grandfather, told me he was born in the only bedroom, weeks too early. They had no money for doctors. They kept him alive by heating the cooking stove in the kitchen all day and night and nestling him in a shoebox. They fed him his mother's milk with an eyedropper. I have family stories on the other side that are worse."

"So much for the *Mayflower*." I cleared my throat. "And I'm guessing cops aren't paid all that well?"

"Will it impress them I've only had a negative balance once this year?"

"It impresses me. I might let you handle my finances."

"I won't fit their criteria." It wasn't a question.

"No, maybe you surpass it. I would never be ashamed of anything about you. I haven't introduced you to Mom and Dad because I didn't want to share you. My parents?" I tried to think of the best way to describe them. "They aren't as snooty as I've made them sound. They're...careful? I don't know how else to say it. They wanted a big family, and they tried for years to have more children after my sister, Wendy, was born. But there were miscarriages, years with no pregnancies. And then I showed up, completely unexpected and, like your great-grandfather, way too early."

"You were a preemie?"

"Big time, and worse. My mom didn't even know she was pregnant. She was in Mexico visiting my sister who was spending a year studying Spanish as a break before college. Mom had given up on the idea of increasing the family. She thought she was starting menopause, but after some symptoms, she discovered she was pregnant and that things weren't going well. The doctors in Mexico told her she couldn't fly home or anywhere. She had to stay in bed and make the best of things."

"So you're an immigrant. That cancels the *Mayflower*."

"I wish I'd stayed long enough to learn Spanish. Mine is awful."

"You started life as a surprise. You've been a surprise to me, too."

I liked being his surprise. "I'm guessing she didn't think she'd be in Mexico long, that the pregnancy would end quickly with no baby. But I stayed put just long enough, although I was still born early, way too early. Which is at least partly to blame for all the heart surgeries I had as a child."

Teo had seen me naked. He hadn't asked about the scars on my chest, but I'd explained anyway. I was beyond embarrassment. When you grow up with something, it seems almost normal, especially something other people rarely saw.

"And so your parents are overprotective," he said. "You were the daughter who almost wasn't."

"I think they were worse with Wendy than with me." And then I told him something I'd never told anyone else. "I came so late in their lives, I think they were done wanting children. Then suddenly, not only did they have a baby they hadn't expected or prepared for, they had one with life threatening health issues. In a foreign country yet. I read once that in previous generations parents believed it was best not to get attached to young children because the mortality rate was so high. In some ways, I think that's what happened with me, and especially for Mom. She distanced herself."

I realized I'd been looking at my hands as I explained. I looked up, and he was now sitting beside me, his chest still bare, the dark hair on his tanned arms soft under my fingertips as I reached out to stroke it. "In the long run, it was better that way," I finished. "Mom was too tired or remote to smother me. I'm not sure which. But I flourished anyway."

"You did." He put his arms around me and held me close. "And nobody appreciates the way you flourished more than I do." Then, despite having made love just a little while ago, we'd fallen back against the sheets, and the conversation about who belonged and who didn't came to an end.

Now traffic picked up and I started forward again. That night and afterward, Teo and my parents had gotten along well. He knew how to ask questions, and he knew how to listen. But he was also a storyteller who could do the voices of his subjects perfectly, and my father, in particular, had loved hearing about his job. If my family had been emotional enough to give a nod of approval, Teo would have gotten one.

Then everything changed.

I pulled up to the Gulf Sands gatehouse and gave yet another new guard my name and status. Inside my parents' house I called my mother's name and followed her voice. I found both of them outside enjoying the sunshine in the walled courtyard.

"I think somebody's starting to feel better," I told my father, kissing his cheek and leaning in for a hug.

"If your mother would just feed me, I'd be up and around in no time."

"I brought you chocolate chip muffins." I held up a finger as my mother started to protest. "Vegan. And banana bread. Plus a couple of quarts of amazing lentil and vegetable soups from the natural food market."

My mother's expression softened. "That was kind."

"That's me. Kind, generous, thoughtful." I smiled. "How is everybody?"

Dad never wants to worry anybody, and Mom doesn't like to admit defeat. So I took their "things are fine" speeches with a grain of salt. I knew they were anything but.

"Your mother tells me your sister has been in touch with you," Dad said, after the ritual questions and answers. "Next time she calls, tell her to call me directly. I don't like this. Nobody at work's heard from her, either."

"Why are you talking to people at work?"

Mom looked unhappy. "That's what I say."

"Dad, just stay off the phone. And Wendy's got her hands full. Let's just leave her alone until she has the situation in—" I hesitated just a fraction of a second, trying to remember where we were pretending my sister was ministering to her college friend "—California."

"Tell her what I said."

"In the meantime, I had some excitement this morning, and since I'm sitting right here telling you, remember there was a happy ending." I recounted the attempted break-in with a few small changes. One, the guy had been trying to break in when he saw me coming up the walk and fled. Two—and related—I neglected to mention the wrestling match.

"The sheriff's department came out to take my statement," I said, wrapping up. "The guy couldn't get in, thanks to you sending Handyman Dave to secure all the locks. The deputy thinks there won't be any more trouble now that the guy, and whoever he's working with, know the house is occupied." I smiled as if I'd just delivered the best of all news.

My mother was the first to speak. "Thank heavens that didn't happen when Wendy and the girls were there."

For a moment I wondered if I'd heard her right. My father

covered up nicely. "Ryan, you're really okay? That must have scared the bejeepers out of you."

My father is the only person I know who can use "be-jeepers" in a sentence and get away with it. "Thank you," I said. "It wasn't the best moment of my life." I didn't look at my mother.

"I only meant that…" Her voice drifted away, and I thought she was finished. But I was wrong. "I'm sorry. You're tougher than your sister," she said at last. "Wendy takes everything to heart. And those little girls. I'm so glad they weren't with you."

"Tougher?" I wondered what she would say if I explained that her "sensitive" older daughter had abandoned her former life because she might be a murder suspect.

"Arlie, Wendy is as tough as nails," my father said. "Something you fail to notice. Under the sugarcoated exterior is a steel rod. And we're talking about *Ryan* now."

He turned to me, done chastising my mother, an event so rare I still wasn't sure I'd witnessed it. "I think you should move back home," he told me.

"I don't think I need to." I patted his hand. "People are already beginning to filter back to Tropicana for the winter, and the town house is as secure as a fortress. I'll use the security alarm, but I think the deputy's right. Nobody's going to break in again. And to be sure, I'll park my car in the driveway for a while so everybody can see somebody's living there."

"You have two young children to worry about," my mother said.

"Something I have not failed to notice." I breathed deeply and controlled the edge in my voice. "And that's exactly why I am going to stay where I am. They're just getting used to me, and they're in a familiar environment at the town house, which helps them adjust. The school's an easy walk, and we can have their friends for playdates." I'd just made up that last part, but it was inspired, and I made a mental note to do exactly that.

Arlie Gracey is not an open book, but with years of practice, I could read her. She wanted to argue, but she knew better. When my father stood up to her, he towered. "If you think that's best."

"Why don't I slice up the banana bread and bring some out here? Herbal tea okay to go with it?"

My father surprised me. "I'll help. We'll leave your mother here to swallow the arguments she knows better than to make. Arlie, stay." As she half rose, he motioned her back to her seat. "I'm supposed to move around."

When we reached the kitchen, I pulled out the banana bread and got down plates. "You're really feeling better?"

"I feel like I've been put out to pasture."

"Just long enough to get fat and sassy again."

"All this is my own fault. I know I have to slow down. I've been hoping to turn things over to your sister, a little at a time, and then ease into retirement. Your mother has always wanted to travel with me at her side instead of meeting me somewhere for a few days."

"Is Wendy the only person who can take over? What if she decides she needs something different than Gracey Group?"

"Has she said that to you?"

"No. But it's a big commitment. With Bryce's job she's more or less a single mom."

"There's always my other daughter."

I laughed. "No chance, Dad. I'd spend my time looking for criminals every time I was supposed to make a real estate deal."

"Perfect place to find some. Maybe more than some."

I'd stumbled into an opening. "I know how hard you and Wendy work. She left a lot of paperwork, and I've been straightening the town house so she won't come back to a mess. She's collected brochures from all kinds of resorts."

"She's probably looking at what they do that we don't. To get ideas."

"Are some of them for sale? Does she make suggestions for acquisitions, too?"

"If she happens to pick up information from our clients that she finds promising, but only rarely."

"I saw a couple of places that looked appealing. I was kind of hoping you planned to buy the one outside Santa Fe. The Golden Aspen Resort and Spa. I've always wanted to go to New Mexico."

"They were for sale last year, which is why she probably had the brochure. I don't know about right now. I think they brought in consultants to do some kind of reorganization, and they pulled it off the market. I never even got around to sending anybody to look at it. I have a guy who does that for me. He has the eye."

I filed that away. It was a nibble. We finished dishing up the banana bread, and Dad left with three plates, while I waited for the tea to steep. Back in the courtyard, I gave everyone mugs and settled beside my mother on the love seat. I told them about the girls, and Mom gave me advice, settling back into her role. Dad told me the plot of one of the books I'd given him, and we chatted about things that didn't matter.

When I stood to go, Mom said she'd walk me to the door. After I kissed my father goodbye, we started through the house.

"I am so glad you're okay, Ryan. I'm sorry," she said.

Since apologies are rare in our family, I knew she really must be. "Thanks."

"It's odd, isn't it, that I just assumed you were fine? Maybe it's because you've come through so much already. You've proved how strong you are, over and over, and I guess I take that for granted."

"That's better than the alternative. You could have squirreled me away in the attic to keep me safe."

"I just believed you were strong and hoped for the best. You never proved me wrong."

We were at the door. I hugged her quickly. And then, after that brief wave of sentiment, I got back down to business. "I think all this uproar is aging me. What do you think?"

She smiled just a little. "You look good to me."

"No plastic surgery to get rid of worry lines?"

She reached up and smoothed my forehead. "Not yet."

"I guess Wendy beat me to it."

"Wendy?"

"She must have had a little tuck here and there?"

"Why would she need to? She's perfect the way she is. Maybe she will when she's a little older."

I nodded. "I guess I'll have to wait."

As always, I was glad to be a journalist. I had learned so many ways to get information. I left with my answers, and with something more. The way my parents viewed me or claimed to was going to be interesting to contemplate.

CHAPTER THIRTEEN

I expected to sleep badly that night. My mother may think I'm strong, but I still have more than my share of nightmares. After being attacked at Wendy's front doorstep, I knew what was coming. Any shock, any scare plunges me back to my internship at the *Seabank Free Press*. As soon as I drift reluctantly to sleep, distorted memories of the worst moments of my life come out to play.

Thanks to my parents' intervention, I got help for my nightmares almost immediately after the night that triggered them, including something called imagery rehearsal therapy to learn how to design new endings. But despite prompting, I had refused medication. Too many friends had become addicted to opioids, and a girl I'd known in graduate school had progressed to heroin, which had been cheaper and more easily available. I'd been afraid if I felt better on medication, I would never quit.

Tonight, if I had been able to stay awake, I would have. Instead, after Holly and Noelle were finally asleep, I raided Wendy's shelf of liquor and made a mug of warm milk with a shot of whiskey. Then I made my way upstairs. I took out a pen and pad and curled up against pillows. Breathing deeply, I wrote down everything that had happened that morning, in as much detail as I could remember. Then I moved back to earlier memories. When my heart started pounding harder, I focused on my breathing and waited until both had slowed before I continued.

Recalling every detail of an event can demystify it. The skeleton is there, but the nerves are silenced. Past events were never completely tamed, of course, but enough so that, with luck, I could channel the familiar nightmare toward one of my carefully crafted endings, which I also wrote down now. If I was careful, aware of possibilities, then I was as ready as I could be. And the good news was that these days, when the nightmare arrived, it hadn't packed half a dozen suitcases and found a room nearby. It was a one-night stay, like a sad reminder of the past, in case I'd forgotten the night four years ago that Teo and I almost died.

The day that John Quayle invited me to interview him started out with a bang. After inexplicably finding Quayle's email on my laptop, I'd gone to see Grant Telford, my immediate supervisor.

"He contacted me on his own," I told Grant, holding up my hands to show I was innocent. "I promise I didn't contact him, and I'm not sure how he got my email address. But apparently he heard I've been nosing around, and he said that it only seems fair for me to talk to him directly."

Grant wasn't much taller than my five-four and grouchy from a restricted diet that left him no extra calories for the pizza and beer that had packed sixty extra pounds on his stocky frame.

"Not your job," he'd said without looking up from his desk. "Not on your contact list."

I was feeling very Jimmy Olsen to Grant's Perry White, but I stood my ground—never Jimmy's strong point. "So what if he decides he doesn't want to talk to a *real* reporter? Or if the mood to talk disappears, or he's silenced by his lawyer? He must still have a lawyer, right? To keep him out of more trouble? What if by the time your *real* reporters come back on the scene, he's as silent as a snake?"

"A rattlesnake shakes its rattles any time of the day or night, lawyers notwithstanding."

I took the chair across from him, though I hadn't been asked. "You obviously think he's guilty."

He finally looked up to glare at me. "I was in Seabank when Becky Drake was murdered, remember?"

"Yeah, and so was I. Remember? That's why you have me doing the footwork."

"Which does not include the big interview. *Capisce?*"

"I'm not sure he's guilty. I haven't turned up one piece of hard evidence to support it."

"Turning up evidence isn't your job, and if you think it is, then maybe you need to spend the rest of your time here color coding our files or making coffee runs."

"My job is to make the job of your *real* reporters easier. Which is exactly what I'm doing and no more. But I'm asking questions and I'm listening. And along the way I'm sorting possibilities. Isn't that why I'm being paid the big bucks?"

"Not for sorting, no."

"He wants to talk to me. Let's consider it a trial run, okay? I'll do the preliminaries and help him see he can trust the *Free Press* to be fair and unbiased. I'll make sure the door's open when someone else takes over."

He stared at me, considering. "You've seen the autopsy photos?"

I nodded.

"Whoever killed that young woman was a very angry person. An out of control person. Someone with no mercy."

"I'll meet him in broad daylight with other people around."

He considered longer. "I'll give you a list of questions. And don't improvise. Basics. And leave him with the idea we're on his side."

"Even if we aren't."

He raised a brow. "I'll be turning this over to somebody with absolutely no information about the case. Somebody who wasn't here when the media went crazy."

"Including the *Free Press*."

"He may hold that against you. Make sure you have a lot of people around. More than a handful. And leave me information about where you're meeting him and when."

"Thank you."

"You can say that afterward, if you still want to." He dropped the Perry White mask. "Listen, I'm serious. Be careful. I have a gut feeling he did it. You won't hear me say that again, okay? But I've been at this for a long time. I know what I know."

"I'll be careful."

"Good, if your father sues for wrongful death, the *Seabank Free Press* would buckle at the knees."

"Okay, now I see why you're worried."

"A good journalist takes everything into consideration."

I left with his assurance that the list of allowed questions would be on my computer in an hour. I knew Grant really was concerned, but I also knew that despite his studied apathy, he still loved the news.

I emailed John Quayle and suggested we meet at a Starbucks downtown, not far from the *Free Press*, and he agreed immediately. We set six o'clock for the interview, and as promised, Grant's questions arrived. They were uninspiring, clearly the opening salvo. Grant wanted me to make Quayle comfortable, kind of like a band no one has heard of warming the audience for the headliners at a rock concert. Being the warm-up act was not the way my particular journalistic talents ran, but there was no point in arguing. I left Grant a thank-you email and told him the interview was at six.

I was meeting Teo for lunch, and once we sat down with his fully loaded Cuban and my veggie pita, I told him my news.

He didn't touch his sandwich. "You told me you wouldn't be going near Quayle."

I unwrapped mine. "That's what I thought, too, Teo. But he contacted me."

"Not a good thing."

I looked up. We'd made no declarations of love, and certainly no future plans. But the signs were already there. And since I was head over heels for this guy, I thought I would be ready when the negotiations began.

"You know what I want to do with my life," I said. "And my choices are a lot safer than yours. I would never ask you not to go out on patrol some night because I was afraid there was going to be more trouble than usual."

"One, Quayle's more than a rumor. I arrested him, remember? Two, he as much as told me he killed Becky Drake. He said everything was his fault."

"He claimed he just meant he should have apologized for his behavior at the fund-raiser. He should have taken her home and waited until she was safely inside."

"That's not what he meant. When he said 'I don't make these kinds of mistakes,' he said it with malice. He thought he was beyond mistakes, beyond guilt. This is the man who ran when I confronted him with Bismarck, the same man I had to haul out of a tree stand."

"If I didn't know Bismarck was really a sweetie at heart,

I'd run away, too." I reached down to pet Biz, who was sitting at Teo's feet.

"Don't be fooled by Biz or Quayle. If I told Biz to attack you, he'd do it in a heartbeat. And Quayle doesn't have to wait for my permission. You know he has a record of violence against women. That was ruled inadmissible because sometimes our laws suck, but you know it's true. Two girlfriends moved away because they were afraid to stay in Seabank after they broke up with him. They thought he'd come after them some night. They gave interviews after his conviction."

"I don't want to date the guy, Teo. I'm doing an interview. I'm meeting him at Starbucks. There will be people around."

"This time, yeah. But what's to stop him from following you home? From following you to work? From finding you somewhere, sometime, when you're vulnerable?"

"Let's see." I ticked off my answers, holding up my fingers as I counted. "The gatehouse at Gulf Sands? The fact that I work daylight hours downtown, where people are always milling around? My good sense?"

"Normal good sense doesn't stand a chance against a psychopath."

"It's an interview. I'll wear my torn-up jeans. No, better yet. I have a Lily Pulitzer dress my mother gave me that makes me look an escapee from an exclusive sanatorium. It will be perfect."

"He may know you and I are together. He may want payback."

"Have you been putting my name up in lights at your apartment again? I told you not to."

"Don't treat this so lightly."

I put my hand over his. "I'm not. I'm sure he only knows me as someone at the *Free Press* asking questions. I'm going to be careful. I'll make sure he doesn't follow me home. This is a one-time thing. You have to let me be me if this relationship is going to happily continue."

"I'd settle for unhappily right now."

"Teo..."

"I don't want to control you, Ryan. I just want you to stay safe."

I wondered if this would be a constant theme. Cops saw criminals everywhere and journalists saw stories.

"I'll call you as soon as I get home, okay? But that's it, Teo. I have to do my job, just like you have to do yours."

"Which Starbucks and when?"

I got up, leaving my sandwich on the table. "Help yourself. You don't eat enough vegetables, and I'm leaving." I picked up my purse, pulled out a ten-dollar bill, dropped it on the table and stalked out of the sandwich shop.

Afterward, I was sorry, but not sorry enough to call and apologize. Neither was I sorry enough to take his phone call later in the day. I was afraid if I did, the argument would start all over again, so I turned off my ringer. Since he didn't leave a message, I decided to wait and call after the interview, the way I'd promised I would. I would apologize then, but I would tell him we both had to set boundaries, and mine started with my job.

At five-thirty I got a text from Quayle saying he was unavoidably delayed and asking if I could do the interview that evening about eight. Since I figured it would still be light outside, I agreed and shot Grant another email, then I went out for fast food and errands to waste the necessary time.

By the time I got to Starbucks a thunderstorm was raging, but an earthquake couldn't have shaken Grant's questions out of my head. As I closed my umbrella, my interview subject was easy to spot. He was sitting near the window gazing outside at the storm. I'd parked at the end of the next block specifically to keep my car out of sight, and even though I was soaked, I was glad I had. I went right to him and introduced myself.

John Quayle was passably handsome, with sandy blond hair and a wide chest. Still, time wasn't going to be kind. He was twelve years my senior and his face and neck were already lined. His hairline was decidedly higher than I'd noted in photographs. Prison was no picnic.

"May I get you something?" I asked. "Cappuccino? A latte? Scone?"

"I'm good. But I'll wait while you get something for yourself."

I had just filled my body with fat, carbs and carbonation, but I wanted to appear casual. I got a cup of decaf and returned to the table with no intention of drinking it.

"I'm curious," I said, as I took the seat across from him. "How did you know to contact me?"

"I figured the paper would get around to rehashing the past. And Misha Reynolds told me you talked to her. She gave me your email."

Misha was the woman who had overheard Quayle fighting with the victim at the fund-raiser. His release from prison was partially due to her insistence she had been coerced by the police. I wondered if her change of heart had come about after agonized years of rehashing and twisting what she'd heard. Did she now hope that by doing Quayle this favor, she could make up for his years behind bars?

I leveled with him. "You weren't on my list to interview. I'm an intern. They just let me do the basics."

"And I'm better than basic?"

I smiled. "Certainly more important. You've been through a lot. How does it feel to be home again?"

"Like I have a target painted on my back."

We continued to talk. He was obviously coming to terms

with his freedom, and all the things that had happened since Becky Drake's death. He seemed pleasant enough, but I thought under the calm facade he was simmering. I wasn't surprised. Years of his life had vanished, and despite his release, too many people were treating him as if he was still a murderer.

I thought it was a good thing I was interviewing him now. I had a feeling Quayle wasn't going to stay in Seabank for long, and this might be all the *Free Press* ever got directly from him.

The interview went well enough, and I stuck to the basics because what would I do with anything else? Tell Grant he'd been wrong not to let me strut my stuff? Quayle seemed to relax as we spoke. I have an excellent memory, so I took few notes, planning to write down most of what was said after we finished. We were there for half an hour, and we were more or less done when he checked his watch. The storm seemed to drift away, but the skies were still gray and night would fall soon.

"I have to be somewhere by nine," he said. "You have enough for your article?"

"Not an article. Just background for one in the future. And you've been helpful."

"You didn't take many notes."

"I have it all right here." I tapped the side of my head. "But I'm going to stay and write it down."

He had a nice smile, the kind that promises that the used car he just sold you will run another hundred thousand miles. I didn't like him, and I didn't feel I'd gotten very far under the surface, or that I even wanted to. But I also knew that someone who'd been incarcerated unfairly might not care about being likable. Sincerity might take a while to relearn.

He stood and I stood, too, holding out my hand. "Thank you, Mr. Quayle. It was nice of you to take the time to set the record straight. The *Free Press* wants to do that. Can they count on you for a more in-depth interview in the future?"

"Why not? Maybe someday the cops will even get around to catching whoever killed Becky. Then you'll have a whole new feature to interview me for."

I nodded, although from talking to Teo, I knew the local cops were sure they'd already caught their man, and he was now walking the streets again. "I'm sure you'll be happy to see that day."

He stopped by the counter and left with a takeout cup, raising a finger in goodbye as he walked out the door. I watched until he had disappeared down the sidewalk. I might have nearly total recall, but memories are better the fresher they are. I stayed to jot more extensive notes, so I wouldn't forget details before I got back to my parents' house.

I thought about calling Teo, but decided to do that on the way home. It might be a long conversation, or so historically short I'd be embarrassed to be cut off in public.

Fifteen minutes later I was on my way to my car. Seabank's downtown area never buzzed at night, and the storm had cleared the sidewalks. Thunder still rolled in the distance, and I guessed pedestrians weren't taking any chances. Cars passed, but headlights were shining now. I walked a little faster and was glad when I reached my car.

I will never understand why I decided to take the back way home. That route was quicker, yes, and there was usually less traffic. But the road, which veered sharply away from downtown before it ended up at Gulf Sands, sometimes flooded after a storm, and I knew that. Maybe I was busy thinking about Quayle, or more likely about Teo, I can't remember. When I stopped at a light on the outskirts of Seabank, I punched in Teo's number but got his voice mail. While I waited I left a message.

"Teo, the interview is finished, and I'm on my way home. In fact I've been sitting at the traffic light at Flamingo and 7th for about three months. Tell your cop friends somebody needs to adjust it or there's going to be a riot." I paused. "Okay, I'm sorry. I shouldn't have walked away before we finished our argument. We need to work this out so it doesn't happen again. Do you want me to stop by tonight? I'm not sure how long you're working. Just let me know." I paused again. "Please don't stay angry. You know how I feel about you."

I put my phone down and followed the car ahead of me through the light that was now green. Ten minutes later I realized my mistakes, and there were two. One, I hadn't remembered the road often flooded. And two, I hadn't checked the weather. Another storm began as I neared the lowest dip in the road. Seabank's sandy soil could only absorb so much water, and besides, the water table here was always high and drainage ditches were always neglected.

By then I was almost alone on the road, everyone else too smart or too seasoned to be there. A lone car was closing in, but I couldn't see any other headlights. I stopped as a lake appeared across the road ahead of me, and I realized my only way home was to go back the way I'd come. The water ahead was rising quickly enough that I was afraid to venture into the edges to make the turn. I needed to back up before I tried, but by now, the car behind me had its nose against my bumper. Clearly he wasn't paying attention to the rising water, and he expected me to keep going.

I honked, but he didn't move, so I flashed my lights. No success.

"Jerk." I decided to try to make the turn without backing up by creeping just as far into the water as I absolutely had to. I did, but the car behind me followed. Now my only choice was to drive through the water, or get out and ask whoever was behind me to back up so I could turn around.

My Chevy Cobalt was old, a high school graduation present from my parents and no longer in production. I wished I had sold it and bought an SUV, but we'd been through a lot together. My first car. Gift from my parents. No more Cobalts on the horizon. Yada yada. Sentiment or not, now it would probably stall if I drove much farther.

Muttering under my breath I ignored my umbrella, useless in the downpour, threw my door open, and stepped out into the puddle and the storm. I dashed back to the car behind me.

Just as I got there the driver opened his door and stepped out.

"Remember me?" This time John Quayle was not smiling. "Does your boyfriend remember me, too?"

CHAPTER FOURTEEN

For once the next morning, I was glad the girls dawdled. Keeping after them kept me busy, and I had no time to process last night's dreams or what I intended to do about them this morning.

While they still dragged their feet, Holly no longer acted as if I had no business in her life, and Noelle was almost friendly. I had a surprise for them. After my first nightmare I'd researched YouTube for videos on little girl's hairstyles. My favorite showed the one-minute variety, which took me closer to five, but that was still an improvement. I put Noelle's hair in a tight ponytail, wrapped a ribbon around it and criss-crossed it to the bottom where I tied the ribbon in a bow. I sectioned Holly's hair into something approximating French braids at the side, and fastened everything with an elastic band and barrettes. Since nobody bit me or called me names, the morning was a win.

By the time I came back from school, a tiny woman named Analena, wearing wireless headphones and a charming smile, was patiently waiting at the front door. She cleaned for Gracey

Group and assured me that she always did the laundry. I had to restrain myself from sweeping her into a fierce hug.

I left as she came downstairs with sheets and towels in her arms. She'd already informed me she would lock the door behind her when she finished. I had no excuse to hang around.

Today as I headed toward Confidence K-9s, I ignored the designer running gear and wore jeans and a dark green pullover. I wasn't going to jog past the kennels. I was going to drive my little Civic right up to the parking lot fifty yards from the front building, get out as if I had business there, and ask whoever I happened to see where I could find the owner.

By the time I arrived, my hands were perspiring, and I felt vaguely nauseous. But the moment to see Teo had come and gone a hundred times, and this time if I lost my nerve, my nieces might pay the price.

I'd combed my hair and put on a little lip gloss, which had probably already disappeared, but I didn't check the mirror. It was too late for major repairs. I got out and started toward the door.

A woman rounded the corner to intercept me. At first she smiled, but her expression darkened as she examined me. I thought she might be the blonde I'd seen on my last jog-by. She was attractive in an outdoorsy kind of way, sandy hair, freckles that blended into a tan, a wedding ring on the hand she lifted to brush a long strand of hair out of her eyes.

"Can I help you?"

I thought it was already clear she didn't want to. "I'm looking for Teo. Is he here?"

"Maybe I can help."

I drew myself to my full height, although it was futile since she was almost a head taller, as well as muscular and fit. "I need to see *him*."

The front door opened, and we both turned our heads.

Teo stepped out. His hair was longer than I remembered, no longer buzzed but starting to curl. He was still slender and broad-shouldered. A khaki-colored T-shirt emblazoned with Confidence K-9's logo hung over dark shorts, and he looked both older and younger than the man in my memory. Younger than the K9 officer who had, while seriously injured himself, killed a man to protect me. Older than the one who'd shared my bed so often and well.

I'd thought of a million possible greetings, none of which covered all the bases. But as my gaze flicked over him, assessing the changes, I stopped at the leg that had been shot out from under him by John Quayle. The leg I remembered was gone, and in its place was a prosthesis starting below his knee.

My head began to whirl and tears welled in my eyes.

By then the blonde had disappeared inside, as if she realized whatever was about to play out would happen with or without her. Teo watched my expression. When my eyes finally met his, he cocked his head. "Nobody told you?"

I shook my head. "Not exactly the kind of thing we talk about at cocktail parties."

"Since when do you go to cocktail parties?"

I blinked back the tears. "I could use a cocktail now. How about you?"

"I was averaging five or six a day until I decided to give up my leg."

"Did your buddies get you drunk every night to help you get through…everything?"

"Unfortunately, I preferred to drink alone. I wasn't very good company. But you already know that."

My fears about the way this reunion would go morphed into something far more terrible. I said the only thing I knew to be true. "This is my fault."

"No. John Quayle's fault."

"You came to my rescue, and if I'd listened to you in the first place you wouldn't have needed to. As it turns out..." I swallowed and looked away. "You were right."

From the moment he'd arranged our interview, John Quayle had probably planned to follow me from Starbucks, maybe just to find where I lived so he could strike later. But a better opportunity had emerged almost immediately. He had stayed well behind me on the road, so that even though I was careful, I couldn't be careful enough. Aided by the storm he'd been able to pull closer, and when I'd stalled at the rising water on the road ahead, he'd seen his chance.

Now I told Teo the same thing I'd told him in the days after Quayle had nearly killed us both. It bore repeating. "After our interview I realized he was angry. He couldn't hide it. I told myself if I had served time for a crime I didn't commit, I would be angry, too. But I was careful leaving. I worked on my interview notes first, then more or less sprinted to my car. On the drive I checked behind me a few times. Then I got this crazy idea to take the rural route home. I thought I'd get there faster. I'd been away long enough to forget how badly it can flood."

"It still does."

I waited, but he didn't say more. "He must have felt like such a winner. He had me and probably intended to take me somewhere and dump me. Most likely the dead me. He probably knew that once it was clear I was missing, you'd look for me. He could take vengeance on both of us, the cop and his girlfriend, the *Free Press* reporter."

I returned my gaze to his. "And the dog who tracked him to the tree stand."

Quayle had nearly succeeded. After I'd left Teo the message that I was sitting at the light at Flamingo and 7th, he had figured out which way I was heading. Even knowing I would be furious, he decided to trail me, just in case. Of course he saved my life. He arrived just as Quayle was wrestling me into his backseat at gunpoint, my hands bound by zip ties.

"Bismarck made it," he said. "I made it. You made it."

I looked down at his leg. "Why did you...?"

He gave the slightest shrug. "I was stupid to hang on to it as long as I did. One day I found myself wondering how I could end my life and make it look like an accident, and I realized the doctors were right. My leg was never going to stop hurting. I was growing too reliant on painkillers, and when I realized how dependent I was, I stopped taking them. But the pain was almost unbearable."

"Oh, Teo—"

He shook his head, as if to say not to pity him. "My leg was never going to be the way it used to be, no matter how many surgeries I endured, and I was never going to work with a K9 unit again. I finally realized I would never be good as new. So I decided just to be new, instead. A brand-new me."

"I really didn't know."

"Yeah, I can tell. I guess you moved on and stopped asking about me." He smiled a little, but it was tight and controlled. "Right?"

I thought about lying, but I couldn't. "No, I was asking, but I guess I didn't ask the right people."

"I don't advertise."

"I may have missed even more. You're married?"

"What makes you think so?"

I let my gaze travel to his left hand, which was unadorned. "The woman who greeted me seems pretty proprietary."

"Janice probably recognized you from old news stories. She's one of our trainers. She's married to our kennel manager."

There was no reason to feel better. My relationship with

Teo had ended years ago. Of course logic and emotion don't always cross paths.

"I don't know how many ways I can say I'm sorry," I told him. "I haven't thought of any new ones since you told me to get out of your life."

He raised a brow. "It helps that on my last day on the job, I made sure Quayle would never terrorize another woman anywhere."

The scene was still fresh in my mind, especially after last night's nightmares. Quayle turning away as Teo's patrol car approached, my futile kick to his hand, hoping he would drop the gun. Quayle turning angrily back toward me, gun still clutched firmly, a shot flying past my head. The slam of a car door, Bismarck's frantic barking. Then a streak of canine fury coming right at us. More gunshots, then Bismarck, who was hit twice, falling to the ground as Teo launched himself at Quayle to separate me from my attacker.

Quayle managed to get off one more shot, the one that had, in the end, been responsible for the loss of Teo's leg. But Teo had already drawn his gun. Cops shoot to kill. Teo had taken the lesson to heart.

When the events of that evening became public knowledge, very few people mourned Quayle. A year later, after an anonymous tip, cadaver dogs searched his mother's property. The bodies of two women were discovered in a pit behind the house. To my knowledge neither was ever identified.

"Back then, I really didn't want you to leave," Teo said quietly. "But I knew you didn't want to be here."

I started to protest, but I stopped. Because Teo was at least partly right. Torn between guilt, sorrow and a bone-deep aversion to the kind of anger that had shaken him, I'd floundered badly, so badly that when he'd pushed me away, I had let him.

I said the one thing guaranteed to prove he wasn't completely right. "I've missed you."

Something flickered in his eyes. "Four years is a long time to miss somebody."

"I'd like to take all the blame, but my phone number never changed. You knew how to find me."

"I wasn't the man you'd known."

"Which man was that, Teo? The one who saved my life and nearly lost his own? The man who did what was right instead of what I insisted I wanted?"

"The one who still knew who he was."

I let out a long breath and my heart seemed to twist in my chest. "We could have shared that. I didn't know who I was, either. Maybe I still don't. But I guess sharing feelings isn't something I'm good at."

"No kidding." He softened that with the hint of a smile.

"We're talking." It was the most I had hoped for.

"We seem to be."

The chance to veer away from our volatile past was right in front of me, so I grabbed it. "And while we're at it, I have something else to talk to you about. Do you have a few minutes?"

"Would you like to see the kennel while you tell me why you're here?"

He opened the door and ushered me inside, where it was comfortably cool in the entryway. A long corridor led off to the left, and individual runs lined it, some with dogs barking for attention, others with dogs comfortably snoozing.

He stood beside me. "This is our boarding wing. Boarders are evaluated and sorted so we know who they can play with in the yard. Some have to be taken out individually for one-on-one."

I stared straight ahead. "Isn't that always the way? The worse they behave, the more attention they get. Same with people."

"We work with each dog to improve manners. But the dogs we trust the least are inside, near the office."

I was trying hard to leave space between us, and he noticed as we started down the concrete passageway. "Don't get too close to the fencing as we walk. Somebody might try a friendly nip."

I walked closer to him, trying not to pay attention to whether he winced with pain or had problems navigating corners. I tried not to pay attention, but of course, I did. And as we walked I relaxed a little. He seemed as comfortable with his prosthesis as I was with my well-broken-in running shoes.

Since I'd had little experience with dogs, I couldn't name breeds, but a couple we passed looked fierce enough that I hoped the chain link fencing surrounding them was as strong as it looked.

"I won't walk you down the other aisles. It's more of the same, but those dogs are here specifically for training." Teo opened a door at the end that was fastened with a chain, and we crossed through to another walkway, this time looking over a large open area. I noted a playhouse complete with tower, a wading pool, a corner shaded by canopy. Instead of grass, the ground was covered by artificial turf.

I was already impressed. Confidence K-9s was spick-and-span, and well organized. There were charts along the walls with names of dogs and instructions, with boxes to initial when a job was finished. The individual care was obvious.

I was surprised by one thing. "Artificial turf? Grass won't grow here?"

"It's easier to clean. We wash it down three times a day. Some dogs prefer the real thing, though, so we have another area with mulch."

"I wouldn't mind being a dog here." We stood together watching the four dogs that were now in the yard romping. One, a collie of some kind, leaped against the fencing to look us over. A young man of about twenty was outside with them, and he came over and shooed the dog away. Teo introduced him as Jim before he went back to what he'd been doing.

"So what did you want to talk to me about?" Teo asked.

"I need a dog."

"The Humane Society has plenty. Somebody there can help you make a good choice."

"That was just my lead-in. I need a special kind of dog. Here's the thing. I seem to be a bad-guy magnet." I gave him an abbreviated version of the attack at Wendy's town house.

"What is it about you, Ryan?"

I wondered the same thing. "The deputy who showed up to take my statement said a dog would be the best deterrent. We already have a security system. But I'm taking care of my sister's little girls for a while. And I want to keep them safe."

"Why? What's up with your sister?"

Teo had never met Wendy. That was a reminder of how short-lived our relationship had been. Or maybe it was a reminder of how territorial I had felt. I hadn't wanted to be diminished by Wendy's splendor.

I phrased my answer carefully. "She's away helping a friend, and her husband's on a nuclear sub somewhere out in the ocean. I'm temporarily Aunt Everything."

"Your parents are okay?"

"Dad just had heart surgery, and Mom's busy taking care of him. So I came home to help out."

"Just how long do you need a dog?"

I stumbled over that. "Well, not forever."

"That covers a lot of territory."

"I don't know for sure when Wendy will come home. So I don't have a good answer. It just depends on circumstances."

He let that go, although I was afraid he'd filed his curiosity away to pull out again if needed. "I don't suppose you're looking for one to take with you when you leave town again?"

"I guess since I work at home a dog's feasible. I probably have room for a small one. But I need something large and fierce right now, a dog so intimidating even raindrops won't fall near the town house."

"And a dog gentle enough to be safe with your nieces."

I realized how foolish I'd been. "You don't happen to have a dog I can plug in to guard the house when I need him and unplug when I don't?"

"You're describing any well-trained dog, a dog who does the job at hand, no more, no less. We train security dogs, and we train them to obey. The thing is, we don't rent dogs. It takes time to train an owner to work with a dog. Mutual respect is involved."

"I fully realize how stupid this sounds. I guess I was feeling desperate."

"Desperate enough to talk to me instead of jogging by?"

I could feel my cheeks heating, but I didn't deny it. "It's a fine road for jogging."

"I almost came after you last time to tell you it was safe to talk to me again."

"I wish you had."

"I liked watching you work up your courage. I wondered if you ever would."

"It wasn't easy."

"Bismarck," he said, as if that was the next sensible thing to say.

I tilted my head. "How is Biz?"

"Recovery took months. We weren't sure he would make

it, but he did. The department retired him, along with me. He sleeps in my bedroom now." As a police K9, Bismarck had always lived in a kennel behind Teo's little bungalow, ready and willing at any moment to go out on patrol with his master.

"I knew he was living with you," I said. "My sources were at least that good, although not the part about sleeping in your bedroom."

"Biz knows you, likes you. He may be old now, but he's plenty feisty. And he's great with children. Janice and Harry have two. He does sleepovers with their kids. They love him."

I tried to imagine having Bismarck in my house, living with me, watching over me. "He saved my life."

"He may well have. But he won't hold that against you."

"You're sure about this? You would trust me?"

"I might. He's in the next building. Let's go see him. If he goes for your throat, it's probably not a good idea."

I put my hand on his arm. Just a light touch, and quick. "You really thought about coming after me when I jogged by? To talk this through so we could be friends again?"

"I wasn't sure a conversation was a good idea."

"And now?"

He shook his head. "I'm still not sure. But it appears we can be civil."

"With all our baggage, you're still willing to help me?"

"It's possible I'm so weighted down by all that baggage I can't see over the top of it."

"No, I think it's better than that. Maybe we've lightened it enough that we can finally move on."

His expression grew serious. "On one condition. If I ever tell you to be careful, and you decide I'm wrong, Bismarck's gone for good. I won't put my dog in danger again, even if you think leaping in with both feet is a great plan for yourself and those little girls."

I heard his ultimatum and knew he was right. "That will work if you're willing to talk through the alternatives first."

"Biz will still remember you. He won't hold the past against you." He started down another hallway and I followed.

Bismarck's owner still remembered me, just the way I remembered him. Would he ever not hold the past against me? I told myself we'd come further today than I'd ever imagined. I would just be grateful.

CHAPTER FIFTEEN

I took myself out to lunch after my visit to Confidence K-9s, sitting at Seabank Seafood overlooking the water and replaying my reintroduction to Bismarck.

Dogs are so much more straightforward than people. He had been asleep in the office when Teo's kennel tour took me there, but when I walked in, he lumbered to his feet to check me out. Then his tail began to wag. And wag. And wag. I'd dispensed with holding out my hand, got down on my knees and held out my arms. He leaped into them, nearly knocking me flat. I was thoroughly licked.

"I guess he remembers you," Teo said. Janice, the blond trainer, walked by and saw me on the floor giggling with Bismarck. Her expression said "dogs are so forgiving," but she couldn't resist a little smile. Who can resist a happy dog?

As for Teo? I was still sorting through my feelings. He seemed at home on his new leg, no longer in pain, no longer fighting a futile battle to pretend he was exactly the same, but I wondered how long it would take me to feel at home with the change. Not because I found the prosthesis distasteful, but because I felt responsible. Teo had moved on, or at least a long way. But for me? This felt like the final assault.

I had caused this terrible injury and all the aftermath. And no matter how many times I told myself that John Quayle was responsible, the truth still breathed loudly in my ear.

Teo had promised to bring Bismarck to the town house in the afternoon with everything I'd need for the days or weeks I had him. We'd gone over simple commands and signals. But watching one of the trainers put another dog through his paces, I knew there had been nothing "simple" about turning Bismarck into the dog who had distracted John Quayle long enough for Teo to take him down.

The dog and the man who had saved my life. The man who had lost his leg and his profession because of me.

I shopped afterward to distract myself, stopping at the grocery store for supplies for tomorrow night. The girls and I were invited to my parents' house, and I'd promised to bring dinner. I planned to enlist Holly and Noelle to help make a vegan meal we'd all enjoy.

Other than cooking, we had an entire weekend ahead of us. With that in mind, after lunch I stopped at a craft store and asked for recommendations. I emerged with red and green headbands to decorate, and instructions and supplies to make reindeer from colored paper and cardboard tubes. Christmas was around the corner. And Wendy's town house needed signs a holiday was on the way.

My final stop was our local discount store, where I bought Frisbees, quick-fill water balloons and a nature bingo game. I hoped we were set.

At home I walked to the school to pick up the girls. The younger Mrs. English was out front making sure children went in the right directions. She smiled when I joined her.

"Holly will be out in a minute. She went back inside to get her sister. Noelle is taking her time this afternoon."

"How's Holly doing?"

"She's not as tired, but she still seems worried."

"I think children always worry when their parents are away. She'll feel better after her mother comes home." As would we all.

"She might benefit from some counseling. But I'd want her mother's permission. Could you have your sister phone the school?"

I told the truth, just not all of it. "I doubt that's possible. Wendy's hard to reach. She's traveling in remote areas."

Younger Mrs. English was no fool. "Got your hands full, don't you?"

"More than I can say."

"I think the girls are lucky to have you."

I thought that was funny since I had no clue how to be an aunt, but as Holly and Noelle came out, older hauling younger, I thanked her. Job finished, Holly left Noelle to drag along behind.

"We have a surprise coming this afternoon," I said.

Noelle perked up. "Is Mommy coming home?"

"Daddy?" Holly asked.

Mentally I kicked myself. The "no clue" thing had reared its ugly head. "I'm sorry, but no. Something else you'll like though."

"Not some*one*." Holly was paying attention.

"Comes with a someone. You'll see."

"I'm hungry," Noelle said, and I waited for Holly to tell her she wasn't. Holly seemed to associate snacking with the onset of a fatal disease. But today she didn't say a word.

At home I heated caramel sauce in the microwave and pulled out a plate of fruit I'd cut up. I added pretzels and set everything on the counter, dipping an apple slice into the sauce in demonstration.

Noelle dug right in. Holly sucked on a pretzel, but even she gave in eventually and started to dip.

By the time there was a knock at the front door, the girls had snacked, changed clothes and done their homework. I knew once Bismarck arrived, they would be unlikely to co-operate with me.

They were happily watching their rationed half hour of television, something featuring rainbow-hued animals with squeaky voices, so neither tried to beat me to the door. In fact they were so deep in TV la-la land, I doubted they even heard the knock.

Teo on my doorstep felt like a gift, even though his visit was business. I had insisted on paying for Bismarck's services. The payment was a barrier we could hide behind, probably forever.

"Biz." I scratched his ears. "You're going to like it here."

"How did your nieces take the news?"

I looked up. He wore the same shirt he'd worn earlier, but he'd changed into sweatpants. I wondered if he was afraid the girls might find his prosthesis frightening, and I felt what was now a familiar pang. Did children ask him questions? Did adults turn away?

He was waiting for an answer. I managed a smile. "I wanted Biz to be a surprise. Will you please come in until we're all settled?" I paused. "Unless you have to be somewhere else?"

"I'm not planning to drop my best friend and run. We'll see how he does. He's not a youngster anymore. He may not take to this the way we want him to."

He and Bismarck came in, Biz by his side, and I led them both into the great room where the girls' show was in its final minutes.

"Here's my surprise," I said. "This is Teo Santiago, and his dog, Bismarck."

The girls rose at exactly the same moment. Holly grabbed Noelle and pulled her close, as if to protect her.

And yes, up close, Bismarck was a little scary. This wasn't the first mistake I'd made today.

I went over and laid a hand on each girl's shoulder. "Bismarck is friendly. He's not going to hurt you. He's my favorite dog pal, right, Biz?"

"He looks like a wolf!" This from Noelle.

"He's not a bit like a wolf." I wished I could tell them how Bismarck had saved my life. But they didn't need stories about bad guys and near-death experiences. This time I saw the mistake ahead of time.

Teo squatted next to Bismarck, as easily as he once had, with slightly different technique. He shifted his center of gravity, swung the leg with the prosthesis a bit, and then squatted down with the other, taking the first leg with him.

"I'm impressed," I said.

"This took a long time to learn, and I won't be down here long." He raised his voice as he slung his arm over the dog. "Girls, Bismarck used to work for the police, and so did I. He's protected me a dozen times. He'll do anything to help the people he loves."

He used Bismarck to steady himself and stood again. "Your Aunt Ryan doesn't even like dogs, and look how much she likes Bismarck."

"I do so like dogs. I just like Bismarck more." I held out my hand. "Holly, you first. He loves to have his ears scratched."

Ten minutes later, after Teo captured their loyalty forever by mimicking the silly voices of their television cartoon, the girls took Bismarck to their bedroom to show him where he was going to sleep. I had no say in the matter.

"They're cuties," Teo said. "I don't remember you saying much about them."

"I probably didn't. I hardly knew them. They're a little prissy. Are all little girls worried about gaining weight and getting dirty?"

"You're asking me?"

Teo had a large extended family. I remembered, sadly, that his parents had liked me as much as mine had liked him. He had brothers, three of them, and a sister. Nieces and nephews were just part of the scenery, and despite feeling overwhelmed, I'd liked them all.

"I am asking you," I affirmed. "How many nieces do you have now?"

"Five. They roll in the mud and sweat a lot, but they clean up nicely. I wouldn't use prissy to describe them. Even the bookworm takes karate lessons."

"Instigated by her uncle, no doubt."

"Every one of them eats more than I do."

"As I remember, you could pack it away."

"Are we going to do this? Pull out all the old memories? To what end?"

"Maybe I'm trying to edge out some of the bad memories with better ones. So when we look at each other, we don't always see a psychopath intent on killing both of us."

"Think that'll work?"

"I don't know. But you're here and Bismarck's upstairs. We must be making progress."

He looked down at his watch. "I need to make tracks. You have everything you need, and I wrote more instructions. My cell number's on the bottom. Call me if you have any questions."

I liked having his cell number. I'd already given him mine. I promised I would take care of Biz.

"Two little girls and a dog. When will you have time to work? Isn't *Out in the Cold* due for another season sometime in the future?"

"You know about my podcast?"

"You're not the only one who asked a few questions." He smiled, just a little, and let himself out the front door.

Teo had been asking questions about me. Maybe he'd even listened to some of my episodes.

I was still smiling when I went upstairs; Bismarck was listening as the girls explained who slept where, whose drawers belonged to whom. I couldn't blame my nieces. German shepherds are intelligent, almost noble. I was sure he understood the essence.

I paused in the doorway. "I can't remember. Have you ever had a dog?"

"Mommy says they're dirty and they smell."

"Bismarck's definitely not dirty, and he just smells like a dog. I think it's a good smell." I realized I was criticizing my sister. "But I can see how some people might not," I added quickly.

"Why did the cop with the funny leg leave him here?" Holly seemed to think this was a perfectly normal question.

I was surprised she hadn't commented on Teo's prosthesis while he was here. "Teo left him here because I told him a dog would be a nice addition for a while." I paused. "And you noticed his leg?"

"We've seen lots of legs like that. And arms."

Their father was military. They'd probably seen plenty of returning soldiers and sailors with even worse injuries.

I made dinner suggestions, but could have offered fried skunk tails and they'd have agreed, just to get me out of the bedroom.

Dinner was chicken nuggets I made from scratch. I had to ban Bismarck when they tried to sneak him food.

After dinner they were still so wound up and excited I resorted to desperate measures. "Instead of a story, would you like to look at your mom's scrapbooks?" Here or not, Wendy was still a powerful presence. I hoped the scrapbooks might encourage them to talk about their feelings.

Noelle was excited. "I would!"

Holly did the classic Holly-shrug.

I retrieved the photo scrapbook from Wendy's bottom drawer and brought it into their bedroom, leaving the other for another time. "Whose bed?"

After they debated, we sat on Holly's. Diplomat and gentleman that he was, Bismarck curled up at both their feet. Noelle plopped herself in my lap, maybe for a better view of the book, or maybe because photos of Wendy made her miss her mother more. Whichever it was, I snuggled her closer and even snuck a quick kiss on top of her little blond head.

I opened the book. "I bet you've seen this a bunch of times," I said.

"No." Holly didn't elaborate.

I opened to the first page of my sister's Kodachrome childhood, a studio portrait of a bald Wendy on her tummy, propped up to smile at the camera. "What a cute baby, huh?"

Noelle squealed in delight. Holly reached over to pet Bismarck. "Does Daddy have a scrapbook?"

"We'll ask your mom when she comes home."

"He showed me pictures once. He liked to play basketball."

She sounded so wistful I wanted to hug her, but I had to take things with Holly one inch at a time.

We progressed through photos of baby Wendy, hair so light it was almost invisible, then as a toddler in frilly dresses, in a ruffled bathing suit, on a merry-go-round with my mother on one side and my father the other. My parents looked so young and happy. Whoever had snapped the photo had tilted the camera, but it was still good enough to include here, even if it was less than perfect.

We graduated to school photos, slowly turning the pages to witness graduation ceremonies, starting in what looked like kindergarten.

There were birthday party photos, too. Wendy had been feted with extravagantly choreographed events. The girls and I paged through themes like Barbie Dolls on Parade and Cinderella at the Ball. There were always loads of kids and tables piled with gifts. During my own childhood, I'd nixed all the hoopla in favor of having one or two friends for a sleepover. I'm sure I was a disappointment to my mother, although in her favor, she never said so.

"Look at all your mom's friends." In addition to dance recitals, school concerts and plays in which Wendy had roles, there were also multiple pages of my sister goofing around with girls her age.

I hadn't been born when the photos were taken, so none of the girls looked familiar. And if Wendy knew any of them as adults, I had never heard them mentioned.

"Who's that one?" Holly pointed to one, a girl with curly dark hair and bangs that spiraled every which way. There were other photos of the same girl on the next pages, hair longer and in pigtails on top of her head, braces on her teeth, cheeks speckled with acne. We turned another page, and while Wendy had apparently never lived through an awkward stage, the dark-haired girl definitely had.

I wondered what kind of girl had been willing to spend her adolescence in Wendy's shadow.

"Snow White and Rose Red," I said.

"What's that mean?"

I tried to remember particulars. "It's a fairy tale about two sisters, one blond and one dark-haired, just like your mom and her friend."

"And like Holly and me," Noelle said.

"Exactly. In the story the girls protect and help a bear, and one day he turns into a handsome prince. After a whole lot happens, he marries the sister with the blond hair, and his brother marries the other." There'd been a few terribly gruesome moments in the Grimm version, which I deleted from this version.

"Does that dark-haired girl have a real name?" Noelle asked.

I had no idea. I reached under the plastic and carefully unstuck one of the photos, but the back was blank. I was curious now. The girl seemed to be Wendy's closest friend. I wondered if my sister was still in touch with her, or if they might even be together now, wherever Wendy was hiding.

"We'll show this to your grandmother. She'll know."

Holly yawned, and we were finished for the night. I tucked them both in, raced through bedtime prayers and gave Bismarck a pat before I left the room.

After I got ready for bed, I curled up with my laptop and went to the internet sites for the *Santa Fe New Mexican* and then to the one for the *Santa Fe Reporter*. The murder of one Vítor Calvo wasn't mentioned. Apparently there was nothing new to report.

I typed Calvo's name into Google and breezed past the first two pages of results. Placement on the page depended on variables like backlinks, site speed, relevance and length of content. I often found the information I needed on page three or beyond.

The website of Calvo's clinic still hadn't posted notice of his death, not even in Portuguese. Some of his former patients had gathered for a cyber-mourning. But nothing I found helped me.

I was thinking about closing down for the night, when the door to Wendy's room widened and Bismarck padded in.

"Well, hello." I'd taken him out before tucking in the girls, and I'd expected him to stay put in their room. But clearly Biz had other ideas.

He came around to the side of the bed, looked it over, then gracefully jumped up beside me, lay his head on my hip and stared at me, as if to say, "You're okay with this, right?"

"You should not be up here."

I could swear he smiled. And what could I do? I owed my life to this dog, and yes, he was a connection to the man I'd once been falling in love with. Was I going to make him sleep where he didn't want to?

"I'm not sure the bed is large enough for both of us," I warned.

He turned over, wriggled a little closer and that was that.

My cell phone rang. I lifted it to my ear.

"Just checking to be sure everything's going all right," Teo said.

I laughed. "You lied to me."

"How's that?"

"You said Biz slept in your room. You did not say he slept in your bed."

"How's that a lie? Why are you interested in my sleeping habits?"

I wondered if there was room for a woman and Bismarck in Teo's bed. "He's making himself right at home."

"You can always push him down."

"Sure, push a dog who's been trained to kill off my bed. You think I'm crazy?"

"Everything else okay?"

"The girls are nuts about him. I hope they don't find out he's sleeping with me."

"I talked to Pete about your break-in. The deputy who took your statement."

"Surly guy? Balding?"

He grunted. "He seems sure it was a one-time thing, that it's a group that makes their living that way."

"Well, now they know the house isn't empty." I paused. I pondered. I finally spoke. "I'm not sure that's all that's going on."

"Like what?"

"There could be more to it, but I'm probably imagining it. Clearly that's what I'm trained for. Ignore me."

He was silent long enough that I knew he was thinking, too.

"We're taking Bismarck to meet my parents tomorrow," I said to change the subject. "Does he sense hostility?"

"Your parents were never hostile to me."

"And, you know, that stunned me."

"Give them some credit."

"Thanks for loaning us your dog, Teo."

"Renting. I'm keeping track of the minutes you have him. The cost goes up and up and up…"

We hung up. I switched off the light and turned on my side. Even with Bismarck snoring beside me, I fell asleep quickly.

CHAPTER SIXTEEN

On Saturday afternoon I learned something else about my nieces. Holly and Noelle were not fans of cauliflower, including the smell of it roasting in the oven for dinner. Forcing children to eat anything that wasn't necessary for their health was not in the Good Aunt handbook. So I promised I would buy Happy Meals on the way to my parents' house if they helped me put together the main dish.

With cauliflower cooling on the counter, I held up the next part of the recipe. "This is quinoa, and we'll cook it in coconut milk with yummy spices. It's white, your favorite color."

Both of them made gagging noises. I wondered what Wendy normally fed them, other than pizza. Still, since neither of them had run from the room, I opened the quinoa and got out the measuring cup for Holly.

"Does Gram know we have a dog?" Noelle asked.

"I thought we'd surprise her." I planned to bring Bismarck along tonight so Mom could see we were well protected, but I didn't plan to warn her. Inside every adult lurks a crafty teenager.

"My daddy likes dogs," Holly said.

Bryce seemed like the kind of man who might, one who hugged his family and friends without fanfare, a man who could command a nuclear sub and still have tea parties with his daughters and their favorite stuffed animals.

"Do you know I was so little when I first met your dad that he used to read *me* storybooks?"

Noelle scrunched up her face, as if the idea that I, too, had once been a child, might take getting used to.

"He reads to us whenever he's home," Holly said. "But he's not home a lot."

"I know you miss him."

"He listens when I talk, but I can't talk to him about everything."

That seemed like a strange thing for an eight-year-old to say, but maybe even at her tender age, Holly had realized that men didn't always want to talk about things that matter to girls.

"Some things are hard to talk about," I said, reflecting her words back with my best interview technique.

"I could get in trouble."

This was the most she had revealed in all the years I'd known Holly. I took a few seconds to come up with a response. "I think your daddy would understand whatever you had to say."

Holly shook her head. "But he's not home most of the time."

She'd made that point twice now. I knew this must feel important to her. "He misses you, too. So does your mom."

Watching her expression, I was reminded of the instant when all the lights snap off during a power failure. Holly was comfortable talking about her father, but her mother, their primary caregiver, was off-limits. Since I had a strong suspicion her sleeplessness was connected to Wendy's disappearance, I made one more attempt to help her open up.

"Missing people is natural. And you weren't expecting your mom to be gone, so that's especially hard to get used to."

Holly met my eyes. "You don't get used to some things, even if they happen a lot."

We underestimate children, assuming their inability to express feelings means they don't have them. I'd just seen a demonstration.

"You're right." I reached out and ruffled her hair. "I bet the times when your daddy is home are the very best times for you." When I waited and nothing else was forthcoming, we launched into measuring the spices we needed for the quinoa.

An hour later we let ourselves into the house in Gulf Sands, casserole dish in hands, along with more vegan cookies, this time chocolate chip to go with raspberry ice I'd picked up at the natural foods store.

My father eyed the dinner suspiciously, but snatched a cookie and told the girls he'd supervise them in the pool if they wanted to swim. I'd insisted they wear their bathing suits to the house, and surprisingly, they agreed.

My mother watched as the three went out to the pool.

"You're good for them." She turned, hands on hips. "When they were staying here, I tried everything to get them in the water."

I was startled by the compliment. "They're loosening up. They helped make dinner and did the cookies almost by themselves."

"Did I just hear a dog bark?"

I had left Bismarck in the car for the moments it had taken to bring the food into the house. "We have a surprise for you." Before she could respond I left and came back a few minutes later with Bismarck on a leash.

"Remember this guy?"

My mother slapped her hands on her hips again. "Is that the same dog? Teo's police dog?"

I motioned for Biz to sit beside me. "Bismarck, remember my mother?"

"You and Teo…?"

"Spoke just long enough for him to agree to rent me Bismarck."

"Rent?"

"I wasn't really in a position to ask for a favor, was I? But I like the idea of having a dog in the house. It makes me feel safe."

I waited for her to tell me to get the dog out of *her* house.

"This is the same dog who…"

"He and Teo retired together. Teo's leg was amputated."

My mother closed her eyes a moment. "Dear God."

"I know, but he's doing great." I heard myself adding, "It should have been me."

"Stop that. All of you, including this dog, were just doing your jobs. And the man who caused all this pain got what he deserved."

With that, she held out her hand to Bismarck. And when his tail began to wag, she told me to take him off the leash. I watched as she called him, and the two headed for the kitchen.

I wandered outside to watch my nieces splashing in the water. My father smiled as I approached. "Has Mom had brain surgery?" I asked.

"Not that I'm aware of."

"I guess you would know." I told him about Bismarck. "And now she's got him in the kitchen while she puts the finishing touches on dinner. And she's talking to him like he's human."

"There are many things about your mom that you don't understand."

"Am I supposed to?"

"Absolutely not." He put his arm around me and pulled me closer. "That's the dog who probably saved your life. And there's no way she's ever going to forget that. He can shed every bit of his fur while he's here, and she'll stuff a commemorative pillow with it."

Touched, I cleared my throat. "The girls love him."

"Have you heard from your sister?"

I shook my head and he didn't pursue it. I thought he probably knew that once we started to discuss Wendy's whereabouts, the conversation would rapidly deplete his already limited energy and strength.

"Holly and Noelle have brightened up since you took over. Thank you."

I was spared having to reply through the lump in my throat, because at that moment the girls got out of the pool.

Dinner was surprisingly well received by both parents, and afterward my father took the girls and Bismarck into the media room to set up *The Muppet Christmas Carol*, which had been a favorite of mine as a little girl. I was pretty sure that, in their hearts, I was still seven years old.

My mother and I cleared counters and put food away. She asked the question I'd been waiting for as we dished up the raspberry ice to take into the media room.

"Have you heard from your sister?"

"Dad asked, too. I haven't. She should be calling soon."

"Will she be home for Christmas?"

"I can't predict, Mom. I wish I could."

"This whole thing is beyond comprehension."

I could hardly argue. "The girls and I made a few Christmas things together this afternoon. But I think I need to buy a tree and decorations for the town house."

"Wendy may reappear, and Bryce is usually on shore over the holiday."

"Be that as it may, it's sneaking up. They can use a little Christmas spirit right now, even if they head back to Connecticut later."

"I have all our old decorations. All the things you and Wendy made in school, the flickering lights you loved. Remember those?"

I pretended I did, because clearly, Mom had saved them with me in mind. "They still work?"

"Your father bought a million replacement bulbs in case they were ever discontinued. But you can have anything in those boxes. I haven't put up a tree in years."

"Well, I think we both need to this year. The girls will expect it."

"I guess we're all the family they have at the moment."

I wondered when, if ever, the girls would head north for a family Christmas with Bryce and Wendy. This year? Next? Never? I remembered the first one Bryce had spent with our family. It was the same visit when Wendy had given me the alligator night-light. My mother had pulled out all the stops. To a four-year-old the house had looked like a fairyland. Tinsel, colored lights, a tree in the entryway as tall as a castle. I'd helped my mother decorate at least a million cookies. And she'd helped me make paper chains to hang in my room, one link for each day before Christmas, so I could remove one at a time and keep track of the coming holiday.

"Do you remember the first Christmas Bryce spent with us? It was the best ever."

"You weren't even in school yet. You can't possibly remember that Christmas."

"How's this? You had a cookie cutter of Santa's sleigh. And we made so many sleigh cookies, we bent it completely out of shape."

"I'm impressed."

"See, even then, I knew I had to pay attention to details."

"What else do you remember?"

In my heart I thought of that year as the Christmas-of-

Wendy. After they married, Wendy and Bryce had traveled far and wide for his career and couldn't travel home. Other years they visited his parents in California for the holiday, because he was an only child. Until his parents died, Wendy and Bryce hadn't made it back to Florida for Christmas. And by the time they owned a home in Connecticut that was large and welcoming enough for all of us, I was in college or grad school, and busy with my own set of friends.

"Wendy took me Christmas shopping," I said. "She bought me a sparkly red dress and shiny gold shoes. And we had candy cane milkshakes."

I was feeling entirely too sentimental tonight. But now I remembered how my sister had dressed me up in my new finery and let me twirl around the living room with my skirts flying and Christmas music playing on the family stereo, while our guests for the evening applauded.

"By the time that night was over, you were tired and very cranky."

"Trust you to remember that."

She actually smiled. "Wendy and Bryce went out, and you wanted to go, too. Instead I tucked you in and read you *The Night Before Christmas*."

"Not that horrifying story about the emperor who imprisoned St. Nicholas until he died?"

She was quiet a moment. "I guess I was worried about your soul." Then, as if on cue, we both began to laugh.

"Wendy thinks you should have been a nun," I said as I sobered. "She's said it more than once. Usually if we're alone having a few drinks." I thought about the few times we'd let down our hair without our parents. They were only memorable because they'd been so rare. But I treasured each one.

"I miss her," I said.

"Because you wish she'd take over again? Or because she's your friend?"

Wendy wasn't a friend. She wasn't someone I'd go to in a crisis, and I would never confess my deepest feelings to her. But she'd been in my life since the beginning, and while we'd never spent the years together that most sisters do, each moment we had spent together glowed in my memory.

"Because she's my sister." I saw an opening to ask about Wendy's scrapbook. "Wendy had a lot of friends, though, didn't she?"

"She had her share." My mother put the raspberry ice back in the freezer and unwrapped the plate of cookies.

"I was looking at some of her old school photos. Are any of her friends still in town? Did she get together with them when she came back?"

She hesitated long enough to make me curious. Had Wendy had a falling out with a classmate that Mom didn't want to get into with me? From years of doing interviews I could tell when somebody was trying to hide something from me. Now I really was curious.

She shrugged, as if to say none of this was important. "One of her friends from the drama club is now the assistant principal of Seabank High. I can't remember her name. I don't know that they ever got together after Wendy moved into the town house, though. Your sister was never a best friend kind of girl. She was nice to everyone. She was popular, but she wasn't in any cliques, never one of the mean girls. Of course you never were, either."

"But I had best friends. Just a few. That was all I needed."

"Wendy had a wide circle. Friends in drama, the band, the church youth group. It seemed like she brought new friends here as often as old."

"Well, there was one girl who kept showing up in the photos." I'd remembered to bring the snapshot I'd taken from the scrapbook, and now I pulled it out of my pocket and held it for her to see. "Is this the principal?"

Mom took and studied it. Her expression changed, and she shook her head. "No, that's Greta. Greta Harold."

I was impressed with her memory. "There are a lot of photos of her."

"I was wrong to say Wendy never had best friends. She and Greta were best friends all through middle school. But Greta's probably the reason Wendy didn't have best friends in high school."

"A nasty fight?"

"No. She died just before Wendy went into ninth grade. Your sister was distraught for months."

Before I could ask more, my father came into the room. "Need help carrying dishes?"

Mom's expression lightened, as if she was glad to leave that particular piece of history behind. "You just want your dessert." She handed him a bowl with two cookies along the side, and picked up two more.

"Ready?" she asked me. "You loved this movie."

I followed behind with the remaining bowls, but as I settled into a leather chair and balanced mine on my lap, I thought about my sister and the trauma of losing a best friend at such a pivotal moment in her development.

I'd never thought of Wendy as someone who had been wounded. But surely Greta Harold's death had changed her. Maybe she didn't trust a world where bad things happened for no reason, and that was, at least in some small part, the reason she was afraid to trust the authorities now.

Whatever part Greta's death had played in making her the woman she was, I felt closer to her. My sister's childhood and adolescence had never been as trouble-free as I had imagined. More than ever, I wanted to help her set her world back to rights. Wendy deserved a happy ending. I just hoped I could help her find one.

CHAPTER SEVENTEEN

My life was falling into a pattern. Where once I'd pondered sound engineering and how much of our story to reveal in episodes of *Out in the Cold*, now I thought about ways to keep my nieces busy and how to sneak vegetables into whatever I cooked for dinner.

Some unseen hand had flicked a switch, and suddenly my career train had been mysteriously routed to the Mommy track, with an unknown destination ahead.

On Monday, as I stood in my local Publix grocery store evaluating the relative cost of tomatoes, I had to admit I was enjoying parts of my odd new life. Now that Holly and Noelle were slowly warming up to me, life in the town house was actually fun at times.

On Saturday night after leaving my parents' house, the girls and I had taken Bismarck for an evening walk and admired the Christmas decorations on neighbors' houses. Tropicana was coming alive, and to prove it, the residents flocking here for the winter were trying to outdo each other with elaborate Florida-themed light displays. Mrs. Santa in a bikini. Reindeer frolicking with dolphins. Today I'd promised we would visit the local discount store so they could pick out decorations for the front door and lights for the podocarpus at the front of the house.

Secretly I hoped if my mysterious wrestling partner returned, he would trip over our electric cords and sprawl helplessly until I could sic Bismarck on him.

I chose my tomatoes and went to put them in my cart when I spotted a familiar face. An attractive silver-haired woman in a navy shift and jacket was coming toward me. She stopped when she recognized me, and I beamed a welcome.

For most of the years of my life, Ella Cramer had been my father's right hand. As a preschooler, I'd perched on her lap, swinging my legs while she taught me to type my name on her computer keyboard. Ella had helped my mother plan every staff Christmas party, and she'd always baked special cookies, just for me. Now I could almost taste them, buttery turtles with pecan legs and chocolate shells, and I wondered if she'd share the recipe.

I moved around the cart to intercept her. "It's so good to see you!"

Her smile was tight, and strangely unwelcoming. "Ryan." She nodded.

Something about her posture said that I shouldn't move closer. "It's been a long time."

Her expression said not long enough. "Your father's recovering?"

This was an odd question, since Ella should know how he was doing. In fact, if I knew Dad, he was probably sneaking phone calls to her every morning to check on things at Gracey Group.

"He's not happy about the diet or the cardiac rehab ahead, but he's gritting his teeth. He looks a little better every day."

She didn't reply.

"How about you?" I asked. "Are you keeping up with everything in the office without him?" And without my sister, I added silently.

Her expression darkened. "I guess you don't know. I was fired. I haven't worked for Gracey Group for three months. I'm a part-time receptionist for a dentist."

I wanted to dive into the nearest display. "No one told me."

"I guess they didn't think it was important." She paused. "And I guess it wasn't. Not to them."

"This is hard to imagine. I'm so sorry."

"Well, I'm glad you are." She nodded, then she disappeared down the next aisle.

In my head I calculated how long Ella had worked for my father. Twenty-five years? Even more? I couldn't imagine what had happened to end that long, productive relationship, but I knew I couldn't ask and upset my father at this delicate juncture of his life. I filed it away as one more thing to worry about.

Back at home I debated plowing through more proposals for *Out in the Cold*'s next season, but with the clock ticking and Christmas right around the corner, I had to concentrate on finding my sister. Uncovering more about her situation might not guarantee she would be home for the holidays, but at least I would have a better idea what, if anything, I could do.

I made a snack and, using a powerful search engine that flirted with sites on the dark web, I started looking for Milton Kerns. I had to exercise more care than usual, but dark web or not, nothing valuable came up.

After a futile hour I made lunch before picking up the search again afterward, this time resorting to a private investigator database. By the time one o'clock rolled around, my eyes were so bleary I shut my laptop and took Bismarck for a run. The two of us returned to find Sophie waiting at my front door.

I gave her a hug after assuring Biz she was a friend. "You didn't say you were coming. Is everything okay?"

"Couldn't be better." She practically glowed. "Hello, Bismarck." She leaned over and held out her hand. "Are you taking good care of everybody?"

He wagged his tail as he sniffed her hand, then wagged some more. Sophie looked up at me. "This is not a dog any man would allow out of his sight unless he had a personal interest in the outcome."

I unlocked the door and escorted her inside. "Don't start."

"I'll tell you my story if you tell me yours."

"Things going well with…" I searched my memory for the name of her new guy and failed. "Mr. Coffee?"

"Ike. Ike Mason."

"A real name seems like a step in the right direction."

"He came to Delray two nights ago and took me to dinner. And today he's having a backyard barbecue so I can meet his daughter and neighbors. That's why I'm here. Now it's your turn."

Sophie was dressed for a luau, not a barbecue. She wore a pink-and-purple dress that wasn't quite a muumuu, but close enough. Her hair was pulled back on each side, anchored by sprays of silk flowers, and her earrings were as long and heavy as wind chimes. She was beaming.

I took out a pitcher of iced tea and poured glasses for both of us. "You like this guy, don't you?"

"He's almost too good to be true."

"You know that's always a warning, right?"

"Remember who you're talking to." She held up her hand and began to tick off what she knew. "Ten years ago his ex-wife found somebody with more money and ditched him. He finished raising their daughter alone in a town inland from here that has one traffic light. He taught middle school—still does—and he's on the board of the local food bank. He resorted to online dating because too many local women were either former students or their mothers."

"And you know his social security number, his traffic violations, and how much money is in his retirement fund." It wasn't a question.

She tossed her head and her earrings tinkled. "If I knew any of those things, do you think I'd admit it?"

We took the tea out to the screened porch. A light breeze moderated the midday sunshine, and we made ourselves comfortable.

"Teo?" she asked, getting down to business.

I told her more about our encounter than I'd been able to on a short phone call, about Teo's prosthesis and the fact I would probably blame myself for the loss of his leg forever.

"Does he blame you?"

I scratched around in my head, replaying our brief interactions. "I think he probably blames me more for leaving afterward."

"You deserted him after all that?"

Sophie could ask because she knew me. "He pushed me away. Hard."

"He was pushing, but he blamed *you*?"

"He lost so much, Sophie. And what did I lose except my patience with him?"

She refused to let me wallow in guilt. "Your sense of security in the world, for starters. You were nearly killed, would have been if that monster Quayle had a better aim."

"I may be eternally paranoid now because of Quayle, but I'm still the one who held on to my profession and all my body parts."

"So how hard did you try to hold on to the man?"

I wasn't sure I remembered. After the nearly fatal encounter,

I'd been so shaken that much of what had happened afterward was a blur. I hadn't been able to sleep or eat. I visited Teo in the hospital, but that had only made my recovery more dicey. When I struggled to talk to him, he'd been either silent and seething or so out-and-out angry that I'd had to leave for both our sakes.

"Not hard enough," I said. "I couldn't imagine he wanted anything to do with me again. But it was more than that. I was just so ashamed and so badly equipped to handle that much emotion." I'd been staring into space. I looked at her. "I guess I thought putting everything behind us was best for both our sakes."

"Did you put it behind you?"

"When I was a kid, whenever I got angry or had any strong feeling, my mother would tell me to go off and be by myself until I calmed down. That's how we deal with emotions in my family. We leave until we can pretend we don't feel anything. Everybody's happier that way. I guess that's what happened when I walked away from Teo. I went away until I thought it would be safe to see him again."

"So is it safe now?"

I started to change the subject, but I realized that was exactly the way I'd been trained to react. I flashed on my nieces, who, judging from my interactions with them, were receiving the same training from their mother.

"No, it's not safe," I said, and it felt good to say the words. "I've missed him every single day."

"Well, that's encouraging. If nothing else, maybe the two of you can finally work through the past. Whatever the outcome."

"Strictly one day at a time. At least we're talking."

"And you have his dog."

Bismarck was lying at my feet, in case Sophie turned out to

be another serial killer. I reached down and scratched his head. "Are we going to giggle over guys the whole time you're here? That would be fun, but is there another reason for this visit?"

"News, of sorts. I found somebody who had access to the guest registry at the Golden Aspen Resort."

Sophie's good at what she does, but this was surprising. "How?"

"Sometimes the simplest way to get things done is the best. I called late last night and asked to be put through to your sister's room. The desk clerk handed me on to the hotel operator, who sounded very young and bored. That was my lucky break. She said there was no guest registered by that name. I told her Wendy was waiting for my call. I asked her to check and see if Wendy might have switched rooms, or if that wasn't true, when she had checked out. She shouldn't have done the latter, I'm sure, but she did. She said nobody named Wendy Wainwright had been registered in the previous weeks."

"Maybe she checked in under Gracey?"

"She checked that, and Gracey Group, too. I told her that the paper I'd written this on was all smudged, and this must be the wrong hotel. I thanked her for her patience, and that was that."

"Are we back to square one?"

"I don't know. Either your sister was never there, or she was there under an assumed name."

"Why would she pretend to be somebody she's not?"

"You won't like the answer."

I knew where Sophie was going, and she went.

"People sometimes use aliases if they're shacking up with somebody they shouldn't be, which, in your sister's case, would be anybody she wasn't married to."

That was a possibility, although I didn't like it. "She would still have to give the clerk a credit card to secure a room."

"Unless whoever she was with presented his."

"There are a lot of maybes there."

"So here's another. *Maybe* that was what happened. But if not? It's not that hard to get a credit card under an alias. She could simply ask her regular credit card company to add whatever name she liked to her account for a second or third card. People do it all the time for family members. And there are always reloadable or single-use credit cards."

"That would take a ridiculous amount of preplanning."

"It sure would."

My head was swimming. "How about a picture ID? Doesn't a hotel ask for one?"

"Depends, but didn't you have a fake ID in college so you could visit your local bar or buy a six-pack? You know how easy they are to come by."

I couldn't imagine my sister slinking through dark alleys to pay a forger to create an ID for her. It was so not Wendy. But, of course, trying to escape the law wasn't exactly Wendy, either.

I thought out loud. "It's also possible Wendy was never at the Golden Aspen, and we have the wrong murder."

The burner phone in my pocket began to vibrate just a split second before it rang.

I was stunned by my sister's timing. "We can test our theory. Wendy's calling." I dug out the phone and held it up.

"Want me to leave?"

For the first time I realized the burner had a speaker button. Wasn't it just like my sister to purchase the best, even for a throwaway? I made a split-second decision. "You stay and listen. Just don't make any noise, okay?"

Sophie put her finger to her lips.

I cleared my throat and answered. "Wendy?"

"Who else?" She sounded tired, but the words were meant to be a joke.

"You're okay?"

"As okay as anybody can be in hiding."

I glanced at Sophie, who was leaning forward to hear better, and I got right down to business. "Listen, I did what you asked. I looked up Milton Kerns. But I don't even know if I'm spelling his name correctly."

"I don't know how it's spelled. The guy's a stranger."

I knew better than to probe that further, since she might hang up any minute. "I haven't found anything, and that's mostly because you're dancing around the truth. You have to clue me in if I'm really going to help. You know I want to. I have some experience. Please tell me everything you can, so I can get down to work."

She was silent so long I wondered if she was going to hang up. But finally, she sighed. "I'm sorry, Ryan Rosie. I really hoped I'd be home by now, and this whole thing could just be a funny story to tell someday. But apparently, that's not to be."

For a moment I couldn't get past "Ryan Rosie." Was Wendy trying to make me feel like a little girl again? Was using my pet name code? *You're my beloved baby sister, so don't think you're going to get the best of me?*

And what could ever be funny about a murder?

Sophie pointed at the phone, and I realized I'd been silent too long. "Look, Wendy, I'm having problems finding any humor in taking care of your daughters while our father recovers from bypass surgery."

"Do you think I'm having a good old time? I'm not lying on a beach working on my tan."

I had purposely mentioned her daughters and my father. She hadn't taken the bait and asked about either. "Then where are you? And when are you coming home?"

When she didn't answer, I took a gamble. "Does this have to do with the plastic surgeon who was murdered in New Mexico?"

"You know about that? Has somebody called there?"

"Nobody's called or contacted me."

"I guess you're just good at digging for details. That's why I called you in the first place."

"Well?"

A deep sigh resonated through the phone. "The whole thing is crazy. Beyond crazy. First, I didn't murder anybody. You have to believe me. But yes, that's why I'm afraid to come home."

"I need the story." I resisted adding "now."

"You have time to listen? It might take a while."

I avoided looking at Sophie. "I do."

"At the end of my trip, I met a woman who worked at Golden Aspen. She mentioned that management was trying to find a buyer after an unsuccessful reorganization last year, and she hoped she could keep her job once it changed hands. She said management was desperate, and the resort would be a bargain for the right company."

My father had said something about Golden Aspen reorganizing. So far I was with her.

"So you went to check it out?" I asked.

"I was in Phoenix by then, and I had some time before my flight back to Florida. She encouraged me to drive over and see the place for myself. She hoped if she helped me, and Gracey Group became the new owner, I'd put in a good word for her. I guess I hinted I would try. Anyway, she told me she would show me around, and I could stay in her guest room for the night. Only, she called when I was practically in Santa Fe and said she'd had an emergency and had to fly to Washington for a week, maybe more, but she told me to take a good look when I got to Golden Aspen. She'd answer any questions when she got back."

"So you registered at the resort and spent a night or two?"

"No, she left a key to her apartment where I could find it."

I was watching Sophie, and she shrugged. Now we knew why Wendy's name hadn't been on a guest list. I felt a wave of relief.

"That just explains how you got there," I said.

"I decided to go ahead and look around. I spent a day checking out the facilities, without telling anybody what I was doing or why. I just wanted to see what looked good and what didn't." She paused, then gave a small, sad laugh. "I wanted to impress Dad. You know how he is. He loves initiative. Either way I'd have a story to tell."

That, too, rang true. Whether Golden Aspen had turned out to be a new acquisition or not, our father would have been proud that Wendy had followed up the lead.

She continued. "I met Dr. Calvo while I was sitting at the bar ordering a drink. I wanted to see how well the lounge was run. I was making notes. It was all innocent. Vítor came up and asked if he could take the stool next to mine, and after one drink we moved to a table in the corner and ended up having dinner there. He was charming, very old-world, and he told great stories about some of the celebrities he'd worked on. I enjoyed talking to him."

"Dinner is hardly a reason to suspect you of murder."

She was speaking faster now. "Who knows? After the meal we were joined by another man, this Milton Kerns person, who was apparently also a guest. Vítor introduced him, but if he said how he knew him, I can't remember. He was pleasant enough. I had another drink with them, but my mind was on the resort, so I wasn't concentrating on the conversation. Afterward I thanked both men and went back to the apartment and packed so I could drive to Phoenix and fly home the next afternoon. I was sleeping soundly when my phone pinged. I was afraid something had happened to one of the girls, so I sat up to read the text. Kerns told me the doctor had been murdered, and the police were probably going to look for me because I was one of the last people to have been seen with him before he was killed."

Sophie was frowning. I watched as she scrambled through her purse, pulled out a pen and scrap of paper and quickly jotted "Had her #?"

I nodded. "Wendy, two things. Were the police already investigating at that point? And why did Milton Kerns have your phone number?"

"At that point I don't think anybody else knew about the murder except whoever killed Vítor. I texted back and asked him to call me. We were on the phone a minute or less. He said after they left the lounge he'd promised Vítor that he'd bring something to his room. I don't remember what. He was talking so fast. A map? A book? He said he got there, and the door was ajar. He peered inside and saw Vítor's body in a pool of blood."

"And he didn't call anybody but you?"

"I guess not. I'm pretty sure the body wasn't discovered by anyone else until the next morning."

"So by then, you were long gone?"

"It's a nightmare. Talk about being in the wrong place at the wrong time."

I winced, thinking it had probably been more of a nightmare for the surgeon. Sophie pointed at her paper and shook it at me.

"Wendy, how did Kerns have your number?"

"I don't know." She paused. "Vítor and I had exchanged

numbers. I figured if I ever wanted a little tuck or lift, he was the man to do it."

"Why did he need *yours*?"

"He told me he gave talks all over the US to women of a certain age who might want to visit his clinic. He was so funny and personable, I knew the submarine officers' spouses' group in Connecticut would love to have him speak at our annual benefit. I asked him to have his office call me once he knew his schedule the next spring so we could arrange a presentation."

Sophie was rolling her eyes, but I ignored her. "No idea how Kerns got your number from him?"

"Maybe he took the doctor's phone when he went into the room. I entered my number in Vítor's phone while I was sitting with him in the lounge, so of course my fingerprints must have been on it. I hope it is gone. Kerns told me that when he saw Vítor's body, he stepped inside to see if he was still alive. When he realized he wasn't, he left. He was afraid he might become a suspect. But maybe when he was in the room he grabbed Vítor's phone. I mean, if the doctor had called him or put an appointment on his schedule, or had Kerns in his contacts for some reason…"

"Or maybe he killed him."

"I know."

"Did you try to call Kerns later? Anytime since?"

"Of course I did. But whenever I try, I get a message saying he's not accepting calls. He probably ditched his phone."

"Maybe he told you to leave because he didn't want the police to know he was with the doctor that night, too."

"I thought of that. But surely somebody saw all of us together. Wouldn't they report we were together in the lounge?"

"But you weren't registered. Maybe he wasn't, either. And if nobody had your names or knew who either of you were…"

"Can you see why I need you to find Kerns for me?"

"So you can turn him in?"

"If I go to the authorities, I want to be able to tell them where to find him. He and Vítor have some kind of history. They seemed to know each other. And me? I was just some woman Vítor met in the bar. If they have Kerns, it's doubtful they'll be interested in me."

My head was whirling, and I wanted to shout at her and tell her everything she was doing was wrong. But my sister always believed she knew best, and if I said everything I wanted to, she would simply hang up. I struggled to keep my tone as even as possible.

"Wendy, go to them now. Tell them what you told me. You had drinks and dinner before Calvo was murdered. So what? That doesn't prove a thing. And the authorities will be able to track Kerns a lot easier than I will."

"I wish I felt as sure of that as you do. But I'm going to wait a little longer."

"A little? You have daughters who need you here. And Mom and Dad aren't stupid. They know something's going on. Then there's your husband."

"How are Noelle and Holly?"

"Christmas is coming."

She moved on, as if that was of no consequence. "You sound doubtful? I'm sorry, but you have to trust me."

Too many things she'd said just barely held together. Did I owe her my trust? Did the lifetime bond of sisterhood mean I had to take everything at face value?

"I trust you, Wendy," I said at last. "But I'm realizing I don't know you very well. In some ways we're strangers, aren't we? I've been looking through your old scrapbooks. I wasn't here yet to share those memories with you. And the only person

I can talk to about you is Mom. I'm just trying to put all this together."

"Really? You think the past will help you do that?"

She didn't sound angry. She sounded surprised but also pleased, as if she thought a closer look at her childhood and adolescence might cure me of doubts.

"Talk to my old friends," she said. "I think one of them is assistant principal at Seabank High now. Her name's Claire. I don't know her married name. She and I were in drama club together. Maybe others are around, too. I've been too busy to reach out. But if you don't trust your own memories of me, ask them for theirs."

My mother had mentioned the assistant principal, too. Whatever I decided, I was sure I needed more information. I concentrated on that, shelving the larger questions. "How were Kerns and the doctor connected? You really can't remember?"

"I was mentally weighing whether it might be worth coming back to the resort as an official representative of Gracey Group. I guess I missed a lot of the conversation from that point on."

"If you think of something, you'll let me know. Because I'm at a dead end here."

"How's Dad?"

She won a point for asking. "He's progressing about the way you'd expect."

"Take care of all of them." Three beeps and the call was over.

I put the phone back in my pocket before I looked at Sophie. "What do you think?"

"I think your sister's story has as many holes as a wool sweater in a trunk filled with moths."

I admired the simile while wondering if she was right. "Like?"

"Nothing she said, not one bit of it, would be worth pulling a disappearing act. The police might question her about dinner with the doctor, but why would they suspect her of murder? Did anybody see her going into his room? Were her fingerprints there? On the gun? Is there any record she and Calvo might have known each other to help establish a motive? And did you notice she never named the so-called employee who invited her to visit and then conveniently didn't show up? She didn't even say what the woman did there."

I hadn't noticed. Everything I'd heard had been filtered through my own concern and, yes, anger that Wendy was putting her family in such a strange position.

"But the story does explain why she wasn't listed as a guest."

Sophie still looked skeptical. "So on the subject of the unnamed employee? If anybody paid attention to the table where the doctor and Wendy were sitting like, you know, the *server*? They would have described her to the police by now. This mysterious woman is probably back. And since we're told she works there, she's probably heard the description of the woman who had dinner with Calvo and another man. And she's probably wondering if that woman is Wendy. And by now she's probably told the sheriff your sister's name."

"If she has, nobody's interested. Nobody's called here looking for her."

"How would anybody who doesn't have my skills or resources get Wendy's home number?"

"Through Gracey Group. The woman knew who she was. Maybe even her cell."

"The cell that's permanently disabled."

I imagined calling Gracey Group in a little while and talking to whoever had taken Ella Cramer's place. What would I ask? *Oh, by the way, has the sheriff called looking for my sister?*

"Did you ever try to get into her voice mail?" Sophie asked.

In the week that had passed, I had tried birthdays and anniversaries as passwords. "No luck. The phone still does that beepy thing when I lift the receiver."

"Somebody in a uniform may have called from New Mexico. Next stop? Your front door."

"I need to check further, don't I?" I got up and she followed me inside. I lifted the receiver. "Thoughts?"

"You are pretty hopeless."

"Ask me anything you want about a cell phone, but I don't own a landline. And remember, no phone bills, so I don't know who the provider is."

"So dial the home number for starters. Area code first."

I knew that much and punched it in, nodding to Sophie. So far so good. I listened to the menu and punched the required 7 and waited. I listened again and shook my head. "Now I need Wendy's code to get the messages."

"Does it tell you how many digits?"

"Six. I've tried every combination I can think of."

"The address here?"

I winced. The address was six numbers. "Well, not that one." I tried it but voice mail hung up on me.

I replaced the receiver. "Even robots don't like me."

Sophie looked at her watch. "Call Glenn. If anybody can help you retrieve her messages, it's our spy guy."

Glenn Peters ran a shop in Boynton Beach named I Spy, which specialized, as the name implied, in surveillance equipment and other spy gear. He had consulted with us numerous times as we considered ways to get the information we'd needed for *Out in the Cold*. I was never sure exactly how legal his suggestions were, but in a world where Russian interference in elections was daily news, I figured that whatever Glenn suggested might, at most, earn us a slap on the wrist.

I walked her to the door and gave her another hug. "Have

a good time at the barbecue. Ike's family and friends will love you."

"If this goes well, I'll bring him to meet you."

When she was gone, I called Glenn.

He never answers his phone, so I left my number and explained what I needed to know. While I waited, I got out the ingredients for chicken chili and prepared it for the slow cooker, which I recognized from my childhood as another hand-me-down from my mother.

The phone rang, and I answered as I dumped a can of corn into the cooker.

"What's up, Ryan?"

Glenn has a great voice, deep, mysterious and sexy. We'd featured him in one of our episodes last season, and afterward I got multiple requests for his photo. In real life Glenn looks more like Georgie Porgie than George Clooney, but the voice makes up for a lot.

We chatted, and then I got down to business and explained what I needed, minus the part about Wendy running from the law.

He told me to wait and went to his computer. "Okay, you say you can get all the way to the security code when you punch in the number?"

"Right."

"Is your sister very techy?"

I hadn't thought so until the burner phone had arrived via a remailing service. "I really don't know."

"Does she mostly use her cell?"

"It went missing."

He made a noise low in his throat to show he didn't believe me. "The easiest thing to try? Some companies use 111111 as their default voice mail code. She's supposed to change it once she logs in the first time. But not everybody bothers. Try that first."

I listened as he followed that advice with a list of other possible numbers to try—123456. *Password*—too many letters, but I was to try the first six and then try it backward. Significant family dates, names of pet—a no go in this case. The list went on.

He told me to call back if nothing worked. Before we hung up I reminded him I was still interested in producing a podcast on spy technology with him as host. Every time I called him I plugged the idea, but it would never happen. Glenn wasn't interested in sharing his secrets.

I don't take luck for granted, so when 111111 immediately unlocked Wendy's voice mail, I lifted my eyes to heaven in thanks.

I punched in the number to retrieve new messages and listened carefully. There were two. One was a perky young woman who asked me if I knew how easy it would be to upgrade all my credit cards. I deleted Miss Perky before she finished. The second was the younger Mrs. English asking Wendy to schedule a conference. Her impatience with my sister rang in her voice. I could relate.

I hung up, disappointed. Since both calls had come in within the past twenty-four hours, I wondered if Wendy was accessing her voice mail from afar and deleting it. As I added chicken breasts to the slow cooker, that raised an entirely new set of questions. Uppermost in my mind? I might not have the number of my sister's burner phone, but if she was calling regularly to access her voice mail, could I leave her a message by calling the home number here and telling her to call me?

Except did I want her to know I'd realized she was accessing her voice mail from afar? Or by bringing up voice mail at all, set her to wondering if I had somehow found a way to listen to hers?

I was sprinkling herbs, when I remembered that a year or so ago I had needed to hear a message I had mistakenly deleted on my cell phone. I'd been able to get to it by paging back through the menu. While it seemed unlikely this older phone would have the ability to retrieve deleted messages, I scrolled through the menu anyway. And luck was my friend for the second time that day.

I went through the steps needed, but I was only able to retrieve one message. The lone call was from a man named Craig, who wanted to know why Kim hadn't been seen at Against the Wind in a couple of weeks.

Funny thing, but now I wanted to know exactly the same thing.

CHAPTER EIGHTEEN

I was learning so much about children. For instance, never let persons who are shorter than you believe they're in control if you take them shopping.

As promised, yesterday after school we had gone to buy Christmas lights. Almost immediately, the one string of lights I had envisioned had morphed into multiple strings to wrap around each tree, roots to top. There were extension cords and needle-like branches involved, and when I'd suggested we backtrack and save all decorations for our indoor tree, I'd been met with such despair that, not only did we now own six strings of outdoor lights, we also owned an inflatable sculpture featuring Santa in a holly-sprinkled bathing suit with a reindeer under a palm tree.

Once we inflated Santa, the sculpture would top my height by almost two feet.

There was good news, though. Now I was Holly and Noelle's favorite aunt, as well as their only one.

I'd decided to get a head start on the lights, since another thing I'd learned was that children have big ideas and little patience. I'd watched a how-to video on YouTube, measured the distance from the outdoor outlet to the closest tree and, since I couldn't count on Mystery Intruder, I'd carefully stretched my extension cord where it would do the least amount of damage. I'd wrapped it around the base of the first tree and was now—I hoped—ready to go. According to YouTube, my next job was to assess the tree to decide what branches should be lighted. Less than a moment passed before I began to wrap. The whole point was just to have something blinking uncontrollably at night when the girls were outside watching.

I was on the ground between trees, butt in the air, when Bismarck, who was keeping me company, began to bark. I pushed out and up just in time to see my dog buddy ecstatically greeting his best friend.

"Darn dog. I had such a great view." Teo did something with his hands and Bismarck immediately sat adoringly at his feet.

"You have to teach me that hand thing." I wiped off my shorts as best I could, but I was pretty sure I was covered in sap and dirt. "And since this is exactly where I was attacked, I'm glad it's you who Biz is greeting."

"I had no idea you were so domestic."

"Yeah, me either. And this is nothing. I had to wrestle my nieces to stop them from buying icicle lights to put along the roof." For some reason I forgot to tell him about the inflatable vacation scene.

"You're kind of getting into this kid thing. So your sister won't be home by Christmas?"

I wanted to tell Teo the truth, but he had been a cop, and a popular one. He was probably still connected every which way except a paycheck to the sheriff's department.

"That's still up in the air." I smiled, as if that was perfectly normal. "So did you just come by to stare at my butt? Or is there a better reason?"

"Better?" He shook his head. "Different. Just checking on my dog."

"You can see how unhappy he is here. By the way, he's a big fan of tea parties."

"Don't tell my students. They think he's a killer."

This was new. "Students?"

"I teach criminal justice at the local community college. Two afternoons a week."

"I bet you're terrific." I felt better somehow. Teo was still using his considerable skills.

"Any new bad guys trying to break in?"

"No, and between Biz and neighbors moving back in for the winter, I doubt there will be. Although since I'm kind of the new kid on the block, I can't tell who's supposed to be here and who's not." We stared at each other, and finally I laughed a little. "I guess uncomfortable silences are to be expected."

"I'm not uncomfortable. I'm just wondering how to invite myself to lunch."

I felt a not-surprising rush of pleasure. "Any way you want to. I have a cupboard full of peanut butter and a fridge full of American cheese. It's not gourmet, but you'll be very welcome."

"I actually brought lunch. Call me optimistic."

More pleasure. "Or smart. I never turn down a meal. You remembered."

"I guess I did. But I guess I wasn't wholly optimistic. I left it in the car."

"I'll wash up. You may have noticed I need to?"

"I like the sap on your nose. At least I hope it's sap." He went to his car, and I went inside to wash. Biz went with Teo.

He was peering into the refrigerator by the time I'd scrubbed and dusted myself back to respectability. "No beer."

"We're an apple juice kind of place. But I can make tea. It'll just take a minute."

"I'll watch." He pulled out one of the stools and sat, leaning against the peninsula.

"Well, it's complex, but I'll outline the steps. What are we eating?"

"Grouper po'boys."

For a moment I was paralyzed. Years had passed, but Teo hadn't forgotten my favorite. "That's awfully nice of you. Could they possibly be from the Shark Shack?"

"Have you been back since you got here?"

The Shark Shack had been our favorite place to eat, and, of course, I had purposely avoided it since coming home. The bar and grill was a local hole-in-the-wall. The owner, Jack, was a retired marine biologist who never missed a chance to promote the importance of sharks in the ocean ecology. I was a convert, although I was careful not to frolic in the water at sunset.

"I haven't been," I admitted. "We had good times there."

"And that's why you didn't go back?"

"I had visions of running into you." I paused. "Buying a grouper po'boy for some other lucky woman."

"Jack sold the place, but the new owner honors all his traditions and recipes. And I don't think I've ever bought another woman one of their po'boys."

I was sure Teo hadn't been alone for all the years we'd been apart. Neither had I, but apparently neither of us had been completely free, either. "It's like a piece of our past. A lot of time's gone by since then."

"And here we are, thrown up on the same shore together. You, me and Bismarck. And to top it all off, one of us may be involved in something she shouldn't be. Ah, the memories."

Road signs appear in our lives. We're walking along, minding our business, and suddenly a sign appears. Sometimes they simply point out the best direction to turn, something we might have known all along. And sometimes they point us in new and scarier directions. I was looking at one of those right now. I could lie or at least cover up the truth. Or I could tell Teo what was going on.

I looked toward the sign that read Goodbye Forever, and I knew that this time, I wasn't going to make that turn.

"I don't know if I'm involved in something I shouldn't be." Even I could tell I was spacing my words carefully, in case I changed my mind between one and the next. "But Teo, I am involved in something."

He didn't look surprised. "I know."

"But do you know what?"

"No clue. Except your sister seems to be somewhere else and suddenly here you are."

I filled the teakettle and set it on the stove. Then I took down the canister of tea bags. "How connected are you to the sheriff's office these days?" I leaned against the counter while the water heated. "I have to know before I tell you what's going on."

"I saw a picnic area over by the swimming pool. It's a pretty day. Want to eat outside?"

I made the tea and rummaged for travel mugs so I could take it with us. I added snack packs of chips and some of the vegan chocolate chip cookies I'd frozen. It might be December, but outside, they'd defrost quickly.

We chatted but said nothing of note until we were sitting among a grove of crape myrtle trees at a round table to one side of Tropicana's pool. The food was spread in front of us, and Teo and I were sitting close together on the shadiest side. No one else was around.

The sandwich was exactly the way I remembered it. I took several bites before I spoke. "This is heavenly."

"So…"

I waited and watched him.

He gave a nod. "I think what you really wanted to know back there was whether I'm required to tell the sheriff or any of his deputies if I'm suspicious about something, or if I hear something that might be suspicious."

"That covers it."

"No, I'm not. But does that mean I won't?"

"I need a promise that if I tell you, you'll keep this to yourself."

"If it puts somebody else in danger, I won't keep it to myself."

"It's more likely that *not* keeping this to yourself might put someone in danger."

"It's interesting, isn't it, that we're picking up right where we left off. Quayle was about trust. This is about trust."

I'd known he would get to that. "I'll trust you if you tell me I should. And I should have trusted you then. I know it, you know it."

"And I shouldn't have come on like gangbusters."

Tears rose in my eyes at that admission. "We have a second chance." I paused and blinked hard. "At trusting, I mean."

He smiled for a split second. "Yeah, I knew what you meant. So trust me and tell me what's up."

"Just so you know, this is Bismarck's fault. I owe you an explanation because you loaned me your dog, and you don't know the whole story."

"You can stop making excuses. I'm listening."

I'd had a few minutes to figure out how to tell Teo why I was suddenly taking care of my nieces. In the end, though, I just told him the story, beginning with the phone call in Delray and ending with the one yesterday.

He didn't interrupt, but he made it clear he was carefully absorbing every word. When I finished, he nodded. "So everything you're telling me is based on what Wendy's said and what you've been able to find out on your own."

"With the help of my coproducer, Sophie."

"Okay. This is harder. Do you believe Wendy?"

As a tween I'd religiously watched *Who Wants to Be a Millionaire*. It was something my father and I had done together if he happened to be home. Fast-forward to today and Teo's million-dollar question.

"She's my sister." It was my best answer, but I wasn't going to win prize money, and I sure couldn't phone Dad for a better one.

"Do you think the break-in here had anything to do with Wendy?"

"I didn't think so at first. But I didn't know everything I know now, either. I didn't know Milton Kerns had Wendy's cell phone number, at least the phone she had the night of the murder. And with that, it wouldn't be a stretch to obtain her address."

"So what would he want that's in the town house?"

"Teo, I'm completely clueless. But if he is after something, it's pretty clear he has some connection to my sister that she hasn't told me about."

He looked surprisingly sympathetic. "Is that the first time you've admitted that your sister might not be telling the whole truth?"

I gave a vague nod, although Sophie had already read between the lines.

"So, do you want my opinion?" he asked.

"I don't know, do I?"

"Probably not, but I'll give it to you anyway. You need to go to the sheriff here, tell him what you told me, and ask him to contact the sheriff in New Mexico and set up an interview."

I debated for less than a second. "Can't do it."

"I figured."

"You have siblings. Would you turn them in?"

"You mean would I turn them in if I worried they were guilty of something, no matter what cock-and-bull story they told me?"

My lips parted to correct him, but I clamped them together. Because, of course, he was right.

"The last time you ignored my advice, you were almost killed and so was I, not to mention the dog at our feet."

"And the last time you treated me like an idiot, I reacted badly, but you gave me little choice because you weren't listening."

We were both silent a moment as the words settled. Finally he spoke. "We aren't good for each other."

"Do you really believe that?"

"I keep trying to. I managed for almost four years."

"Yeah, me, too." I leaned closer. "Do you have any advice I might actually be able to follow?"

He didn't rise and leave me sitting there. He didn't argue. I had expected one or the other. Instead he sighed. Then he leaned forward, too, and he kissed me. A brush of his lips, lasting only a second or two, but as momentous as any in my life.

"Maybe we should just be good *to* each other, and see what happens," he said.

My brain was frozen, but my body was a river of fire. I cleared my throat. "That will be much easier." I tunneled my fingers through his hair and brought his face closer for a second kiss.

He finally sat back. "Now that we're even, finish your sandwich. I have to leave in a few minutes."

I'm not sure what we talked about while we finished our lunch. I probably babbled. I had hoped we might find a way to be comfortable with each other again, a way to stop blaming each other, a way to stop feeling guilty. I hadn't dared to hope that after everything and all the time that had passed, we might still find our way back to love.

We cleaned up in silence and headed back to my unit. We were careful not to touch. He didn't hold my hand. But I felt the new intimacy like a warm cloak.

As he bent over to say goodbye to Bismarck, I put my hand on his arm. I'd just thought of something I needed help with, and it was another way to show that I trusted him.

He straightened. "I'm busy tomorrow," he said, "but would you like to run by my place on Thursday? This time *with* me?"

"I'd love it."

"Aren't you going to ask me how I run with a prosthesis?"

"Okay. How do you run with a prosthesis? Faster than me or a whole lot faster?"

He grinned. "What were you going to say?"

"Can you break into a medicine cabinet for me?"

"Unexpected question. Why?"

I debated, but again, I told the truth. "The girls' teachers are complaining about how tired they are at school. And Holly said her mother gave them allergy medicine before bed. Anyway, I want to be sure there are no prescriptions in the cabinet that they ought to be taking. And it's locked."

"You haven't asked your sister?"

"Our conversations are about her problems, not about her daughters."

"Do the girls miss her? They must."

I hedged. "Noelle does. Holly's more a daddy's girl."

"And speaking of Daddy?"

"Out at sea, God knows where, in his submarine keeping the world safe from nuclear weapons *with* nuclear weapons. But I do know how to text him. I just don't think I want to do anything until I know more."

"Are you worried that whatever's in the cabinet could be the reason for the break-in?"

"I wasn't until you just brought it up."

"Let's take a look."

We climbed the stairs with Bismarck zigzagging behind like a border collie making sure we headed where we were supposed to. In the master bathroom Teo looked at the cabinet, arms folded in front of him. "This isn't the original."

"I know it doesn't match."

"Did your sister install it?"

"No telling."

"Got nail clippers?"

There were several different sizes in the drawer beside the sink. I pulled out two and put them on the counter. Teo chose one and flipped out the nail file attachment. Then he inserted it into the cabinet lock.

He fiddled with turning the file until he seemed satisfied. Then he jiggled it slowly and gently, and finally he turned it once more. The cabinet door swung open.

He put the clippers back on the counter. "There you go."

I whistled. "I am so impressed."

"That's all it took? I wish I'd known."

He moved back so I could examine the contents. Teo watched as I pulled out prescription bottles, one after another, reading the labels silently, and finally followed with an economy-size bottle of a generic antihistamine. I stared at the collection on the sink, and I didn't know what to say.

"Do you know what you're looking at?" Teo's tone said that he did.

I knew. I might have to look up some of the prescriptions online, but I was almost certain I was staring at enough tranquilizers and sleeping pills to knock out all of Seabank for a night.

Teo picked up several of the containers. Then he laid a hand on my shoulder. "She has a drug problem."

I didn't deny the evidence, but another answer occurred to me, and it was worse. The containers sitting on the bathroom counter were a possible clue why my nieces had been so fatigued at school, why Holly had too often fallen asleep at her desk, and why going to sleep was so difficult.

My sister might well be drugging her daughters.

CHAPTER NINETEEN

We Graceys aren't a drop-in kind of family. In the years I've lived in Delray Beach, I've never driven to Seabank just to surprise my parents. And whenever I visited Wendy in Connecticut, we made elaborate arrangements, consulting a multitude of calendars before selecting a date.

This pattern has history. After my mother moved my eighty-five-year-old grandmother to a retirement community in Seabank, she and Nana still made appointments to see each other, arranged between Nana's bridge games and Mom's yoga or Pilates. While I've never asked if they arranged my grandmother's death to suit their schedules, I've always wondered.

All this is to say that late Wednesday morning, when I realized my mother was standing unannounced at the town house front door, I wondered if the sky had fallen. Where was Chicken Little when I needed him most?

"Are you busy?" she asked before taking a step inside.

I had been. I'd finally taken a morning to do some much-needed work, but I wasn't going to waste such an unusual opportunity.

"Never too busy to see you." I gave her an awkward hug.

Arlie Gracey can take in everything around her in one sweeping glance. Today she swept before she spoke. "The place looks good."

I was ridiculously pleased. "The girls help me pick up before bedtime."

"How do you manage that?"

"With a whip and chains."

She smiled stiffly. "They weren't what I'd call cooperative when they were with us."

"I'm reading them the Paddington books. The sooner we finish cleanup, the more time I have to read."

"You'll be a good mother."

"Yeah, well."

She gave a decisive nod. "You can get pregnant. You'll just have to be carefully monitored."

Heart valve replacement, and other assorted surgeries, won't make pregnancy or childbirth easy, but I'd been told that with the right level of care, I can probably pull it off safely. Still, there was a larger issue.

"First I need a good man."

Since she had no answer for that, I moved on and offered her tea or coffee.

"Coffee would be nice. We're not drinking it at home anymore."

"Good. I could use a cup, too."

She followed me into the kitchen. "I don't suppose you've heard from your sister."

I was surprised Mom hadn't called out the cavalry to find her older daughter. She could certainly afford to. The fact she was letting me run with Wendy's disappearance was as odd as any of the many things happening in our lives. I could only guess she was suspicious that things were worse than I'd told her, and wasn't ready for details. Lately even her questions were perfunctory, as if she hoped my answers would be, as well.

I told her I had no new information for her. In my mind, "for her" changed a lie to a fib, although the nuns who educated me might not have noted the subtle shades of gray.

"You're much neater than she is," Mom said.

Being told I was better than Wendy at anything was as good as receiving a trophy. "Am I?"

"I dropped something off one day, and there was clutter everywhere. Piles of papers, dirty dishes. It was right before Analena was due. I felt sorry for her."

I took out pods and filled the coffee maker. "Maybe Wendy was having a hard week. I have a taste of how tough her life is. Work, kids, a husband gone most of the time. I guess a few piles here and there were natural."

Mom perched on the same stool Teo had used. "She was the neatest child. Neater than I was, if you can believe that. The kitchen smells good, by the way. What did you make for dinner last night?"

"Spaghetti sauce and meatballs. Noelle can roll a mean meatball."

"And they like cooking?"

I nodded. "Do you remember all the nights you and I cooked together?"

"Apparently they were productive. Now you're passing on what you learned."

"Trying. Noelle remains convinced a tablespoon is a spoon that's been left on the table." I ventured what might sound like criticism. "I don't think they cook much with their mom."

"I don't think Wendy cooks much period."

"See my prior statement. Work, kids, husband at sea."

"I tried to cook with Wendy, too. We did sometimes, but your sister was always so busy with school activities."

I hadn't been as busy, and now I was glad. "Those were our best times together."

"I never knew what else to do with you. Wendy kept me so busy, I never had to think about what to do next. But you? You were so self-contained. You were happy by yourself, doing whatever appealed to you. And I was afraid to interrupt."

"Afraid?" I put the first mug under the coffee maker and pushed a button. Coffee poured out and smelled delicious.

"I don't like being unsure of myself," she said.

That being true, I couldn't imagine a worse scenario for Mom than our lives at the moment. Wendy vanishing. Dad undergoing surgery. Unsure and insecure were the watchwords of our days. Of course finding a cabinet filled with controlled substances hadn't helped me feel any more secure, either.

I decided to go back to my sister's housekeeping. Could neglecting dishes and dusting be a symptom of drug abuse? Or was Mom, who cleans up after her vast array of cleaning ladies, judging my sister by her own unusual standards?

I set the first cup of coffee in front of her. "So when did Wendy go from being a neatnik to a slob?"

She sipped as I made my own, and I had the feeling she wasn't trying to remember, she was trying to decide how to explain. She didn't speak until I'd made myself as comfortable as I could on the second stool facing her.

By now she was staring into her cup. "Wendy changed after her friend died. It was a very emotional, a very *difficult* time for her. The last thing I wanted to do was nag, so I didn't. I never found the right time to insist she start cleaning up after herself again, and she got used to letting things go."

"You didn't tell me what happened to Greta." I had imagined a car accident, or some fatal childhood cancer, but she surprised me.

"It's not the kind of thing I would have told you about, not unless I had to. But it might help you understand your sister. Greta drowned, and Wendy was there."

"That's awful. In a pool?" I was afraid to ask if the pool had been ours.

"It's a terrible story. Greta and Wendy were thick as thieves. They were pretty girls, popular and smart. Wendy was prettier, and I'm not saying that because she was my daughter, but Greta was interesting. You know what I mean? One of those girls who'll turn heads later in her life. Striking, I guess."

"Most girls would settle for turning heads."

"She went through an awkward stage, which your sister somehow bypassed."

"I've looked at the photos in Wendy's scrapbook. Greta was outgrowing the awkward phase when the photos stopped."

"She was such a nice girl. Polite, funny. I loved her sense of humor. Once she brought me a bouquet of daisies, and when I looked closer, I realized she'd hidden a chocolate bar in the middle. She knew I loved chocolate and I didn't want anybody to know what an obsession it was. That was priceless, don't you think? How many girls that age pay attention to something like that?"

"She sounds really special." I sipped and waited.

"Her parents moved away after she died. I tried to stay in touch, but we were a reminder."

"Did this happen at our house?"

"Oh, no, thank God. Both houses had pools. In the summer the girls were either in the water at our place or Greta's. And sometimes they went to the beach with their other friends. Wendy was the stronger swimmer, though. By the time she was eight, she was competing on the swim team. The Harolds moved here from somewhere in New England. I don't remember where, but not the coast. So Greta didn't start lessons as young as Wendy."

She was meandering. I had a feeling she didn't want to get to the bad part. "I know how careful you are. You were always around when I was in the pool. Even when I was a teenager."

"It just makes sense. But nobody was watching the night Greta drowned. Nobody but Wendy, and she couldn't save her."

"What happened?"

"They sang in the chorus. It was one of the activities where Greta surpassed Wendy. She had a gorgeous high soprano and thought she might like to sing professionally someday. Anyway, that's neither here nor there. The chorus had their end of the year bonfire. Somebody's family had a house on the bay, and they got permission to build the fire on the beach, roast marshmallows and hot dogs—something nobody is allowed to do today. Both girls were there, and after they ate, they went for a stroll. The sun had set and nobody saw them leave. The chaperones said they would have stopped them if they'd known, but Wendy and Greta sneaked off."

When she didn't start up again, I prompted a little. "So it was dark…"

"Greta decided she wanted to swim. She thought it would be fun. Wendy tried to talk her out of it. She warned her not to go in, because she knew Greta wasn't a strong enough swimmer to take that kind of chance."

"But she went anyway?"

"Greta started swimming away from shore, mad because Wendy wouldn't go in with her. Wendy yelled at her, but she wouldn't come back. So Wendy decided to run back and get a chaperone. Before she could get even halfway, she heard Greta screaming, and Wendy knew she was in trouble. She ran back and jumped into the water to find her, but she couldn't. She said it was like Greta had never been there. And by the time the authorities got to the beach to help search, Greta was gone for good."

The story was awful enough. I could only imagine how much worse reality had been. "Did they find her body?"

"Farther up the beach, but not for another hour."

I felt so sorry for everyone involved, Greta most of all, of course. Wendy, who hadn't been able to stop or save her best friend. The parents of both girls. The chaperones. Every other student at the bonfire.

"The other night you said that Wendy was distraught afterward. I can see why."

"She was in a daze for months. She didn't want to finish the final week of school. She didn't want to go to parties or activities. So we rented a house for the summer in the North Carolina mountains. I found a counselor to work with her, for all the good it did."

"I'm sure staying in town would have been worse."

"Some people blamed her. Some of their friends said Greta's death was Wendy's fault, that she should never have sneaked off with her. But others said it was Greta who wanted to sneak away. Pretty soon everyone who knew the two girls had taken sides. It was terrible for your sister."

"And the next year?"

"She started high school, and some kids in her classes were from other middle schools. She found her feet socially again, but she never had another close friend, at least not one like Greta. She'd have a couple of girls over to spend the night once in a while, but the next time the girls would be different."

"Equal opportunity friendship."

My mother sat back. "She was never the same. I'd catch her staring into space at the oddest times. I had to nag her to finish schoolwork, but eventually that improved, even though she never concentrated as well. I think that's where the messy habits began. She just forgot to clean up after herself, like her mind was elsewhere."

One thing stood out for me. "I'm amazed nobody ever told me this."

"It's a hard story to repeat, Ryan. Wendy just wanted to move on, so that's what we did. The Harolds moved away almost immediately. Wendy and Greta's old friends found new interests and new friends in high school. At first there was talk of a service project to honor Greta, but nothing much came of it. I think some club raised money for swimming lessons for kids who couldn't afford them. But that only lasted a year or two. Your father established a college fund for Greta's younger brother, but I don't think her parents ever touched a cent."

"They blamed Wendy?"

"I think it was more that they wanted to move on. To this day, though, I think Wendy blames herself. If they had stayed with their other friends and hadn't taken that walk down the beach. If she had convinced Greta not to go in the water. Or if she'd gone into the water, too, maybe Greta would have been okay, or she could have saved her."

All this had happened before I was born. Did any of it reflect on Wendy's situation now? Had she learned to care less about other people because she'd seen how painful caring could be?

How much emotional damage lurked behind Wendy's lovely smile? Was she using tranquilizers and sleeping pills to keep it at bay? Or worse, was she using tranquilizers and sleeping pills for respite from her children, who demanded so much of her? I couldn't believe any of it.

"Please don't ever tell her you know," my mother said. "It's not something we talk about. In fact, let's talk about something else now."

Not talking about things that mattered was another part

of my family heritage. This time, though, I had to introduce another unpleasant subject. "I ran into Ella yesterday at the grocery store."

"Oh."

When nothing else was forthcoming, I capsulized the encounter. "I wish I'd known that she's no longer working for Gracey Group. I made a fool of myself. What on earth happened?"

"I'd planned to tell you the next time you came home."

Of course she'd never expected a homecoming under these circumstances. "So why was she fired?"

"She *wasn't*. Fired, I mean. Your father arranged for her to take an early retirement. She left with her pension, and all her health benefits until she turns sixty-five."

"Well, somebody thinks she's got plenty of work left in her. She's a part-time receptionist for a dentist."

"Yes, Dr. Borgman. He's an orthodontist. Part-time is probably a good idea. Ella was forgetting things, making mistakes and then insisting other people were at fault. Your father felt the job had become too complex and stressful for her. I promise you, everyone tried to help her, your sister most of all. She even volunteered to take some of Ella's work if Dad just let her stay. But in the end he hired a young man to replace her, and Carl does his job without complaint and takes orders, something Ella wasn't doing well."

"She wasn't taking orders from Dad?"

"No, the problem was taking orders from your sister. Ella had known Wendy since she was a little girl, and then suddenly, Wendy became the person Dad worked closest with, instead of her. Plus Wendy became her immediate supervisor. The reorganization made sense, steps to help Wendy take over Gracey Group one day. But Ella retaliated. She put off important projects Wendy assigned, then claimed Wendy's requests had come in too late. Finally she missed a big deadline for a project with your father, too. He had no choice but to let her go."

"Wow. I'm sorry. She was like family."

"But she wasn't family."

No, "family" was somewhere hiding from law enforcement. I moved on to a safer subject. "So tell me where you think we should put the Christmas tree."

We spent the next fifteen minutes deciding Christmas details. Neither of us wondered out loud whether Wendy would be home by then or not. We were planning a holiday without her, just in case.

When we finished, Mom insisted she had to leave, and I walked her to the door. "I've been wondering," she said, "do you need to get back to Delray at some point for your job?"

For the first time in days, I'd put aside both Milton Kerns and Wendy Wainwright and spent my morning working on *Out in the Cold*, slogging through a list that would have been easier to complete in Delray Beach.

"If I can find a way, I do need to go back for a day or two to put my head together with some of our crew. We have details to consult on."

"What kind of details?"

"Sophie—you remember Sophie?" I went on after she nodded. "She found a cold case a bit north of Seabank. She sent me the background, and now we're both intrigued. A little boy went missing about ten years ago, and the authorities believed they might have found him. Only before they could do a DNA test, he disappeared again. If we do this one, we'll be following the story in real time, as the search progresses. We'll do the background, talk to all the suspects, his family, his teachers. We've found some interesting side developments we can explore. It's the kind of case we've been looking for."

"I still remember how surprised I was when you became obsessed with crime in college, and later with reporting it."

"I'm more obsessed with justice."

She smiled, as if she were proud of me for noting the difference. "When I think about it, I shouldn't have been surprised. Do you remember that right after your dad and I married I worked on a newspaper?"

"I don't think I would have forgotten something like that."

"You probably thought it was too dull to remember, and the job was short-lived. I covered weddings and school board meetings. If I was really lucky, I got to attend city council sessions, but only if there was nothing worth noting on the agenda. I thought I was putting in my time so I could move up to something more interesting, like crime or politics."

"You could have covered both in one fell swoop."

She smiled a little. "I got pregnant with your sister before I could uncover one good story. Suddenly I had a whole new career path." The smile disappeared. "Maybe I should have kept the job. Maybe then I wouldn't have measured my success by how perfect my daughter was."

"You can't blame yourself for anything Wendy does."

"I don't even know what she's doing."

I realized then that she'd said daughter, not daughters. I also realized it hadn't been a mistake. "By the time I came along you were less interested in perfection? Or after my difficult entrance into the world, did I just seem hopeless?"

"No, by the time you were born I was more interested in you and less in myself."

"I'm not sure what that means."

"I didn't need a project when you were born, Ryan. I just needed a daughter."

We were poised on a precipice, but neither of us were ready

to jump or retreat. I cleared my throat and moved back to her career. "So I come by my journalistic talents honestly."

"You come by your *interest* honestly. I never got far enough to know if I had talent, but more important? I understand how much you're sacrificing for Wendy. I have an idea of the pressure you're under."

I was touched. "I'm dealing okay."

"Would it help if Dad and I take the girls this weekend so you can go back to Delray? He's a little depressed. Holly and Noelle would cheer him up. We'll watch *The Polar Express*, and I'll have somebody set up our tree so the girls can decorate it. Then they can bring the leftover ornaments here to decorate yours when you come back. It'll be good for all of us."

My nieces were getting used to me, and we were establishing routines. But Mom's offer opened another door, one I could explore on Friday night. If I dropped Holly and Noelle at my parents' house after school, I could do a little detective work in the evening before I drove to Delray. Then I could head back to Seabank on Sunday afternoon and still be the one getting them ready for school on Monday morning.

When I didn't answer immediately, my mother resorted to her voice of steel. "I think it's a good idea."

"It is. Thank you. That will be great. But just so you know? Your talents of persuasion have been passed on to your granddaughters." I slung my arm over her shoulders and guided her out the door. "Before you leave, let's swing by the garage so I can show you what the girls made me buy. Did you know that Santa's a sucker for a tropical vacation?"

CHAPTER TWENTY

On Thursday morning I promised myself I would work on *Out in the Cold* after my jog with Teo. I had to make sure all my appointments were in place for the weekend, and that I had all the necessary information to meet with the most vital crew members. This plan left me enough time to do a few side trips before I met him at Confidence K-9s.

Today my nieces were ready right on time. This close to Christmas, school was more fun with plays, recitals, and arts and crafts projects. Sadly, our Christmas preparations had hit a snag. When I backed out of the garage with Bismarck beside me, Santa and respective tropical scenery were a puddle of vinyl on our front lawn. To circumvent tantrums, I promised both girls I would pump them up as soon as I got home.

I had carefully mapped my route to Confidence K-9s, and after I dropped them off, with the dog as my copilot, I navigated to a section of town in the western suburbs. Most houses here were window-dotted rectangles with tile roofs and carports. Some yards were patches of sand and weeds, while others were well-tended St. Augustine or Centipede grass, sporting poinsettias interspersed with garden gnomes and Christmas elves. The neighborhood was solidly working class, and not that different from my own in Delray Beach.

At a stop sign, I checked the street names again as a woman inched through the intersection using a walker that sported tennis balls on the rear legs. If I was lucky, a man named Craig Leone lived two blocks away. I'd traced him here using the phone number that had shown up on Wendy's deleted voice mail.

I'm always surprised what I can find out about someone after a few minutes on the internet. Forty-five-year-old Craig was either divorced or separated, because he and a woman with the same last name lived at separate addresses now, while last year they had lived together. He was also a father, and definitely a man who'd strayed from the straight and narrow at least one time too many. Without half trying I'd been treated to the specifics of a brief stint in our county jail.

I wasn't sure what I'd find today, but I knew what I was looking for. I was hoping to find the maniac who had jumped me at Wendy's town house. I had no intentions of confronting him. If Craig was my culprit, I would turn over his address to the police or get advice about what to do from Teo. If I found a complete stranger, then I'd figure out how I could talk to him about my sister. Of course, I wouldn't talk here at his house. I would do it in public, at Against the Wind. I thought the chances were probably excellent that I'd find him sitting at the bar tomorrow night. In his message Craig had sounded like a regular.

Once the woman with the walker was safely across, I made my way to the right block, where the house I sought was second from the corner. I pulled over to the shoulder one house away.

Craig Leone's yard was shabbier than his neighbors'. My high school botany teacher had relished field study, and I could still identify crabgrass and nutsedge—with a few sandspurs thrown in—sprouting in tufts.

The concrete-block house needed a fresh coat of shell-pink paint. Plastic flamingoes and a birdbath had been optimistically placed under a front window, so at some point, somebody at this address had cared. But as I watched the man working on a motorcycle at the top of the gravel driveway, I doubted the happy homemaker had been Craig himself. The muscular tattooed guy with the shaved head and beer belly, the very same guy who appeared to be tearing the motorcycle to bits with his bare hands, wasn't a flamingo kind of guy, although he might chew the head off a live one on a dare.

Motorcycle man might not be the only resident at this address, but I had seen Craig's mug shot online. This was Craig Leone, and now, in person, I could see he wasn't my feisty intruder. He was larger and broader in every way.

My next job was to discover how he knew my sister.

With stop one completed, I moved on to stop two. The quickest way to get to Against the Wind would have taken me right through the intersection where John Quayle made his last stand. I went the long way, parking on the street in front of the bar, a building that had obviously entered the world as a mechanic's garage. To the left was a pawnshop, complete with metal bars crisscrossing every shiny surface. To the right, a used-car lot looked like a final resting place for junkers. Against the Wind was perfectly situated to draw customers from the neighborhood.

The bar was fronted by a parking lot with spaces just wide enough for motorcycles. Where signs advertising motor oil and radial tires had once hung, new signs for Milwaukee's finest framed glass-paneled doors that had probably opened to separate bays. Since there were no Hells Angels or the local equivalent milling in front, I got out and crossed the parking lot to peek inside. The bays had been converted into one long room, with a bar against one side and half a dozen tables on the other. The space in the middle housed two pool tables. Most interesting of all, the bar rested on three motorcycles, evenly distributed to hold the weight, or at least to look as if they did.

The message I'd intercepted on Wendy's voice mail might have come from a wrong number. But if my sister was hanging around Against the Wind at night, an entirely new and troubling set of questions had to be asked. Tomorrow, I would arrive sometime after eight and wait to see if Craig Leone showed up. If he did, I would find a way to ask about "Kim."

For now I'd seen enough. The neighborhood might be seedy, but the street was well-lighted and traveled. Saturday I would have to rise early to get to Delray Beach in time to make my meetings, but visiting Against the Wind would be worth the inconvenience.

My third stop, an independent pharmacy, was along my route to Confidence K-9s. I'd never filled a prescription here and probably never would, but I hoped the pharmacist in the tiny strip mall had time to talk to me.

The roped-off parking lot, shared with an abandoned taqueria, was in the midst of being repaved, although at the moment, no one was working on it. The temperature was only sixty, so I parked on the street under heavy shade and left the windows down for Bismarck. He was more than capable of scaring off bad guys who reached in to unlock a door.

Purse tucked under my arm, I carefully made my way inside. The store was crowded with medical supplies and equipment, but not with customers. Unlike chain pharmacies, there were no aisles of gift items or snack foods, and I didn't see a single greeting card. Homeopathic remedies, though? The store had a remedy for everything from acne to whooping cough.

At the back only one pharmacist was working behind the

counter, busy mixing, shaking and labeling. When he finally looked up, he moved to my section and peered at me over frameless glasses. A man nearing the age of retirement, mostly bald, neck spilling over his collar, he thoroughly looked me over before he smiled.

We chatted a moment. I told him the day was still pleasantly cool, and that I'd easily found parking on the street. Then I pulled a plastic bag out of my purse and handed it to him.

My lie seemed harmless. "A friend is renting out her apartment over the winter, and after she left town she realized she hadn't cleaned out her medicine cabinet. The renters come next week. I have her spare key, and she asked me to mail any prescription drugs to her."

He held up the bag. "This is what you found?"

I nodded. "Thing is? I don't think she has a problem with illegal drugs. Nothing like that. But there seem to be an awful lot of..." I held up my palms. "Narcotics? Sleeping pills? I looked some of them up, and now I'm worried."

He opened the bag and moved pill bottles around, setting them on the counter after he examined each one, until he had a neat little row. "Quite a collection. And you're right about what they are."

"Some of them are pretty outdated. So maybe she's not taking them often."

"I hope you're right." He swiped the bottles back into my bag. "If she left without this stash, hopefully they aren't that important to her. People fill prescriptions and don't finish them. Eventually they get more. They pile up. That could be what's going on here. But she shouldn't be mixing these. Does she seem foggy or unusually tired?"

"I honestly don't know." My mother hadn't said anything to lead me in either direction. On the other hand, Mom looked at Wendy through rose-colored glasses.

"Maybe she has problems sleeping," he said.

"Could be."

"If she is mixing prescriptions, adding this to that because the sleep medications aren't working, then she could be in trouble."

"I'm going to mention that. She won't like it, but she needs to know."

"People die mixing drugs, or drugs and alcohol. With some of these prescriptions, even over-the-counter drugs could be fatal in high enough doses."

I made a face to show him how horrified I was. "Like what?"

He ticked off a couple I knew and then added, "Diphen-hydramine."

An economy-size bottle of diphenhydramine resided in Wendy's medicine cabinet. "What's that?"

"Most commonly? Benadryl. It makes some people sleepy, although not everyone, and in the right dose it's safe enough by itself. Mixed with other medications, though, it can make patients feel dizzy and disoriented."

I nodded to encourage him, because he was doing my work for me. "She did have a large bottle in the cabinet."

"Want a sad story? Not long ago a baby died when his caretaker gave him an adult dose to knock him out. It was all over the news. So even for an adult, mixed with some of these drugs?" He brushed his hand over the bag and shook his head. "I hope your friend's doctor warned her."

The store was warm enough, but I was chilled to my bone marrow. "Adult doses must be very different than doses for children."

"Different doses and different drugs. Drugs for adults aren't always tested for children." He handed back the bag. "Are you really going to send these to her?"

"No, I'm going to flush them all down the nearest toilet. I'm not taking chances they could be intercepted. She'll just have to go to a local doctor and get a new prescription if she needs something."

I thanked him and left. How much Benadryl had my sister been giving her children for their allergies, which so far, from my own observations, seemed to be nonexistent? Had Wendy been drugging her girls with anything else?

I wondered if I was being paranoid. Maybe Wendy hadn't connected the problems the girls were having on school mornings with a drug given at night. Maybe she'd been busy adjusting dosages, trying, like any good mom, to find the perfect solution to whatever problem she'd been addressing.

Or maybe not.

I put the possibilities out of my mind for the moment. Wendy wasn't here to tell me, and right now her absence was the larger problem.

My head hurt.

I made the rest of the drive and parked in front of the kennel office, stripping off the jacket that covered my tank top. As we jogged, Teo and I would warm quickly.

Somebody buzzed Bismarck and me inside, and dogs in the nearest kennels barked and howled in greeting. Janice, who was coming down the hallway, smiled stiffly and told me where to find Teo, then stopped to talk to Bismarck, who appeared to think she was pretty swell. She rose a notch in my estimation. Bismarck is a great judge of character.

Teo was out on one of the lawns tossing Frisbees to two beautiful silvery dogs with bobbed tails. When he saw me, he let himself out and fastened the gate behind him. Bismarck got most of his attention, but he did smile at me first.

"Gorgeous dogs," I said, trying to focus on the dogs instead of the man.

"Australian shepherds. Blue merles. Their owner thinks they need more training, but what they really need is exercise."

When he finished roughhousing a little with his best canine friend, he stood and gave my outfit the once-over. I was wearing one of Wendy's gifts, lavender-and-black-patterned running shorts and a lavender tank with mesh inserts. Very little of me was left to the imagination, although Teo might harbor enough memories to make up the gap.

"Nice duds."

"It's going to warm up. Still want to go?"

"Sure. I figure you need to run the other way on the road and see what's at the very end."

"Your local taxidermist?"

"My house."

"I assumed you lived here."

"No, Janice's family lives in the ranch house at the edge of the property. They keep an eye on things when I'm not on-site."

"So, you're ready?"

He smiled as if reading my mind. "Do I need to change my clothes? My *leg*?"

I winced. "I was not going to ask."

"If I ever decide to try out for the Olympics or just want to ramp up my workout, I might need something more efficient, but this leg's high-tech and all-purpose. It's fine for jogging."

"How long did it take to become *fine*?"

"A year and a half of physical therapy. A lot of appointments with a prosthetist, which are ongoing, a lot of adjustments, a lot of exercise. A whole lot of falls. I ended up on my nose or ass more times than I can count." He paused. "A lot of money."

"You forgot a lot of prayer and a lot of cursing."

"More of the latter than the former. My mother did most of the praying."

"I said my share of prayers for you, Teo, even though I didn't know everything that was going on."

"You were praying?" He sounded surprised by the act, more than the recipient.

"All those years of Catholic school come in handy."

We walked along the corridor and out the gate to the parking lot. "I did say some prayers after I killed John Quayle," Teo said.

Now I was surprised. "Asking forgiveness?"

"Forgiveness for saving your life? Never. Asking God why He created someone like Quayle in the first place." We were walking faster now, and in a moment we broke into a slow jog with Bismarck running happily beside Teo.

"Did you get any answers?" I asked.

"The usual lack of them, unless you count a greater sense of peace with everything that happened. I don't know why people like Quayle exist, if they're born or made or somewhere in between. But I do believe that trying to stop them from hurting other people is a calling."

"Training dogs for protection and security work seems like a good way to do that. Teaching criminal justice seems like a good way, too."

"So does bringing cold cases to light so they can finally be solved."

I was pleased he thought so, and warmed by such an immediate answer. "They aren't though, not most of the time. Podcasts like ours, television shows, special newspaper series? Too often the cases were cold for good reason. Real evidence remains scanty. Investigators pull the cases back into the sunlight for a while, then shove them into folders and file them away again. Not usually because they don't care. Because they have to concentrate on the ones they might actually be able to close."

"So you don't think you're doing any good?"

I thought about that for a little while before I answered. "Not all police departments are good ones, so the publicity can make them take notice. Whatever we can add to a case might pay off someday. And there's always the chance we'll hit the jackpot."

"A gambling woman."

"Not just that. I also like to think people learn to be careful from listening to true crime reporting, that they pay attention to the way a crime happened, and they're more alert in their everyday lives. They may not be able to spot a psychopath, but they may consider the possibility."

We continued to chat as we ran, moving to more comfortable topics. Eventually we passed Marvin's Masterpieces, and I was disappointed that instead of my long-imagined unicorn, Marvin had a well-preserved longhorn steer on display in front of an oversize barn beside an undersize house.

Teo gave the steer a nod. "Meet Houston. Marvin loved that old steer. When Houston finally went to that big cattle range in the sky, Marvin hauled his carcass into the barn with a tractor and spent weeks preserving him as a memorial."

"A friend of yours? Marvin, not Houston."

"Marvin prefers animals over people, but sometimes I can entice him out of his workshop if I promise to listen to lectures on the relative values of glass eyes versus acrylic."

I was beginning to tire at exactly the point when Teo slowed to a walk and pointed ahead. "My place."

The house was raised off the ground on brick pilings, with a wide shaded porch surrounding the front and the sides. I thought there must be a second story because there was a gable in the sloping tin roof.

"Wow, this is cute. Isn't this what they call a cracker house?"

"The main house was more of a shack than a cracker, but what was left after a century of hard living was redesigned by a local architect who added the second story and porches, adjusted the slope of the roof and lived here himself for a while. It's small, but it has a lot of living space."

"Plenty, I'd say."

"I was lucky to find it and luckier to buy it. Not everyone

wants to live this far from Seabank, and Marvin and Houston scare off the rest."

"What's in the back?"

"A screened porch. I have coffee out there every morning to watch the wildlife. It's all woods behind me. I've bought enough acres to keep a developer from eyeing the rest."

"I can see you here." I paused. "But maybe not. It's isolated. You never really liked to be alone."

"I'm surrounded by people and dogs all day long. These days I like having a retreat."

"I have people around me, day and night, but luckily I live alone in half a duplex. Unfortunately, my wildlife lives in the other half, rides a Harley-Davidson and shows up around midnight, sometimes with lady friends."

"I have something to give you. And I have lemonade to go with it."

I needed something to drink. I pinched my tank top and wiggled it to create ventilation as I followed him inside.

The entryway was fronted by stairs up to the next floor, along with a woodstove that probably heated the entire house. Past the stairs, a great room spread back to the screened porch, with a kitchen and dining area to the right and what was probably a bedroom to the left. The open floor plan made the space feel larger than it was, but it was still cozy, with different areas well defined by casual furniture.

He pointed toward the back. "I'll get the lemonade. Try the screened porch."

The porch was furnished with vintage rattan, the style of sofa and chairs common in the fifties and sixties, disdained in the decades afterward and sought after by collectors now. The cushions were earth tone florals appropriate anywhere from the Adirondacks to the Everglades. Potted hibiscus added more color, and just in front of me, a lemon tree was beginning to fruit. There were still enough blossoms to lightly scent the air.

Teo dropped off two icy glasses of lemonade and returned with a plate of bakery cookies, settling next to me on the sofa, one seat cushion between us.

I helped myself to a cookie. "This really is a small piece of heaven." The woods behind the house were dotted with large oaks hung with Spanish moss. Between porch and woods, a patio fronted a small yard planted with flowering shrubs.

"I never cared where I lived before," he said. "I wasn't home often enough to worry. Now it seems important."

I turned so I could watch him. "I've never taken the time to do much with my place. Appearances are so important to my mother and sister. I think I made a conscious effort to be sure they weren't important to me. Then a couple of months ago I went to an art show and fell in love with an artist's work. There's something about her beach scenes that I love. So I bought one, two little girls in bathing suits playing on a beach at twilight, and I hung it over my sofa. Now I think about what to add next, which is dangerous, because my place is the size of this porch."

"I started noticing how colorless my apartment was when I had to spend so much time there during recovery. Somebody told me about this house. I had money from a worker's compensation settlement. That's how I was able to put a down payment on the kennels, too. I made an offer on the spot."

"Good call."

He set down his glass, hardly touched. "I didn't bring you here to show you how great my new life is. I have something for you."

He started to stand, but I held him back. "Is it? Great, I mean?"

He cocked his head. "Parts of it."

"You seem to like what you do."

He waited. I didn't know what else to say, but I tried. "You've been through a lot." I wondered if I could have come up with anything lamer if I'd tried for a month.

He finally smiled. "When I said I like being here alone, I meant it. Is that what you want to know?"

I shrugged. "This is all very confusing."

"Good. You spend so much time sorting and reporting facts. Just let whatever is happening here move at its own pace."

"I don't want you to get hurt again. Me, either."

"Are you planning to hurt me?"

"I didn't plan to the last time, either."

"Quayle pulled the trigger. I survived *him*. I plan to keep surviving whatever you throw at me."

He got up and this time I let him. We'd said enough. And maybe he was right; maybe it was time to simply let things happen.

I had no idea what he would bring back, but I didn't expect a lone piece of folded paper, edges frayed where it had been ripped from a spiral notepad. I doubted we'd had to jog all this way for a sheet of paper that would have fit in his pocket.

He held it out. "I still have friends in the sheriff's office."

"Yeah, I met one of them."

"I figured I could do this much."

I unfolded the paper and stared at three names and a few scrawled sentences to go with them. Then I looked up. Nearly two weeks had passed since my life-altering phone call with Wendy. While most days I felt like I wasn't making any progress toward helping her, these three names could be a huge breakthrough.

"I have a feeling this isn't the way your friend should be spending his time," I said.

"For the most part arrest records are public."

Records might be public, but even though Sophie had amazing snooping skills, she didn't have access to all the resources that the sheriff's office did.

Each of the three names were some variation of Milton Kerns. Someone named Milten Cairns, a man in his seventies, had been arrested for breaking into a Philadelphia ATM, but never charged. I realized Wendy hadn't said how old the man she'd met in New Mexico was, but this didn't feel right.

The second name was Milton Kernbauer, eighteen, who'd been arrested for drunk and disorderly at a fraternity party in South Carolina.

The third was a man named Alexander Milton Kearns—I noted the *a* in the middle—called Alex or sometimes "Ex" on the street, who had been arrested for assault after a confrontation at a ski resort in Vermont. There were other minor offenses.

I stared at the name of the resort. It was all too familiar. The Autumn Mountain Club belonged to Gracey Group, or at least it had years before. I rarely kept up with my father's business dealings, but I remembered this one because we'd traveled there when I was a teenager. I'd had my first skiing lesson with an instructor who'd been a hunk to boot.

At the time of his arrest, I noted that Kearns had been an employee at the club. There wasn't a lot more information, except his birth date—he was forty-six—and birthplace.

"Costa Rica." I looked at Teo. "This third name just might be the guy. In our first phone call Wendy said he was from Costa Rica." I didn't mention Kearns's connection to Gracey Group, and I wasn't sure why. Maybe I just needed to process the possibilities and do that alone.

"So there you go."

"I really appreciate this. I can do some targeted sleuthing now."

"If this is the right guy, he may be a murderer. You're not going after him alone, are you? If you find him?"

I could see from his expression that this might be the question that moved our relationship along or destroyed it before it even began.

"I don't plan to risk my life or anybody else's. I don't plan to underestimate Kearns or overestimate my ability to stay safe the way I did before." Then I addressed the most important part of his question, even though it hadn't been voiced. "I'll let you know whatever I plan to do. I promise."

He gave a short nod. "I'll be here if you need me."

As we prepared to jog back to Confidence, I had a thousand things to think about. But one was paramount.

Alexander Milton Kearns had worked at what was, or had once been, a Gracey Group resort. Had we owned the club when he was arrested? And if we still owned it when Wendy began her job as the Gracey Group concierge, had my sister come in contact with Kearns during visits to the resort?

Was Kearns really a stranger, as she had claimed, or had Wendy known him for years? If so, what were they doing together at the Golden Aspen Resort and Spa on the night that Vítor Calvo was killed?

I knew they hadn't bumped into each other while waiting for massages or mounting their horses for a trail ride. But I sure hoped something similarly coincidental was true. Because if not, maybe Wendy had gone to the resort to meet Kearns in the first place. And if so, what had happened?

Sophie or I would be able to dig up a photo of the guy on the internet, quite possibly his mug shot. We had a name and, soon, a face. I hoped she could use what I'd found and give me some answers. But I was afraid we'd just have far more questions now.

CHAPTER TWENTY-ONE

Convincing Holly and Noelle that a weekend at my parents' house would be fun was surprisingly easy. Wednesday evening Mom had called and asked their opinions on what kinds of Christmas cookies they should make together. When she promised they might have to climb a ladder to help decorate the top of her tree, she had them in the palm of her hand. The smaller tree and simpler decorations we bought and set up on Thursday felt like a warm-up. With all the fun at my parents' house, I might never be able to wrestle them back to Wendy's town house again.

I debated whether to bring Bismarck to Delray Beach with me, but on Friday after school, I dropped him off with the girls. Since the shopping trip, Bismarck sported a red bow on his collar complete with jingle bells. Luckily, he's a good sport. Despite the humiliation, he still carried his head high.

"This will do your father good," Mom said, as I lingered on her doorstep before heading to my car. The girls were somewhere in the house giggling loudly, and I could hear Dad's booming baritone followed by a recording of "Jingle Bells." "He's worried about your sister."

My father has good sense. He also has a heart that's healing from major surgery. The two don't mix well. "Maybe she'll call him soon," I said.

"We have every kind of resource to help her. Whatever is going on. Please be sure to remind her."

Wendy had been missing in action for almost two weeks, but it probably seemed longer to my parents. There wasn't a darned thing I could do about that except continue trying to find her.

On the way back to the town house, I thought about the other parties who should be crumbling under the weight of Wendy's disappearance. But while Noelle often asked about her mother, Holly never did. And when I explained that Wendy would be home as soon as possible, Holly's expression seesawed between skeptical and furious.

Holly did ask about her father, though, so when I got home and checked voice mail, I was sorry the girls had missed a call from their dad. I wasn't sorry when I listened to it.

Bryce's message hadn't been meant for them. His voice was scratchy and distorted, and while I knew he wasn't calling from under the water, he might as well have been. I had to listen twice. But I finally pieced words together. First he complained that my sister wasn't answering her cell phone. Then he continued.

"Wendy, why haven't you signed the papers the way we agreed? This has to be settled."

After that there was so much distortion that I wasn't positive, but I thought he said that she wouldn't be able to reach him. In the meantime she was to move forward and soon.

I was sorry I hadn't been here. Except what would I have said? Sorry, Bryce, but Wendy's off God knows where, and I'm taking care of your daughters, who I hardly know. In the meantime I'm lying to everybody to cover your wife's you-know-what?

Had Bryce been purposely obscure because he didn't want the girls to know what he was talking about, in case they heard? Were he and Wendy selling their house in Connecticut? Were they drawing up a will, and afraid that talk of death might frighten their children?

Like any journalist I'm the queen of possibilities. So the worst one popped right up. Did Bryce want a divorce? Was it possible that Wendy had moved herself and the girls to Florida to make the legalities more difficult?

One thing was clear. Bryce didn't know his wife was hiding from the law. For the first time I wondered if Wendy was arrested for murder, what might happen to Bryce's security clearance and job? Was that part of her decision to hide out until the coast was clear? Was Wendy trying to protect her husband? If so, her disappearance might be admirable, but I'd heard Bryce's voice. Bubbling through the long-distance distortion, I'd heard anger. If Bryce was already upset with Wendy, what, if anything, had she done? If he was divorcing her, why? Was everything that had happened in New Mexico just part of a longer chain of events?

Normal people considered one, possibly two scenarios when confronted by a problem. People like me? We fell asleep at night adding possibilities to lists as long as Rip van Winkle's beard. I filed this particular list away for later. Tonight I just needed to find any connection between Craig, Kim, my sister and Against the Wind.

Just.

Never having visited a biker bar, I debated what to wear. I didn't want to look like a biker chick or a wannabe, either of which might create a whole new set of problems. I was planning to present myself as a friend of Kim's. The Craig I'd seen ripping apart a motorcycle struck me as a guy who wasn't looking for the All-American girl. So even mere acquaintances of Kim's were probably a little glittery, a little sexy. I called my fashion consultant, who picked up right away.

"I found a photo of this Kearns character," she said instead of hello. "A mug shot, so it's not the best quality. I sent you the link. Close-cropped reddish-blond hair. Freckled complexion. His ears stick out, but he's good-looking."

I thanked her and promised I'd check him out. "I'm going to do some research at the biker bar tonight. Tell me what to wear."

She asked for the possibilities, so I went to the closet and listed what was hanging there. She made a noise not unlike a teenager's dad when his daughter presents her first boyfriend for his approval.

I tried to cheer her up. "We can do this."

"Doesn't your sister have anything you can wear?"

"She's a head taller. Plus she's an officer's wife and a lady." The words weren't out of my mouth before I remembered Wendy's stash of sexy undies.

I hadn't paid much attention to the clothes in my sister's closet, except for the pockets, but now I pulled my own additions closer to the door and started sorting through Wendy's.

"Wow," I said in the middle of whatever Sophie was telling me about colors that would suit me.

"I gather you're not complimenting my fashion brilliance," she said.

I held up a camisole that was heavy with silver sequins. On the same padded hanger hung lipstick-red satin pants so narrow that if Wendy had worn them, some willing assistant had poured her into them.

"I didn't really notice before. There's a whole new Wendy hanging in this closet." I described my finds.

"Put down the phone and see what else you come up with."

By the time I returned, Sophie was humming Ravel's "Bolero." She was just getting to the part where I always have to turn down the volume. I wasn't sorry to interrupt. "She's got a little treasure trove of sexy clothes in here. Everything interesting is hidden under suit jackets and smashed between mommy dresses."

Ever practical, Sophie moved on. "Can you wear any of it?"

"Way too long and way, way too glitzy. But I bet my big sis makes a real splash when she's out on the town."

"And the question is where she goes and with whom."

"I've got to get moving."

"Black's never a bad idea," she said in parting.

I settled on black pants and camisole, and a red shawl of Wendy's that made me look like a flamenco dancer. But I rolled the shawl and flung the ends over one shoulder and that helped. Even though my knowledge of biker bar dress codes was sadly lacking, I would neither stand out nor blend in. And Kim, whoever she was, would be proud to say she knew me. I troweled on twice as much makeup as usual, slipped a couple of photos in my handbag, and I was ready.

On the drive over I gave myself one more chance to tell Teo what I was up to. He wanted to help, and I wanted him to. But Craig wouldn't talk to me with Teo in tow. A man and a woman approaching a stranger in a bar would look like a setup. I would tell Teo whatever I discovered the next time we were together. Meantime I would park on a busy street and be surrounded by people inside the bar. Finally I would drive some crazy route on the way home to be sure nobody followed me. I would be safe.

Against the Wind was hopping. Still two blocks away, I could hear the strains of Steppenwolf's "Born to be Wild" along with hoots and hollers. I wondered how many times the song played every hour. I bet I'd hear it again before my snooping ended.

When a car pulled out right across the street from the bar, I did a quick U-turn and pulled in before somebody else nailed the space. Double good luck? My car was directly under a streetlight. The sleuthing gods were with me.

Tonight, motorcycles were lined up neatly along the parking strip at the front of the bar. Careful parking probably prevented a lot of fights. Two old guys with gray beards and ponytails were working on a monster chopper at the end. Two younger guys with a blonde in a not-so-artfully torn tank top were lounging against the side of the building. Her bleached hair was scrub-brush short, and her earrings were shoulder-length chains. My earlobes ached in protest.

Inside I made my way to the bar under a shower of colored light. I wasn't sure Christmas had provoked this seasonal display, or whether the owner thought his world needed color year-round. But lights were strung from every rafter, and a life-size Santa sat at the end of the bar, *on* the bar, with a beer mug in his robotic hand. Every so often he lifted the mug to his lips and chortled. I was surprised no one had ripped Santa open and torn out his mechanical heart.

I grabbed the only empty seat, swinging myself up to a metal stool. My legs could no longer reach the floor. Neighbors on both sides seemed harmless enough. On my right, a guy with a crew cut and an eye patch was reading email on his cell phone. On my left a woman with hair confined in a million long braids was conversing with a man in a tweed jacket who looked like an Oxford don.

By the time the middle-aged bartender finally got to me, "Born to be Wild" was playing again. "Haven't seen you here before." He swiped the space in front of me with a rag that had seen a lifetime of duty. I'm not a psychologist, but one look told me this guy probably thought drinking hemlock was just one short step below working here.

I ordered a beer on tap. I wasn't planning to drink it anyway. "First time here," I said. "I'm looking for somebody. Kim."

I had a photo of Wendy ready, and I laid it on the not-quite-clean counter. "Do you happen to know her?"

"Why?"

That wasn't quite as good as "no way," but I was encouraged. "I told her I'd meet her here."

"Pretty crowded." And with that, he took off.

A minute later my beer was in front of me, but before I could ask him anything else, he'd scooped up my five-dollar bill and left again.

The woman beside me turned. She had smooth skin the color of chestnuts. "Isn't he a sweetie?"

"I bet he's on his way to pick a fight with somebody, so he can put an end to all this."

She laughed. "Picking a fight's easy here. So you're looking for somebody?"

I slid Wendy's photo toward her. "Are you here often? I told Kim I'd meet her tonight, but I'm either early or late."

"You never been here before?"

"Kim's thing, not mine."

She lifted the photo and held it closer. I made a guess she was nearsighted and no fan of glasses. She handed it back. "She looks kind of familiar."

I told my heart to stop skipping. "I don't know how often she comes."

"It's not the best place to look for guys. I've already got one, so I'm safe." She nodded behind her. "Shooting pool. He makes enough in an hour here to take me somewhere nicer on Saturday."

"American enterprise. Gotta love it."

We chatted awhile and eventually she showed "Kim's" photo to the tweedy guy, who seemed to know everybody.

As it turned out he owned a national chain of cycle shops, and nobody here was going to mess with him.

My new friend translated whatever tweedy guy mumbled after looking at the photo. "He said he's seen her here, but not tonight."

I didn't know what to feel. After all, I was here to find answers. But I had hoped that nobody would recognize my sister.

Immersed in thought I hadn't realized my seatmate had finished, but now I saw she was waiting for a response to something she'd said. "I missed that last part." I moved a little closer, as if the noise around us was the problem.

"He said that guy who just came in might be able to help." She swiveled and pointed to her right.

The news was getting worse, along with the crowd. Craig Leone himself was pushing his way through to take a newly vacant seat not far away.

Craig Leone might be able to help. Leone himself, who seemed to think the woman in my photo was named Kim.

I thanked her, wished her well and before I lost my courage, I grabbed my beer and gave up my seat. I wandered over to the pool tables first, to give Leone time to settle in. I assessed the players and hoped the guy in a black leather jacket and faded jeans was the boyfriend. Because as I watched, he cleared the table.

The music changed to something by the Rolling Stones that everybody but me seemed to know. A guy with bad teeth and hair edged by and pinched my butt before I could move away. "Start me up!" He winked, but he was so drunk his eyelid only made it to half-mast.

I shoved him away. "Pinch me again, and I'll start you on your way to Seabank General." I punctuated with a word I rarely say. The guy beside him jerked him toward the other side of the room. I had a feeling he had to do that often.

I reached Craig without further incident. The seats around him were taken, but there was a space just large enough for me to squeeze into. "Hi, you Craig?"

He turned and looked me up and down. Up close he was even more intimidating than he'd been in his yard. "Yeah."

"Somebody over there told me you might know where Kim is tonight."

He didn't answer, so I pulled out the photo I'd shown the others and held it out. "This Kim."

His gaze dropped momentarily. "Who are you?"

"A friend." I pulled out the second photo as evidence. Wendy and I were arm in arm, the sun shining brightly all around us. My father had snapped it the last time we were all together. I held it up for him to see. "I'm supposed to meet her here, but I don't see her. I hate to wait if she's not coming. Know anything?"

So much time passed before he spoke that I nearly walked away. But finally a darker expression crept over his face. "I haven't seen her. But if you happen to? Tell her no more games. She can go—"

I didn't blink at the stream of profanity that revolved around an anatomically impossible act. I waited until he finished. "Apparently if you two were together, you aren't anymore?"

"You want to talk to somebody who might know, lady? Somebody who cares?" He pointed to the far end of the bar, just shy of where Santa was chuckling in his beer. "Go talk to him." He got up and pushed past me. I grabbed his seat and set down my glass. Then, as if I was just examining my new surroundings, I finally looked in the direction where Leone had pointed.

The guy next to Santa was lean but broad-shouldered, his skin darkly tanned from the sun. From his profile I noted that his nose was long, and his cheeks sported neatly trimmed stubble. Maybe

I hadn't gotten a great look at the man who'd attacked me on the town house front porch, but now I stopped breathing.

This man was wearing a leather vest over a shirt with an insignia of some kind, and he had enticed the bartender into conversation. As he leaned forward, I slid off the stool and made my way through the crowd to the door. Outside I took a deep breath and started down the street. I didn't want to go right to my car, in case he'd followed me, but I stayed as close to the road and passing traffic as I could. At the first traffic light, I crossed and looked behind me. So far so good.

I started back, staying low behind the other cars parked along the road. I may not have been entirely out of sight, but neither would I attract anybody's attention. Nearly there, I stopped behind a navy blue pickup. I watched the front door of Against the Wind for the man I'd spotted, but he didn't emerge.

I tried to talk sense to myself. The guy had been some distance away, with colored lights above us. I could be imagining the resemblance. As I made even more room for reasonable doubt, my gaze dropped to the truck in front of me.

The words painted on the passenger door were familiar. I'd seen them before, on the day I'd been attacked. I'd seen them on this truck, parked a few units down from Wendy's town house. I wasn't imagining that the guy in the bar was all-too-familiar.

"Carrillon Roofing." I breathed it more than said it. I took out my phone and snapped a photo, which included Carrillon's phone number.

Then, with even more care, I scuttled to my own car, and when I was sure no one was paying attention, I pulled out, and began a circuitous route back to the town house.

In the end, though, all my twists and turns and backtracking made no sense whatsoever. If the guy at the end of the bar was indeed my attacker, he already knew where I lived.

CHAPTER TWENTY-TWO

Friday night, despite the security alarm, I slept fitfully. Every noise, a car on the road, a wood stork perching noisily on the master bedroom sundeck, woke me until I finally went downstairs and slept on the sofa. I left my gun in the glove compartment, but sleeping with it had been a temptation.

The moment I'd gotten home, I'd picked up the phone to call the sheriff's office and tell them I'd seen my attacker, but that was as far as I'd gotten. Wendy and Kim were the same person. As Kim, my sister hung out at a biker bar, and the guy who had tried to break into the town house was a regular who knew her. After all, I'd learned the God's own truth from that most reliable of witnesses, Craig Leone. It seemed clear that the attempted break-in was somehow related to my sister, and for now, the less attention any law enforcement paid to Wendy, the better.

I also considered calling Teo, but once again, I had to protect my sister, at least until I found out what was really going on. And truthfully, I wasn't excited about recounting my visit to Against the Wind. At dawn, I got up and packed the few things I would need for my trip to Delray Beach, locking the town house and turning on the alarm behind me.

When I pulled out of the garage, I discovered the town house finally had neighbors. An older man in a tracksuit and Cubs' cap was searching the bushes between us, most likely for his newspaper.

I got out to close the garage and introduce myself, and paid close attention to his expression when I told him I was Wendy's sister. He said she had moved in after he'd left for Chicago in May, and I was relieved. Maybe he could have told me things he'd seen as Wendy's neighbor, but I was glad we were starting fresh. He wasn't as foolproof or cuddly as Bismarck, but another set of eyes in the neighborhood was a good thing.

I listened to a variety of true crime podcasts on the lengthy trip to Delray Beach, checking out the competition. By the time I arrived, I'd formed a long list of things we should never do at *Out in the Cold* and a short list of things we might want to try. Of course now that we'd triumphed once, the pressure was on.

I convened two different meetings with crew members, and Sophie and I took comments on the case we had zeroed in on. The feedback was positive and we were that much closer to moving forward if Sebastian was in agreement. I had time scheduled with the big boss on Sunday, and I expected to be able to convince him.

Sophie and I went out for lunch before afternoon meetings, and on the walk to one of my favorite local dives, she caught me up on Ike and the family barbecue. "His daughter is a sweetheart. My girls will love her."

"And Ike?"

"Also a sweetheart." Her smile almost stretched to the rhinestone earrings twinkling in her earlobes.

We settled on stools at the counter and made our order. I

realized how much Teo would like this place. It wasn't the first time since arriving here that I'd thought about him.

While we wolfed down fish tacos, I told her about last night. Sophie waited until I'd finished my account before she commented. "Do you have thoughts about what your sister was doing there?"

The question was so low-key, so neutral, that I was stumped for what to say. A part of me had been prepared to go on the defensive.

"I'm out of ideas. I'd like your help."

"She's using an alias. We could start there." She turned up a palm in question.

"Okay."

"So she doesn't want the clientele of a biker bar to know her real name. That makes sense to me. You?"

"I had a fake name all prepared last night if I needed one."

"How well-known is she in Seabank?"

I had no idea. Wendy had graduated from high school decades before. Nobody ages so well they are instantly recognizable.

I felt my way to an answer. "She works for Gracey Group, but I'm doubtful the people she works with would party down at Against the Wind. Certainly my parents' country club friends wouldn't."

"Still, it's taking something of a chance. Just to be there, I mean."

"What else?"

"Why would she pretend she's somebody she's not?" When I didn't answer, Sophie went on. "And we aren't just talking about the fake name. You found clothes you hadn't expected, and they hint at a different identity she might use at the bar. Because it adds spice to a dull routine? Because it's a chance to try on another kind of life? Because even getting caught could be interesting?"

"How so?"

"Adrenaline high. A chance to make up a great story."

She was using "story" instead of "lie" to be tactful. "What else are you thinking?"

"I'm wondering how she managed to go out at night with two little girls at home."

"My parents?"

"I'm assuming she wouldn't tell your parents where she was really going. Would she use old friends as an excuse?"

My mother had said Wendy wasn't socializing with old friends, so I knew that wasn't it. "She might have asked Mom to give her a break so she could go out to dinner or a movie. And she's perfectly capable of finding babysitters."

"Have the girls mentioned a sitter?"

I had asked Sophie for help, but now I realized I didn't want it. I knew where she was leading, and I wasn't ready. I shook my head. "Can you think of any *good* reason she might show up at a biker bar?"

"An innocent pressure release? She has the girls, a tiring job, an absent husband."

I had forgotten to tell her about Bryce's phone call. I did. Quickly. She nodded. "Okay, something's going on there."

And how could I refute that? Instead I looked at my watch. "I'm going to I Spy to see Glenn before the next round of meetings, and I'd better leave in a minute. You'd be welcome to come. I'm going to ask him about tracing Wendy's calls."

"I'll let you do that alone, but you'll tell me what he says?"

I promised I would, refused an invitation to dinner with her daughters the next night because I planned to drive back right after my meeting with Sebastian, and told her I'd see her in an hour.

She held me at arm's length. "When you really want to talk about this, let me know."

I sighed. "She's my sister."

I drove to Boynton Beach and parked in front of Glenn's store. I Spy wasn't quite a hole-in-the-wall, but neither was it easy to find from the street. The windows were darkly tinted, the signage was subtle. He didn't like walk-ins. Most of his customers found him on the internet and had good reasons to shop there.

Glenn was a licensed private investigator, and he had an office in the back of the store. One time I'd arrived while he was explaining how a young woman could discover what her husband was *really* doing every time he claimed to be checking on his mother. She was suspicious because her mother-in-law had accused her of keeping him from visiting. I didn't have a lot of hope for that marriage.

Today Glenn was alone with his technical devices, shelves and shelves of them against dark gray walls. He sold cameras and video surveillance equipment hidden in everything from AC adapters to teddy bears. I was particularly fond of the models with night vision, and was still trying to come up with a good reason to buy the bird feeder. Maybe if I found Wendy and all turned out well, I'd tell her to buy it for me at Christmas.

Other shelves sported GPS trackers of every shape and kind, monitors for cell phones and landlines, and another personal favorite, bug and camera detectors to help root out all the previously listed gadgets.

My favorite spymaster greeted me with the sexiest male voice in the Americas. "Good to see you," he rumbled. Thirty-something Glenn was short and squat with a Winston Churchill nose, but in the dark, would any woman care?

He gave me a careful hug. I was never quite sure if he was

hugging me or patting me down, but I understood. Glenn made paranoia pay.

"I hear you're staying on the other coast," he said when he stepped away.

I suspected he knew everything about me. "I'm taking care of my sister's children. And I have a bit of a problem."

The other sexy thing about Glenn is that he listens without interrupting. Of course who knows what he does with the information? I gave him the most abbreviated version of what had happened with Wendy, but didn't add my growing suspicions.

"She doesn't want me to get involved. But I want to help. Is there any way, any…device I can use to trace her calls?"

He didn't have to think. "Nothing. It's a burner phone. She's blocking the number. You don't even know what state she's in. Even if the cops were involved, they'd have problems finding her."

I had expected this, and he saw my disappointment. "Ask leading questions when you talk to her. Ask if she needs you to send her warmer clothes? Promise you'll send them through the remailing service—which is a good one, by the way. Ask if she's getting enough to eat, staying where she can sleep enough? And listen for background noises when she calls." He shrugged. "I'm sorry, but with what you've told me, that's all I've got."

We both knew it wasn't enough. Before I left I asked him to show me his latest finds, and we chatted as we toured the shelves.

The afternoon meetings went well, and after we had finished with every crew member I'd been able to snag, Sophie and I were in agreement. If Sebastian approved, we had our case. She went off to waste her snooping talents at a cash register, and I went home to the duplex, locked all the doors and fell deeply asleep on the sofa, only waking up once to heat a can of soup for dinner and strip off my jeans before I crawled into bed.

I woke early the next morning. Florida dawns can be spectacular, and Sunday morning's promised to be no exception. Since my morning was free, I bought a takeout breakfast and drove to Gulfstream Park.

After I found a parking spot I strolled between sea grapes down a boardwalk to the beach, spread a towel on the sand and waded a short distance as the sky turned a marbleized apricot and, at last, the sun peeked over the horizon.

Wendy was not a fan of sunrises. Once when we were both visiting our parents, I'd made her come with me to see what I like to call the "Seabank Special." Off a point not far from the house where I grew up, dawn sets the sky on fire. To get there, walking through tall brush is required, something else Wendy doesn't like. But I'd dragged her along, and when we got to the beach and dawn lit the sky I turned to watch her expression. She was looking at her cell phone screen.

"I don't suppose you're about to take a picture?" I asked.

"I missed a text last night. I was just checking." She looked up. "I've seen sunrises, Ryan. I came with you, didn't I?"

Now as I watched the sky brighten and three pelicans fly across the sun, I wondered why she *had* come that morning. To keep the peace? To show she was a good sport? To stay on my good side? I wondered if I had ever really seen my sister clearly.

In my work life, I was surrounded by eccentrics, and certainly not just the sources I interviewed for our podcast, or the crew, like Sophie and Glenn, who followed their bliss wherever it led them. Sebastian Freiman, *Out in the Cold*'s executive producer and backer, was eccentric in his own way, although his eccentricities made him one of the richest men in Florida.

Among other things, Sebastian owned a chain of weekly newspapers, which he devoted to stirring up controversy, as well as making sure that justice prevailed in courts and police work. Like our podcast, I'm not certain the newspapers were earning their keep or if he cared. Although I knew he started life with a trust fund, I'd never discovered all the ways Sebastian multiplied his birthright. I'd just seen plenty of evidence of the way he spent it.

Right now I was looking at one of them. Sebastian's house—better described as a mansion—made my parents' luxurious home in Seabank seem small and insignificant. The house was saffron-colored stucco with a red tile roof, inset tile mosaics and beautiful wrought-iron balconies and doors. Inside there were at least six bedrooms—I'd counted that many once on my way to his upstairs office. The property itself stretched from ocean's edge to Lake Worth lagoon. Today I'd faced down two security guards to get this far.

Somebody once told me that Sebastian bought the house to help an old friend when it was about to go into foreclosure. However it happened, he made good use of it and threw amazing parties. Invitations were nearly as coveted as those to soirees at nearby Mar-a-Lago. Twice Sebastian insisted I attend. Since I grew up with parents who entertained lavishly, I knew exactly how to enjoy myself. I smiled, schmoozed, and when I could, I escaped with a plate of gourmet tidbits, one glass of white wine and another of whatever red came most recommended by the bartender. Then I'd sit behind a palm tree to people watch.

It wasn't a bad way to socialize.

Now Sebastian's housekeeper let me in and motioned me to the parlor to the right of a huge foyer dotted with priceless art and sculpture. I stayed where I was, trying to imagine how easy it would be to steal this collection. I didn't want it. I just wanted to know how an art thief might proceed.

The fact that I was now standing under Sebastian's priceless Murano glass chandelier plotting a burglary was little more than a fluke. Fresh out of grad school, as well as courage after the John Quayle encounter, I had drifted to Delray Beach to work on the crime beat at one of Sebastian's weeklies.

Trying to find my feet again, there had been too many hours in every day. Six months in, on the verge of starting over somewhere more exciting, I met Sophie at the local grocery store. She's a chatterer, my Sophie, and the store was nearly empty. I told her what I did, she told me her hobby was crime research and internet sleuthing, and we became instant best friends.

Just for fun we decided to create a podcast about a local jewelry store heist. By criminal standards, the crime was mediocre, a theft that had netted the burglars less than a thousand dollars in merchandise. But between us, we found some interesting angles, and a friend with a recording studio. We wrote and recorded the podcast for entertainment, never expecting anything to come of it. But when we finished, I played it for some of my colleagues and wondered out loud if it would be an interesting addition to the paper's lackluster website.

Three weeks later I was called to a meeting at this very house, with the boss I'd never met. I thought my command performance might relate to an unflattering story I'd written about a local politician. I hadn't expected to like Sebastian Freiman, who was known to be outspoken and domineering. Instead I fell under his spell immediately.

The Sebastian I met was a distinguished silver-haired man in his late fifties, wearing jeans and a polo shirt and munching a bagel as he strolled into the foyer. He had one for me, too, along with a travel mug of coffee, and even better, as we walked around his extensive grounds, he told me he liked our podcast. He asked if I'd like to inaugurate a series that he would bankroll and promote through his papers, as well as his other contacts.

I was so taken aback I had to finish my bagel before I could answer. I told him I couldn't do a podcast without Sophie, and he told me to hire her and whoever else I needed, but not to assume the money wouldn't dry up if it was spent too freely. It wasn't quite that simple, but nearly. When Sebastian wants something, Sebastian almost always gets it.

Today he didn't keep me waiting long enough to finish plotting my crime. He joined me from some room beyond the foyer and came to stand beside me. He's a head taller than I am, and as physically fit as any man in his income bracket who golfs and works out with a personal trainer. He was wearing khaki slacks and a pale yellow sport shirt, along with a vintage Patek Philippe watch with a brown leather strap. One of two ex-wives had given it to him, and he'd kept it after the divorce because, as he'd told me, unlike the marriage, the watch would hold its value forever.

"Good to see you," he said, although he, too, was staring at his foyer art collection.

"I'm plotting a heist."

He played along. "Great idea. I'd rather have the insurance than the art. Some dark night I'll slip you inside and help you load the truck."

"It would be boring that way. I couldn't get one good podcast episode out of that."

"So now you're planning to provide your own material?"

"No need, I guess. There's such a wealth of it out there."

"You've chosen something to work on?" He held up his hand to stop me. "I thought we'd talk onboard. It's a beautiful day to be out on the water. You're game?"

I had been on Sebastian's yacht one time, a long day with people I had little in common with, although the food and liquor had been spectacular. Of course if Sebastian wanted me out on the water, out we'd go.

I followed him to the lagoon side of the property where a long dock extended into the water. The yacht was nowhere in sight, but several smaller crafts were.

"We'll take the runabout." He pointed to the end of the dock.

I was relieved this was not a party, but surprised at his preference, a small red bowrider comfortable for only a few people. I shouldn't have been. Sebastian does what he wants, and not to impress others. It was a perfect day for cruising slowly along the lagoon.

At the end of the dock I stepped in, and after he cast off, he followed, motioning to the swivel deck chair beside his in the cockpit. The bowrider had a wraparound windshield, and bench seating in the helm. I stowed my handbag in a mesh net against the side that was nearest me and settled in to enjoy.

At first, as we cruised slowly along a shore dotted with spectacular homes, Sebastian acted as tour guide. I learned that the lagoon was twenty-one miles long, with two inlets to the ocean, so what had once been fresh water had turned brackish, creating an estuary favorable to the growth of sea life. Although the lagoon had been polluted and abused through the centuries, now both the government, private citizens and environmental groups had come together to restore what they could. Oysters, birds and fish in abundance had followed.

He pulled farther away from shore, out of a no wake zone and into a channel where he could crank up the outboard engine. I was enjoying the sun on my head and shoulders, the gentle motion of the boat and whatever cool spray dared to breach the windshield. When Sebastian asked me to tell him about the case we wanted to explore, I was happy to do it. As always, he asked insightful questions, but my answers seemed to satisfy him.

"Send me what you have, but so far, so good," he said.

Pleased, I told him about another idea for a short series on Florida's Stand Your Ground law. I wanted to keep listeners tuning in while we tackled our new cold case idea. I'd already done the footwork, taking suggestions from my former journalism professors for students who might like the job of researching and writing scripts.

"Still a work in progress," I said, "but I think we could have something to start with in six months or so."

He seemed interested in that, too, and again, I promised to send him everything I'd done so far. We chatted casually and after a while, he made a wide circle, and we started back the way we'd come.

"You're able to work while you're in Seabank?" he asked.

The question was only fair. I wasn't making a fortune, but I was getting paid. "To be honest, not as much as I want."

"Why don't you tell me what's really going on."

I didn't know what to say. Sebastian is both astute and crafty. He also has long arms that can reach into every corner of somebody's life and extract whatever he needs. On the plus side, he's also capable of absolute silence when it's called for. Sebastian really doesn't answer to anybody.

"My sister's disappeared." I glanced at him. He wasn't watching me, but he sure was listening.

"Why and where?"

This was a man who could help or destroy me. I knew if I equivocated, or worse, lied, he would probably know. From that point on he would never trust me again.

"This is in confidence, Sebastian. Is that okay?"

"Off the record then."

One journalist to another I told him about Wendy, from her first phone call all the way to Friday night's visit to Against the Wind.

"I know it sounds bad," I said, finishing my explanation. "But you'd have to know Wendy to realize how impossible this is. She's got everything going for her. She's beautiful, kind, thoughtful—" I nearly stumbled over that remembering how little thought she'd put into what her absence might be doing to our parents or her daughters. "She's smart and savvy, and she always plays by the rules," I finished.

"Then this is particularly hard for you, isn't it? Because you know her so well, and you're afraid for her."

I was grateful he understood. "I feel helpless, along with wishing I could shed some light on whatever's going on."

He asked a few more questions, but my explanation seemed to satisfy him. "Do what you can on the podcast. You're making headway even if you can't work as hard as you want right now. Just keep me up to date."

I was happy when he changed the subject, happier still that he hadn't offered to help find Wendy. Having Sebastian involved would focus attention where I didn't want it.

We were not far from his dock when he cut the motor, and we drifted as waves lapped gently on the sides of the boat. "Our neighborhood blight," he said, pointing at a house set back from the water with only a roof visible through the trees.

I saw peaks and spires that reminded me of Hogwarts Castle. "Kind of creepy. What's it like in full view?"

"Creepier. And there's a story to go with it. Want to hear it?"

"You're asking a journalist if she wants to hear a story?"

Sebastian has a nice laugh, deep and round. It's rare and nicer because of it.

"There was a murder there in the 1950s. The house isn't

actually too much older than that. It was built by an English-man named Jonathan Peele, the youngest son of an earl, who wanted to re-create the manor house where he was raised. Rumor says he was chased out of England by older brothers and told never to return."

I was sorry we couldn't get close enough to see it better. "What did people think of Peele and his little castle?"

"I'm told they didn't think well. He was haughty and some-thing of a recluse and when he came out of hiding, he insisted everyone call him the Honourable Jonathan Peele. He mar-ried a young woman from New York, and then, mysteriously, she simply disappeared. Nobody knew what had happened to her, but years later, another wife took her place. And when he decided to introduce her to local society, that's when the murder occurred."

Having grown up in Florida, I was surprised I'd never heard this tale. "This sounds like a lurid gothic novel. Or something very Agatha Christie."

"It does, doesn't it? A huge party was staged, and everyone of note was invited. Most likely every guest wanted to see the new wife and learn what had happened to the old one. But the night of the party, they were greeted by security guards who turned them away. It seems Mrs. Peele—or would she be 'Honourable,' too? Anyway, she'd taken sick, and the master of the house was at her bedside with a local doctor and didn't wish to be disturbed."

I was entranced. The story was fascinating, and Sebastian told it well. "I assume she died?"

"Unfortunately, yes. And when her body was carried out, the police went straight in and arrested Jonathan Peele. Even-tually he was convicted of her murder, later ruled a death by arsenic. The house was abandoned for years, then sold and nearly demolished until it was saved and turned into a small hotel by a young couple from California."

"What happened to Peele?"

"He died in prison, but five years ago, the maid who had attended both wives, admitted that she had poisoned them. She'd been hopelessly in love with Peele and wanted him for herself. Everything had worked against him, of course. He was unsympathetic. He had isolated himself, and there were stories about his past in England, along with the house itself, which everyone believed was a hopeless eyesore. He was tried in the public eye and convicted long before any court heard his case."

I digested everything, hypnotized by what had the makings of a great PBS series. "What a story, Sebastian. I can't believe I haven't heard it before this."

He was silent so long I thought he was finished. Then he turned to me. "You haven't heard it because I just made the whole thing up."

I stared at him.

"You believed every ridiculous word I told you, because it came from me. It never occurred to you I might lie. Maybe eventually you would have questioned it, looked it up and found no mention of the Honourable Jonathan Peele anywhere on Wikipedia or beyond, but for the moment, I had you hook, line and sinker."

I didn't answer, so he went on. "Did the details make sense? If we got closer to shore, you'd see the house is actually fairly ordinary, once the trees aren't blocking it. Ostentatious, yes, but what isn't in this neighborhood? Would you have gotten closer just to check my story? I don't think you would have made the effort. You wanted to go with the easiest explanation. And you thought you could, because you trust me. You can't imagine why I might lie to you."

"There's got to be a point to this," I said, but I already knew what it was.

"You don't take anything with the podcast at face value, Ryan. You're relentless and thorough, and you question everything. That's why the first season of *Out in the Cold* did so well. Between you and Sophie, everything is examined, even when you're leaning a different way. So why did your guard slip today? Why did you absorb my story without questioning anything I said?"

Of course we were no longer talking about the youngest son of an earl, nor had we ever been. We were talking about the younger daughter of Dale and Arlie Gracey, and the older one, too.

I heard myself repeat what I'd said to Sophie. "She's my sister."

He started the motor again and angled his way down the lagoon. Only when we pulled up to his dock did he reply. "Those are not words to live by, Ryan. You know that, don't you?"

He was right, and worse? I was afraid putting family ties aside might be the hardest thing I would ever have to do.

CHAPTER TWENTY-THREE

On the way back to Seabank I didn't listen to podcasts. I had plenty of noise in my own head to keep me company.

Sebastian hadn't told his bogus fairy tale to ridicule me. He'd wanted to teach me a valuable lesson, and it had worked. Sophie had tried, too. But even though most of the time my family values privacy over intimacy and evasion over candor, we are still a family. Could I be the one who destroyed it?

By the time I pulled into the town house garage, I could no longer pretend that Wendy's virtues, the same ones I'd listed for Sebastian, were anything other than a younger sister's illusions. I had always seen Wendy from a distance, even when we were standing next to each other. I had assembled my view of her from occasional thoughtful moments and gifts, and from my parents' accounts. I knew about her achievements. I knew how many people admired her. But did I know her heart?

At the town house I showered and changed before I left for Gulf Sands to pick up my nieces. Just in case my mother hadn't fed them, I stopped by the grocery store on the way.

Fifteen minutes later I was heading for the checkout line when I saw Ella Cramer, dressed casually today. I decided she must live in the neighborhood, too, and unless one of us wanted to change grocers, we had to clear the air.

She started down the pet food aisle when she saw me, and not far from the cat litter I caught up to her. "Ella?"

She turned, one hand still on the handle of the shopping cart. "Yes?"

"I feel bad about the last time I saw you. I had no idea you weren't at Gracey Group now, but you've always been one of my favorite people. I just wondered if we could maybe heal the tension and share a cup of coffee? My treat?" I nodded to the market café by the deli.

"I'm sorry, I have other things I have to do."

I figured those other things were in the same category as untangling yarn or clipping toenails. "We don't have to linger. You could give me your recipe for your wonderful turtle cookies." I smiled, but she didn't. "Or maybe you could just be honest with me and tell me what in the hell happened."

"So you can go straight back to your father and tell him I'm complaining about the way I was treated?"

"He just had bypass surgery. We're going out of our way not to upset him."

"And your sister?"

"She's out of town, and by the time she gets back, this will be old news." I paused. "Old news I don't plan to recount to anyone in my family."

"I still don't see the point."

"Please?"

As I was growing up, Ella kept a supply of Tootsie Pops in the bottom drawer of her desk, just for me. They had been our secret, but she'd never been able to deny me if I asked nicely. Apparently the habit had held.

She sighed. "All right."

She didn't speak again until I was sitting across from her at the café. I watched her carefully doctor her coffee. One packet of sweetener, one thimbleful of cream. She stirred so hard I was afraid I might get sucked into the whirlpool.

I started, hoping to get her talking. "I can't help thinking there must have been a big misunderstanding. My father valued you above all his employees."

"Not above your sister."

I nodded, as if that made sense. "So Wendy was part of the problem?"

"Part?" Her laugh was humorless. "Your sister claimed I made a mistake, a huge mistake, one guaranteed to cost Gracey Group a small fortune. She told me the due date on a project had been changed, so I had more time to complete my part. Of course when the project wasn't finished by the real due date, she went to your father with evidence that I'd screwed up the timing for everyone."

"She had evidence?"

"I don't have to tell *you* that evidence can be misinterpreted." She paused, and then she leaned forward. "Or manufactured."

I nodded again. I was beginning to feel like a bobblehead doll. "So it was just one incident?"

"Heavens, no."

I waited, hopeful she'd continue without prodding, and boy, did she. First a whirlpool, and now, a tidal wave.

"Wendy wanted your father to think I was slowing down, or worse. To be blunt, she wanted Dale to think my mind was failing. For a while, even I began to wonder. Paperwork disappeared off my desk, documents I was sure I'd left there, correspondence I had to answer. Computer files were erased or damaged. Once a set of figures I had taken an entire morning to gather ended up in the recycling bin. Even worse, not everything I'd accessed to assemble them was still on my computer. So I had to reconstruct and print out the entire document again, while your father and several valuable clients were waiting."

"That must have been awful."

"I wasn't the one who finally located the original. Another employee found it and handed it over to Wendy. Of course she couldn't have been sweeter or more helpful. I must have had a late night, she said, or I'd been working too hard. She certainly wasn't going to tell Dale what had happened."

Ella's job at Gracey Group had been complex, with many different facets. My father had always said she did the work of three people, and he couldn't begin to imagine how she kept everything so neatly compartmentalized in her head. Maybe Ella's position really had become too complicated, and she hadn't wanted to complain. Or maybe the constant changes in technology had finally gotten to her, and she hadn't kept up with the best ways to proceed.

But worse than a simple age-related slowdown? Maybe my sister had discovered a good reason to send Ella on her way. And that's what I needed to know.

"Did you and Wendy have disagreements? Did she have a reason to want you out of the office?"

She looked at me as if I were a stranger. "Are you asking if there's a possibility your sister might have had a good reason to want me gone, something that has to do with her and not me? Or are you trying to find an excuse for what she did?"

"I'm just trying to get to the truth."

She reached for her purse. "It's over and done with."

"Ella, it's not really over and done with." I struggled with the best way to phrase the next part. "Will you tell me if

Wendy directly influenced Dad to get rid of you? My mother told me the opposite."

"Your sister is very good at saying one thing and meaning something different."

"You have no reason to help me, but I'm trying to figure out a few things. I need to know if you think Wendy set you up or had reason to."

She got to her feet. "There wasn't and isn't anything wrong with my mind, Ryan. You and Wendy have a special relationship. You think I haven't always known what you are to each other? I'd really be a fool to think you want to discover the truth. No matter what your father or anybody else thinks, I'm not now nor have I ever been one."

I watched her walk away, and despite wishing differently, I knew that my *special* relationship to Wendy might be taking a hard hit in the near future.

By the time I arrived, Holly and Noelle were ready to go. Maybe Bismarck was happier to see me than they were, but they were happy enough. I admired the newly decorated Christmas tree, gave the elder Graceys hugs, and shepherded the girls and the dog to my car before Mom could recite another list of things to do for them in the coming week.

"I thought Mommy might come home with you," Noelle said, as I pulled away from the house.

She sounded so forlorn I had to clear my throat. "No, sweetie. She's still away."

"She needs to come home."

"No, she doesn't," Holly said.

"Holly, Noelle's entitled to her feelings," I said.

"So am I!"

I wondered if taking Holly aside when we got home would turn up new reasons for her anger. A certain amount seemed reasonable, possibly even healthy, but Holly was moving well beyond that.

I asked them about the cookies they'd baked with my mother. I hadn't yet checked out the tin she'd sent home with us. Neither of them answered.

I continued trying to find a way to lighten the mood. "How did Bismarck do?"

"He's limping," Noelle said.

"Is he?"

"She just said he was," Holly said.

"Indeed she did." I thought of an idea that would be good for Biz and me, since it might channel Holly's energy in a better direction. "I'll tell you what, let's eat, and then maybe we can take Bismarck to Teo's to see if something's wrong. You can see where all the dogs live. Sound good?"

A grunt from the backseat was answer enough.

Inspired, I called Teo from the car and he said it was fine to stop by, so I offered to come right away and bring dinner. Twenty minutes later the girls and I were at Confidence K-9s.

Teo met us out front, accompanied by a little blond girl Holly's size. She was wearing sweatpants and a hoodie, and unlike every stitch my nieces owned, her clothes didn't match.

"Meet Fiona," Teo said, "Janice and Harry's daughter. I'm babysitting while they do some shopping."

Fiona said a shy hello, then she asked the girls if they wanted to see her house and pet beagle. They were off like a shot.

Teo was dressed like Fiona, only his clothes were cleaner. "I paid her so I could get you alone."

"They'll be okay?"

"We'll walk over in a minute. I thought we'd head to my place. I have a table and silverware."

"Don't get your hopes up. Strictly grocery store deli food."

"Manna from heaven." He went to the rear door of my car

where Bismarck was still sitting between the two booster seats. He gave a command, and Bismarck gingerly stepped down to the floor and even more gingerly to the ground.

Teo stood back and called him. Bismarck was indeed limping. Teo scrambled to the ground and examined his old friend. The longer the examination took, the worse I felt. I hadn't been at my parents' house to supervise, and I shouldn't have trusted anyone else to make sure he was okay.

"I don't think it's serious," Teo said at last. He pushed away from the ground and got to his feet, gracefully enough, but with effort. "I think he pulled a muscle. I'll give you some meds for the inflammation. Just make sure he takes it easy for the next week or so. He's not a young dude anymore. If the limping gets worse, I'll take him to the vet for an X-ray."

"I was gone for the weekend, and he was at my mother's house with the girls."

He pulled a treat out of his pocket and held it out for Bismarck. "And somehow you still had time to slip in a visit to Seabank's most notorious biker bar."

I jammed my hands in my pockets. "How did you know that?"

"Bad news travels fast." When I didn't answer, he shook his head. "Remember Jim, the kennel tech I introduced you to? Well, he remembered you, and he happened to be there Friday night."

I had planned to tell Teo about my escapade, a decision I'd made on my trip home. So now I did, leaving out nothing. "And don't tell me I should have taken you with me," I finished. "If you'd been there, no guy would have talked to me."

"You didn't have to invite me, Ryan. You're a big girl. But it would have been nice to know where you were heading, in case you disappeared, like your sister."

The fight went out of me. "We're revisiting old issues, aren't we?"

"No. But when you put your life in danger after you've already involved me, it would be nice to know where you are. You see the difference between that and me timing your trips to the grocery store, right?"

I saw his point, but I had to make sure he was able to live with what I'd learned. "I'm not telling the sheriff's office I saw the guy who attacked me. For one thing, it'll be my word against his. But whatever the circumstances, this guy knows Wendy. And I don't want to draw attention to her disappearance. Can you live with that?"

"For now."

"Well, there's more, if you want to hear it." I didn't wait for an answer. I plowed into my talks with Sophie and Sebastian, ending with my grocery store coffee date.

He let me finish before he spoke. "You're having trouble with this, and that makes sense. You're starting from zero, and now you have to get up to speed again before you make progress."

"I've told myself to take Wendy's story at face value, that if she's been lying, she's only trying to protect our family. Now?" I stopped, shaking my head.

"Do you trust me?"

I trusted him completely, but I didn't trust that he had Wendy's best interests in mind. When I didn't answer, he folded his arms. "You're going to have to decide, Ryan. Because, like I said, you've involved me already. I'm not risking my life or my dog's life again by not being up to speed. Either you tell me everything you learn, so I can help, or you tell me nothing. We can call this relationship quits now, and you can leave Biz right here, with no hard feelings. Or you can take your chances with both of us."

"Can't we spend time together, even if I don't share everything?"

"This thing with Wendy is too big a part of your life to shut me out. We can partner on this, and see where that leads. Or you can be completely on your own. I'm not going to push. You choose."

"She's my sister," I said, for the third time that weekend. And maybe three really is a charm, because this time as the words escaped, I realized that sisterhood was no excuse.

I stepped closer and rested my fingertips on his arm. My hands felt like ice, but his skin was warm and pliant. "She's my sister, but you're the one who can help me get to the bottom of whatever's going on. No more secrets. I'm sorry."

He nodded. "Let's get the girls and eat. I'm starving."

The drama seemed to be finished, and I was grateful. "I brought chicken and a couple of salads. Nothing exciting."

"The company's not half bad." He draped an arm around my shoulders, and pulled me close.

I looked up at him, deciding. Then I rose on tiptoe and kissed him, slowly and thoroughly. "The company's stellar," I said at last.

We walked to Janice and Harry's house together, his hip brushing mine and my heart thumping in time to our footsteps.

CHAPTER TWENTY-FOUR

I woke up on Monday morning resolved to unmask the real Wendy Gracey Wainwright. If I couldn't do it face-to-face, maybe I could get a clearer picture from people who had known her. My Wendy was thoughtful and caring. The picture Ella had painted was much darker, but I recognized some of it. Wendy was determined to succeed, and had been from the time she was a small child, but at what price? If somebody got in her way, would she use any means to stop them? And what might that say about Vítor Calvo's death in Santa Fe?

I couldn't ask my parents if their older daughter was ruthless and destructive. In so many ways they had built their lives around Wendy's perfection. But was that the real story?

After breakfast I went upstairs to shoo my nieces into the car and found Holly sitting on her bed, cell phone to her ear.

"Daddy, we miss you. Can't you come home?"

I stopped in the doorway. Noelle was cuddled next to her sister, tears streaking her cheeks.

Holly was pleading now. "But we miss you, and it's Christmas!"

Galvanized, I moved across the room. "Let me talk to him when you're done."

I let her finish the conversation, which moved from begging to resignation. At last Holly thrust the phone in my direction. "Bryce?" I asked.

Reception was less than perfect, but I heard his voice between crackles. "Ryan? Is that you? Holly said you were there."

"Yes, will you hold on a minute? Please don't hang up."

I told the girls to get in the car, and for once, they didn't argue. Both were sadly subdued. When they were out of earshot, I put the phone back up to my ear.

"Bryce, what's going on?"

More crackling. "Where is Wendy?"

By now I could teach a course on the art of half-truths. "She ran into difficulties while she was away for work, but she should be back soon. I told her I'd watch the girls in the meantime. She didn't want Mom and Dad to cope with them right now. You know my dad had heart surgery?"

"How's he doing?"

Bryce hadn't called my parents. My mother had used national security to explain his uncharacteristic disinterest, but I wondered if sneaking around the ocean, polishing nukes, was a real excuse, or if Bryce had purposely avoided them.

"He's recovering," I said. "Slowly but surely."

"I'm glad. I like your parents."

"I'm beginning to wonder if you and my sister like each other. I heard the message you left on the house phone. If I'm going to stay here and take care of your girls, I'd like to know what's going on."

"I'm surprised Wendy hasn't told you. We're getting a divorce. It's been in the works for a while, although she's suddenly dragging her feet."

If my parents had known about a divorce, I was sure I

would know by now, too. Had Wendy hoped the problems would blow over? Worse, was she afraid to explain what had happened?

I asked the one question no polite person would, but after all, I'm a journalist. "Why?"

"That's our business."

"Not anymore. I'm taking up the slack while you do your job, which makes it pretty hard to do my own, by the way. At the very least, I need more information, so I can figure out how to deal with the girls when they find out."

"Let's just say your sister has plans for her life that don't include me," he said after a long silence.

"What kind of plans?"

"That's all I intend to say."

"Do her plans include her daughters?"

Silence again, then a barely audible sigh. "That's negotiable."

"Negotiable? With money?"

"I have to go. I'm only in port temporarily."

"I need to be able to reach you if something happens here, Bryce. You may have an important job, but you're their father, and Wendy's almost impossible to get hold of right now."

He didn't ask why. He didn't even seem surprised, as if whatever inexplicable actions Wendy took these days didn't matter. "You can email me." He rattled off an address that was just short enough to remember.

"I'll send you my cell number and email address," I said. "Please stay in touch."

"Take care of my girls. And thank you." He disconnected.

I grabbed what I needed for the day and found my nieces in the car. I hoped the Mrs. Englishes had something fun planned.

By the time I dropped them off, I knew where I wanted to

start my quest. I did a quick search on my cell phone and found a woman named Claire Durant listed as one of two assistant principals at Seabank High. She looked to be about Wendy's age, an attractive African American woman with penetrating dark eyes. I wasn't going to win a sleuthing award. The other possibility was an older white male.

I decided not to call for an appointment. Instead I stopped and bought two lattes, one for me and one for my new best friend Claire.

I hadn't attended Seabank High, so the building was unfamiliar. After showing ID and explaining my reason for being there to the security guard, I found my way to the office. The high school opened later than my nieces' school, so few students were milling about.

The woman at the front desk looked like she'd lost all her illusions. She wasn't impressed when I explained I hoped to see Claire before school began.

"She's probably getting organized for the day. Would you like to make an appointment?"

I flashed my dimples. "I won't take up much of her time. I'll be in and out, I promise."

"Why do you want to see Mrs. Durant?"

I played my trump card. "I'm a journalist, and I have some questions about a former student."

"I—" The secretary looked up, and then beyond me. "Mrs. Durant, this young lady would like to see you. Do you have time?"

I turned and saw a more stunning version of the woman pictured on my cell phone. Claire Durant wore a red-and-black dress, with oblong gold hoops in her ears that set off a pixie haircut.

I set the lattes on the counter and held out my hand. "I'm Ryan Gracey. You went to school with my sister, Wendy."

She stared at me a moment, not as if she were trying to place me, but more as if she were trying to absorb me. The sensation was an odd one, and I wondered what had triggered it.

When she finally extended her hand, the handshake was the best kind, firm but not bruising. I grabbed one of the lattes and held it out to her. "I thought you might like one of these while we chat."

She smiled a little and took it. "What can I help you with?"

"It's a bit personal."

The smile died a fraction, and her gaze flicked to the clock to our right, then back. "I only have a few minutes."

"She's a journalist," the secretary warned.

"I am," I agreed, "but this is off the record."

"This way." Claire Durant lifted a section of counter and ushered me into an office at one side of the reception area. I was happy when she closed the door.

I had prepared a story, this time an all-out lie because I was feeling a little desperate. "Thanks for seeing me. You did go to school with Wendy, right?"

She sat behind her desk and motioned me to the chair in front of it. "We were in drama club together, and probably a few classes."

"So you knew her pretty well?"

Her smile was perfunctory, more of a placeholder than an expression of delight. "More or less."

"Did you know she's living in Seabank again? Temporarily, at least. She's working at Gracey Group, and she wanted to be closer to our parents."

"I think I heard she was back."

I was glad I wasn't a tardy Seabank student, or one who'd been caught cheating on a test. I launched into my lie. "I want to have a surprise party for her. It's been so long since she lived here, she's kind of a fish out of water." I realized that was a mistake. No one would ever describe my sister that way.

Claire seemed to know that. "Has she made any attempt to find her old friends?"

"I don't know. I'm just home temporarily. But when I talk to her, she seems lonely." That, too, was out of character, so I hurried on. "She has little girls, so she's not getting out a lot, and of course, the job. So I'm hoping I can gather a few old friends for a surprise party, and help her reestablish contacts."

"That's an interesting approach."

"I was hoping you might be able to put me in touch with some of her high school friends. I don't have her yearbook, so I'm fairly clueless. And besides, I don't know who stayed in town and who didn't."

Claire didn't reply. I hoped she was forming a guest list for my counterfeit surprise party, but I was doubtful. "Can you help?" I prodded.

She shook her head, and the hoops in her ears swayed gracefully. "Why are you really here, Ryan?"

That took me by surprise. "I told you. I'd like to find some of her old friends."

"Her old *boy*friends?"

I had no idea where she was leading. "Not particularly."

"Do you have a personal reason for wanting to know who Wendy went out with in her senior year?"

I tried to process this odd turn in our conversation. "I'm not sure what you mean."

Claire picked up a pen and tapped it on her desktop. "I don't think this is anything I can be involved with."

"I'm sorry. I just thought you might know some people who'd like to see Wendy again."

"I don't know who she was close to. She always had a lot of boyfriends." She emphasized "lot."

"I don't think I ever said boyfriends. She's married." Although not for long, if Bryce had his way.

Claire tapped harder. "I'm afraid you came to the wrong place. Secrets aren't easy to keep, but I do my best. You'd be surprised how many I know. High school can be a hotbed of intrigue." She dropped the pen—or more accurately flung it to the desktop—and stood. Obviously we were finished. "I'm sorry I can't help you."

She started around her desk, to usher me out, then she paused, as if considering something. She went to the nearest wall and bent to search a crowded bookcase. Finally she pulled out a hardcover volume and thrust it at me.

"You said you don't have her yearbook. This might answer some questions then. One of our parents found this copy at a yard sale and bought it for me. It's our class yearbook, Wendy's and mine. I have my own copy at home. You can have this one."

I had no choice but to take it. "Thank you, I think."

"Your sister was a star in the drama club. You might start there." Claire opened the door to her office. I followed her through the reception area and out into the hallway, where she gave a parting nod.

"I hope you find what you're looking for, Ryan." She was gone before I could say anything more than goodbye.

In the parking lot I debated what to do next. I decided to head to the same beach where I'd tried to show Wendy the Seabank Special. The point wouldn't be crowded today since effort was needed to walk through the brush, and the beach itself was narrow and often slick with seaweed. Only those of us who'd discovered the glory of sunrise there, or knew that sand dollars could sometimes be found fifty yards from the shore, ever returned.

I parked on the street and got a blanket out of the back. Then with blanket, yearbook and latte, I made my way down the narrow, sandy path to the beach. This morning it was relatively free of debris, and I spread the blanket several feet above the waterline.

I didn't open the yearbook immediately. The sun was well and truly up, but the reflection in the water was enchanting, dancing, sparkling light rippling along with the waves. Not far away, a pod of dolphins was having breakfast. While I finished my latte I watched them leap and dive, following their school of fish until they were too far away to see.

Finally I opened the yearbook. It had belonged to a girl named Diana Gordon, whose name was printed in small, cramped letters on the inside of the cover. I wondered why anybody disposed of their adolescence at a yard sale. All these years later was high school still an unpleasant memory? Had she left not only Seabank, but Planet Earth? I certainly hoped not. I was beginning to feel like a voyeur.

The opening pages were dotted with scribbled notes, the kind most yearbooks have. "I've loved knowing you," or "Can you believe we're graduating?"

I looked for a cheery message from Wendy, but didn't find one. Had the girls been friends or even known each other? If their homerooms had been organized by the first letter of surnames, they should have been together.

I paged through nostalgic photos of the school, empty hallways, the gym, study hall. Following these were page after page of students doing a variety of things. I looked for my sister in a trio of cheerleaders, two suspended high in the air, but she wasn't there. Wendy would have fit on that page, blinding white smile, lithe figure. I did find her in the homecoming court, looking spectacular in a long, pink sheath slit to her thigh.

I didn't see sports or clubs, which were probably in the

back, and I couldn't identify my sister in other casual photos, so I kept turning pages.

I reached the senior photos. Seabank High is a large school with almost two thousand students, making Wendy's many achievements that much grander. With so many students, the senior photos were small, sixteen to a page. Her graduating class had dressed as they saw fit. The boys wore jackets and ties, while the girls wore their Sunday best. As I flipped pages, I saw a multitude of bare shoulders and low necklines, probably the reason the nuns at my school had opted for the traditional academic drape and pearls.

Diana Gordon was at the bottom of a page. Among pretty girls who looked their best, Diana stood out, and not in a good way. Her brown hair had been permed into a frizzy cloud surrounding a long, narrow face. She wasn't smiling. In fact she was squinting, as if she'd insisted on being photographed without her glasses. She was wearing the type of high-necked, long-sleeved dress I associated with polygamous cults.

Poor Diana had deserved a second photo shoot. I was beginning to understand why her yearbook had ended up at the yard sale.

My gaze moved to the opposite page, where I expected to see my sister. My parents still have a large canvas print from Wendy's senior photo shoot on a wall in their den. While that photo, showing Wendy against the railing of a footbridge, wasn't the one in the yearbook, it was magnificent. In contrast, when my turn came, I'd declined the extras. Mom and Dad dutifully displayed my lone head shot in a nice frame on a shelf. My mother still brings up my defection whenever the opportunity arises.

Wendy's photo was easy to find, but not for the reasons I'd expected. It was the only photograph on the page that had been defaced. My sister's radiant smile was barely visible under scribbles so violent, they had gouged a hole.

"Whew!" I stared at what remained. Since the yearbook had belonged to one Diana Gordon, the perpetrator was clear. Had Assistant Principal Claire seen the damage? Was this why she'd given me the yearbook? Was she making a point about how little my sister was admired?

I paged through the rest of the senior class to see if Diana had destroyed anyone else. But while I saw the usual sweet notes in the margins, everyone else's photos were undisturbed.

Determined now, I continued to turn pages. Sports took up a large section. While she might not have been a cheerleader, my sister had been right on the front row of the pep squad. I came to music and found Wendy with her flute in band. I didn't see another photo of Diana. High school had not been her moment to shine.

Finally I arrived at drama club.

The first few pages showed scenes from two plays the club had staged that year. The first was unfamiliar, and I didn't see Wendy's photo or name. The second was a one-act adaptation of Ibsen's *A Doll's House*, and Wendy wasn't listed there, either.

I turned the page and this time I spotted my sister immediately, but then, she would have been impossible to miss. Along with the music department, the drama club had staged *L'il Abner* as their big show. The entire left page was devoted to a profile photo of Wendy as the ravishing Daisy Mae. She stood on stage with her breasts thrust out. Daisy Mae's off-the-shoulder polka-dotted top and tight shorts covered just enough flesh. Had one additional inch been exposed, the administration would never have allowed the play to go forward.

I wondered if this photo was the reason my parents had chosen a private Catholic girls' academy for me. Even in high school, Wendy had managed to exude both sensuality and class.

On the right page, L'il Abner faced Daisy Mae. I studied him next. The young man was neither slight nor bulked up, with an athletic body that was probably still filling out. His curly hair was black or almost, which was perfect for the role, and his wistful expression, in a ruggedly handsome face, was engaging.

I wondered if the drama teacher had taken one look at both Wendy and this boy—Sean Riley—and planned the musical around them. They were striking together and perfect for their roles.

For some reason Sean looked familiar, but I didn't know why. When Daisy Mae and L'il Abner were cavorting around the Seabank High stage, I hadn't even been born.

The next pages showed half a dozen scenes from the production. I paged through to the last one. The finale, again a full page, was a love scene, a close-up between L'il Abner and Daisy Mae. The two were entwined, gazing deeply into each other's eyes.

I couldn't shake the feeling that Sean was someone I knew. Or maybe I'd even seen the older Sean, working at our bank or managing a local restaurant. I noted dimples, deep enough to be seen in this more intimate pose.

Then, as my eyes began to lose focus from staring so hard, I knew exactly why he seemed so familiar.

Sean Riley looked like me, or rather, I looked like Sean Riley. In fact the resemblance was so striking, I was stunned I hadn't seen it immediately. But some part of me had denied the truth, even refused to see it, because the answer seemed so impossible.

Sean Riley couldn't be my twin, and he was not my older brother. My few cousins were distant, both in relationship and miles. The only other possibility was obvious. Sean Riley was my father, and the woman I'd always believed to be my sister, was, in fact, my mother.

CHAPTER TWENTY-FIVE

This wasn't the first time I'd blinked and the world around me had changed. The night that John Quayle wrestled me into the backseat of his car was the first. Even though Teo couldn't save me this time, I found myself driving toward Confidence K-9s.

Somebody buzzed me in, and I found him in the office, in conversation with two of his trainers, whose names I couldn't remember.

Teo took one look at my expression and stood. "We're done here?" The men took the hint and nodded to me as they left the room.

"I'm about ready for lunch. We can go to my place," he said.

I hadn't spoken and still didn't. I followed him to his car, a small SUV that was good for carrying dogs and easier for him to climb in and out of.

For a cop and a tough guy, he was surprisingly intuitive, so he didn't press me. "How's Biz doing?" he asked instead.

"Probably sleeping on my bed right now."

"How are you?"

"I'm a mess."

"I kind of thought so." He pulled into his driveway and parked. "Food, then talk. Right?"

"Right."

In the kitchen he pulled cold cuts and cheese from his refrigerator and we made sandwiches. We took our plates out to his patio and dusted off a round table in the shade. Teo took the seat beside me so we were both facing the woods, although I didn't think the scenery had motivated him. He had sensed correctly that it might be easier for me not to look at him.

"So, is this about Wendy?" he asked.

I picked up my sandwich and took a bite while I considered how best to begin. By the time I swallowed, I knew I just had to tell the story. So I did. My trip to the school, my talk with Claire Durant, the yearbook. All while I stared into the woods.

"So the original owner of the yearbook defaced your sister's photo?"

"That's a mystery I haven't solved and probably never will."

"If she was the one who had the yard sale, maybe she's still around."

"Or maybe she was moving and getting rid of everything. I guess I can look for her if I need to."

I could see he was watching me, and I turned a little. "I found a photo of Wendy with a boy. They were in a play together, *L'il Abner.* She was Daisy Mae."

He waited, but his eyes telegraphed concern. I considered putting my arms around him and just letting him hold me. Because that's why I'd come. Not to tell him about this new piece of the Wendy puzzle.

Instead I took a breath. "I couldn't figure out why he looked so familiar. But finally I got it. It was like looking into a mirror, Teo. My dark hair, the shape of my face, my nose, even my dimples. And suddenly my whole life fell into place. This boy—Sean Riley's his name—is my father, and you know what that means? That means Wendy is my mother. Not my sister. My *mother*. Do you remember the story of my birth? How Wendy was doing a gap year in Mexico, and Mom went to join her? Then she discovered she was unexpectedly pregnant and had to stay in Mexico because she was in danger of miscarrying? I was born prematurely. Or so I've been told."

"Whoa…" He shook his head.

"You don't believe me?"

"Sure, I do. I just don't believe they kept something that important from you."

"Well, they kept it from everybody. Although now when I look back on my conversation with Claire Durant, I'm sure she realized the truth the moment I told her I was Wendy's sister. She seemed genuinely taken aback when I introduced myself. I guess it was like seeing Sean Riley again, only in drag. And I bet she thought I was there to discover my father's identity."

"She didn't tell you?"

"No, she gave me the yearbook. Maybe she thought I'd find whatever I needed to on the pages. And if I didn't? Maybe I didn't really want to know."

"Maybe she wanted you to realize it slowly."

"Now everything's coming together. Yesterday Ella told me she knew all about my special relationship with Wendy. I thought she meant we were sisters, so of course, I couldn't be objective. But no, she knew the truth. And how many other people do? The fact that Wendy only rarely came to Seabank and never went out with old friends or introduced me to them? The fact that my parents moved across town and sent me to a private school instead of Seabank High?"

I rested my face in my hands, and Teo put his arm around me. "Take a deep breath. There's a lot to think through."

I was crying, and I hadn't even realized it.

"It's too early to point this out," he said, "but I'm going to anyway. Your mom and dad kept you. They raised you. They wanted you."

"My *grandparents*, you mean? What else were they going to do, leave me by the side of the road after Wendy gave birth? They aren't the kind of people who let others carry their burdens."

"Has anyone ever said you were a burden?"

I was too wrought up to think clearly. "They certainly never saw me the way they saw Wendy. She was the child they'd dreamed of having, and I was the one who came along too late to waste energy on."

"Ryan, do you know how many people want to adopt a baby? It would have been easy for them to find a good home for you, one with any attributes they wanted. Heck, look how cute you turned out."

I turned to blast him for making a joke, and saw how much he cared. He was trying to make me smile, or at least stop crying. I cried harder.

He drew me into his arms. "You are something else, lady. No matter who your mother is. Nothing about you has changed except the circumstances of your birth."

I cried on his shoulder. "Holly…and Noelle are my sisters."

"Technically half sisters, only they aren't."

"What does that mean?"

"Ryan, your parents are your parents, and your sister is your sister. The girls are your nieces. You are their aunt. The only thing that changed is who gave birth to you. Not who raised you, loved you, made sure you got all the surgery you needed and stayed in the hospital while you did. Not who saw you all the way through college, even when you were probably a pain in the ass. Dale and Arlie love you. They consider you their daughter. I'm an outside observer, but I've seen it up close.

Maybe raising you was a little harder than raising Wendy. They were ready to start a different kind of life, but apparently not ready enough. Because they became parents again, told the world you were theirs and treated you like you were."

"They never treated me the way they treated Wendy."

"You need to confront them, then. You need to find out exactly what happened and how they felt about it."

I pulled away. "You think I could talk to my father about this? He's recovering from heart surgery. This is not what he needs."

"Then talk to your mother."

He handed me a napkin, and I wiped my eyes and then my face. "Put yourself in my situation, Teo. Can you?"

"Of course not."

"Wendy is my mother. Wendy is running from the law. Wendy wants me to find some mysterious ex-con so she can pin a murder on him, or at least turn him in to the sheriff so she can come home unscathed."

"It's complicated. I get that. But put that aside for now and go see your mother. Tell her what you learned. Show her the photo. Pay attention to everything she says and doesn't. You have to."

"I know."

He reached for me again, and this time he kissed me. I leaned into the kiss, so glad for his warmth and the familiar feel of him against me.

I finally pulled away. "You've always been here for me when I need you. And you know what? You never let me be there for you."

"It's a guy thing."

It was such an inane response, so ridiculously superficial, that I had to smile. Of course, a smile was the point. I put my hand on his cheek, and he closed his eyes. "I promise from

now on I'll be there if you need me, Teo. Any time, any place.
Even when it's not easy."

"Settle this. Find your answers. Then let's see if we can be
together without drama." He opened his eyes. "Do you want
to finish your lunch?"

I shook my head.

"I'll pack it up, then I'll take you back to your car. I can
finish mine at the kennel."

"I'm not ready to face my mother." I paused. "Mothers.
Neither one of them."

He rose. "Take some time to think. But you need to talk
to Arlie. You see that, right?"

"Yeah, and I will."

"I'm a phone call away."

I wanted him closer. I wanted him where, at that very moment, Bismarck was warming my sheets. But he was right. I
had too much drama in my life, and I couldn't let the leftovers
spill into his. I couldn't let Teo become an antidote for angst
and suspense, or ever think that he was.

I stood on shaky legs and made a decision. "I'll talk to Mom
in the morning, after I've calmed down a little, and I'll let you
know what happens."

"I'll be waiting."

"That's more than I deserve."

He cupped my chin and kissed my nose. "You deserve
everything, Ryan. Don't sell yourself short. Start with your
family and find out what you already have."

CHAPTER TWENTY-SIX

I knew better than to talk to my mother at home because my father wasn't healthy enough to hear our conversation. I didn't want to invite her to a restaurant, either, where others could eavesdrop.

Instead, on Tuesday morning, when I knew my dad had a regular cardiac rehabilitation appointment at the hospital, I waited in the back of the parking lot until I saw my parents' silver BMW pull into a temporary parking spot designated for patient drop off. After they went inside, I drove up to the curb so that when my mother emerged, she would see me immediately.

Five minutes later she was as surprised as I'd expected, opening the passenger door and peering inside immediately. "Are you okay? The girls?"

"I need to talk to you. Please get in."

"But I'm parked—"

"I know. I saw you drive up. I'll take you back to your car when we're done."

She frowned. "I'm not really dressed for—"

"We're just going to walk. Please get in."

She frowned, but she lowered herself to the seat and slammed the door, grabbing for her seat belt. "This must be about Wendy. Is she—"

I cut her off. "I haven't heard anything new, but yes, it's about Wendy. It's about you. It's about me. We're going over to Glade Springs Park, unless you have some major objection."

She didn't answer, so I didn't change course. Neither of us spoke until I had parked my Civic at the end of a row and gotten out. As Mom emerged, I opened the back door and got out Diana Gordon's yearbook and slid it under my arm. I met her on the sidewalk. She glanced at the yearbook, then focused her eyes straight ahead.

I started walking. "I thought we'd take the path along the lake. It's shady, and long enough for this conversation."

"You have certainly piqued my curiosity. You seem angry."

"I don't know what I am."

I started down the sidewalk, choosing the lake fork once we reached the path. The morning was gray and cool, the air scented with the possibility of rain later in the morning. Not a lot of people were in sight, although the ten-thousand-steps crowd would probably arrive when the skies cleared.

"You need to slow down," my mother said after a few minutes.

I didn't realize how fast I'd been walking. I stood and waited for her to catch up. My mother looked tired today, and even though, as usual, she had taken the time to apply makeup and add a long silver chain over her cotton sweater, both seemed haphazard. Despite my sense of betrayal, I felt a pang of sympathy for her. She had a lot on her plate. Dad, Wendy, and now, having to deal with mysterious me.

I wondered if the weight of all these problems reminded her of the day my sister had announced she was going to have a baby. Had Mom and Dad learned of the pregnancy before Wendy graduated? Lying in bed last night after looking up my father on the internet, I'd done the math. I had been born in January—unless that, too, was a lie—and I had been two months premature. Give or take a week, most likely I was conceived right before or after Wendy donned her cap and gown.

I started down the path again, but slower. "I was given this yearbook by Claire Durant. She's the assistant principal at Seabank High. You mentioned her recently."

"I had forgotten her name."

"I thought it might help to know Wendy a little better. I thought Claire might have some insights."

"I can't imagine how Wendy's life as a teenager could have any bearing on her decision not to come home."

"Investigating means turning over every stone. And this time? Well, under the Claire Durant stone, I hit pay dirt."

"I can't imagine what you mean."

I glanced at her, and I had a strong feeling she did know. "I saw the picture of Wendy in *L'il Abner*. Interesting, isn't it, that nothing about Wendy's big moment of glory made it into her scrapbooks."

"I don't think I finished them. I guess I got tired…"

"I guess you got *careful*. Because anybody looking at the photo of her costar in the play, and then at me, would know that Sean Riley is my father. And after that, they would make the leap that, since it's doubtful you and Sean had an affair, Wendy must be my mother."

Mom was silent, and we walked a few minutes until we approached a bench by the water. She touched my arm. "I need to sit."

Anger was bubbling inside me, but not enough to refuse. I perched on the edge of the seat and turned to the page with Sean's full-length photo. Then I rested the yearbook on her lap. I wasn't sure what I was expecting. Denial? Explanation? Tears? What I wasn't expecting was silence.

"I've had this conversation with you a million times, but only in my head," she said at last, closing the book without even looking at it. She set it beside her. "None of them went well. I could never figure out how to tell you how all this happened."

"That's where you went wrong, trying to make the story palatable. Just try the truth. No icing, no sprinkles. Just the plain, simple truth."

"It's figuring out where to start that stops me every time. Do I tell you how amazed I am that such a terrible time in our lives turned out to be such a joy? Do I admit that your father and I threatened to banish Wendy from our lives forever if she didn't go through with the pregnancy?"

"She wanted an abortion?" I wasn't surprised. While my parents are march-through-the-streets pro-lifers, I am pro-choice. I have no idea what Wendy's stance is, but had I been Wendy, seventeen years old with college and a whole new life ahead of me, I would have considered abortion, too.

Of course, I was glad she hadn't gone through with it, even if my parents' strong opinions had been the only reason. Because here I was, dealing with the aftermath, but sitting here. Alive.

Mom finally answered my question. "Your sister didn't know what she wanted, Ryan. Wendy wasn't used to bad luck. And that's how she saw the pregnancy. She gambled and lost, and she couldn't believe it. An abortion was the easy way out. And maybe she was too used to easy. Maybe we'd made her too used to it."

"What about Sean Riley?"

"Wendy refused to tell us who the father was. We really

had no idea until you began to grow into that young man's spitting image."

"So you moved across town and sent me to Catholic school so nobody else would see the resemblance?"

"That was part of it, yes. But not all. I wanted you in a school that was safer than Seabank High, somewhere values would be an everyday part of your education, the way they hadn't been for your sister."

"It's a joke to think that sitting through Mass every morning does much to tamp down hormones. Girls at our school got pregnant, too."

"I was willing to try."

I couldn't throw that back at her. I'd loved my school. The faculty, nuns and laypeople alike, had challenged me on every level. They'd helped me see I could be anybody I wanted. They'd helped me emerge from Wendy's shadow because they hadn't known her.

I changed the subject. "Sean Riley is dead. Did you know that?"

Mom cleared her throat. I glanced at her, and she looked away. "The Gulf War. So few casualties, really, but yes, Sean was one of them."

I'd learned the news last night on Google. How could I mourn a young man I'd never met? He'd been a sperm to Wendy's egg, nothing more. But still, I had cried more than a few tears. The opportunity to meet my biological father had exploded right along with the land mine that had killed him.

"His family is large, and they aren't wealthy," she went on. "He was a smart boy, handsome as all get out, and he could sing like a Broadway star. I heard he won scholarships, but the money didn't stretch far enough. So he enlisted. He was counting on the GI Bill when he got out."

"He gambled and lost."

"After he died I had no proof he was your father, but I was beginning to suspect. You weren't even in preschool, and even then, you looked like him."

"Do his parents know about me?"

"They still live in Seabank, but I could never find the right way to tell them."

"That's sounding familiar."

"What if I was wrong? What if Sean wasn't your father? Wendy still refuses to talk about it. What if I got the Rileys' hopes up or worse, what if my revelation ruined the way they saw their son? In their eyes he's probably a hero. And then there was you, and yes, Wendy. The truth would have gotten out, and both of you would have been forced to live with the result."

I was in no mood to agree with her. "Why don't you start back at the beginning?"

She took a deep breath. "By the time she was a senior, your sister was hard to control. She was sure she knew exactly what she should do and with whom. The fights were wearing. And when we didn't agree with her, she found other ways to get whatever she wanted. Of course, other parents were having the same problems. Our situation wasn't unique."

I heard her making excuses for Wendy. "Were she and Sean a couple?"

"No, that's why nothing came together for a long time. She went out with one boy, then another. In her class everyone seemed to go out in groups, like pack animals. I thought that was good, that it was less likely she'd find herself in any trouble."

"And then, wow, the big prize."

She took my hand, which surprised me. "Of course, at first we didn't see her pregnancy that way, sweetheart. We were devastated. We wanted the best for your sister, and instead she couldn't start college when her friends did. We had to make up a story. We had to find a way to protect her, and then we had to send her to Mexico to live with old friends for the first six months of the pregnancy. They took her on as their au pair."

"She went along with that?"

A shadow crossed her face. "Wendy knew if she didn't carry the baby to term, she would no longer be welcome in our house."

"How Victorian. You threatened her? Forced her? What were her choices?"

"When she had sex with Sean Riley, she made her choice. And neither your father nor I could have lived with a different outcome. In the end, she agreed that having the baby and giving it up was the right thing to do. Once we helped her see that nobody would ever know, and that in years to come, she could look back at what was, yes, something of a sacrifice—"

I couldn't believe her wording. "Something? *Something* of a sacrifice?"

"We raised your sister to believe that life is sacred. How would she have felt if she'd gone through with an abortion? She would have regretted it until her dying day."

I was in a peculiar position, of course, since this time, my best interests had been in line with those of my parents. Yet I wondered if Wendy regretted my birth every bit as much as she would have regretted the alternative. Living in a foreign country, taking care of the children of acquaintances, counting down the days until labor began, and then returning with nothing to show for those months of isolation except stretch marks? I couldn't even imagine it.

"Finish the story," I said.

"We told everyone that Wendy wanted to travel. She'd taken four years of Spanish in school and was fairly proficient. So she told her friends she was going to spend a year in

Mexico, traveling with family friends and polishing her language skills."

"And people bought this?"

"Like I told you, she had lots of friends, but none I'd call close. And your sister is so good at making people believe her. By the time she embellished her story, I think her friends were sorry they weren't going with her."

"And then..." I held up my palm. "She was supposed to give me away?"

She bit her lip. I tried to remember if I'd ever seen her do that. Clearly, this part was going to be hard.

She moved into it slowly. "My plan was to go down to Mexico for the final trimester. I told everybody we were going to travel together for a few weeks, that once Wendy went off to college, she would be off to new and fabulous things without me. So I packed my suitcases and flew to Mérida, in the Yucatán, where Wendy joined me. It was remote enough we were sure she wouldn't run into anybody we knew, and they had an excellent hospital and medical care."

"And the adoption?"

"We set that up ahead of time with a Catholic agency." She gave the tiniest smile. "You were in high demand. Wendy chose your new family from half a dozen possibilities."

"Is that supposed to make me happy?"

She began to flip the cover of the yearbook back and forth, until she realized what she was doing and folded her hands. "We moved into an apartment near the hospital. We'd planned to do some light travel, but she wasn't feeling well, so we stayed put. And then, just a month after I got there, she went into labor."

"The problem baby."

"You had problems, yes, far too many problems. You were so tiny, and so terribly sick. The hospital was good, but, in my opinion, no hospital would have been good enough. Unfortunately, you were much too sick to move, so we had to stay in Mérida. You needed surgery right away. And, of course, an adoption was out of the question while we waited to see if you pulled through. After all the trauma around the pregnancy, Wendy was mentally exhausted. She was finished with her part and anxious to go back to the US. So we spoke to the dean of the college where she'd been accepted, and we were told she could attend the second semester."

"She went off to college and left you behind?"

"Your sister distanced herself. From the beginning she realized she wasn't going to keep you, and she didn't want to watch you struggle."

By now I was beginning to see. "You had already told people back in the States that you'd gone to a doctor in Mexico, found you were not only pregnant but pretty far along."

"A change of life baby, yes. And I told them the pregnancy was high risk, so when I came home with empty arms, no one would question it. It was all an excuse for staying long enough to see Wendy's real pregnancy to conclusion. If things had gone as they should have, after the birth Wendy and I would have seen you safely to your new parents and flown home together."

"Why this elaborate charade? Why not just leave me there and call once in a while to see if I made it?"

"Wendy flew back and started school, and I stayed with you. At first I told myself I had to be there to make sure you got the best care until you were well enough to meet your new family. But even when you started to improve, the couple refused to come to Mexico and see you. Of course that set me wondering how committed they were. Your father flew down whenever he could, and after a month he flew in a pediatric cardiac surgeon for your second surgery. It was touch and go, but finally, after two months, it looked like you really were going to make it."

She'd stopped, as if remembering that moment, so I nudged. "And?"

"And I just couldn't let you go, Ryan. I finally faced the truth. We could have given our friends any number of excuses why I didn't come home at the same time your sister did. Instead, right from the start, the story I'd chosen had made it possible to come back with a baby. *My* baby. From the beginning I'd left that loophole, just in case."

"Why? Did you want to wave Wendy's mistake in her face for the rest of her life?"

She covered my hand with hers, but briefly. "Ryan, it was much simpler. You see, by that time, you were mine in every way. I'd held you, fed you, talked to you for hours, sung to you. You knew my voice. You knew my touch, my smell. The nurses said you thrived whenever I was with you. Quite simply, I fell in love with you, and then your dad did, too."

"You mean my grandfather."

"No, Dale Gracey is your dad in every way that matters. And I am your mother."

I tried not to be swayed. "And the adoptive family?" I guessed the answer. "They didn't want a baby with all my problems, did they? And if they didn't want me, who else would? Was guilt a part of bringing me home? You couldn't abandon me to a system that might fail me?"

"Every day I say a prayer of thanks that the adoption fell through. I can't imagine what kind of people they must have been. But by then I wouldn't have let them have you, anyway, not even if Jesus Himself had come down to vouch for them."

I sat silently for a while. She was answering my questions, but only as I brought each one to the surface. I had guessed much of this as I had time to reflect through a long, difficult night. But now I dug out another.

"So how *did* Wendy feel about you bringing me home as your daughter?" I turned. "And be honest. I need to know."

She looked uncomfortable, but she nodded. "Not happy. Between Mexico and the United States there were a lot of legal documents to wade through, and that went on for months, so your sister had to be involved for some time."

I hadn't thought of that. "You and Dad are listed as my parents on my birth certificate."

"After an adoption, the original birth certificate is amended."

"You adopted me?"

"We wanted to be your real parents, your legal parents. Wendy was more than ready for that part of her life to be over. She didn't want reminders."

"Maybe she didn't want to share you and Dad with a sickly infant, either. She'd had you to herself for her entire life. You doted on her. You were at her beck and call."

"I can't tell you for sure. After we brought you home, Wendy mostly went her own way. Oh, she came home from college occasionally. Sometimes she held you, even played with you or fed you. She would buy you cute little gifts, but she never treated you like you were hers. And she never stayed long. For years she found other places to be, other things to do. Part of that was Seabank, more or less the scene of the crime—"

"And part was me." I wondered if knowing I was hers had just been too tough emotionally. Or was I simply an annoyance? After her marriage Wendy had waited a surprisingly length of time to have Holly and Noelle. Had the thought of another pregnancy and childbirth been such a horror? Had she only succumbed because Bryce had insisted, and she hadn't wanted to lose him?

"Did you know she might react this way?" I asked.

A mockingbird in a nearby pine began and ended a complicated aria before she turned to me. "I'm afraid we did. She tried to persuade us to give you up. She made threats. She was still very young—"

"Stop making excuses for her!"

She closed her eyes. "You have a right to be angry, but Ryan, please understand what I'm about to say. We knew bringing you home, pretending to the world you were our daughter, would create a divide in our family. We knew that some people would guess, and you might even find out the truth before you were ready. We knew Wendy would not forgive easily, but we brought you home anyway. We knew we could never forgive ourselves if we didn't. And we knew—" Her voice caught, and my mother, who never cried, suddenly had tears running down her cheeks. "We knew we would mourn your loss forever. And so, we made a choice between you and your sister."

They had chosen me. They had chosen a baby with serious health problems, not knowing whether I would need more surgery in the near future, not knowing if I would survive. And despite that, they had chosen me over the daughter they had raised for eighteen years, the daughter they had doted on, the daughter whose entire childhood had been documented, preserved and treasured in the pages of scrapbooks.

"Ryan Rose." This time she took my hand, threaded her fingers through mine, and held it tight. "I have never, not once, regretted that decision."

We sat that way, as I tried to believe her. I wanted the conversation to end on that note. But I knew it couldn't.

"I grew up in your house. And I heard stories about how perfect my sister was. I never measured up, and I knew that." I freed my hand and held it out to stop her from interrupting.

"You were never cruel, but you had less invested in me. That was clear. Maybe you were just older, weary—"

She interrupted anyway. "I was both, yes, and so was your dad, but that had nothing to do with the way we treated you."

"So what did? Because there was a difference. Don't pretend otherwise."

"Of course there was. We treated you differently because we understood how many mistakes we'd made with your sister. I realized we had to change the way we raised you."

She was no longer attempting to explain away Wendy's faults. "Well, you certainly did change."

"You don't think it was a struggle? Especially at first with your health problems? It would have been so easy to shelter you, to hover over you the way we'd hovered over Wendy and guided every step she took. We wanted to wrap you in cotton. Every time you got winded from running, or forgot to take your meds, or refused to do anything the easy way, we wanted to grab you and store you in a closet until you finally grew good sense."

I thought about John Quayle. "You would have had to wait a good long time."

Her smile was watery. "If you ever have children, you'll understand how much you want to protect them. But we realized we had to let you find your own way, the way Wendy should have been allowed to find hers. Your sister rebelled after a lifetime of being told what she should do and how she should do it. We knew we had to let you make mistakes, try this path, then that one. We had to let you fail, so ultimately you could succeed."

"Succeed? I'm the imperfect daughter, remember? Not good advertising for your parenting skills. I'm not even your real daughter. I'm an illegitimate granddaughter with an imperfect heart."

She turned and put her arms around me, pulling me close, even as I resisted. It was so odd, so un-Arlie, that I finally let her. I felt myself relax unwillingly against her. The tears on my cheeks were my own.

She stroked my hair a long time before she spoke. "Oh, sweetheart. I can't imagine how you could say something like that and believe it. Don't you realize we never, never saw you as less than who you are? We loved you as a daughter, just the way you were, right from the moment you were born. In our eyes you were and are absolutely perfect."

CHAPTER TWENTY-SEVEN

When I arrived home, Teo was parked in my driveway, car seat cranked back and Latin jazz playing on the radio. I parked on the street and tried to sneak up on him, but he still had a cop's instincts. Just as I stuck my head through the front passenger window, he opened his eyes and smiled.

"'A Deeper Shade of Soul,'" he said. "Ray Barretto. My mother heard him in concert once before I was born. She still talks about it."

"Latin jazz was a favorite at my house, too."

He brought his seat back to driving position. "Name one song."

"'The Girl from Ipanema.'"

"Name another."

"'The Girl from Ipanema Goes Walking'? 'The Girl from Ipanema Just Doesn't See'?" I turned up my hands in defeat. "My father played that song as often as he could get away with it. Now the two of you have something to talk about after he trashes his diet."

He clicked off the music and came around to join me, leaning against the side of the car with his arms folded. "That's promising. Both that you expect me to speak to your father in the future and that you're planning to *keep* speaking to him."

After the morning's confrontation, I was wrung dry. So I leaned against the car, too, and edged closer until our shoulders touched.

"I had a talk with my mother."

"And you're still calling the Graceys your mother and father, unless you're talking about the woman formerly known as your sister."

"Did you ever read *Horton Hatches the Egg*?"

"An elephant's faithful 100 percent?"

Not every man would admit a children's book had made a lasting impression. I inched closer. "I loved that story. Horton the elephant did everything required to make sure an egg hatched after an irresponsible bird abandoned it."

"I mostly remember the story because my mother called the bird a lot of bad names. Mamá is very maternal. She can also cuss like a sailor, usually in Spanish."

"I like your mother. Maybe she'll give me Spanish cursing lessons."

"Be careful what you wish for."

Now our hips were touching, too. "When the egg finally hatches, after weeks of horror for poor Horton, the creature that emerges is half elephant and half bird. The little bird-elephant and Horton return to the jungle together for a happily-ever-after."

He slung an arm around my shoulders. "Are you planning to live in the jungle with Arlie and Dale?"

"If I have to. I know who my real parents are."

"So is Wendy the bird?"

"Only if the bird was barely out of high school and forced to lay the egg when she didn't want to."

"They forced your sister to go through with the pregnancy?"

"They made it impossible for her not to. I can't support what they did on a lot of levels, but you know, Teo—" I opened my arms wide, whacking him softly in the chest. "Here I am."

He squeezed me closer. I absorbed his comforting warmth before I told him the rest. "When they decided to tell the world I was theirs, the decision opened a rift between them and my sister. They knew it would, but Mom says that by then, they also knew she and Dad would give me the best home."

I would tell him the rest later. For now, I knew exactly what I needed to do. "Tropicana is a great place to run. Want to try it with me?"

"I thought you might need to. I'm wearing my running shoes." He lifted his flesh-and-bone leg and wiggled his foot.

"You always wear your running shoes."

"I fell flat on my face a lot at the beginning. I don't let vanity get in my way."

"You know, someday if you fall, I'd like to be there to pick you up."

"And if I won't let you?"

"I'll keep asking. You can't scare me off."

He touched my cheek. "You got those dimples from your dad. You know that, don't you?"

Last night I'd texted him the archived article from the *Seabank Free Press* about Sean Riley's death, complete with a photograph of Sean in his camouflage battle uniform. "I always wondered where they came from. No one else in the family has them."

"I'm sorry he never knew you."

"Once I'm ready, I may go see his parents. I guess they're officially my grandparents. But I need to find out more about them. I don't want to be an unwelcome reminder."

"You could never be unwelcome."

That was enough sentiment to make my insides quiver again. I needed to work off the emotion coursing through my body. Teo understood. He grabbed my hand and pulled me away from the car, and in a few moments we were out on the street.

Once we hit our stride, he spoke. "How's Biz this morning?"

"Probably mad we didn't bring him. I'm sure he's already figured out you're here."

"Still limping?"

"Not that I've seen."

"I think those little girls gave him a workout. I'll check on him when we get back."

Our pace was now in sync. Somewhere between slow to medium, arms swinging gracefully—at least I hoped so. Ominous clouds were gathering forces to take over the sky. I mentally mapped a route through the streets that wouldn't take us too far from the town house, in case the heavens opened.

"I'm sorry if the girls are responsible for the strain," I said. "But Biz is helping them loosen up, so I hate to set limits. You ought to see them at the park tossing balls for him, or a Frisbee. They even roll around on the ground. They're not very good at any of it, but they sure love the activity."

"He's good for them. You're good for them."

"Wendy may not think so when she comes back and takes over."

"When…"

He was right. The word was wrong. "If."

"That's a big step. Semantics, maybe, but still."

"She's the one who nudged me to talk to Claire Durant. Do you think she hoped Claire would drop the bomb she's my biological mother?" Saying that out loud felt odd, even distasteful. But disloyal? I wasn't sure anymore.

"It's an interesting question. Does Bryce know?"

I hadn't asked my mother, and I hadn't asked if Wendy ever wanted to tell me the truth. "I have a lot of questions for later," I said, "after I've absorbed the answers I got today. But let's say she did want me to find out, or at the very least, she isn't worried that I might. What could be her reason?"

"You're exploring new territory here. Do you really want my help?"

"I have to get to the truth, whatever it is. I have to know so I can protect Holly and Noelle."

"And your parents."

I nodded. "So if Wendy wanted me to figure out she's my mother, why?"

"I think you already know."

I did have a theory, and I could see he wanted me to be the one to voice it. I watched the road more carefully than I needed to. "Because if I know she's my mother, not my sister, I may be even less likely to turn her in if I think she's guilty of murder."

"Does that seem like a real possibility to you?"

"That I'd walk away and let a murderer go free?"

"Not what I meant, and I don't think you'll know the answer to that until you're faced with the question."

I moved down a notch to the less challenging one. "If she's hoping for greater loyalty from me, maybe revelations are coming that require it."

At the end of the block we turned left, then left again, circling back to my street. I moved over to the side, off the bumpy pavement to a well-trampled path beside it. Grass and spongy soil made running here easier, and I knew that from this point to the town house, there were no real obstacles.

I felt the first drops of rain when we were still a block away. We picked up speed, but I didn't want to sprint. Teo's leg was good enough for jogging, but I wasn't sure it was up to a race. We were doing fine. Even the worst of the rain held off, until we hit a dip in the ground where previous rains had washed away soil. I jumped over it without thinking, but Teo slipped, and suddenly he was facedown on the grass.

What else could I do? I plopped down beside him, the rain falling faster. "Fancy meeting you here," I said. "You okay?"

By then he'd flipped to his back. He was breathing hard but looked fine otherwise. I did the only sensible thing. I propped my hands on each side of his head, leaned over and kissed him. Hard. He put his arms around me, and the only thought that managed to worm its way through a haze of desire was that I was glad we were off the road.

"You know," I said, when I propped myself just high enough to see his face. "When I said I wanted to pick you up, I didn't mean right away. You could have waited until we were inside."

"I stubbed my toe. That doesn't happen often."

"Too bad. The result was so much fun."

"You have raindrops in your eyelashes."

"You look a little worse for wear yourself."

He held up his hands to look at his palms. I saw they were red, but not even skinned. I leaned over and kissed one, then the other. "And now I get up, extend my arm, and even if you don't need it or me, you don't refuse either."

I did exactly that, positioned myself over him, with one foot on each side of his hips, and held out my hand. He took it reluctantly, sat up, then in one smooth motion he pulled me down on top of him again. "This is so much more fun."

I squirmed, but he wrapped his arms around me. "We have to get up sometime, Teo. This is a public place. And I saw lightning."

He slid his hands under my T-shirt and his thumbs under the bottom of my bra. He kissed me again.

I gave up being practical. This felt exactly right, even as the rain fell harder. I was consumed with memories of other moments like this. I remembered, too, where they had always led and how good our lovemaking had been, right from the beginning.

Only when the distant thunder grew louder, and my bra was in danger of being unhooked in somebody's front yard, did I finally wrench myself away, get back to my feet and hold out my hand again. This time he let me help him up.

Rain was now falling in earnest, but I couldn't stop smiling. "You didn't injure anything, did you?"

"No, but Peg's not so fond of getting wet."

I laughed at the nickname. "Peg Leg?"

"She's a ravishing beauty, my Peg. She's worth every penny I spend on her."

"Did you really slip?"

"You'll never know."

I punched him, and then I took off for home. He came, too, and we made it under the overhang just before the heavens opened and lightning split the sky.

Inside Bismarck greeted us, so happy to see Teo that he immediately forgave us. Teo checked him thoroughly and pronounced him greatly improved. Delighted, I went upstairs to wash my face and comb my hair while Teo washed in the downstairs bathroom with his sidekick in the doorway. I thought it was possible, even probable, that the fall had been staged to take my mind off the drama in my life. For a few minutes, at least, it had worked.

Mostly, the aftermath.

I came downstairs in time to find Bismarck on a great room sofa. I watched as he was told to get down by his handler, who was meaner than I was. Biz wandered off to nap on the floor by the front door. I was sure I heard him sigh.

Teo turned down my offer of lunch, so I poured water for both of us and handed him a glass. "If Peg doesn't like getting wet, does this mean you never shower? Not that I've noticed much of a smell..."

"Peg takes a break. Sometimes I use a crutch, sometimes a chair, I have grab bars. I shower as often as you do, probably more considering what I do every day."

"You handle everything well. To me it all seems a part of who you are now."

"I miss the leg, but I don't miss the life that went with it."

"How can that be true? You loved your job. You were a hotshot."

"I lived on adrenaline. If I wasn't having an adventure, even a bad one, I wasn't alive. That was part of what I had to get used to. Slowing down, letting my heart beat at a normal rate, thinking about things that didn't have to do with chasing bad guys. Not risking my life isn't as exciting, but it has its own rewards. I sleep at night. I eat regular meals. I see more of my family. The only thing more dangerous than being a K9 officer is undercover narcotics. My time was coming."

"And the life you have now?"

"I'm good at it. I make a difference for dogs and people. And I can go home and look at the stars every night and not worry that my phone will ring and I'll be called out again."

"Then you have everything most people want."

"Not everything."

I knew better than to pursue that.

We went out to the screened porch to watch the rain, and neither of us spoke until the storm began to move away.

"Do you have more trips to Against the Wind planned?" Teo asked.

Luckily, I could give him the answer he wanted. "I found what I needed and more than I wanted."

"If you want my opinion?" He waited until I nodded. "I think you'd be wise to keep Bismarck close. There's more going on here than you know. And whatever happens next could be more dangerous than just getting flattened at your front doorstep."

I'd had a lot of other things to think about since that morning, but now I went back to that scene in my imagination, visualizing everything that had happened. "The roofer? The guy I saw at the bar? What was he doing here? Was he prowling around because he knew Kim wasn't home? Maybe he wanted to break in and steal whatever he could. I think he might have tried before." I told him about the hanging screen.

"Maybe he was looking for something specific, rather than something he could pawn or sell quickly."

I had thought of that, too, and something worse. "Is it possible Wendy hired him to break in and grab something she left behind?"

Teo gave a low whistle. "You're thinking on a new level."

"The old one wasn't working."

"You've probably looked around here pretty thoroughly. Have you seen anything Wendy might need badly enough to persuade this guy to break in?"

Mentally I went through all the rooms I'd searched, and shrugged at the end of the tour. "She has good jewelry. But I can't think of anything else, unless wherever she is, she can't live without her Bloomingdale's catalogs."

"It could be the jewelry, but you could use another set of eyes. Want me to take a look?"

I flashed Sean's dimples in gratitude. "That would be terrific, and I'll look again, too."

"Why don't you start in the garage and kitchen, and I'll look out here and then in the great room. Afterward we'll trade."

I hadn't really checked the garage, which was conveniently empty of anything but yard tools and garbage cans, since I had parked on the road. I left Teo to search with the help of his nosy canine friend and opened the door. The storm was nearly gone, and the garage was bathed in a soft gray light that helped me see into every corner. I walked along the walls, noting everything, lifting a few flowerpots on a shelf and feeling behind them. A backup battery for the wireless system blinked cheerfully. The electric panel was an old friend because I'd opened it a week ago to flip a circuit breaker.

Nothing turned up in the garage, or in the half bath off the mudroom. The mudroom itself had a few empty hooks, and a narrow shelf with two baskets holding flip-flops, packs of tissues and a school library book. So far the book was the only treasure of the day.

Teo wandered in as I opened the louvered doors to the laundry area. By now the washer and dryer were old friends, too. I wasn't going to find anything here, except maybe a missing sock.

"You about done?" he asked.

"Close. Did you find anything?"

"Three quarters and a dime between the cushions on the porch."

Behind me I heard the tinkle of change hitting the counter. I scrunched farther into the narrow space beside the washer-dryer combo and looked behind it. "Nothing here." As I backed out, something snagged my hair and I set it free. Looking up I saw that the culprit was an electric box, similar, but not identical, to the one in the garage.

I edged backward into the kitchen. "Teo, is it common to

have more than one breaker box in a house? Because there's one in the garage, too. I had to flip a switch last week."

He joined me. "No, it's excessive." He reached around the appliances and swung open a smaller metal door on the front of the box. The smaller door read Voltage Conditioning System. He gave the same low whistle he'd given before, his special "this is new" whistle.

"What?" The inside of the box was different from the one in the garage, smaller, with an electric diagram on the inside of the door, and then against the larger door, two fuses, something called a voltage compensator, and more diagrams, along with the universal danger sign below them. "It looks like it's specific to something. Maybe the washer and dryer? Maybe a voltage conditioning system, whatever that is, is normal in a laundry area?"

"Not even close."

"Then what is it?"

"A wall safe."

I paged through memories of the inventory at I Spy. I'd seen a wall safe hidden behind a picture frame. Glenn might even have said hidden safes were a hot seller. But this one didn't look familiar.

"How do you know it's a safe?" I asked.

"Because it's not what it says it is. It has a door we can't get beyond and lots of camouflage. I've never seen one exactly like it, but I've heard gun owners buy them. They're big enough for a handgun. I don't suppose you can call your parents and ask if they installed it for their tenants."

"I don't suppose I have to. A gun safe? I can guarantee they didn't. Like the new medicine cabinet, either a former tenant installed it…"

"Or your sister did."

"Can we get into it?"

"If that was easy, what would be the point?" Teo moved closer and pointed to voltage compensator. "This is how you set the combination. It takes four numbers, which probably equals a thousand or more choices."

"Do you plan to stand there today and tomorrow trying all the possibilities?"

"Not much chance of that."

"Me either." I had a feeling this safe was the reason roofing guy had paid me a visit. And if that was true...

"If this is what your guy wanted, he probably knows the code," Teo said, beating me to it.

"I was just finishing that same thought."

"We could ask him for it."

If any of this was true, my sister had probably given Mr. Carrillon Roofing the code, and I couldn't think about that now. I preferred consulting Glenn, who was less likely to flatten me than roofing man. I told Teo to take five while I found my cell phone and called him. I left Teo staring up at the safe, as if he hoped the right numbers would suddenly come to him.

Glenn answered immediately, and I listened closely before I hung up and went back to the kitchen. "He says to try the usual things, but there's no easy way to break in. If I want him to come over next week, he'll take a look. No guarantees, though."

Teo stood back, and I tried variations of Wendy's birthday, the birthdays of the girls, mine, my parents. I finally stepped away. "No go."

Teo closed the doors to the laundry area. "Do you want to wait for him? It sounds like a long shot."

By next week I would have to tell my mother what was going on. Wendy might be hiding out in an ashram or dead. And the girls would be getting out of school for winter break.

Teo read my expression. "I'd bet on the roofer."

He was right, although my stomach was knotting at the thought. "I'll call Carrillon. At the very least we need to learn the guy's name."

I saw the question in his eyes. "I'm not going off half-cocked, Teo. I promise. If I have to confront this guy, I'd like you to be with me. If you're willing. Are you?"

"I'll stand by you. You stand by me."

I stroked my fingers down the side of his cheek, already just a bit rough, although he'd obviously shaved that morning. "I pick you up. You pick me up. Or better yet, we congratulate each other for not falling in the first place."

"We're always going to fall."

I touched his lips. "Then let's fall together. Deal?"

He kissed my fingertips. For the moment, it was answer enough.

CHAPTER TWENTY-EIGHT

The continuum between truth and lies was becoming more than a philosophical problem. Every day was a new tug-of-war. Truth whenever possible. Half-truths for love or safety. And finally, lies, if absolutely needed.

As a fraud investigator, I'd learned to spin believable stories with little or no basis in fact. Sometimes lying was the only way I had been able to protect our consumers. That skill had continued to serve me well on *Out in the Cold*. Now, once Teo left, I put my dubious skills to work.

Carrillon was a small company. I told the woman who answered the phone that I needed an estimate on a new roof for my waterfront estate. If you have to resort to lying, go for broke. I told her I thought I might have talked to one of their roofers, and described my attacker. Did the guy sound familiar and could I drive by and see one of Carrillon's jobs in progress?

She told me the guy was probably Jonah Greer. She gave me an address, and said the crew would be working there until late afternoon.

I texted Jonah's name to Teo. An hour later I cruised by

the address, and saw the now familiar Carrillon pickup parked in front of it. This time I called Teo and we made arrangements to meet there later, after I dropped the girls at my parents' house.

Teo had been busy, too. "I had a buddy check Greer's record. He's not a career criminal. A DUI, a bar brawl, and my friend thinks he remembers a domestic abuse complaint that was later dropped. But he's been in enough trouble that he won't want more."

I hoped he was right.

Just before four, Bismarck and I parked in front of a vacant lot at the end of the block. I'd been told to bring my canine buddy, and I appreciated his warm bulk beside me. I walked halfway up the block to join Teo, who had parked closer to the house, a Mediterranean-style two-story, with a fountain spurting half-heartedly in front.

"I got here about half an hour ago," Teo said. "Two of the crew are still working, but one of the other guys just left. A blond, not your guy."

"He's not my guy." I paused, and then went for it. "*You're* my guy."

He smiled a little, but he was still staring up at the roof.

I stared, too. "What's the plan?"

"If you recognize him, we can confront him here, or we can follow him and confront him wherever he stops."

This neighborhood was either on its way up or down. I couldn't tell. Some of the houses, like this one, were well cared for, but others were run-down and in need of more than a new roof. Still, it didn't look like a street where anybody would give us trouble.

"I say give the neighbors some excitement. Unless the second guy on the roof hangs around."

"Let's wait in my car and see."

We climbed in, and I settled back while keeping my eye on the roof. Bismarck panted over my shoulder. I hoped he wasn't drooling.

"Did you ever do stakeouts?" I asked. "Before you joined the K9 unit?"

"Nothing in the world more boring."

"Try getting little girls to take a bath and brush their teeth."

"That bad?"

"Last night Noelle lost her first baby tooth when she was brushing, so after I tucked her in, I had to get on the internet and see what the going rate is for the tooth fairy. Every day I fly blind. I know so little."

"What is the going rate?"

"What did your parents give you?"

"Fifty cents?"

"You and I were cheated. Just so you know, these days the proper amount is tied to the S&P 500."

"You're kidding."

I slapped my hand over my heart. "I'm not. The amount goes up with the health of the economy. You think I didn't do my research?"

"So what did *you* get?"

"I was born after you, and my father has more money than King Midas. But he was careful not to spoil me." I paused, but he poked my shoulder with his fist. "A dollar, okay? Two for molars, but guess what kids today are getting?"

"A Porsche and a vacation home in the mountains?"

"Four bucks. And get this. Some parents give up to twenty."

"Not my kids."

I turned to look at him, eyes wide. "You have kids?"

He grinned. "I'm going to be strict but fair."

Teo would love his kids to death, and his whole family would be involved in raising them, including a host of cousins who might not share even a smidgen of his DNA. His parents and most of his siblings lived northeast of Seabank, near Lakeland but that wouldn't stop anybody.

"You should have seen Noelle this morning when she checked under her pillow," I said. "Wendy missed the excitement. So did Bryce. They should have been the ones to play tooth fairy."

"It's possible your sister may miss a lot more."

"Like Christmas." I'd been giving the upcoming holiday more than a little thought. "I'm going to have to play Santa, too. And they both have birthdays next week. My mother's going to throw a party for them. Luckily, nobody can do that better." I had taken my eyes off the house, but now I glanced back at the roof and no one was there.

I pointed. "Showtime."

He leaned over to get a better look out my window. "There's the other guy coming around the house. Not yours."

The guy coming into view was short, unlike my assailant, with long black hair tied back in a ponytail and a scruffy goatee. I couldn't believe our luck. He was leaving, and if the other roofer really was the intruder, then we would be alone with him.

Goatee guy got into an old green sedan parked a few car lengths in front of Teo's SUV and roared away, hip-hop serenading the neighbors.

"And that leaves Jonah," I said.

"Let's meet him in front. I'll get Biz."

I stepped out, and in a moment Teo and Bismarck were on the sidewalk beside me. We walked to the driveway on the side of the house and waited. Moments later, Jonah came around from the back carrying a ladder on his shoulder. Jonah, the very same guy who had pinned me to the town house porch.

Same long nose. Same tanned scruffy cheeks. Same height and weight. He was even wearing what might be the same hoodie.

My knees suddenly felt like rubber. "Fancy meeting you here," I said loudly enough for him to hear.

He looked surprised but not worried. He hadn't yet made the connection. "You need something?" Jonah had a strong drawl, with the slow lengthening of vowels I equated with the Deep South. His gaze flicked to Bismarck who was standing at attention next to Teo.

I took a step closer, so he could see me clearly. "Do I look familiar?"

Teo moved up beside me, but he didn't try to stop me.

Jonah shrugged, the ladder rising into the air and settling down again. "I'm going home, and you're in my way."

"Kind of like you were in mine when I tried to get into my house a couple of weeks ago. You know, *Kim's* house?"

I watched as he made the connection. Then he dropped the ladder in the driveway and turned to run. With a shouted command, Teo sent Bismarck after him, stopping the dog with another command when he was only a few feet from Jonah's leg. I had to give my intruder credit for good sense. He had stopped, too. In fact I thought his feet might be sending roots right through the concrete. I wasn't even sure he was breathing.

"He's a trained K9," Teo said, as if they were having a casual conversation. "Used to work for the sheriff's office. I can put him through his paces to show you."

"Who the hell are you?" He turned slowly, glanced at me and then back at Teo. "You've got me mixed up with somebody else."

Teo gave Bismarck another command and now, snarling, the dog inched even closer.

"I could never use my dog this way if I were still a K9 officer," Teo said. "But you know, I'm not. So these days I have more latitude. You know what else? I don't think you're going to report me. Because, well, you have your reasons not to draw attention to yourself, don't you?"

I could almost see Jonah thinking. He looked at the dog, at his truck, at Teo, who smiled and nodded pleasantly. "You wouldn't get far," Teo said. "He loves a good takedown."

"What do you want?"

Teo nodded to me. "The lady wants to ask some questions."

"Just so you know," I said, "the sheriff has your description, and I would love, *love* to tell them that I found you, and who you are. So if you do run, that's the plan."

"I don't think you're going to tell anybody anything, lady. That's Kim's house, not yours. I was just looking for her. I did some handyman work, and she said she might need more."

"You were hiding in the bushes. Did she need help with the gardening?"

"What kind of work did you do for Kim?" Teo asked.

Jonah didn't respond until he glanced down at Bismarck, who looked ready to lunge. "I installed some stuff. That's all."

"Stuff like a medicine cabinet?" I asked.

He gave a short nod.

"How about a safe that doesn't look like a safe."

"No law against that, is there?"

"There is a law against breaking into one," I said.

"You think I'd need to break in? I'm the one who set the lock."

Jonah knew the combination. I wanted to dance a jig.

Teo's tone was still casual, two buddies discussing a boring football game. "So now, back to why you were prowling around. Why you assaulted this woman. Why I shouldn't tell my dog to drag you around a little."

"Kim asked me to look for something."

"In the bushes?" I asked.

"You trying to be stupid? Inside!"

"In the safe," I said. "The safe you know the combination to. But apparently you didn't or couldn't get through the town house doors. Why was that?"

He was silent, but his eyes never left Bismarck.

"I think my dog's getting tired of waiting," Teo said. "He's a little short on patience."

"I had a key," Jonah said. "Kim sent it to me. But it didn't work."

My conversations with Wendy had been so short that I'd never mentioned changing all the locks. Nor had it been important enough to tell her, not with everything else going on.

I summed up. "So you were supposed to go inside, open the safe and take something out? Why? What?"

"That's Kim's business."

"No, it's mine, unless you'd prefer the cops."

He backed up, but a snarling Bismarck followed. I could almost read the dog's thoughts—and I was sure he had them. Biz was like a little kid begging for an ice cream cone.

Jonah came to a halt, holding up his hands, although that would never have stopped Bismarck. "Nothing was against the law. She asked me to do this. It's her house! She told me to send her everything inside except the money. She told me there was cash in the safe, and I could have it all as a thank you, as long as I sent her the other stuff. When she got it, she was going to send me a little more."

Teo mimicked Jonah's voice exactly, as if he was trying it on for size. "Nothing was against the law. She asked me to do this."

As always, I was impressed at his abilities. "Kim sounds remarkably generous. All that for using a house key, opening a safe you already know the combination to and mailing her whatever you found, minus the cash. How did she know you wouldn't just keep everything else?"

"Kim knows I wouldn't do that to her."

For the first time I heard warmth in Jonah's voice. He'd nearly stumbled over "her."

"You like her, don't you?" I didn't expect an answer. "Maybe more than like."

"Where were you going to send everything?" Teo asked.

"Someplace north of here."

I was pretty sure I knew even more. "Cross City?"

He looked surprised. "So?"

Risk-Free Remailer seemed to be doing a booming business. I plowed on. "Jonah, that's your name, right? Jonah Greer? Since you never got inside, you couldn't send anything to Kim in…Cross City. What does she say about that? Is she still waiting?"

While I didn't think Jonah was the brightest star in the Milky Way, he had proved he wasn't stupid. He could see that Teo and Bismarck weren't kidding.

"I don't know," he said. And he looked like he meant it.

"How come? You haven't told her?"

"No."

"Her phone's not working, right?"

He shrugged, which meant yes.

"Hasn't she tried to call you?"

"She might have."

"What does that mean?" Teo asked.

"I got a couple of calls from a blocked number. Maybe it's her. I don't know."

"But you didn't answer?"

He almost looked sheepish, and I understood why. "You don't want to tell her you failed, do you? Nobody likes failing somebody who means something to them. Plus Kim has a temper. She wouldn't be happy. So you were hoping you could find a way to be successful after all."

"Like I would say that."

I smiled a little. "I know Kim pretty well. And I know that guys like her a lot. I think you like her. A lot. And you want her to think well of you."

He just stared at me, or almost stared. Every once in a while his gaze darted back to Bismarck.

"Did you two have a thing going?" Teo asked. "Maybe you're hoping for more? Like, I don't know, ending up together?"

"Kim's a party girl. You think I don't know that?"

I made a guess, and not a wild one. "So you were just one of the guys she slept with. There were others like, you know, Craig Leone, but you hoped for better from her."

"None of your business."

As if on cue, Bismarck growled.

This time Jonah didn't flinch. "You got nothing on me. I was doing a homeowner a favor, that's all. You go to the cops again, and I'll tell them I was just coming back around the house that day after trying to use the house key she gave me, and you startled me. That's all. I took off because you started to scream. That's it. Nothing happened."

"I'm sure Kim will back you up." I laid a finger on my cheek. "Oh, wait. She's not answering her phone. And she's going to be pretty upset you failed. She might not be the best alibi."

"I'm leaving."

"Want my dog to drag you to your truck?" Teo asked.

"Give us the combination," I said. "That's it. You give us that, and I won't tell the sheriff I found you. I won't even tell Kim you gave it to me. Although, you know what? If I were you, I really wouldn't answer calls from blocked numbers for a while. Because she's going to be pissed when she doesn't get her stuff. And when she is pissed…" I shook my head. "She is no fun at all."

He could curse, our Jonah. He could make a career out of it. When he finished I was still standing, and he was shouting. "Who are you anyway?"

"The woman who's going to call the sheriff if you don't give me that combination." I inclined my head toward Teo. "And this is the guy who just heard your story and will back me up if you try to come after me." I pulled my phone out of my pocket and waved it in his direction.

"Four numbers, and they'd better be right," Teo said.

"6-6-8-6!"

Noelle was six and Holly was eight, so it was possible these were familiar numbers Wendy could remember.

"Did you come up with that, or did she?" I asked.

"Her. And now, I'm going."

He didn't hold any of the cards, but Teo nodded and called Bismarck to his side. "Walk away nicely," he told Jonah.

A minute later the Carrillon Roofing truck peeled away from the curb and sped down the street.

I waited until it was out of sight. "Think that will be the last we see of him?"

"He knows we're going to open the safe and get whatever's inside, so his reason to break in is gone. Set your security alarm at night, but I think he's out of the picture."

Since Teo was still standing beside me, I reached for his hand. "Thank you." I squeezed it.

"Bismarck was the hero."

I stooped and rubbed behind the dog's ears. "You can live with me forever, boy. Just so you know. Don't tell Teo."

"What's next?" Teo asked.

I straightened and met his eyes. "A good cry?"

"I'm sorry."

"Mentioning the other guys Wendy slept with didn't faze him. He sure didn't try to defend her honor. Now do we know the reason Bryce wants a divorce?"

"Maybe. Although if she came back to Florida after he initiated proceedings…"

"That means she was probably cheating on him in Connecticut, too. Bryce said she had other plans for her life. Those were his words. Apparently the plans included sleeping with scuzbags."

I gave a sigh meant to cleanse my body of poisonous thoughts, but, of course, out they spewed anyway. "She was sneaking off to Against the Wind while she was living here. That's a fact now. Who was taking care of the girls when she did?"

"Hopefully somebody."

That left so much room for possibilities, I could only sigh again. "Or some*thing*. Like a medicine chest full of drugs." I thought of poor Holly, falling asleep at her desk, of the many teacher conferences Wendy had avoided, of Holly's antipathy toward her mother.

"She can't have them back," I said. "I won't let her."

Teo didn't argue. "Let's go back to your place and open the safe."

"You'll come? This isn't your mess."

"You're planning to steal my dog. I have to stay alert." He put his arm around me and squeezed. "One step at a time. If you have to, you can tell the girls' father what you've learned and let him take it from there. Will he want custody?"

I really didn't know. Bryce couldn't take care of two young children and play with nukes, too. Of course there was also the matter of his security clearance.

Teo was right. Getting too far ahead of myself served no good purpose. I started toward my car. "One step at a time."

By the time I opened the garage and drove inside, I was no more ready to open the safe than I had been. Teo parked in the driveway and followed me, closing the garage door and locking the one into the house behind him.

Without a word I walked to the kitchen and threw open the louvered doors. "I think we should do this now. I promised my mom I'd pick up the girls before dinner. She and Dad have a party. His first outside social engagement since the surgery. It's local, nothing too strenuous... I'm babbling."

"Yep, you are."

"I hate this."

"Of course you do."

He stepped aside and let me do the honors. I punched in the numbers Jonah had given us: 6-6-8-6. Part of me hoped he had made them up, although that would have meant another confrontation. As it turned out, though, Jonah had told the truth. I wondered how often that happened.

I swung open the door. A handgun swung with it, hanging from a built-in holster. I was struggling to see things as they were. At the same time, I wasn't going to tar and feather my sister unnecessarily. "Lots of homeowners keep guns," I said. "I have one in my glove compartment right now."

"What?"

I turned. "You should understand why I keep a gun better than anybody else."

"Do you know how to use it?"

"What do you think, I carry it around as a souvenir?"

"Are you a good shot?"

"Good enough." I stepped aside and motioned for him to take it. Teo took down the holster and pulled out the gun. "You don't need two, do you?"

I shook my head.

He checked to be sure the safety was on, then he examined it. "SIG Sauer, a nice little gun. Single action. Six rounds." He removed the magazine, racked the slide and ejected the cartridge. Then he held the gun up to the light and checked to be sure it was empty before he set everything on the washer. "It was fully loaded and ready to go. At least your sister kept this where your nieces couldn't get to it."

"Do you think Jonah was supposed to mail the gun with whatever else?"

"More likely he was supposed to keep the gun."

He was probably right. Wherever she was, if Wendy needed one, getting one was easy enough. With the gun no longer a threat, I reached into the safe and pulled out an envelope of cash, which, at a glance, looked to be around $200. Jonah's price tag was high. I handed it to Teo and pulled out passports, Wendy's and one for each daughter. For a moment I thought I was finished, but at the bottom, behind the ledge, I felt something smaller. Although it hadn't immediately been visible, the safe contained a flash drive.

I backed out and held it up.

Teo looked interested. "The possibilities there are enormous."

I slipped it into my pocket. "If I can't figure out how to download this, my friend Glenn can. I can overnight it to him."

"The passports may be just as interesting. Especially your sister's."

"Was she thinking about taking off somewhere with the girls? To prevent Bryce from having them?"

"Does Wendy seem like someone who would work that hard for sole custody?"

"Bryce told me her plans for the girls were negotiable."

"Check her passport stamps. Let's see where she's gone."

I'd thought of that, too. Whatever information the flash drive held would take time to discover. But the passport was in my hand.

It looked fairly new. I opened it and flipped past the first page to see Wendy's photo staring back at me. Unlike most, the photo was a good one. She looked every inch the sophisticated naval officer's wife.

I thumbed through to the final pages for a record of the countries where she had traveled. A few months ago she had been to Jamaica to visit one of Gracey Group's resorts. My mother had kept the girls for a week, and Mom had sounded wrung out afterward. As expected, I found a Jamaican stamp.

What I hadn't expected were the two right before it. Brazil. Both entry and exit stamps, on pages opposite Brazilian visas. Not only had my sister been to Brazil, she had been twice, one year apart, once for a week, another for two.

As I held the passport up for Teo to see, he watched my expression. "What are the chances Wendy's trips to Brazil had nothing to do with Vítor Calvo's death?" I asked.

"There are still an awful lot of unknowns."

He was being kind. We were no longer proceeding one step at a time. I felt as if I'd just been dropped miles into enemy territory.

I closed the passport and picked up the ones belonging to my nieces. I thumbed through and found nothing of interest. "I'll put these somewhere safe." I paused. "Somewhere Wendy and friends can't get to them if they come looking."

"What's next?"

"I have to pick up Holly and Noelle, but the next time I get Mom alone, I'll ask if she knows about the trips to Brazil."

"Why don't I come with you? We'll take the girls out to dinner. Then maybe drive around and look at the lights."

"Everything is such a mess! Why are you willing to be part of all this? Didn't I mess up your life enough the first time?"

"Apparently I'm a sucker for punishment. Or you. Can't tell which."

I couldn't look at him. "Does it matter? They seem to be inextricably linked."

He reached around me, closed the safe and pocketed the gun and ammunition. "Life was pretty dull until you came back into it."

"Teo, you told me you liked dull. You sat right here on my porch today and said that."

He put his arm around me and guided me toward the door. "You, of all people, shouldn't believe everything you hear."

CHAPTER TWENTY-NINE

One more thing I had learned about lies? They have a shelf life. You can plump them up with more of the same, smile when you utter them, insist all is well, but only for so long. At some point, lies expire.

I knew this from firsthand experience. A week had passed since Teo and I had opened the safe. I'd just spent most of the day with my parents, who had royally entertained my nieces and the little girls in their classes at a joint birthday party, and the expiration date on the lies I'd told them was about to come due.

Luckily, with some people I could tell the truth and nothing but, and I was with one of them now.

Teo pulled his SUV into my driveway, and turned off the engine. "You have two sleepy little girls here. I think you'll need some help getting them inside."

I peeked behind me and neither girl looked all that sleepy to me, but I was delighted to have an excuse to invite him in. "I'll handle them if you handle all the presents."

Both Holly and Noelle had birthdays during the week before Christmas, and a celebration had been in order. All afternoon my parents' quiet lanai had rivaled a college football game for noise. From a comfortable patio chair at poolside, I'd watched overly chlorinated water churn like waves in a tropical storm as two dozen little girls swam for balloons filled with trinkets. Teo had been kind enough to keep me company.

"Finding places for everything is going to be a challenge," I said.

"Mommy doesn't like our room to be messy." Noelle, who still believed her mother was coming home soon, sounded worried.

I waited for the inevitable, which was Holly telling Noelle to be quiet—or worse. But Holly seemed less worried these days, and while she still refused to talk about her mother, she was less apt to force silence on her sister, too.

"We'll make sure we keep everything neat." Fully awake now, both girls unbuckled their seat belts and scampered to the front door clutching some of their favorite new treasures.

"Forget what I said about sleepy. Looks like you have some night ahead of you," Teo said, stepping down from the driver's seat to join me.

"Stay. We can get them in bed after they calm down, and the rest of the evening might be ours..." I flashed my dimples and stopped just shy of wiggling my eyebrows.

"You think you'll get them in bed anytime soon?"

All right, it was doubtful. The birthday party had started with caterers flipping sliders and hot dogs on my parents' outdoor grill. After lunch and before the mermaid birthday cake, a pack of poodles wearing silly bathing suits had arrived to entertain. Finally, each of the two dozen guests had gone home with a sand pail painted with her name containing a colorful beach towel, rhinestone flip-flops and a blow-up beach ball that read "Thank you for coming to my birthday party."

Both Holly and Noelle had been too excited to be sad that their parents weren't there. My overachieving mother had known exactly how to manage their special day.

Unfortunately, she'd left tonight in my incapable hands. Now I pretended I knew all about children. "I'm going to wrestle them into pajamas, and they'll go right to sleep." I linked my arm with his. "But really, I'll understand if you want to leave." I grasped his arm tighter, so moving would be a challenge. "You already went above and beyond the call of duty."

"I might have enjoyed a moment or two."

He had loved the whole thing, laughing and dodging water balloons, even pretending to be a pirate when one brave little girl asked about his leg. He was a natural, an experienced uncle, and sometimes, at heart, a kid himself.

I pulled out all the stops. "You might enjoy a moment or two of the upcoming evening, too. Besides, there's a dog inside who's dying to see you."

"Maybe I'll come in for a little while."

Successful, I disentangled myself and went to open the back of the car. "I'll get an armload."

Weighed down like a pack mule with board games, a fancy spa set, a fairy garden and two American Girl paperbacks, I made it to the front door, noting the predictable demise of TropiSanta, once again a sad vinyl puddle. "Key's in my front pocket," I told Holly.

She fished it out and eventually all of us, plus the loot, made it inside. The girls divided the spoils and started hauling them upstairs. I turned on schmaltzy Christmas carols and flipped a switch in the great room so the tree lights sparkled.

After another trip to plug in the outdoors lights, I noted Teo conferring with Holly at the head of the stairs. "Coffee or something stronger?" I asked.

"How about both?"

"Done." At the well-stocked liquor shelf, I pulled out Irish whiskey. Then I selected dark roast pods and started the coffee maker.

Since the afternoon we'd confronted Jonah Greer, Teo and I hadn't seen much of each other, although he'd made it clear that when I needed him, he'd be available. He'd been letting me know that this was my life, and he wasn't going to interfere. And he was letting me come to terms with Wendy's life in my own way.

Between the girls and the holidays, I'd spent whatever hours were left researching *Out in the Cold*'s next podcast. Sophie and I had taken several trips north to interview principals involved in the new case. We'd also done on-site records searches, and snapped hundreds of photos of buildings and settings relevant to the story. We were on our way, but, of course, not fast enough.

And every evening after the girls were in bed, I'd delved deeper and deeper into the dark web. Sophie was searching for Milton Kearns, too, but so far, both of us had come up empty-handed.

Disappearing was an art form practiced by criminals, the battered and stalked, and those poor souls who wore aluminum-foil hats and stuffed cotton under their doorways. I Spy made a killing selling how-to manuals. The lighter reads advised staying off social media and investing in a shredder. The more serious explained how to misdirect investigators, how to find a job that paid under the table, and how to buy everything under the guise of a legal but otherwise spineless corporation.

Wendy and Milton Kearns seemed well informed. But from prior investigations I knew there was hope. The longer any-who might not share even a smidgen of his DNA. His parents and most of his siblings lived northeast of Seabank, near Lakeland but that wouldn't stop anybody.

"You should have seen Noelle this morning when she checked under her pillow," I said. "Wendy missed the excitement. So did Bryce. They should have been the ones to play tooth fairy."

"It's possible your sister may miss a lot more."

"Like Christmas." I'd been giving the upcoming holiday more than a little thought. "I'm going to have to play Santa, too. And they both have birthdays next week. My mother's going to throw a party for them. Luckily, nobody can do that better." I had taken my eyes off the house, but now I glanced back at the roof and no one was there.

I pointed. "Showtime."

He leaned over to get a better look out my window. "There's the other guy coming around the house. Not yours."

The guy coming into view was short, unlike my assailant, with long black hair tied back in a ponytail and a scruffy goatee. I couldn't believe our luck. He was leaving, and if the other roofer really was the intruder, then we would be alone with him.

Goatee guy got into an old green sedan parked a few car lengths in front of Teo's SUV and roared away, hip-hop serenading the neighbors.

"And that leaves Jonah," I said.

"Let's meet him in front. I'll get Biz."

I stepped out, and in a moment Teo and Bismarck were on the sidewalk beside me. We walked to the driveway on the side of the house and waited. Moments later, Jonah came around from the back carrying a ladder on his shoulder. Jonah, the very same guy who had pinned me to the town house porch.

Same long nose. Same tanned scruffy cheeks. Same height and weight. He was even wearing what might be the same hoodie.

My knees suddenly felt like rubber. "Fancy meeting you here," I said loudly enough for him to hear.

He looked surprised but not worried. He hadn't yet made the connection. "You need something?" Jonah had a strong drawl, with the slow lengthening of vowels I equated with the Deep South. His gaze flicked to Bismarck who was standing at attention next to Teo.

I took a step closer, so he could see me clearly. "Do I look familiar?"

Teo moved up beside me, but he didn't try to stop me.

Jonah shrugged, the ladder rising into the air and settling down again. "I'm going home, and you're in my way."

"Kind of like you were in mine when I tried to get into my house a couple of weeks ago. You know, *Kim's* house?"

I watched as he made the connection. Then he dropped the ladder in the driveway and turned to run. With a shouted command, Teo sent Bismarck after him, stopping the dog with another command when he was only a few feet from Jonah's leg. I had to give my intruder credit for good sense. He had stopped, too. In fact I thought his feet might be sending roots right through the concrete. I wasn't even sure he was breathing.

"He's a trained K9," Teo said, as if they were having a casual conversation. "Used to work for the sheriff's office. I can put him through his paces to show you."

"Who the hell are you?" He turned slowly, glanced at me and then back at Teo. "You've got me mixed up with somebody else."

Teo gave Bismarck another command and now, snarling, the dog inched even closer.

"I could never use my dog this way if I were still a K9 of-body tried to stay under the radar, the better the chance they would slip up.

Unfortunately, the flash drive I'd found in the safe was still with Glenn, who was trying to decrypt files that had been encrypted by a master. So far he hadn't been successful, but in his eyes, that just made the challenge more fun.

I *had* discovered new information about Wendy from my mother, although more was still an arm's length away. Without explaining about the passports, I'd told Mom I had an old appointment book of Wendy's and wondered about certain dates. She had answers. During the first stretch when my sister had been in Brazil, she had told my parents she was in Texas at a seminar. In fact Mom remembered flying to Connecticut to take care of the girls, and Wendy had come home looking puffy and exhausted.

Bryce was home on leave during the longer trip. He'd flown the girls to California to meet distant relatives, and supposedly Wendy had gone off to visit college friends and do a little traveling on her own. Mom remembered because she had sounded so much happier, so rejuvenated, by the time she returned.

My mother had the memory of an elephant. But "Brazil" hadn't been uttered. My parents didn't know that Wendy had gone to Rio for procedures, quite possibly under the skilled hands of Dr. Vítor Calvo.

I didn't want to think about all the parts of my sister's body Vítor Calvo had monkeyed with.

Wendy hadn't called again.

By now the second cup was filling with coffee, so I ran upstairs to see what Teo and the girls were doing.

I found my nieces building a tent with their top sheets and towels. Teo and Bismarck were in the center.

I watched from the doorway as the giggling grew louder and the thumping of Bismarck's tail did, too.

"Aunt Ryan! Can you help me tie these?" Holly held up the ends of two sheets.

Three weeks ago Holly wouldn't have asked me for a glass of water after a week in the desert. "What's the problem?"

"They keep slipping!"

"I'll hold, you tie."

She favored me with a big smile, and I was reminded how much she looked like her father—the father who was aware that something was happening that I wasn't sharing with him.

I lifted both sheets by the hem and winked at Teo, who was reclining against the wall like a desert sheikh.

"Don't get too comfortable," I warned. "You still have to get out when they're done."

He draped an arm over his canine buddy and closed his eyes, the picture of bliss.

I wondered if Bryce ever horsed around with his daughters. When I moved in, the girls had been prissy and subdued, as if nobody ever dared to tickle them or mess up their hair. But since then, they had both blossomed so much. I wanted to believe those seeds had been planted by their father.

Bryce had sent me a handful of carefully veiled emails. I was sure email from a nuclear sub wasn't private, thus the need for skillfully worded platitudes and questions, but his meaning was clear. I had sided with my sister in the divorce, and I was shielding Wendy from him as well as his lawyer.

If only. As bad as that sounded, the real scenario was so much worse.

Downstairs I finished the coffee, adding cream and a slug of the Irish to both mugs. I was working on hot chocolate for the girls when Teo and Bismarck came down, too.

I held out coffee for Teo and a dog biscuit for his sidekick. "I was preparing to pay ransom."

"When those girls start to crash, they're going to crash hard."

"At least they won't need baths tonight. Do you think if I yell upstairs and tell them to get into their pajamas, they'll hop right to it?"

"If that's hot chocolate, you can bribe them."

I went to the foot of the stairs and yelled his suggestion upstairs. When nobody argued—or responded—I figured they were congratulating themselves for having such an outstanding aunt.

Back in the kitchen I offered Teo another pass on the evening's festivities.

"What do I get if I stay?" he asked.

My heart beat a little faster. "After you help me pump up TropiSanta, we can lie on the floor of the great room and watch the Christmas tree lights."

"Yeah, I saw the lights. It's a good thing I'm not prone to seizures."

"Those are the very same lights I loved as a child. My mother carefully stored them for me, along with every Popsicle stick ornament I ever made. And from this day forward, they'll be on every Christmas tree I erect, until my mother either moves to Alaska or forgets how much I loved them when I was four."

"Too bad that woman never paid attention to what you loved or needed, isn't it?"

I toasted him with my cup. All the little things I'd discounted, things as simple as saving Christmas lights, were beacons I couldn't ignore. Arlie Gracey had been the mother I needed, no more or less.

"Has she told your father that you know who gave birth to you?" he asked.

I liked the way he'd phrased it. "At this point I don't think she wants to mention Wendy to Dad. If it weren't for his health and the holidays, he'd be rallying flocks of private investigators."

"After watching your mother orchestrate the party, I'm more surprised that *she* hasn't hired a dozen professionals."

"I asked her to trust me a little longer."

"And she's buying it?"

"I don't think she'll be patient forever."

"And the girls' father?" He finished with the most obvious question. "Does Bryce really care what's going on here?"

I'd gone over that in my head, with no clear result. "Bryce is infatuated with his job. What kind of man disappears for months at a time and leaves his family behind? Can I blame Wendy for not wanting to play second fiddle to a nuclear sub for the rest of her life?"

"To answer the first question, a man or woman in the military disappears for months. It's part of the job. Nobody lies about that when you enlist." Between high school and college, Teo had done a stint in the army as an MP, so he knew what he was talking about.

"That may be true, and Wendy knew Bryce's life plan when she married him. But maybe reality was harder than she thought."

"Has she ever complained that he's away too much of the time?"

"When you're with my sister, she makes you think her world is absolutely perfect."

"A high pedestal to fall from."

I was building a case against Bryce in my head, although I wasn't quite sure why. Now I tried to be fair. "I'm assuming he misses the girls. I've sent reassuring emails with photos. But from his responses, photos and reassurances aren't cutting it."

"Have you considered he might make a surprise arrival?"

"Some part of me hopes he will. And then once we're face-to-face, I can tell him the truth."

"You're ready to do that?"

"How much longer can I breathe platitudes and reassurance? The only reasons he doesn't know the whole Wendy story are distance and a job that requires superb concentration. But nobody stays underwater indefinitely."

"I don't know about that. Some of those little girls in the pool today had me worried."

I was glad we were moving to something more positive. The party was living proof that good things could still happen in the midst of turmoil.

I heard tramping on the stairs, and in a moment two little girls in mismatched pajamas were in the kitchen, too.

Mismatched was new and different. Holly and Noelle had been carefully schooled to look pretty and sweet, even when they were asleep. Today both girls were taunting the fashion police.

"Purple polka dots and orange stripes, Holly Jolly! Wow!"

"It's our birthday. We should be able to wear anything we want," Holly said, challenge in her eyes.

"I couldn't agree more."

"Mine match. They both have puppies, see?" Noelle lifted the hem of her cocker spaniel shirt as evidence.

Her pants sported circus lions complete with lion tamer, but this wasn't the moment for a lecture on animal families. I lifted her to a stool and set hot chocolate in front of her. Hours had passed since the cake, so I was hoping tummies weren't going to rebel.

When they were finished, I took Noelle upstairs to brush her teeth, while Teo and Holly went outside to pump up TropiSanta, who would be flat by morning. After Noelle put away her toothbrush, I perched on her bed, and she surprised me by plopping into my lap. I wrapped my arms around her. "So what do you think, Mermaid?"

"Holly said today was her party because she was born first."

"Holly can be so silly."

"Are you sure it was my party, too?"

"Your friends were there, right? Your name was on the birthday cake. Half the presents were yours."

She relaxed and grinned, her missing tooth a reminder she was growing fast. "I never had a birthday party like that before."

Not many children ever would, because Arlie Gracey couldn't be cloned. But the girls were usually silent about what had gone on in their home before Wendy disappeared, so I probed a bit. "What kind of birthday parties did you have?"

"I don't think I had one. Maybe once when Daddy was home."

That was more than I usually learned, but then Holly, the appointed secret keeper, wasn't in earshot. "What was it like, do you remember?"

"Mommy threw out my presents. She said they were cheap. I told her they were still mine, and she got madder."

"Well..." I hugged her harder. "Some people get cranky at parties. But not you, right? And we're going to keep every single present you got today. I promise."

Noelle hugged me back, then she leaped off my lap and went to sort through her treasure again, which was piled haphazardly on the floor at the end of her bed. I went downstairs to see if niece number two had finished outside.

By the time TropiSanta was merry again, I calculated we had maybe ten minutes before the girls disintegrated. I got Holly upstairs, teeth brushed, and finally, both of them into bed. Teo joined us for the tuck-in.

As he stood in the doorway and Bismarck reclined at my feet, I said the usual prayer and asked the girls what they were thankful for. The party came out on top, but Noelle said she was thankful for me, as well.

I cleared my throat. Twice. "And I am very, very grateful I have two silly little nieces."

They asked Teo for a story, and he told them the true story of a dog who tracked a little girl who was lost in the woods.

Twenty questions later, the girls were finally ready to close their eyes. The story was the perfect happy ending for a long, exciting day. I kissed them both and, at their request, so did Teo. Then I turned off the light and we tiptoed downstairs.

Bismarck elected to keep the girls company. He was snoring by the time we left the bedroom.

In the great room I pulled Teo down next to me on the sofa and told him what Noelle had said about Wendy.

To avoid the blinking splendor of my heirloom lights, he leaned his head back and closed his eyes. "You've got your hands full there."

"Noelle's no trouble."

"Hands full trying to keep your sister out of trouble with her daughters."

"It doesn't come up often," I said. "They don't talk about her, at least not to me. There's a pact of some sort, like they know they'll get in trouble if they do, or something bad will happen."

"You're going to miss them once you're out of the picture."

I turned on my side so I could see him better. His skin was alternately red and green, but I could ignore that. "I'm not planning to be out of the picture. Never again. If they aren't with me, I'm still going to make sure they're okay. Nobody's going to get between me and them."

"So they're kind of a package deal for the lucky guy who gets you?"

"I have no idea what's going to happen with my sister. She might never come back. Bryce might stay submerged and ask me to raise them on my own."

He didn't frown, not exactly, but he opened his eyes. "Is that what you want?"

"It's too early. It's hypothetical."

"You seem more and more sure your sister's not a good mother."

The largest part of me was still waiting for a miracle. I wanted to learn that every conclusion I'd reached about Wendy was wrong, but even the most optimistic part of me knew better.

"You look at home here," he said, when I didn't answer. "You never used to."

"Here, in the town house? Here, in Seabank with my parents? Here riding herd on two little girls?"

"The journalist with a million questions."

I ticked off my answers on my fingers. "I couldn't wait to leave Seabank after high school. I couldn't wait to leave Florida, for that matter. Then when I came back, after... everything that happened, I thought I'd never want to be here again. Now?" I paused. "It's all good. Who'd have thought?" I wiggled my fingers in the air.

"I am assuming, and it's only an assumption, that some small part of that has to do with..."

I waited for him to say "me."

"That talk with your mom," he finished.

I was disappointed. "The talk, yes."

"You'll make it through the holidays?"

"Things are a mess, true. It's doubtful either of the girls' parents will surface, but Christmas can be about the rest of us. I'm going to do my darnedest to make it a good one." I paused. "I wish Christmas was going to be about you, too. But I know you have to spend time with your own family."

"I'm heading north tomorrow, coming back New Year's Eve."

"We'll miss you."

"I'm sorry I'll miss the holidays with the girls." He smiled just a little. "And maybe you."

He hadn't said as much, but Christmas was in the air, and I was more hopeful that somehow we were finding a path back to each other. "I wish I could be your Christmas present."

"Better than a pony."

I was encouraged. "Better than a trip to Disney World? Universal Studios?"

"You're setting the bar a little high." He threaded his fingers through my hair and pulled me closer. I nestled against him, and I wasn't sure whose lips found whose. I sighed with pure pleasure.

"I need a drink of water."

Laughter rumbled through Teo's chest. I pulled away and turned to see Noelle, head cocked, watching us.

"You have a water bottle beside your bed," I told her.

"You didn't fill it."

"Did you ask Holly to help you?"

"Holly's asleep."

Since I knew her sister's sleeping habits—or lack of them—I doubted it, but I got to my feet. "Okay, I'll come up and do it."

"Right now?"

I sighed. "Immediately."

"You were kissing."

Teo laughed again. "We sure were."

"Was I supposed to see?"

"You were supposed to be in bed asleep."

"I'm not sleepy."

"Of course you are." I held out my hand. "Up we go."

Five minutes later I was downstairs again. A slender package wrapped in silver paper and gold ribbon had taken my place on the sofa.

"What's this?" I lifted it and sat down where it had been. "Is this my Christmas present? Because yours is under the tree. Want me to get it?"

"Just put this with the ones I already stuck there for the girls. You can open it Christmas Day."

"What fun is that?"

He looked uncomfortable, and I laughed. "You're afraid I won't like whatever this is, aren't you?"

"My sister Luella helped me pick it out."

"So Luella knows that you and I are, you know, hanging out again?"

"She does now."

I held up the box and shook it. "I won't need a hazmat suit?"

"My family doesn't blame you for anything."

"So if I see them again, they won't all make the sign of the cross at the exact same moment?"

"Behave, and just open the present, okay?"

I slipped my finger under the ribbon and pulled it to one side, and then I carefully pulled the tape from the paper.

"You're short on wrapping paper? You're going to use that for something else?"

I laughed and took my time folding the paper, setting it beside me to expose a shiny white box. This was too delicious to rush. I slipped my fingers under the top of the lid.

"Aunt Ryan, Bismarck's snoring!"

Teo nudged me with his elbow. "Don't look now, but there's a little girl standing across the room. And not the one who was here a few minutes ago."

I set the box on the carefully folded wrapping paper. "What would you like me to do about it, Holly?"

"Can I sleep in your bed?"

"Yeah, Aunt Ryan. You didn't have other plans for your bed, did you?" Teo asked, nudging me again.

Considering how unlikely it had been that Holly would fall asleep quickly, sadly I did not.

"Go ahead," I told her. "But when you wake up tomorrow morning, don't be surprised to find you're back in your own."

"Will you tuck me in? Can I sleep with your lamp on?" I got up and handled the questions one at a time until we were upstairs, and she was tucked in, a night-light plugged in beside the door, and soft music playing to speed her into Dreamland.

Downstairs I went through the moving-gifts-and-sitting-down ritual. "How do married people manage to conceive more than one child?"

"Open it fast before Noelle shows up again."

"You are terrified I won't like whatever it is, aren't you?"

"Just open it."

I put the box on my lap and slowly lifted the top. A silver oval on a fine gold chain lay on top of white cotton. Inside the oval, which was open in the middle, stood a tiny three-dimensional German shepherd, modeled in gold. The dog was familiar.

I lifted the necklace and held it to my chest. "It's so beautiful. He looks like Bismarck."

"Close as I could get. You like it?"

"No, I love it." I wasn't a fan of glittery jewelry, but this necklace was classic, simple enough that I could wear it anywhere, anytime. And when I wore it, I would always be reminded of the dog who had saved my life and nearly lost his own.

And, of course, the man.

"Will you help me?" I held it out and turned so he could put the chain around my neck and clasp it. I turned back to him. "How does it look?"

"You look beautiful."

I kissed him, wrapping my arms around his shoulders. "You haven't seen my gift yet."

He kissed me again, until I was pressing into the cushions behind me. "This isn't it?"

"You don't even have to open mine. It's not actually in the box under the tree, anyway. The real thing will be delivered after the holidays."

"I'm all ears."

I nibbled on his earlobe, to prove his point. "It's a sofa."

"I have a sofa."

"For Bismarck."

"You bought Bismarck a sofa?"

"It's especially made for dogs. It's so comfortable I'd sleep on it, if I was, you know, a dog. It'll be perfect at the foot of your bed, so when I'm at your house, in bed with you, Bismarck will have another place to sleep."

His dark eyes danced. "You are so sure of yourself."

"You know I'm just waiting until you're ready, Teo, and the girls are somewhere else. Because all systems are go here."

"Aunt Ryan!"

"Coming!"

He laughed, and then he kissed me before he stood to leave. *"Lo bueno se hace esperar."*

"That's not fair. My Spanish is worse than rusty."

"Next year I'll give you lessons instead of jewelry." He smiled. "Good things come to those who wait."

As I walked him to the door and wished him a final Merry Christmas, I didn't have to tell him I was counting on it.

CHAPTER THIRTY

I kept Holly and Noelle busy over the holidays. We spent Christmas Day with my parents, and the next walking nature trails with the new backpacks and binoculars my father had given them. Two days later I treated them to Legoland, their big gift from me. The park was colorful and cheerful, my main criteria, plus none of the roller coasters were scary. We ate kid food, shopped for souvenirs and lapped up the entertainment at the official Legoland hotel.

By the time they were back in school, I had a new appreciation for stay-at-home moms.

"Eventually you forget what it's like to sit on the toilet without somebody banging on the door," Sophie told me, after I'd regaled her with anecdotes. "I still lock mine, just in case."

For the first time since the beginning of the holidays, we were observing our regularly scheduled morning phone call. We'd tried to catch a few moments when my nieces were occupied elsewhere, but Sophie had been busy, too. She and Ike had taken a quick Caribbean cruise over the holidays, which

I'd just relived with her. My Sophie had stars in her eyes—or more accurately her voice.

"I woke up one morning and there were two little girls and a German shepherd in bed with me," I said. "I was an inch from going over the side."

"It's a good day when you don't."

The social portion of the call was finished. Both of us had work ahead.

"I'm at a dead end with Wendy," I said. "Bryce called Holly on Christmas Day, and then after he spoke to Noelle, he asked her to put my mother on the line. My *mother*. When she hung up, Mom was livid. I've avoided her ever since. If this goes on, I'll have to change my phone number."

"Did he tell her about the divorce?"

"Let's just say she wasn't coherent afterward. At the least he must have told her I'm not being straight with him. She said he wants the girls to move back in with her and Dad."

"What did you say to that?"

"I told her the girls are happy with me, and we aren't going to upset them with another move. Luckily, it was late in the day, so we left, and I haven't talked to her since."

"Don't you think it's time to tell her at least some of what's happening? And him?"

"It's not the kind of thing you blurt over the phone to a nuclear submarine commander, is it? Especially if his calls are monitored."

"Are they?"

"I don't know that they *aren't*."

I wasn't looking forward to sitting down with Mom and telling her that her older daughter was involved in a murder, but Sophie was right. I hoped I wouldn't have to tell her everything else I'd learned, at least not yet. I wanted to keep my conversation with Jonah private, along with my suspicion that Wendy had partied with way too many male admirers at a biker bar.

Most especially I hoped I never had to tell her about the scary assortment of drugs in my sister's medicine chest.

"Are you going to talk to her today?" Sophie asked.

I was still scurrying for a reason not to. "Not only is she going to be upset, she'll want to call the authorities. And who can blame her? I'm stuck, and I don't know what to do next."

"She might be able to get information about Kearns's job at the Autumn Mountain Club, since that's where he probably met Wendy."

I'd done enough research to know that Gracey Group still owned the club, but I hadn't wanted to call and give my name, in case my call got back to someone in our main office or worse, my father. Instead I'd tried to get information by calling and pretending I was an adoptee who had put my birth information on an adoption registry. Wasn't it simply amazing that Milton Kearns had done the same, and all his information matched mine? Now that I was so close to finding my father, could they help me locate him?

The office manager had insisted that all employee information past and present was confidential. Even though I gave Meryl Streep a run for her money, I still hung up a failure.

In turn Sophie had tried to locate the employee who Wendy claimed had led her to the Golden Aspen Resort and Spa, but with so little information, she'd been unsuccessful, too. The staff had been in and out on holiday vacations, and between the murder and rumors the resort might close its doors, half were already gone or scrambling for new jobs.

"Anything else?" I asked.

She told me she planned to follow up on a couple of leads about places Kearns might have worked. "But even if they pan out," she warned, "the leads aren't recent enough to be helpful, unless they point me somewhere else."

At least that was something. "Where are these places?"

"One's a bar in Alabama. The other's in Canada."

"Would Canada be a good place to hide out?"

"It's not where I would go."

"And where would you go?"

"In January? Somewhere with sunshine and beaches."

We hung up, agreed that we should both keep searching.

My plan for the day was to hunt down Ella and insist she speak to me one more time. Sophie felt there was more she could tell me if she just would. I wasn't sure that anything my sister had done at Gracey Group was relevant to her disappearance, but as always, I wasn't sure it wasn't.

I hadn't paid close enough attention when my mother had mentioned the name of the dentist whom Ella worked for, but I did remember he was an orthodontist because my teeth had ached in tribute. Now I checked online and recognized Borgman's name at the head of the directory.

I called the office and Ella answered. Her greeting, a little too high, a little too precise, was easy to identify. I cleared my throat, mumbled "wrong number," and hung up. Then I changed into something more presentable than the leggings and T-shirt that had gotten me this far, and hopped in my Civic.

Dr. Borgman's office wasn't far from the grocery store where I'd learned Ella was no longer working for my father. Luckily, Borgman had not been my orthodontist, so I didn't have to resort to yoga breathing.

Inside, Ella was sitting in the front behind a counter, and she rose to greet me, until she realized who I was.

"Why are you here?" she said.

"I need to talk to you."

She leaned over the counter and lowered her voice. "I don't need to talk to you."

"I'm sure you're busy. I'll wait." I glanced behind me where an older man was sitting in an armchair. "You have *Women's Health*. I forgot to renew my subscription. And *InStyle*. I really am in luck. I could hang out here all day."

"Don't plan on it."

"I could really use your help." I leaned closer, too. "And for the record, I know my sister manipulated my father to fire you." I didn't really know, not unequivocally, but it was more than a stab in the dark.

"Will this get you off my back for good?"

"I certainly hope so."

She considered. "The office is closed from one to three. I'll meet you out front at one."

Other than snatching her by her pretty lavender scarf and hauling her over the counter, I had no options. "Please be there, Ella. I really need your help."

She narrowed her eyes. My work was done.

The closest coffee shop, Eyes Wide Open, was featuring buy-one-get-one-free lattes. I took my laptop inside, and by the time I'd roughed out an introduction for the first episode of *Out of the Cold*'s interim podcast, I was tuned for takeoff. An email from Glenn came in just as I was shutting down my computer. The subject line read: "Secure connection needed."

I hoped he had finally accessed the files on Wendy's flash drive. The subject line didn't scare me. Glenn had used the same one on an email of three moose looking out the windows of a car with a human body strapped to the top. Glenn was a member of both the National Rifle Association and People for the Ethical Treatment of Animals. Go figure.

Ten minutes before one I went back to Borgman's office and found an empty space on the curb in front. I parked and leaned against my car, watching to be sure Ella didn't sneak away. To her credit, she came out precisely on the hour, and headed straight for me.

"I have until two."

"May I treat you to lunch? It's the least I can do for strong-arming you."

She started down the sidewalk, past palm trees and street lamps. "You haven't changed all that much. You used to smile at me like that when you wanted a piece of candy."

"Think of lunch as payment for all the Tootsie Pops."

"And you were always bullheaded." She paused. "But at least you were clear about it. You didn't simper, and you didn't smile, and you didn't lie."

I knew who she was describing. I took a big chance. "When you talked about my special relationship with Wendy, I thought you just meant that she was my sister."

"Oh?"

"Now I know the truth. When did you figure it out?"

"Your mother and father's story was transparent to anybody who looked closely. But I had to give Arlie credit for coming back with you. I'm sure that sister of yours wasn't happy about it."

"Wendy spent so little time with us when I was growing up, she never seemed remotely like my mother."

"I used to watch her whenever she had to be with you. When you were both at Christmas parties and other social occasions, she paid attention to you if other people were watching. She liked to show you off. Then, once you were both out of the spotlight, she ignored you."

Ella's characterization was so cruel, I didn't know what to say. But a kaleidoscope of images flashed through my mind, as if they'd been stored there, waiting for the right moment.

She was right. Even my beloved alligator night-light? Bryce

had been in the doorway watching when Wendy presented it to me. He'd been looking on, probably thinking what a perfect wife and mother she would make.

"Oh, God." I shook my head.

"You don't think it's true?"

"No, I think it *is* true."

She stopped walking, and for the first time, she actually looked sympathetic. "Your sister is very good at projecting whatever image will get her what she wants, Ryan. Do you know the worst? For a while, after things started going crazy at work, I actually wanted to be wrong. I wanted to be the one at fault. I cared too much about your parents to want them to suffer. But eventually they will. Because Wendy is good at pretending, but not good enough. She's going to be brought down sooner than later. And they'll have to cope."

We were standing in front of a small café advertising fresh mozzarella and other assorted Italian delights. "Here?" I asked.

We went inside and ordered at the counter, taking drinks to a table in the back until our sandwiches were ready. My stomach was in such turmoil I knew I would have to take mine home.

"Was that what you wanted to tell me? That you know Wendy's your mother?" Ella unwrapped her straw and thrust it with such force into her glass that I felt sorry for the ice cubes.

"I told you so you would know I've been in the dark," I said. "And I still am. I need your help."

"You should talk to your sister."

"I'm not sure she'd give me the straight scoop. And she's still out of town."

I could almost see Ella calculating how long my sister could stay away and still be valuable to Gracey Group. I wondered if I should offer her a job on the podcast. Between Ella and Sophie, nobody would ever be safe.

"So?" she asked.

"Did you learn something about Wendy that you didn't share with my father? Anything so serious she would manipulate events to have you fired?"

"Carrying details back to your dad won't change anything. My termination was official, and my attorney approved all the paperwork."

I knew I had to tell her some part of the truth or she wouldn't help. "I need to know what Wendy was up to back then, because she's disappeared."

The server brought our sandwiches, and I watched as Ella played with her sub, looking between layers, moving the shredded lettuce to cover the surface, adding vinegar and oil from the bottles on our table. Finally she looked up.

"She was having sex with our clients, the men she was supposed to be working with to organize tours and visits to the resorts. And if you say I told you, I will deny it."

I contemplated my sandwich and finally forced down a potato chip.

"Okay," I said. "And you know this...how?"

"A personal email to Wendy was routed to me by mistake. The details were quite...revealing. A second instance was reported to me by the manager of our resort in Barbados. Apparently your sister was so indiscreet, he was getting complaints from other guests. He was concerned about Gracey Group's reputation."

"You didn't tell my father? You had proof. Why not?"

"Because I was a fool. I went to Wendy instead. I hadn't come to terms with who she really was, and I told her she needed to be careful, that some of the things she was doing had been misconstrued."

"You thought the email was, what, a lie?"

"The man who had emailed was somebody your father really didn't want to do business with. I thought he might be trying to frame your sister."

"And you thought the manager in Barbados had misinterpreted behavior?"

"No. He was a trusted employee, and by then I was suspicious. I thought about it over a long weekend, and then I spoke to Wendy. If anything was going on, it was important for her to know that she was being watched. By the manager, by me. I was such an idiot. I'd worked with your father so long that I never considered he wouldn't listen if I was forced to tell him what I knew."

In my experience honest people often couldn't comprehend the dishonest kind. They believed if they just made things clear, right would triumph. Until recently, I'd been one of them, at least as far as my own family was concerned.

Ella was waiting for my response. I plowed through it. "I'm guessing Wendy quietly went behind your back and framed you so that my father would never believe anything you said about her."

"She proved she wasn't just deceitful, she was experienced. Of course the email I'd saved to protect myself disappeared from my computer and our server. The flash drive I'd backed it up to went missing, and the manager in Barbados was fired for stealing cash from a hotel guest."

It was hard to believe my sister's reach had extended as far as Barbados. But all of this was hard to believe, and I couldn't discount any of it.

"Did you try to tell my father what was going on?"

"I did try, but by then it was clear he wasn't going to believe a word I said."

Dad had rejected Ella's story, but now I wondered if it would help him accept the truth, if or when things with Wendy finally came to a head.

"I'm sorry. I keep saying that, but I am." I touched her hand, which was still hovering over her sandwich. "You didn't deserve any of this."

"If all this comes out in the open, and your father realizes he fired the most loyal employee he'll ever have? If somehow that little miracle occurs?" She looked up. "I don't want my job back. I don't want anything from any Gracey, except to be left alone."

"I won't bother you again. You gave me more than I had a right to know."

"I don't think you're anything like Wendy, if that's any comfort." Ella picked up her sandwich and took her first bite.

Maybe it was a comfort, but not much of one. I stood, left my sandwich on the table hoping she would take it home for dinner, and walked out of the café.

At home after lunch with Ella, Glenn's email was no surprise. He asked if I wanted him to send the two dozen or so photos he'd retrieved from the flash drive, while also implying it would be a bad idea to do it over the internet. I was in no mood to wait, so I took my chances. When I had finished clicking through them, I knew that Ella had only discovered the tip of the iceberg.

I also understood why Wendy had hired Jonah to empty the safe. Six men, probably all Gracey Group investors of one kind or the other, were now prime candidates for blackmail. It didn't take an experienced investigator to realize what Wendy, in various stages of undress, had planned.

I wondered if the photos were just insurance, something she'd planned to tuck away and pull out if her other life plans fell apart. If so, the disintegration had begun. I wondered if Bryce had caught her with a fellow officer or two while she was honing her covert photography skills. But even with a divorce, Wendy was still in line to take over Gracey Group, pay herself an extravagant salary and live happily-ever-after.

Of course, if Bryce ever explained his side of the divorce to Mom and Dad, it was possible our father would fire her. Then she would be left with nothing.

Except the flash drive.

Since everybody who invested in Gracey Group properties had a substantial income, the photos were as good as gold bullion. Some, if not all, of the men in the photos would probably give Wendy whatever she asked.

My sister, the capitalist. If this scheme hadn't been so sleazy and despicable, my father would've been proud.

Since I hadn't eaten, I grabbed crackers and cheese from the refrigerator and went out to the screened porch to stare into the woods beyond.

Was I surprised when the burner, my constant companion, began to buzz? Wendy and I had once been linked by an umbilical cord. No matter how I regarded our relationship, we would always be connected. I could almost hear her thoughts. The holidays were over, and she didn't have to pretend she'd been depressed and lonely without all the people she loved so well.

I put the phone to my ear. "Wendy..." I waited.

"Are you alone? Can you talk?"

"Yes to both. I'm on the screened porch. Where are you?"

As expected, she ignored the question. "It was horrible missing the holidays."

"I'll bet." I waited.

"The girls... They're okay? Did Bryce come home? Did you tell him about me?"

"The girls had a good holiday. Bryce didn't come home. And so far I haven't told him anything. But I'm at the end of my lies, and the next time I talk to him, I'm going to be honest." I paused just a second so she wouldn't begin speaking again. "Honest like he was honest with me when he told me you two are getting a divorce. Only you aren't holding up your end of that bargain, are you?"

She sniffed. Her voice was teary. "I should have told you myself."

"You think?"

"You have no idea…" More sniffs. "I'm raising those beautiful little girls alone, Ryan. He's never there. I'm supposed to do it all. Work, be Mom, be the perfect submarine commander's wife. I just couldn't do it anymore. I thought if I asked for a divorce, maybe he'd come to his senses."

Although he hadn't exactly said so, I wondered if Bryce had been the one asking for the divorce. "It's going to be pretty hard to get a divorce if you're hiding from the police. Maybe you should come home and straighten this out."

"You sound so distant."

"I may be. As far as I know, you could be in Australia hanging out on a cattle station."

"I mean emotionally."

"I'm sorry. What would you like me to say…Mom?"

She gasped. I had to give her credit. This time she actually did sound surprised, but how could I tell if Wendy was acting from genuine feelings or faking them? I wasn't even sure she had feelings.

"So…you know?" she asked in a small, sad voice.

"Yep, you led me right to the truth. It took a while, but I saw my father's photo in a yearbook, and it all came clear."

"I loved him, you know. Sean was such a sweetheart."

"I'm curious why you never told Mom and Dad his name?"

"I didn't want to ruin his life. He had such big plans."

"Like enlisting so he could get killed in the Gulf War? It never occurred to you that if you married him, or at the very least admitted the truth, Dad might have hired Sean at Gracey Group? Or sent you both to college?"

"I...guess I didn't think of that."

I thought it was more likely that Wendy hadn't known exactly who my father was, not until I'd turned into the spitting image of Sean Riley. The thought stung, but it made sense. Claire Durant had intimated as much. My sister, she'd said, had always had a *lot* of boyfriends.

"Well, thanks for giving birth to me," I said. "I'm glad you went through with it."

"I was seventeen, Ryan. I did my best. And I didn't want to give you up, but Mom and Dad made me. Then I had to come home and pretend I was your sister. It was horrible. You have no idea."

Anger boiled inside me, but a small, rational voice told me to stay calm. In order to get to the bottom of everything, Wendy had to continue to call me.

"I'm sure it was tough." My tone was credible, if not warm.

"I wanted to tell you, I promise, but Mom wouldn't allow it. She didn't want you to know. I guess even now, after all these years, I still couldn't go against her. She spent all those years raising you, and what was I going to do? Waltz in and tell you I was your real mother? So I let you go on a little quest, hoping you might realize the truth."

"Why the subterfuge? So I wouldn't tell Mom I learned it directly from you?"

"That, and because I think people ignore whatever they don't really want to know. I thought that you'd only figure out the whole truth if you were ready. And if you weren't, you would stop looking and push whatever you'd learned aside so you could go on believing what you always had. I didn't want you to be hurt. I love you." Now that I had stopped filtering every word through the bonds of family, I could hear everything she didn't say. *I want you to believe this because I need your help. If I pretend to love you, you can't turn me in.*

I had a brand-new appreciation for all the people I'd ever investigated, all those poor souls who had repeated far-fetched stories they'd been told by somebody they loved, never imagining they were passing on lies.

"So you sent me to Claire."

"Everything else is so awful now, I wanted that one little thing. For you to know. For you to love me for the person I really am in your life."

I almost hung up. But on the patio table in front of me was a drawing of pink reindeer that Noelle had made for me. She'd drawn it right after we'd had the Santa Claus talk, something, like the tooth fairy, that her parents should have been there to handle. Luckily, I'd avoided the truth—nobody did that better these days. Sweet little Noelle still believed the man in the red suit slid down the chimney every Christmas Eve, or in our case, sneaked in through the garage.

The drawing and the reminder of Noelle and Holly helped. The girls and my parents had to be my focus.

I squeezed out my reply. "I'm sorry everything is so awful. I'm sorry you missed Christmas with the girls."

"Did you make it a good one?"

I dug my fingernails into my palm until I knew I'd drawn blood. "Yes, but everybody missed you."

She sniffed again and while she sniffed, I lied. "We're close to finding Milton Kearns."

"Are you?"

"We are. But Wendy, I have to know the truth."

I took a deep breath. I had rehearsed what I would ask her if and when she called again. I had decided not to tell her about catching Jonah, or about opening the safe. And she certainly didn't need to know my friendly spymaster had managed to decrypt the photos on her flash drive. But I did want her to know something else.

I couldn't let her know I had her passport, so I lied yet again. "I checked with the Gracey Group travel agent. You've been to Brazil. Twice. I'm guessing you went for cosmetic surgery. I'm also guessing Vítor Calvo might have been your doctor. So his death at the same resort you were evaluating in Santa Fe seems more than suspicious. Is that why you're on the run?" I paused for one more second. "Or are you running because you really did murder him?"

"I didn't!"

I had to admire how she poured a ton of outrage into three syllables. "Okay, but were you meeting him there? Was that why you were at the resort?"

"No."

"When you were in Brazil, was he your doctor?"

"Listen, I had two small cosmetic procedures at his clinic when I was in Brazil on vacation. I love Rio. I loved getting away for a little while. It meant nothing. But yes, he was my doctor. So that's why when I saw him at the resort, I asked him to have a drink. It was 100 percent innocent. He was charming, and he even pretended to remember me. But don't you see? That connection, as vague as it is, makes it more likely the police will come after me."

"It really does, doesn't it?"

"Yes, it does! Thank you."

"And everything else is the same? You're not holding anything back?"

"I am not. I'm sorry I didn't tell you right up front. But, to be honest, I was a little embarrassed I'd had surgery. I didn't want to admit it."

"I can see that. It just doesn't help when you lie to me."

"I won't anymore. Look, just find Milton Kearns. Then we

can get the police to question him. Then I'll talk to them and tell them everything I know. Hopefully I can finally walk away."

"Well, like I said, we're getting close."

"Where is he?"

"It's complicated. But the next time we talk, maybe I'll have good news."

"Ryan, take care of your…sisters."

I disconnected when I heard the familiar beeps. But I didn't move for a very long time. I sat staring at pink reindeer and plotted what I would do next.

CHAPTER THIRTY-ONE

When I arrived in Gulf Sands, the Christmas decorations in my parents' front yard were being carefully removed to go back to a nearby storage facility. The realistic topiaries with velvet bows and handblown bulbs that had flanked the door, and the twin golden reindeer as tall as my nieces were now under the care of two energetic young men with T-shirts that read "Stohr and Moore: Store More."

Not surprisingly, Mom was supervising from the porch. "Don't forget the three nutcrackers on the lanai. Remember they have moving parts."

The guy wrestling the last reindeer into the truck made one final adjustment. "They're already in the truck. We'll be finished in a few minutes." The back of his T-shirt said he was Jerry Moore. When the other man turned his said Greg Stohr. The gimmick was cute.

Mom didn't say anything to me until I was standing beside her. "The girls are back in school?"

"As of this morning. I only have an hour before I pick them up, but I need to talk to you. Without Dad overhearing."

Adding that last sentence was key. Her expression changed from austere to worried. "Bryce is very upset."

"He should be."

Her eyelids fluttered, and for a moment I thought I might need to steady her. But she straightened. "Your father's napping. We'll go out by the pool."

She thanked the men and handed Jerry a check. Obviously a tip was included, because he looked delighted.

Through the house and out to the lanai, she didn't say a word. But when we were seated in the shade, she wasted no time.

"You've been hiding things from me since the day your sister disappeared. But how can you keep her husband in the dark, too? He's the father of those girls. He has every right to know what's really going on with Wendy because it affects them. And I am tired of waiting!"

"Before you recommend Bryce for sainthood, you need to know he hasn't exactly told the truth, either."

I had her full attention so I plowed on. "A divorce has been in the works for a while. In his defense, he probably thought Wendy should be the one to tell you. Apparently she said she'd go along with it, but now he can't find her to move the paperwork along."

"A divorce?"

"He told me himself, and Wendy confirmed it."

She looked stricken, but that didn't stop the questions. "When? You've talked to her again?"

"About half an hour ago. For the first time in a month."

"You don't know how to get hold of her? You can't call her and tell her to talk to Bryce and straighten this out? Is she staying away because she doesn't want him to serve the papers?"

"I'm going to start at the beginning, but it's not a pretty story, Mom."

"You think I haven't guessed that much?"

Touching traditions didn't apply today. I covered her hand. "I'm going to tell you what Wendy told me, and then I'm going to tell you what I think about it. I'm not trying to make you choose between daughters. You need facts, and then you can make your own decisions."

"Get it over with."

I started with Wendy's first phone call. I could see Mom was prepared to hear that Wendy's absence was all about the divorce. She wasn't prepared to hear that her older daughter might be accused of murder.

When I finished, she seemed dazed, as if she was trying to fit my words into a more acceptable pattern. "Wendy could be right," I said. "She might be pulled into a murder she has nothing to do with. It can happen."

"But if she didn't know him, if she was just staying at the same hotel that night..."

"Unfortunately, that part's not true." I told her the basic details of Vítor Calvo's murder, then about Wendy having a drink with him earlier in the evening. "She denied knowing him and said he was just a nice guy she met in the bar, but today the story changed. She admitted she'd been to Brazil twice to have cosmetic procedures at his clinic. So that connection makes it even more likely the sheriff might be interested in her."

"Brazil? When did she go to Brazil?"

I explained and waited for Mom to insist I was wrong, that Wendy would never lie to her that way. Instead she shook her head, but not in denial, more as if she hoped a good shake would set the facts straight.

Sadly, the shake dislodged more questions. "Why is she telling you this? She wanted you to take care of the girls because at the time I couldn't, I see that. But why is she telling you about the murder? If she lied about Brazil, surely she could have lied about her reasons for not coming home."

"Not easily. Look how suspicious you've been. And she involved me because I have contacts and experience. She thought I could help her find the man who had drinks with her and the doctor that night."

I finished telling her about the events right before Calvo died and Wendy's explanation for why she was at the resort in the first place. Finally I told her about Milton Kearns.

"Wendy claims if the police can find and talk to Kearns and nail down his story, she won't be a suspect."

"Why hasn't anybody in New Mexico contacted your father or me to find her? Or Gracey Group? Have you spoken to anyone from the sheriff's department?"

"So far I don't think they've identified her as the woman with Calvo that night."

"Then she can come home. Why doesn't she? She's not a suspect."

"Wendy thinks it's a matter of time until someone comes forward and leads them to her. When that happens, she wants to be able to give them Kearns. She thinks that's the only way she'll be safe."

"Do you believe this?"

We'd come to the hardest part. "No."

"Why?"

I wasn't about to go into all the sordid details—Jonah, the attempted break-in, the safe and the photos. Instead I sorted through what I knew and ended up with the common denominator.

"Wendy can't be trusted, Mom. I'm sorry, but she's lied, and I've caught her more than once. She's done other things, worse things than lying. She claims she had nothing to do with Calvo's murder, but I can't take that as a given."

She could have asked a dozen questions, most notably what I meant by "worse things than lying." I'd fully expected her to, so the question she asked instead surprised me.

"And what will you do if you find out she's lying about the murder? What will you do if she had something to do with it?"

I squeezed her hand—she had never moved it from mine. "I don't know. She's family. She's my sister and my mother, and your daughter and the mother of two little girls I love, who are not my nieces but my half sisters. It's as complicated as that. And I'm pretty sure she's counting on our convoluted relationship to keep me from sharing what I already know with the police."

Mom was staring into space. Her eyes were glazed, not teary. I thought she was in shock.

She finally met my gaze. "Your father."

I squeezed her hand once more, then sat back and folded my arms. "He's not like you. He never saw our flaws, and if he suspected we had any, he protected us. He always adored Wendy. She could wrap him around her little finger."

"So could you."

"But he was grooming her to take over Gracey Group. And that means everything to him."

"His rehab's gone better than anybody expected. He has more energy, and pretty soon he's going back to work part-time, whether I tell him he can or not. I've asked the Gracey Group staff to stay away and not mention Wendy's name if he calls them. But very soon I won't be able to stop him from getting to the bottom of things. Maybe it is time for some professional intervention."

"If a private investigator found her, what would you do? Try to talk sense into her? Threaten her if she doesn't come home? Help her escape somewhere she'll never be found again?" I paused for emphasis. "Turn her in to the authorities?"

Her head was turning side to side. I knew that feeling.

"What do we tell your father?" she asked at last.

"I think you should tell him about the divorce, and then tell him Wendy's gone off on her own to think things over and doesn't want anybody in the family involved. She especially doesn't want Bryce calling or emailing, because she needs to figure things out without him. You can tell Dad she calls me whenever she has something to say, but otherwise we need to leave her alone until she's ready to deal."

"I suppose that has enough truth in it that it doesn't sound like a fairy tale."

"Sophie and I are doing everything humanly possible to find her and get to the bottom of what really happened."

"You're looking for this Kearns creature?"

"We're trying."

"And what will you do if you find him?"

I'd given that careful thought. "I'm going to talk to him on my own. I'm going to get his story, and then I'll decide what to do."

"If you alert that man he's been found, he'll take off again. And I hope you don't plan to talk to him in person. He could be dangerous. He could be the one who killed the doctor."

"I'll be careful."

"You've said that before."

"I did learn a few things after John Quayle nearly killed me."

"What does Teo say about this?"

She wasn't asking because Teo was a man, which would have infuriated me. She was asking because Teo had been a cop and a good one.

"We'll talk it out," I promised, "and I'll listen to whatever he says as long as he listens to me."

"Why didn't you tell me all of this right from the start?"

"Are you happier now that you know?" I waited. "That's why," I said when she didn't answer. "I hoped she would come back quickly, and I would never have to explain. But honestly? As time's marched on, everything has gotten uglier and more complicated. And now there's no longer a way to spare you."

I glanced down at the fitness tracker buckled to my wrist and saw it was time to get Holly and Noelle. I got up to leave. "Think about everything, and we'll talk again soon."

"You are going to let me know what else you learn." Mom still looked dazed and unsure, but the last had not been a question.

I leaned over to kiss her cheek. "Thanks for trusting me so far. I know it's been hard. Just trust me a little longer. I'll keep you in the loop whenever I can. I promise."

Ten minutes later I was parked in the pickup zone at the girls' school waiting for the final bell, when my phone rang. After our long conversation that morning, I was surprised to see the caller was Sophie.

I spoke first. "I just told my mom what's going on."

"How'd she take it?"

"It's hard to tell. She's a Gracey. But two things stand out. One, she didn't follow up on some of the things I hinted at. Maybe I hit her hard enough for one day, and she'd reached her limit."

Sophie made noises of sympathy, and I plowed on. "Two, she didn't defend Wendy." Mentally I backpedaled through the conversation. "I don't think she did, not even once."

"What does that tell you?"

"At the least? That Wendy hasn't always been truthful with her. At the most? Mom isn't discounting the possibility that Wendy really was involved in the murder."

"That sounds grueling."

From inside the school the final bell rang. The girls would be out in the next few minutes. Two teachers I didn't know opened the double doors before they took their places on the steps.

"I'm sure you didn't call to hear my progress report," I said. "What's up?"

"I hope you're sitting down. Alabama bore fruit and I traced Kearns to a bar with the same hotel chain in Albuquerque. He was working there for six months or so before the murder, but he quit just before it happened. That means it's possible he was still in New Mexico when your sister was."

"So now we know where he used to be."

"The trick was locating him anytime, anywhere, in the past year. The rest fell into place. He quit his job in Albuquerque because he got an offer to become the head bartender at an ecotourism resort near the Tortuguero National Park."

"Tortuguero?" It didn't sound familiar.

"In Costa Rica, on the east coast not far from Nicaragua. It's literally in the middle of nowhere. Not a road to speak of that will take you all the way. You can fly in, but January's a popular month and flights might be hard to get. The best way is by flying into San Jose, then booking a seat on a bus, followed by one of the resort boats."

"I guess if he wanted to be inconspicuous, that might be the place."

"Someone in his family owns the resort where he's working, a brother-in-law or an uncle. I can't tell. Anyway, Kearns is there now, and he's going by Ex, not Milton. Get this. The resort has a Facebook page, and they update it every day, interviews, videos, photos. I'm going to steal their social media person for *Out in the Cold*. Last night they posted a photo of him with three other employees, mixing drinks on camera. It's definitely him. I compared it to his mug shot."

"Why would he allow anybody to put his photo on the internet?"

"He didn't know? He figures he's so far away, nobody who matters will see it? He doesn't know Wendy's looking for him? He's assuming the cops won't fuss with extradition unless they have proof he murdered Dr. Calvo? And maybe he feels safe because he didn't do it."

Sophie's lists of possibilities were even longer than mine, and today every one came with more questions. "He couldn't be somewhere easy to get to. Like Key West."

"Nope. And if you're going to Costa Rica, Ryan, I'd go soon. Anything could happen, and he could split. How's your Spanish?"

"Two years in high school."

"Bummer."

The girls were heading down the steps toward me now. I thanked Sophie and disconnected. Holly and Noelle looked worn out. A plan was forming in my head, and the first step was to skip going home for a while.

"Is anybody in the mood for a milkshake?" I turned as I spoke, in case they'd relapsed to nonverbal responses. But "yes" was absolutely clear. We stopped at my favorite local drive-in, one of the few that had remained after an eruption of chains.

The girls still weren't adventurous, but Noelle had graduated from vanilla to strawberry and now Holly asked for chocolate. I ordered pistachio for myself.

"How about if we swing by the house, get Biz, and then go see Teo?"

"Bismarck needs a milkshake."

"We'll let him lick our cups. Deal?"

Minutes later schoolbags were on the kitchen counters and everyone, including Bismarck, was back in the car heading toward Confidence K-9s.

"Does Teo know we're coming?" Holly asked. "Is Fiona going to be there?"

"If she's home from school, she probably will be." I heard a loud rattle and figured that Bismarck was taking care of milkshake residue. "Tell me about school."

They did, and I managed to eke out details to keep them busy until we pulled up in front of the kennel. "We'll go inside and see if Teo's here, then you can find Fiona."

Teo's SUV was parked to one side, so I was encouraged. One of the kennel techs let us in, and pointed toward a training yard. Janice was coming from that direction, and she volunteered to take the girls and Bismarck to her house to hang out with their new friend.

Teo was alone in the yard with a massive black dog who I guessed might be at least part rottweiler. The dog was leashed and didn't look happy. I stayed back from the fence so as not to distract them. As I watched, Teo said something and the dog raised its head to stare suspiciously. Teo's next word was "now."

The dog stayed where it was.

Teo patiently repeated the sequence. This time I realized the first word was the dog's name. "Bluff." Again the dog stared at him, but this time when Teo said "now," the dog moved toward him. Teo reached in his pocket for a treat and gave it to the dog along with a "good dog!"

They repeated the sequence four times. The fifth time when Teo said "Bluff," he added "to me." Bluff went to him immediately.

I watched for minutes as Teo lengthened the leash until he and the dog were a good distance apart. Sometimes Bluff came and sometimes he didn't. But by the end, Bluff was coming nearly every time.

The young kennel tech who'd let us in went into the yard, and waited beside the door until Teo shortened the leash again and slowly walked Bluff toward him. The tech said his name and "to me." Bluff went to him, and after the tech gave Bluff a treat, Teo gave the young man the leash.

I waited until Bluff and the tech were gone before I moved closer. "That was interesting. You do basic training yourself?"

"Only when a dog's dangerous."

I didn't like the sound of that. "Dangerous?"

He came out and locked the gate behind him. "We take in the occasional death row dog when we can. Let's just say Bluff had a particularly difficult life, and it showed. But Harry saw the great heart underneath and rescued him just an hour before he was due to be put down. If we can get him on the right track, he'll make a great security dog."

"What if you can't?"

"I should have said when, not if."

Now I was worried. "Would he attack you?"

"Ryan…" He smiled warmly, obviously a bit pleased at my reaction. "This is what I do. I've worked with plenty of aggressive dogs. I'm good at it, but it's not always safe. We're prepared if something goes wrong. You notice I had some-body nearby?"

"I'm sorry, but, you know…"

"I've lost enough body parts already?"

"I was not going to say that!"

"To what do I owe the pleasure of this visit?"

Dogs were barking in the runs lining the walkway, and I wanted a quieter place to talk. "It's kind of noisy."

We ended up at an outdoor table in the shade inside one of the play areas. It was quieter, even though a couple of smaller mixed breed dogs were chasing each other in circles.

"So?" He lowered himself to the bench, and I sat beside him.

"Sophie found Kearns." I told him the details, ending with his new name.

"Are you relieved?"

"I don't know what I am except positive I have to go to Costa Rica."

"You could tell the Santa Fe cops who he is, where he is and let them take it from there."

"And how can I do that without telling them how I know he's involved?"

"Make an anonymous call. Some departments have a hotline. Wasn't that why Wendy said she wanted to find him? So she could turn him in?"

"She called today." I told him everything she'd said, and added that I'd finally told my mother most of the truth.

"So what do you take from all that?"

This was not the brash young man who had insisted he knew what was best for me. Both of us had learned a lot in the intervening years. For instance, looking at him now, I realized that I was in love with him.

And wasn't it just like me to realize it or, rather, to admit it to myself, when life was rapidly falling apart around me?

I looked away and tried to focus. "I could talk to the police, but if I do, I'm out of it. I won't be able to talk to Ex myself and figure out how much of Wendy's story is true. And if she finds out I turned him in without alerting her, she might disappear forever."

"Not if the authorities tag him for the murder."

I met his eyes. "If it was that simple, Wendy would have gone straight to the cops the moment she heard Calvo was murdered. You figured that out a long time ago, didn't you?"

He didn't deny it. "I had nothing to lose. You had everything."

"I need to talk to him myself. I know it might not be a hundred percent safe, and I know he might take off afterward. But unless I do, I won't know the full extent of her lies, and I won't know how best to protect Holly and Noelle and my parents."

"You're assuming that Ex won't lie. That whatever he tells you will be gospel."

"Okay, it sounds stupid. I get that. I told you I'd be up front. I just wanted you to know what I'm planning."

I waited for him to tell me I was walking into danger again, and that yes, the one thing I'd said that rang true was that my plan was stupid. Instead he took my hand, turned it over and lifted it to his lips.

He kissed my palm before he spoke. "You want me to come?"

"Pretty much more than anything."

"You want me for my language skills?"

"That, too. But I want you because…I don't want to go without you."

"You couldn't ask?"

"Are you kidding? You really should avoid me."

He squeezed my hand and dropped it. "I tell myself that, but it's not getting through."

"You don't have to come, Teo. Why should you? I'll understand."

"You're getting closer to asking me. Try harder."

I sighed. "Will you come to Costa Rica with me?"

"When?"

"You're not teaching until the new term starts, right? So as soon as I can get reservations and make arrangements to get out to the resort where he's working."

"Immediately then. Yeah, I'll come."

"I'm not going to cry." I sniffed. Hard.

He put his arm around me and pulled me close. "Go ahead and practice. No matter what Ex tells you, you have more tears ahead."

CHAPTER THIRTY-TWO

I had no doubt Costa Rica was charming, and I was sure we would see plenty of it on our way to the resort in Tortuguero tomorrow. But by the time Teo and I drove to Miami, went through body scanning at security where Peg was swabbed for explosives and drugs, and waited for two hours in the airport, I just wanted the trip over with. After we finally boarded, took a three-hour flight to San José, stood for an hour to get through customs and headed outside to find transportation to our hotel, we were both so exhausted we could have been anywhere. San José was a metropolitan area with a population of more than two million, the usual traffic and congestion near the airport, and very little to distinguish it from other tropical cities I'd visited.

Unfortunately, my own exhaustion was eclipsed by Teo's. He was in pain. That was clear, even though he refused to talk about it.

The trip had come together quickly. My mother agreed to take my nieces. I found two seats on a nonstop flight, and both Teo and I were able to dig out our passports and pack in two days.

When I'd chosen a hotel by the airport, I'd gone for a well-known chain that probably had hotels in heaven and hell, since they had everything in between. I assumed we wouldn't get into our room until it was nearly dark, and tomorrow we were leaving after breakfast to catch a bus to a boat to a… I didn't want to think about traveling again.

"Almost there," I said, as we got out of the shuttle. "And into our room soon."

We were at the door by then, but he stopped. "Our room?"

"The hotel is overflowing. I was lucky to book one."

"Did you try to book two?"

I couldn't tell if he was pleased or upset. "Well, it seemed silly. But, it's a suite, so there's a pullout sofa. That's kind of like two rooms. I mean, I thought it was pretty darned close, to be honest."

"You can stop anytime."

"I can sleep in the lobby. Or the bathtub."

He looked pale and beyond caring. My heart sank. "Sit. I'll register."

He didn't argue. He took a seat on a chair in the center and closed his eyes.

I didn't try my pathetic Spanish. The clerk spoke excellent English, and she checked us in quickly. I'd put everything I needed in a backpack and handbag, but Teo had a rolling suitcase and a small pack. Before he could stand I grabbed the suitcase. "We're on this floor."

I walked ahead of him and had the door open by the time he arrived. The suite was spacious enough. If sleeping apart really was in the cards, it could be done.

"Why don't you lie down," I said.

He went into the bedroom and sat on the edge of the bed. "I have to remove my prosthesis."

"By all means."

"I don't need help."

He was angry, and so many things suddenly became clear. "I figured you could do it on your own, Teo. Is it bothering you?"

"Yes, it's bothering me. Sitting, standing, walking, not walking—" He swiped his hand through the air to take care of anything he'd left out.

"Okay, how do you get around without it? I'm assuming there's a better alternative than hopping on the other leg if you need to get to the bathroom, or drink a glass of water."

He was gritting his teeth. "I have crutches in my suitcase."

"They fit? That's pretty amazing."

He got up and went to get it, and while he was gone I turned back the covers and fluffed the pillows.

Once he was back I took the suitcase from his hands and set it on the other side of the bed. He more or less collapsed on the sheets and stripped off his jeans—boot cut and wide enough to slip on and off without a lot of difficulty. He wore boxers beneath.

I opened the suitcase, taking out what had to be adult crutches, although they looked like they would fit a child. "Here you go." I looked closer as he pulled them apart. "They're retractable? Hey, those are cool."

"Are you finished pretending this doesn't bother you?"

"You're the one who's bothered." I came around and sat beside him. "Why didn't you take your prosthesis off on the plane?"

"Ryan..." He shook his head.

"Teo..." I mimicked, then I nodded. "Lie back. Make yourself comfortable. I'll do the honors. How hard can it be?"

"I'll do it. Just leave."

"Do I pull?" I paused. "No, wait. Now I remember. There's a button somewhere at the bottom, a pin. Then I pull."

He started to push me away, then he stopped, cocking his head. "How do you know that?"

"YouTube. I have a natural curiosity, and now I have more than general knowledge about below-knee amputations and jazzy new legs." I felt around his ankle and discovered the pin on the side. "May I?"

His expression softened from angry to annoyed. "You are a nutcase."

"You knew that going in, buddy." With that I pushed the pin, and Peg slid off. What was left of the leg he'd been born with was covered with layers of sock-like material.

"The padding makes the prosthesis more comfortable?"

He lay back against the sheets and stared at the ceiling. "It makes it fit so what's left—"

"Residual leg?"

"Yeah, or call a stump a stump."

"So the sock thingies make Peg fit with no rubbing."

"You are just full of questions."

I lay down on my side and turned so I could brush his hair back from his forehead. "So with all this protection? What's hurting?"

He didn't look at me. "It sounds crazy."

"Even more interesting."

"Pain in the foot they took off."

I schooled myself not to show even a hint of sympathy, which I knew he would hate. "Phantom pain. I've heard of that. What happens?"

"Sometimes it feels like the Inquisition is pulling off my missing toes with pliers. Sometimes it's more like I stuck them in a light socket. Today? Both."

That sounded awful, but I kept my voice as light as possible. "How often does it happen?"

"More at first. Rarely now."

"The trip did it?"

"Probably."

"You have meds? Can I get them?"

"Over the counter, and I've taken them. I don't go with the heavy stuff. I gave that up with the leg."

"Will it help if I massage it?"

He propped himself up. "Why are you doing this?"

"What?"

"Trying to make this sound like no big deal."

"Pain is always a big deal. But if I'm too casual, it's your own fault. You've made the amputation sound like nothing since the day I found out about it. You've been a big macho guy. But guess what? It's huge. To you especially."

"I've moved on."

"I don't care if you have half a leg or no leg or three legs. You're here. Against all odds we're here together. I'm crazy about you. I'm crazy about Peg. She's a star. But if I can do anything to help you feel better? I'm in."

"I can handle this on my own."

"The last time you needed me, you pushed me away. I went because I was a mess, too, and I didn't know what else to do. But this time, I do know. I'm not going anywhere. Lie back."

When he didn't answer, I got up, circled the bed and stood over him, hands on hips. "I'm going to channel Arlie Gracey. Please don't make me."

He lay back, and I perched on the edge and began to peel off the layers protecting his leg. When I was finally down to bare skin, I took a long look. Then I trailed my fingers over it.

He sat up and tried to push me away.

"Uh-uh-uh." I grabbed his hands.

"What am I going to do with you, Ryan?"

"I have an excellent idea for exactly what you're going to do when you're feeling better. So, let's hurry that along. Will it help if I massage your leg? Get ice? Do a little naked dance to take your mind off the leg-that-went-away?"

He almost smiled.

"I'm going to try something. I want you to relax and listen to my voice. Can you give me one chance?"

He was fast losing the strength to argue. His face was pale and scrunched in pain, and his expression said he would try anything if I would leave him alone afterward.

I hoped a piece of the truth would help us both. "I had terrible screaming nightmares after, well, you know. That's the most common symptom of PTSD."

"I didn't know."

"I was in therapy for a while. Actually quite a while. Did you know that men and women experience trauma differently? Not always, but often enough. Men get angry. And women? We just go dead inside." I stopped chattering and let that sink in. It described what had happened to both of us so well, and the way it had worked against our relationship.

"I was furious," he said, which surprised me. "Sometimes I still am."

"I was trying to be strong for you, but I was a wet sponge. And at night? I'd go to sleep and see Quayle coming toward me with that…that look on his face." I shook my head to make it go away. "Anyway, my therapist taught me to change parts of the nightmare, and eventually it worked. I got to the point where when the Evil One appeared, he would be wearing a dunce cap, or a silly mustache. And that would break the spell. I'd wake up, and even if I wasn't smiling, at least I wasn't screaming."

He grasped my hand. "I'm sorry."

"Let's see if a little visualization can help you relax, okay, and maybe soothe your leg? Will you try it?"

"Can I imagine you in a dunce cap?"

I was glad he could joke. "May I try?"

"Will it get you off my case?"

"It's possible."

He closed his eyes, and I took that as a good sign.

"We're both going to pretend you still have your whole leg. I'm going to touch and kiss the right leg first. Pay attention to how it feels. And then I'll going to touch and kiss the left one. You're going to imagine it feels exactly the same. And your toes and your foot will begin to relax."

"This is not an accepted therapy."

"Of course not. I'm making it up. But we might hit the jackpot."

I stroked his intact leg, slowly working my way down. Then I followed the path with my lips. My fingertips and my lips remembered the feel of his skin, the heat, the resilience.

"If you think that's relaxing, you have another think coming," he said.

I stopped kissing and pressed a little harder with my fingertips, massaging gently as I went. "Work in progress."

I fell silent, slowly moving toward his knee, taking my time. Once I got there, I started to hum softly, something tuneless and, I hoped, soothing. I kissed his knee, and then below, circling his leg with my fingers and thumbs, brushing gently but not too gently. By the time I got to his foot, I thought he might be relaxing a little. He seemed more pliant, more willing to let me slip a hand under his heel and gently massage his toes.

Minutes had passed. I'd taken my time, and now I started with the other leg. Instantly he tensed. I hummed louder, and slowly massaged above the knee. His thigh was as hard as concrete, and I worked slowly, digging in with my fingertips. Even though I couldn't tell if he was relaxing, I pretended he was and told him so.

"You're letting go. That's great. You can feel your leg relaxing all the way down to your toes." I moved my hands lower, and then bent and brushed kisses along his knee, and lower until I was kissing the stump. He didn't stop me, and that was powerful incentive. No matter what else happened, we had crossed that line and we'd never have to look back.

"You can feel my hands moving lower," I said softly. "My fingertips are stroking your calf and it's so relaxing. I can feel every fiber relaxing. Your muscles are letting go, the skin is softening, like jelly." I imitated the therapist who had worked with me on my nightmares.

Finally I graduated to his toes. "Your toes are tense, nearly cramped, but as I massage them, they begin to relax. Before, the big toe was as rigid as a fence post, but now, it's beginning to bend. In fact you can bend it a little yourself, and then more. And now? Now you can easily bend it without my help. Slowly, ever so slowly, all your toes are beginning to straighten and align, and the tension is easing. The pain you feel is easing, too."

Finally I'd run out of things to say and do. I sighed, slid the imaginary foot—which almost felt real to me—back to the bed, and wiggled up until I was lying beside him.

"Do you feel any better?"

He turned over, opened his eyes and pushed me down, covering half my body with his. He bent lower and kissed me, and then, with a groan, he rolled to his back.

"I don't feel any worse." He reached over and pulled me close until I was snuggled against him. "Did you really see Quayle in a dunce cap?"

"Let's just say I came close, but it makes a good story. I did learn how to wake myself up before he got to me. That was huge."

"This was… What you just did… It was huge for *me*. Even if the pain's still hanging around. Thank you for touching me."

I took a moment to swallow tears. "Maybe you just need a little more time to let everything wash over you, Teo. Your brain's probably sorting out all the bum signals."

He closed his eyes.

I got to my feet so I could cry in the hallway. "I'm going to the front desk to see about takeout. Think about something wonderful and try to relax those toes, okay?"

I slipped on my shoes and found my handbag. In the public restroom I gave in and cried until no tears remained. Then after I washed my face, I searched the main part of the hotel for food to bring back to the room. It wasn't simple, but I managed to get sandwiches and bags of plantain chips with bottled drinks.

As it turned out, I had plenty to eat. Thirty minutes later when I got back to the room, Teo was sleeping like the dead.

I spent the night on the sofa bed in the other room, afraid to wake him.

We were on the boat heading to the resort before we talked about the night behind us. Teo looked rested, and said whatever pain remained was under control. Before we left our room, I gave him privacy to get Peg back in place, a process more complicated than removing her. Peg plays hard to get.

The long bus ride to catch the boat had been bouncy but scenic. Teo told me he'd been to Costa Rica once before, and I told him I'd like to come again under better circumstances. Other than that, we slumped against each other and tried to get more sleep.

The boat was comfortable, and we'd been allowed to tag

along with a tour group, so the pace was just slow enough to give us a chance to enjoy the wildlife. A guide narrated from the front, but we sat by ourselves in the back.

"Thanks for last night," Teo said.

"You may not remember, but nothing happened. At least nothing more exciting than a kiss."

"Plenty happened. Thanks for being there for me."

"You missed a great chicken sandwich."

"That's not all I missed."

I tucked my arm under his and took his hand. "If you play your cards right, tonight could be better. If I happen to be in the mood."

His laugh was tantalizing. "You probably saw me at my worst."

"If that's your worst, we're in good shape. But for the record, I didn't see a single thing to deter me from getting you naked tonight."

The narration halted just as I said the last words. Teo laughed and I blushed. I put my head on his shoulder and stared out at the scenery.

I'd made reservations for two nights at the resort where Alexander Milton Kearns, now known as Ex, presided over several bars. Two nights was the minimum, and I'd thought we might want to observe and assess before we challenged him. By the time the boat pulled into Toucan Village, we'd been treated to dense tropical foliage with sightings of spider monkeys and crocodiles. I recognized some of the many birds as Florida friends, but not all. The woods along the canal were alive with movement and song.

We got out and collected our bags, making arrangements for a return trip on Sunday morning. The buildings seemed simple, almost primitive, but the grounds were lavish and the resort sprawled in every direction. Above us, though, the sky was turning darker. They didn't call this rain forest for nothing.

After sitting so long Teo was ready to walk. "Let's look around while the tour group registers."

We left the backpack and suitcase at the front desk after a rapid stream of Spanish passed between Teo and the clerk, a middle-aged woman as trim as my mother.

"What did you tell her?" I asked as we walked away.

"I asked for a quiet room. I told her we planned to make noise all night long."

Of course he hadn't told her any such thing, but I winked, as if I believed him. "Did you tell her I always scream your name?"

"Who else's?"

I slipped my arm around his waist, and we made a show of pretending to be lovers or honeymooners. For me, no acting ability was needed.

"I thought we'd look for the bars," he said. "And with luck, the bartenders."

Signs in the reception area, a large open room with decks and covered walkways, pointed to a total of three bars. The first took up a wall on one side of the dining room. Another was by the pool, and the last was in a gazebo with a roof thatched with palm fronds that stood alone looking over the river.

The dining room and its bar weren't open. We were too late for lunch, and it was too early for dinner. The bar by the pool was doing a brisk business, so we sat on a stool and ordered beer and Costa Rican tamales cooked in banana leaves instead of corn husks.

Ex wasn't there, and the two young women behind the counter weren't in need of anybody's supervision. We finished what passed for lunch and moved on to the gazebo, which was closed until five.

The skies took that moment to open. There was no warning patter of raindrops. One moment we were dry, and the next we were drenched. We sprinted to a covered walkway leading back to the reception area, got our luggage and directions. As we were leaving, I could swear the receptionist winked at me.

"Wow." On the walkway again I watched rain sluicing off the roof to the ground beyond us.

"Mariana said that the sun took a vacation last week. But she thinks this should pass soon."

"Seems like a great time to take a nap, since we can't sight-see."

"They do a jungle walk at six and another at eight."

"We'll be looking for a different kind of wildlife about then."

Maybe Teo really had told Mariana a quiet room would be best, because she'd given us one so far from the lobby that at one point we had to backtrack and read more signs. But when we finally reached the correct walkway, I was delighted. Our room faced jungle, and the walkway in front of it, with two plastic chairs, wasn't shared by another room. The key was in the lock.

The resort billed itself as ecotourism. In keeping with that, the room was not luxurious, but it was spacious and clean, built from a wood that gleamed with a golden luster. And while the room contained nothing remotely resembling technology, there were a couple of outlets and a small area where we could hang clothes. A wide-bladed ceiling fan lazily churned the air and was as close to air-conditioning as we would get.

The bed took up half the room. And there was one. No sofa bed to retreat to tonight. "Again," I said, "they only had one room when I made the reservation."

Teo gave his suitcase a push and it rolled to the wall. He put his arms around me and slipped off my backpack. "One room is perfect."

"So what should we do while it's raining? I can't imagine bird-watching."

He brushed my hair back from my forehead and kissed it. Then my nose, an earlobe, another, my cheek and finally, my lips.

"Do you remember how good sex was before everything happened?"

I felt warmth flooding through me that had nothing to do with rain forest heat. Suddenly my knees refused to lock. "How could I forget?" I saw what he wanted to say, but couldn't.

"You were afraid things might be different because of the missing leg." I kissed him gently and smoothed my hands under his shirt to feel the solid expanse of his back. "Things are different, Teo. You are so remarkable. I want you more than I did then, even if I don't deserve you. Don't you know I love you?"

I put a finger on his lips when he started to speak. "You don't have to say a thing. Whatever love means? It definitely means good sex will be great sex. I am so thankful you're back in my life. Just don't let me blow it this time, okay?"

He smiled a little, then he reached for the hem of my T-shirt and slowly eased it over my head. I returned the favor, then I unhooked my bra and tossed it to my feet so I could feel his body, skin to skin.

We found the bed. Peg and every stitch of clothing made a mountain on the floor beside it. We kissed and touched and moved in ways I remembered and ways that were new, but every bit as perfect. I gasped when he entered me, and I wanted to hold him there forever.

The rain beat down on the metal roof of our little bungalow, and what had once been good was magnificent.

CHAPTER THIRTY-THREE

We made love, took naps, then made love again, making sure it was as perfect as we'd thought. We finally rose and took showers. Apparently ecotourism was code for minimal hot water, but I didn't care because I had a man balanced against me to keep me warm.

As we stepped outside to find our way to dinner, Teo spotted a pair of toucans I'd missed. But when he pointed, I saw two exquisitely beautiful birds at the edge of a small clearing in the trees, their yellow chests and prominent rainbow-colored beaks unmistakable.

"They came by the name of this place honestly," he said softly.

I was prepared to watch all evening, but after a few minutes they flew away. I wondered if the management mapped out their route.

Teo put his arm around me and we made our way to the dining room. While we waited for a table, I examined the three people standing behind the bar. Two men were dark-haired and short. The woman with them seemed to be serving, not mixing drinks.

Teo had been watching, too. "We have all night."

Dinner was a buffet of fresh vegetables, fish, several kinds of rice and a delicious assortment of small desserts. We ordered wine with our meal, and were shown to a table at the edge of the room near the bar.

"Eat slowly," I told Teo. "Let's wait him out."

Unlike the toucans, Kearns didn't show. By the time we were lingering over cups of delicious local coffee, no one who looked remotely like the mug shot was in the room either serving or eating.

"What next?" I refused yet another coffee refill and couldn't swallow one more bite of a delicious passion fruit mousse.

"We hang out in the gazebo bar. This time of night I don't think we have to worry about the pool, but we could swing by on the way and see if the bar's still open."

The pool bar was closed, and only a few people were enjoying the water. We strolled arm in arm, and at one point Teo pulled me into the shadows and kissed me. I was sorry we had other things to do tonight.

The gazebo had been transformed. Strings of lights glowed over and around the thatched roof, rafters and posts. The bar itself was softly lit, but not so softly I couldn't make out the faces of the two bartenders. They were experts, shaking, pouring, taking orders with smiles. One was a woman with short blond hair, and the other a thin, dark-skinned man with hair pulled back in tiny braids.

We found a table away from the lights subtly illuminating the surrounding gardens. Several dozen people were enjoying the soft guitar strumming of a young man who occasionally added his voice. At one point a sound more distinctive and soulful than a pack of coyotes rang through the air, and he stopped playing and waited.

"Howler monkeys," Teo said before I could ask. "If we're

lucky, we'll see some before we leave." If I hadn't known what they were, and the monkeys had howled while I was sleeping, my sadly creative brain would have woven the eerie sounds into a nightmare.

We both ordered the ubiquitous Cerveza Imperial lager, and since we were biding our time, half an hour later our glasses were still nearly full.

I gestured to the gardens. "Is Puerto Rico this beautiful?"

"A few years ago I went back to the area where my mother's family was from, near Ponce. They call it *La Perla del Sur*, the pearl of the south. She can trace fragments of her ancestry back to the French Creoles who fled the Haitian revolution. Ocean and hills and beautiful old buildings. I'll take you there someday."

That was as close to talking about our future as we had come. Our reunion was still tentative, like a fledgling poised uncertainly on the edge of its nest.

He asked me about the podcast, and I told him about the plan for our second season. He said he would make calls if I wanted, that he knew a few cops in the department we were researching. Delighted, I asked him about the classes he was teaching, and he described a few of his students.

I captured his hand. "We're on our way back from the abyss, aren't we? Somehow we've found lives we can be happy with. You have the kennel, and your house and your teaching. I have the podcast, my friends…" My eyes held his. "My nieces."

"You're in trouble there."

"What would you say if I ended up raising them?"

"I would say it's not my decision. And it may not be yours, either."

"Let's just pretend that you and I are finding our way back from our *mutual* abyss. Together. Would Holly and Noelle be a strike against that?"

"This is all theoretical—"

I sat back. "Spoken like a cop."

"But theoretically," he went on, as if I hadn't interrupted, "how could two wonderful little girls ever be anything except another reason to be happy?"

I beamed at him. And that's when I noticed a man strolling into the lighted area beside the bar and greeting a group of patrons with nods and pats on the back.

"Bingo." I inclined my head. "Look who just showed up."

He took my hand, as if we were deep into an intimate tête-à-tête, and then he turned and signaled the woman who had brought our drinks, as if that had been his intention. "Another for both of us?" he said, even though our glasses were far from empty. I watched his gaze flick to the bar and settle on the man we'd come to see.

"So, now we keep an eye on him," Teo said after the server left. "In a minute I'm going to move beside you, like I can't stand to be this far away."

"Were it only true."

"It is, but making eyes at each other isn't the reason we're here, right?"

"What if he leaves?"

"He went behind the bar. What's he doing now?"

"Talking to one of the bartenders." I smiled at Teo, as if he'd said something funny.

"Okay, I'm coming around. Pretend you're thrilled."

"I'm so good at pretending." I sat back and focused on him, a slight smile, eyes sparkling. None of it was hard.

Teo pulled his chair around and took my hand and kissed it, cuddling beside me. "Now we can both keep an eye on him," he said, his mouth against my ear. "What's he doing?"

"Looks like he's mixing drinks."

"I bet he'll be there until the bar closes."

"Are we going to stay awake that long?"

"I wouldn't miss this for the world."

An hour passed. As impossible as it seemed, I was hungry again. We ordered a platter of fresh vegetables, crackers and cheese. I fed Teo bites from the platter, and kissed him in between.

"Keep that up and we might need to adjourn to our room," Teo said.

Kearns had been conversing with patrons at the bar as he served. Suddenly he came out from behind. "He's leaving. Are we going to follow him?"

"Not yet." Teo was watching, too. As we both looked on, Kearns began to visit tables, spending a minute or more at each one.

"Customer satisfaction survey," I said. "But he'll be over here before long."

"It he asks where we're from, don't say Seabank."

"Delray Beach," I said.

"Fine. Me, too."

"Honeymooners?" I wiggled my eyebrows.

He held up his hand. "No ring."

"Just lovers, then."

"Just?"

I laughed. "Lovers on fire?"

"Tell him we're here to relax. And then look at me the way you did this afternoon."

"How hard will that be?"

His laughter rumbled through my body in all the places it was meant to.

We studiously ignored Kearns, but we didn't converse, afraid, even without consulting each other, that he'd think he was interrupting. As we sipped and listened to the guitarist, he finally made it to our table. I looked up and smiled, but mentally I was checking his features against the ones in the mug shot. He was definitely our man.

"How are you enjoying this beautiful evening?" Alexander Milton Kearns had a nice smile and an open, friendly face, although he was built like a bouncer, not a bartender. With his reddish hair and freckles, he looked like a product of Ireland, but I knew from a little research that Ticos, the name for native Costa Ricans, came from a wide variety of ethnic backgrounds.

"You sound like you're from the United States." I held out my hand. "I'm Rose, and this is my friend Matt."

If Teo was surprised at our new names, he didn't show it. "Great place here," Teo said, offering his hand, too.

"I'm Alex, but my friends call me Ex. Yeah, I've mostly lived in the US, so I come by the accent honestly."

"Ex for excellent? Extraordinary?" I hoped my dimples were on display, even if my clever repartee was on vacation.

"All the above. Is this your first time here?"

"Matt's been to Costa Rica, but this is a first for me."

"Have a wonderful time then. Make sure you schedule some of our nature walks." Ex was already glancing toward the next table. He wished us a good evening and said if we needed anything, to let him know.

I needed plenty, and I planned to do exactly that.

If Teo and I hadn't been keeping track of our friendly bartender, the evening would have been perfect. Still, I was sitting in paradise with the man I'd nearly lost. Even with a confrontation hanging over our heads, our surroundings were magical.

The guitarist finally called it quits for the night, and I went to tip and thank him. I stopped by the bar. "When do you close?"

"We'll call the last round soon. But you're welcome to sit here as long as you'd like. We do turn out the lights at midnight. And we dim the ones along the walkways, so be careful going back. Artificial light confuses the wildlife."

I thanked him and went to tell Teo. "Not long now," I said. "In a little while I'm going to disappear. I'll be in the shadows watching. When he leaves, you look at your watch, like you're ready to call it quits for the night, and follow."

When the call came for final drinks, I signed our check. Ten minutes later, Teo got up, kissed me and headed toward the reception area.

The server cleared what was left on all the tables, and I punched a text into my phone, as if waiting for Teo to return. In a few minutes the other bartenders wheeled bottles of liquor toward the dining room for storage, and just ten minutes later, after clearing and cleaning the bar, Ex called it quits for the night. I watched him unfold louvered shutters over what remained of the liquor supply and fasten them with a lock. He dimmed the lights before he took off, but I was more interested in his direction. I stood, looked at my watch and headed the same way.

I would bet on Teo—missing leg and all—if a fight was in the works. Still, we were in somebody else's country. What would we tell the authorities if a fight ensued? That we'd waylaid a Costa Rican citizen because we thought he might be involved in a murder, even though we had no proof and very few facts?

By now Ex was thirty yards ahead of me, and I walked faster.

Just as I wondered where Teo was, Ex stopped in the middle of the path to remove a shoe. He held it up and shook it, as if he'd picked up a briar or stone, and at the same moment Teo appeared, coming toward him from the other direction. As I approached, I pulled out my phone and held it up when I was close enough that Ex had spotted me.

"This is something different. A smartphone holdup?" He was smiling, still the friendly bartender.

"I just want to show you a photo." I held up the phone. My sister stared back at him.

"Remember her?" I said. "Wendy Wainwright sends her regards."

CHAPTER THIRTY-FOUR

I gave Ex just enough time to process the photo before I spoke again. "Wendy asked me to find you, only I'm not sure whatever she plans next is a good thing. I don't know if you murdered Dr. Vítor Calvo, or if something else happened that night."

He was no longer smiling. He turned, still holding his shoe, as if he planned to take off, but Teo was standing in his way. "Don't go yet." Teo put his hand on Kearns's shoulder. "We're just going to talk."

Ex reached up to grab his hand, but Teo changed his stance and stepped behind him, where he was harder to dislodge.

I switched from Wendy's photo to the text I had punched in at the table, holding it out again. "I've put everything I know about you into this. How you worked at one of my father's resorts. How you were with my sister in New Mexico the night Calvo was murdered. Where you are now and what you're doing. Unless you agree to talk to us, this will go out to the authorities in Santa Fe."

"What good is talking to you going to do?"

This time, honesty was the best policy. "I'll tell you, but can we do it somewhere else?"

"I'm fine right here."

Teo dropped his hand. "We're not trying to frame you," he said, then he followed with a stream of Spanish. Ex looked surprised, then answered in Spanish before he turned to look at me.

I had no idea what had been said, but his expression was a shade more promising.

I took advantage. "Wendy's my sister, and she really did ask me to find you. But I only tracked you down because I want to hear your side of what happened."

He gave a skeptical laugh. "You don't trust your own sister? You're not planning to turn me in?"

"Sister or not..." I realized the irony, since Wendy fit better in the "or not" category. "We're in your country and you have the power. No cop is going to take what we tell them seriously. Your family owns this resort. We're foreigners. By the time somebody in New Mexico looks into this, you'll be somewhere else."

"So tell me again. Why should I speak to you?"

I held up my phone. "This might not work immediately, but it's a first step."

"I saw some benches," Teo said. "Better to be comfortable."

Ex was weighing his options. I had to alter the balance. "If I had to make a guess, Ex? I'd say Wendy used you. And one thing I've learned since Calvo's murder? She's good at that. In fact she's using me right now. That's why I ended up here."

He didn't look convinced, but he started toward a wildlife viewing area not far away. I trailed behind him, and Teo stayed close to his side.

Three benches formed a U on a square platform, surrounded by gardens. Beyond the end of the walkway, a body of water somewhere between a puddle and a pond sparkled in the moonlight. No rooms were nearby. I was glad both Teo and I had finished our showers with insect repellant.

He lowered himself to the bench in the middle, and Teo and I flanked him. The lights along the walkway were already growing dimmer.

Ex went right to the heart of things. "Your sister is a liar and a murderer." He looked at me, as if expecting a protest.

No matter what I suspected, his opening salvo caught me by surprise.

Teo leaned forward, guessing that I needed a moment to recover. "Why don't you start at the beginning, like how you got involved with Wendy?"

Ex's gaze flicked to Peg. "What happened to your leg, man? You a vet?"

Teo gave a slow nod. "Yeah, and I was a cop. I took a bullet from a murderer...seconds before I killed him."

I managed a deep breath. "So how long have you known my sister?"

I could see Teo's story had affected him. "We met at a resort."

"The Autumn Mountain Club."

"You seem to know an awful lot."

My tone was friendly. "The better to trip you up, my dear."

"We hit it off."

"Hit it off. You liked the same music? You both liked to hike? She was fun in bed?"

Gone was the friendly bartender. "Are you going to listen?"

"Yes, but I need to understand. Was it casual or something more?"

"Some of both. She seemed to like me. I knew her father owned the resort. She came on to me."

"Maybe you felt you didn't have a choice. Like you said, our father owned the resort. Maybe your job was on the line?"

He didn't take the easy way out. "Nothing like that. We had fun whenever she was there. And after a while, it just turned into more."

Ex should either be responding to casting calls, or he was telling the truth. "You were falling in love? Was she?"

He glared at me. "Do you know her at all? She thought I was a big, dumb cluck. We had fun together, and she figured if she ever needed me, I'd be there."

"How long before you figured that out?"

"Give me some credit, lady. Right from the start. You have to know people to tend bar. It's better than a psych degree. She was never going to leave her husband and kids for me. I was just supposed to be there when she showed up."

I wondered how anybody's standards could be that low. "So, were you? There for her, I mean?"

"When I could be. But she underestimated me. She thought I wasn't wise to who she was, but I guess the way she used people was part of her charm."

"So you saw her on and off?"

"And every time that I assumed she was out of my life for good, she'd call and ask me to meet her someplace new. She always paid. It was like she knew what she had to do to keep me on the string." He turned to Teo. "You know women like that?"

Teo ignored the attempt at male bonding. "You must really have had a thing for her."

"It got to be a game. I wanted to see what was going to happen next."

I decided to move the time line to the present. "So this went on for, what, years?"

He gave a slight nod. "I moved around, took a couple of

different jobs, but she always knew where to find me. Then a long time went by when I didn't hear from her. I decided it was time to come back to my own country, time to start over and find a better life. So I quit the job I had in Albuquerque, arranged for this one and got ready to move home."

"How did you end up in Santa Fe with Wendy?"

"She called one night, and she said she was sorry she'd been out of touch. She wanted to make it up to me. Seeing her one last time seemed like a goodbye present, so I said sure. She told me I was going to love the resort where we would stay, that it had these cute little casitas scattered over the hills, and we would have one all to ourselves. I didn't tell her I was moving here. I thought maybe I'd change my mind about that if, you know, things went well."

Teo took over. "Do you have a different opinion now about why Wendy invited you to the resort? Not just for a good time, but maybe for something else?"

"Sure. She knew Vítor Calvo was going to be there, and she wanted to kill him. I don't know why she wanted him dead, but she did."

I drew in a sharp breath, but Teo went on. "So you think that's what she planned all along?"

"It's the only thing that makes sense."

"How do you know?" I asked.

He sounded almost earnest now. "Here's what happened, and you can believe it or not. On the phone she told me she was going to Golden Aspen to look over the place for Gracey Group, kind of like a secret shopper. She asked me to register and get an extra key for her, and she would pay me back in cash. She said it would be better if we weren't seen together, in case somebody figured out who she was."

"So you registered. Did you use your own name and credit card?"

"No."

"But you were able to register?"

"I found a way. I wasn't going to charge anything, so it didn't matter what card number I gave them. I had cash and I paid in advance. I had some outstanding traffic violations, so I figured it would be better not to use my own license and name until I paid them off."

I looked at Teo, who shook his head slightly, as if to tell me to move on. I remembered Sophie's lecture about fake IDs. How many times had a patron left a credit card or license on this man's bar and walked off without it? Pocketing the credentials of somebody he resembled might have been easy.

I moved on. "If you weren't going to be seen with her, what was the point of being there?"

"Come on, lady. We weren't there to socialize. It was no big deal. I checked in and texted her where I was. She joined me, and we ordered room service."

I didn't want to hear what else they did. "What happened then?"

"The next morning she said she was going to look around, make notes and stuff, talk to employees. She said there were some good hiking trails and I ought to enjoy my day, that I'd see her later in the afternoon. After she left, though, I decided to go down to the lobby and get information about what else I could do. I had to pass the bar, and I saw Wendy inside. She was arguing with an older guy. Turned out, he was the doctor."

"Were they loud? Is that how you knew?"

"Loud enough, and she was waving her arms. At one point he pushed her away."

"Did you confront him?"

"No. The fight—and that's the right word—was dying down by then. She backed away, and he turned to leave. I knew we weren't supposed to be seen together, and since it looked like the trouble had ended, I watched from the doorway. She left by another door, and Calvo came out my side. He looked upset, even bumped into me without apologizing."

"Was anybody else around?"

"It was close to the lobby, but I wasn't paying attention to anything but the fight."

"Did you hear anything that was said?" I asked.

"They were across the room. I couldn't hear Wendy, but when he started in my direction I heard the doctor tell her she'd better leave him alone, or she would be sorry."

"So he threatened her."

"That's what I thought at the time."

"But not now?"

"He's dead. She isn't."

A chill coursed down my spine. Teo asked Ex to go on.

He was speaking faster now, in a hurry to finish. "I gave her some time to calm down, then I went back to the casita. She was already there. I told her I'd seen her fighting with a guy in the bar, and she said he was a surgeon from someplace in South America. She claimed she knew him because he'd been interested in investing, and she'd shown him around one of the Gracey Group resorts. She claimed that he got drunk and attacked her, and she barely got away. Since then he'd been stalking her, and this wasn't the first time he'd showed up. Calvo was part of the reason she'd asked me to register for both of us, just in case, but somehow he'd found her anyway."

"You believed it," Teo said.

"She was crying. I had to work to calm her down. And, you know, I'd never seen her that way. Wendy was a good-time girl. She never worried about anything."

"Did she say why she didn't call the police the night he attacked her or later when he started stalking her?" I asked.

"She was afraid her side of the story would reflect badly on your father and the company."

I exploded. "And so, even though she was in Santa Fe with you, having a little tête-à-tête—one of many, apparently—you thought her reasoning made sense? Because, you know, it seems to me that shacking up with you might reflect badly on my father and Gracey Group, too."

"Let him finish," Teo said, putting his hand on mine. "Ex knows he made a mistake."

Ex turned to me. "That sister of yours is the biggest mistake I ever made!"

"Please go on," Teo said. "You can understand why this is hard to hear."

We were playing good cop, bad cop, and we hadn't even arranged it. Reluctantly I sat back and folded my arms.

For a moment Ex seemed to debate whether to continue.

"I'm sorry," I said. "It is hard."

He gave a short nod. "She finally calmed down, and she said she wanted to be alone, only she was afraid he might come after her. I told her I had a gun in my car. I'd driven from Albuquerque, and I usually carry it in the glove box. She asked me to bring it to the room, just in case. The gun's registered, perfectly legal, so I did. I told her I'd stand guard, but she said she needed an hour alone. She was going to write down everything that had happened that morning, and send it to her lawyer. Then he could decide how she should handle things."

Neither Teo nor I commented.

"So then—" he blew out a long breath "—then I told her she could have the gun while I was gone, and I showed her how to use it. I loaded the bullets myself. I explained how to handle it. At first she didn't want to touch it, but eventually she picked it up. She said she could never pull the trigger, but maybe just pointing it at Calvo, if somehow he got inside, would be all she'd need."

Wendy hadn't needed instructions. The gun in her safe was proof. But she'd played along, acting the part of the frightened, helpless female, and he'd bought it.

Or else his entire story was a lie.

"You left her there alone?" Teo asked.

"She insisted."

"We all make mistakes."

Ex put his head in his hands. "I walked around the grounds looking for Calvo, to make sure he wasn't lurking. I figured it would be good to know where he was staying. So I talked to one of the maids, gave her a little money, and she told me which casita was his. When I went back to the room, Wendy was napping. I figured the worst was over, and we were leaving the next day anyway. Things improved after she woke up. I put the gun in the room safe, just in case. We had drinks and dinner in the room, and she made nice. I fell asleep way too early, but I figured I'd just had too much to drink, and Wendy said she was tired, too. She got into bed with me."

He looked up. "And that was the last time I saw her. I woke up before dawn the next morning, but Wendy had disappeared, overnight bag, the whole nine yards. For a while my head was pounding so hard I couldn't remember where I was or why. And then, little by little, everything cleared and I started to worry something terrible had happened to her. I got up and went to the safe to get my gun. It was gone."

"Do you think she drugged you?" Teo asked.

"I can hold my liquor, and I hadn't had more than two drinks, maybe three. The evening was fuzzy, but by then my head was clear enough to figure out what must have happened. I threw on my clothes and took off for Calvo's casita. I wasn't sure who to worry about, Wendy or the doctor. The sun still wasn't up, and nobody else was around. When I got there, his door was ajar. I went in and Calvo was on the floor, blood pooled all around him."

He paused, and Teo leaned forward to encourage him, though neither of us spoke.

"My gun was lying next to his body," he said. "The one I'd loaded myself, so even if the gun had been wiped clean, my fingerprints would still be on any bullets that hadn't been fired. I'd been arrested once, so my prints were in the system, and the gun was registered to me. I realized that I'd been well and truly set up."

We waited, but he didn't continue.

"If I was in that situation, here's what I would do," Teo said. "I would grab the gun and make sure everything I'd touched since entering was wiped clean. Then I would go back to my room, pack, wipe down that room and get the hell out of there. All before the sun rose."

He nodded. "Pretty much. Except when I went back to our room to grab my clothes, I saw that the jeans I'd worn the day before had blood on them. She must have taken them with her to Calvo's casita and afterward dumped them on our closet floor, grabbed her own things and left. But not before she slipped his wallet and some kind of fancy watch in the jeans' pocket."

"You still have them?" Teo asked.

"You're kidding? Gun, wallet, watch, jeans? Buried somewhere along the Turquoise Trail on the way back to Albuquerque. The only mistake she made? She didn't use enough of whatever drug she slipped me. I'm sure I was supposed to sleep until the maids arrived."

When neither of us knew what to say, Ex went on. "So that's what happened. Except all the parts where I just went along with whatever she said because I was crazy about her. If you want to believe something badly enough, you do."

Silence fell, except for a flute-like trill of a bird in the forest canopy beyond us, and the whirring of insects. "Yeah," I said at last. "Sometimes you do."

Ex got to his feet. "When I was pulling out of the resort parking lot, I heard sirens coming from the other direction. I probably got out just in time."

Teo and I stood, too, and I told Ex a detail he apparently didn't know. "Somebody called housekeeping and asked for more towels. The maid went to deliver them and found the body."

"Your sister." He thrust his hands in his pockets. "You know I'm just going to disappear again, don't you?"

"Nobody can predict what's going to happen next," Teo said. "If I were you, I'd keep an eye on the news."

"You mean in case Wendy has an attack of conscience and admits she killed him? That's never going to happen. I'll be on the run for the rest of my life."

"Whether you're telling the truth or not, I'm not going to tell her where you are," I said.

I don't think he believed me. "So? You found me. Someone else will do what you did."

"You said it yourself. Extradition is tricky."

"You think I'm worried about the cops? I don't want to end up like Calvo." Hands still in his pockets, he headed back the way we'd come.

Teo and I stood shoulder to shoulder until he was no longer in sight. "Do you think he's telling the truth?" I asked as the darkness closed in around us.

"What do you think?"

I was struggling to put everything together. "Right from the beginning Wendy was after me to find him. That's all she wanted. She claimed she wanted to tell the police where he was."

Teo was still staring into the shadows. "If you told her tonight that you found him, what do you think would happen?"

I didn't want to answer.

"I think her reason for wanting to find him is simple. It's all about the gun," he said.

"She wanted to know where the gun ended up."

"Everything hinges on whether Ex is telling the truth. But if he is? If things had played out the way she'd planned, and the sheriff had found the gun beside the body, along with everything she planted, then your sister could have gone home and resumed her life."

"Because Ex's fingerprints were on the bullets."

"But if Ex took the gun and disposed of it, she had two choices. To disappear forever, in case he came forward or someone at the resort identified her, or to find him and make sure he never told anybody what happened that night. Because if he did tell his story, for whatever reason, it wouldn't be as simple as his word against hers. Wendy's the one who knew Calvo."

Teo turned to me, sympathy in his eyes. "You'll have to decide where you're going to go with this, Ryan. I know it's a lot to think about tonight."

I had already decided. "There's only one thing I can do, but I know you're not going to like it. I'm going to find and talk to Wendy. I have to. It's the only way my family will ever have closure."

He was silent so long, I thought he was mentally listing all the reasons that was impossible, but I was wrong.

"Then maybe I can help you," he said.

CHAPTER THIRTY-FIVE

The day after I returned from Costa Rica I finally met Ike, a gorgeous specimen of the nearly-fifty crowd. He was sandy-haired, with broad shoulders and chest, and a terrific smile. Since we were having dinner on the water, he was wearing a bright tropical shirt that looked great with Sophie's chartreuse sundress. Best of all, when he looked at Sophie, his expression said he'd won the grand prize in a once-in-a-lifetime giveaway.

"Teo's coming tonight?" Sophie asked after introductions were finished.

"He's meeting us there." Teo had gone ahead to choose the perfect table. He had his reasons.

In addition to being a hunk, Ike was brave enough to teach middle school and obviously liked kids. "Does Bismarck need a walk before we go? Mind if the girls show me your neighborhood?"

"Perfect. I still have to get ready, and my mother's not going to be here for another half hour."

Theoretically Mom was coming to babysit, but she was really coming to grill me about the trip. I wasn't looking forward to our conversation.

Holly and Noelle took to Ike immediately, and by the time they left, they were chatting happily, Holly in charge of the route and Noelle clutching his hand.

Sophie followed me upstairs and flopped on my bed. "Something's cooking, isn't it?"

"Yep, at my favorite restaurant. My favorite *noisy* restaurant." I looked down at the jeans I'd been in since returning from Costa Rica. "I'm taking a quick shower. Be back in five."

When I returned in my robe and clean underwear, Sophie looked up from her lap. "Ike gave his phone to Holly so she could document their tour. The video's adorable."

"Maybe I'll send it to Bryce."

In a conversation that morning, I'd given Sophie a quick overview of the trip, and the things Ex had told us. Now she looked sympathetic. "Something tells me you won't be saving it for your sister."

I dug through the closet. I hadn't done laundry since my return, but I found a denim skirt and knit shirt, both clean and unwrinkled, my only standards.

"How much evidence will I need before I feel sure Ex was telling the truth, or at least most of it?" I asked when I emerged, clothed if not zipped or buttoned.

"Loyalty's a hard habit to break."

"As much as Teo loves his own family, I'm not sure he understands. He's trying to help me put Wendy and everything she's done behind me, but he still thinks like a cop. He always will."

"Let this play out, Ryan. That's all you can do."

The front door slammed, and Bismarck woofed to tell us he was back.

"Gram's here!" Holly shouted up the steps.

"Oh, joy." I finished dressing and combed my hair.

"You can think about what to tell her over dinner," Sophie said.

"I'm going to need something stronger than wine."

"Martinis on me."

Downstairs we greeted Mom, who was in the middle of showing her granddaughters the new board game she'd bought them. After Ike was introduced, and before the front door closed behind us, she managed to get me to one side. "I'll be waiting to hear about the trip."

I put my hand over hers. "Listen, no matter what, don't answer the house phone tonight. Okay?" I had turned off all the ringers, but I needed to be sure.

"Are you going to explain why?"

"It's complicated."

"The new normal."

At Seabank Seafood Teo had managed to secure the same patio table where I'd sat with my nieces. I made the introductions, and Sophie hugged Teo like an old friend. We chose seats so our guests had the best view of Little Mangrove Bay and the last vestiges of sunset. Tonight the band on the other side of the patio was playing light rock, and the air was filled with laughter and conversation. We added to the cacophony as Sophie and Ike asked Teo about Confidence K-9s.

Our server, a bearded blond with a man bun, arrived with a basket of hush puppies, and Sophie ordered lemon drop martinis for everybody. After he left, I suggested bowls of Key West chowder, followed by a couple of giant seafood platters. When he returned with the martinis, Teo made the order and added two pounds of boiled shrimp to arrive immediately.

Once we were alone I got down to business. "Teo has an idea for finding my sister."

Sophie was instantly intrigued, and Ike knew enough about Wendy's disappearance I could tell he was interested, too.

Teo took over. "A friend in the sheriff's office explained a sneak attack he uses to locate suspects who've moved away. He has to have their former address, and it only works if their mail is being forwarded."

"Is Wendy's?" Sophie asked.

"Not yet."

"This is getting good."

Teo smiled at her enthusiasm. "He sends a letter to the last address he had and types 'return service requested' over the address. And here's the important part. The post office doesn't forward the letter. Instead they *return* it to him with the suspect's new address on a sticker. The person he's trying to find is never notified."

"Moral to the story," Ike said. "If you want to keep your location a secret, keep it secret from the good folks at the post office."

We waited to continue until our server set a bowl of cold shrimp on ice in front of us. Sophie was ready with a question for me.

"But you're still getting Wendy's mail at the town house, right?"

"We're hoping to change that tonight."

Her eyes were dancing now. She loved a good challenge.

I filled in details for Ike, since I knew Sophie wouldn't have shared most of this, if any. "There's a safe in the town house laundry room with things inside that my sister wants. A friend of hers was supposed to help her get them. He had a house key, but it didn't work, and he couldn't break in. Let's just say that under pressure, he gave us the combination."

"She's hitting the highlights," Sophie said.

I finished up. "This guy, Jonah, was supposed to send most

of what was inside the safe to my sister by way of a remailing service. My sister is probably frantic to find out why she never got it."

"We know Wendy is still checking voice mail on the home phone—she's deleting messages." Teo changed to his best Southern drawl. "So tonight, she's finally going to hear from Jonah."

He sounded exactly like the renegade roofer. I clapped silently.

He grinned at me. "I'm going to block my number, then I'll call the town house and leave a voice mail from Jonah." He turned to me. "What about your mom?"

"She won't answer. I told her not to."

"Perfect." He paused. "Ike, want to help?"

"Sure."

"Be my drinking buddy. When I point to you, say something like 'hurry up, Jonah.'"

Sophie looked proud to know us. "That's why you chose this place. The band, the conversation."

"And the food," I added, "which will be here soon, so let's roll."

Teo pulled out his phone and punched in numbers. From my seat beside him, I could just hear Wendy's recorded "leave a message."

When Teo spoke, he sounded enough like Jonah that I had to stop myself from turning around to check.

"Hey, Wendy, this is… You know who it is. I'm out of town, but so are you." He forced a nervous laugh. "You aren't answering your cell phone, but luckily I got this number when I was, um, doing repairs at your place. Anyway, I got what you wanted. I sent you everything a while ago, but it came back in the mail, right when I was leaving."

He stopped and pointed to Ike who leaned over the table.

"Hey Jonah, hurry up!" He sounded appropriately tipsy. The guys were enjoying themselves.

Teo gave Ike a thumbs-up. "Anyway, the address you gave me was no good. Don't worry, though, the stuff will be safe until I get home." The band cranked up their volume, which was perfect.

Teo spoke louder. "Jeez, can you hear me? This place! I've been thinking. You've been gone a while, so the post office must be forwarding your mail. When I get home, I'll mail the envelope to your house in Seabank and the post office can forward it. It's one of those padded kind. You can't miss it. I bet you'll be happy to get it, one way or the other."

I thought he was done, but he added the perfect touch. "I guess I won't see you again, but remember when you get everything, you still owe me a little cash for those…repairs. You know where I live."

Teo put his phone back in his pocket and picked up a shrimp.

"Bravo!" If the phone call worked, my sister, anxious for the passports and flash drive, would go to the post office, wherever she was staying, and fill out a change of address card. And in a couple of days, her mail would stop coming to the town house. I reached over and kissed Teo's cheek. He put a shrimp in my mouth.

"So if she does decide to forward her mail, what happens next?" Sophie asked.

"I've already written a letter." I took a sip of my martini. "And if you're willing, I'll give it to you when you drop me off tonight. Once I'm sure Wendy's mail isn't coming to the town house, you can mail the letter in Delray. The envelope is all typed up, and your house is the return address. If, for some reason, she actually gets it, she'll think I was visiting you."

I didn't tell them I had struggled with what to say, and in the end, had simply scrawled, "Call me, please."

"Of course I'll mail it," Sophie said. "Think it will work?"

Teo detailed the problems. "It's a long shot. We're counting on Wendy to have her mail forwarded, and then counting on the post office to do their job correctly. We're also counting on Jonah not to answer any strange calls in the next few weeks, in case Wendy tries to get hold of him."

Three possibilities that could spoil everything.

"Is she going to believe the remailing service made a mistake and returned Jonah's package?" Sophie asked, nailing the fourth. "Isn't that unlikely?"

"Everybody makes mistakes," I said. I hoped we hadn't made one tonight.

The seafood chowder arrived, but not before Ike clapped Teo on the back. "I don't know this Jonah guy, but you sure convinced me he was sitting right here."

The two men grinned at each other. Sophie winked at me, and I made a conscious effort to put my sister behind me for the rest of dinner and enjoy our beautiful evening together.

In the shadows of the restaurant parking lot, Teo kissed me good-night. "I'm going to be out of town for a little while, working with a police department in the Panhandle. You'll let me know if this works?"

"You know I will. If it doesn't? I'm still going to find her."

"I know, but if this works, please don't go alone. It's not safe. Think about it."

And that was the problem. He was right. I shouldn't go alone, but I knew I couldn't go with him and still expect Wendy to tell me anything. The dilemma was all too familiar.

"I'll do nothing but think about it," I said. "Trust me." I kissed him again before I got into Ike's car. Back at the town house, Sophie stopped in just long enough to get the letter that might give us Wendy's address.

Finally I was alone with Mom. We sat together in the great room, her back as straight as a fireplace poker.

"Don't bother trying to make it sound better. Just tell me what this Milton Kearns told you."

So I did. By the time she left, she knew the bad news from Costa Rica, if not every detail. But I'd also reminded her that so far, we only heard one side of the story. As I had expected, she'd stood up for Wendy and pointed out Ex's poor reliability. I respected her for spreading her wings over her baby chick and fighting off predators. But I also respected her for the last thing she said before she left.

"No matter what she's done, Wendy's my daughter. I'm going to stand by her, Ryan, the same way I'd stand by you. But if any of what that man said is true, even half of it, we have hard times ahead."

By then Mom looked exhausted. I put my arms around her. She let me.

A few minutes later I stood in the driveway and watched her drive off before I closed the door. I felt wrung out from tonight and all the decisions ahead.

"Aunt Ryan!"

The girls often woke and called me. It wasn't a nightly occurrence, but usually after a trip to the bathroom or a glass of water, they'd go right back to sleep. This was different. Holly sounded terrified.

I raced up the stairs and found her sitting at the top. She wasn't quite awake, and not quite asleep. I reached for her, sitting close, and held her against me.

"Hey, it's a bad dream, sweetheart. But that's all. Just a dream. You're home and I've got you." I held her tighter.

"Mommy wasn't here."

I stroked her hair. "No, Mommy's gone. But I'm here, and I'll take good care of you."

"No, Mommy was gone. Before. When I got up."

For a moment I actually wondered if somehow my sister had gotten into the house, and Holly was trying to alert me. Of course, that was impossible.

"It was a dream. It doesn't matter."

"It does! She put us to bed, and we were supposed to sleep. But I felt sick. I threw up all over my sheets. And I got up to tell her. I knew she would be mad, but I couldn't sleep that way. And my stomach hurt and my head was so dizzy."

I wondered if Holly was talking in her sleep. Despite that I started to tremble, as if my body knew, before my mind, what was coming. I held her even closer. "Of course you couldn't," I said.

"But she wasn't anywhere. Nobody was here. Just Noelle, and she wouldn't wake up. Mommy wasn't anywhere. I looked all over. I was so scared. I cried and cried, and finally the door opened and she came back."

Holly looked up at me, and I saw she was wide awake now. "There was a man, and they were laughing. He wasn't Daddy, but he kissed her. I ran downstairs, and she was so mad when she saw me, she shouted at me to go back to bed. I told her that I threw up, and she pushed me, and I fell, and she told me to sleep on the floor."

I scrambled for the right thing to say. Could I pretend this was only a dream? But how awful for Holly to be told that what she remembered so clearly had never happened. She was sure it was real. How could I destroy her faith in herself or in me?

As I held her, and all the facts came together in my head and worse, in my aching heart, I knew the scene she'd recounted was no dream. It fit all too well with the things I'd already learned about my sister.

"What made you remember?" I asked, pushing her hair back from her wet cheeks.

"I thought you were leaving. I heard the door close. I thought you were gone."

"I would never, never leave you in this house alone. I was just saying goodbye to Gram."

"Mommy left us alone. After the night I got sick? I tried to stay awake every night and listen for the door. Sometimes I couldn't. But sometimes…"

"Sometimes you did." I was crying now, too, my tears falling against her hair.

"She went away and left us a lot."

"I'm so sorry, sweetheart. Children should never be left alone. Your mommy was wrong to do that."

"She told me not to tell anybody, especially Daddy."

"Thank you for telling me anyway. That was the right thing to do, and your mommy was wrong to say otherwise."

"She said bad people would come and take us away if I told. Will they?"

"No chance. I won't let them. Your daddy won't let them. Gram and Grandpa won't let them."

"Then why did she say that?"

I no longer knew the reason my sister did anything, but it wasn't my job to make Holly hate her mother. Sadly, Wendy was well on the road to making that happen on her own.

I felt my way. "Sometimes people do things they shouldn't, and then they tell lies to cover up. And sometimes when people are unhappy, they do bad things. Maybe your mommy is unhappy. It's still very, very wrong to leave kids alone, no matter what. But it might explain it a little."

"Can we keep living with you? Until Daddy comes back?

What if Mommy comes home? Will she make us live with her? Will she take us away?"

"You don't have to worry. If she does come home, it won't be for a long, long time, and your daddy and I will make sure we're the ones taking care of you, no matter what."

"Noelle misses her. Noelle cries because she's gone. But I don't miss her. I hope I never see her again."

I sniffed back more tears. I remember Noelle's hidden stash of Wendy's discarded objects, so lovingly assembled. "The best thing we can do is try to make your sister happy whenever we can. And you, too. Just remember I'm not going to let anything bad happen, okay? You can sleep at night and not worry. That's a promise."

"Can I sleep in your bed?"

"With Biz? Sure."

"I love you, Aunt Ryan."

There was no hope of damming tears now. I cried and held her. "I love you, too."

Just weeks ago I'd wondered how I was going to cope with Holly and her sister. I'd only come to take care of them because Wendy had demanded it. My nieces, my *sisters*, gifts from the universe that Wendy had thrown away like the weekly trash.

I would fight for these children, no matter what that meant, no matter where it happened or why. If my parents tried to protect Wendy, I would still find a way to keep her from Holly and Noelle. Forever. Even if I had to take both girls and run.

If I'd had any lingering doubts about my sister, I no longer did. Our final battle had begun. And I was ready.

CHAPTER THIRTY-SIX

Sitting in my rental car across the street from the Pronghorn post office in southwestern Utah, I had to admit that Teo had been right. Stakeouts were the absolute pits, and worse? This one gave me too much time to think. Other than turning on the engine to heat the car, sipping hot coffee from nearby Pizza Pleasures or snuggling under the extra blankets I'd borrowed from my bed and breakfast, there wasn't much to do.

For three days I had parked in the same spot to watch post office patrons come and go with their mail. And for three days I had considered and reconsidered how best to bring an end to this chapter in my family's life.

I was beginning to recognize the regulars. First thing every morning two middle-aged men in cowboy hats strode inside together, leaving the engine running on an ancient Dodge pickup. About an hour later a dark-haired mother dragged two protesting preschoolers inside, probably afraid if she let go of their hands they would leap into the snow banked outside the parking lot.

My favorite was a regal old man with a cane, silver knob

glinting in the winter sunlight. He came precisely at one o'clock and held his head like a king. Yesterday he'd slipped on a patch of ice, but as I grabbed my door handle to cross the street and help, he scrambled up and continued inside. I was glad I hadn't offered my services. He wouldn't have liked it.

I thought about texting Teo to tell him that so far the stakeout hadn't been successful. But I didn't. We had only seen each other once since dinner at Seabank Seafood, and the encounter hadn't gone well. Just before my flight to Las Vegas, I'd stopped by the kennel to return Bismarck. While my mother had volunteered to keep both dog and girls, Holly and Noelle had gone to Gulf Sands alone. With no reason to break into the town house, Jonah was no longer a threat. Bismarck's days as our security dog were over.

At Confidence K-9s Teo had met me in the parking lot, leaving me to wonder if he no longer wanted me inside. He'd nodded a greeting before he leaned over to speak fondly to his favorite canine, then he straightened and inclined his head in question.

"I hate this," I said. He knew what I was talking about, since I'd told him what I planned to do on the phone that morning.

"So you're really going to confront Wendy?"

As careful as my sister had been from the very beginning, she had not anticipated that the postal service would be her worst enemy. If she didn't move on before I got there, I knew I would find her in Utah.

"I got a good flight from Fort Lauderdale, so I can swing by Delray and pack a few winter things before I go. I'll fly into Las Vegas and drive to a little town called Pronghorn. It's not far from Bryce Canyon, and it's supposed to be beautiful country, even in winter. I was lucky to find a place to stay."

"Yeah, lucky."

"I can't imagine Wendy hiding in a place like that. She's

not the outdoor type. And there's nothing to do this time of year except enjoy the snow."

He didn't answer. I grimaced. "You're not going to help here, are you?"

"You don't want to hear what I have to say."

"It's not that I don't want to hear it, Teo. I just have to do this my way."

"Believe it or not, I know."

"But it makes you angry."

"No, I'm not angry. I am…" He shook his head. "This place you're talking about? You say it's in the middle of nowhere? Doesn't that strike you as risky?"

"Aren't *we* more important than whether I go or stay? I have qualms, but my family has to move on. No matter what Wendy says when I see her, I need to protect her daughters."

"That's what it's come down to now? It's not about proving she's innocent?"

I shook my head. "I remember those days like they were, what, last week? Now, it's about getting her out of our lives."

He looked as if he wanted to say more, but he didn't.

I moved closer and kissed him quickly. Then I bent down and hugged Bismarck. "Take good care of him. I'll settle up what I owe you for dog rental when I get back. Just let me know."

"Meet her in public."

"And don't let her follow me back to my B and B. I know. I won't. I'm going to be careful, but she won't hurt me. I'm her sister and her daughter."

"And squishy good feelings saved Vítor Calvo?"

Of course, he was right. Calvo's murder had been premeditated and his killer cold-blooded. "I guess I'll know the answer very soon."

"Let me know what happens." He'd touched my hair, just

the lightest stroke, then he'd turned, called Bismarck to walk beside him and together they had gone into the kennel.

And now, I was many miles away doing exactly what Teo didn't want me to.

Besides watching for Wendy and making up stories about post office patrons, this morning I played another game. I made bets with myself. How long could I continue my stakeout? It was Friday, and if Wendy didn't show up by tomorrow morning, then maybe I had wasted an airline ticket. If she really wanted what she thought Jonah was sending, she should have checked for it by now. She'd gone to the trouble of renting a post office box and having her mail forwarded. So where was she?

Of course, if I could think like Wendy, I wouldn't have to wait at all.

Another hour passed. I was afraid to get more coffee, which even when freshly made was muddy and bitter. In the time it would take to grab another cup, Wendy might come and go.

Services at the Pronghorn post office ended at three on weekdays and noon on Saturday. The lobby, where the postal boxes resided, was open twenty-four hours, but the boxes were too small to accommodate anything other than regulation size envelopes. Wendy must know she had to retrieve anything larger at the counter, and no later than noon tomorrow.

Today, if she didn't show by three, I could safely drive the miles to my B and B, make a dash for the bathroom, rest until five, and then return to town to take over my usual booth at Pizza Pleasures. For my evening's entertainment I could spend the next two hours eating a small cheese pizza, chewing so slowly that the staff probably wondered if my jaws were wired shut.

There were three restaurants in Pronghorn, and two were closed for the month of January. Since Wendy wasn't much of a cook, even if she didn't pick up her mail, I hoped she might eventually show up at Pizza Pleasures. I would haunt the place all weekend and somehow try not to draw attention to myself.

At noon I ate the sandwich I'd picked up on the way into town. At twelve-thirty I walked up and down the sidewalk, keeping watch and keeping warm. Since I was clothed in a down parka past my hips, and my head was covered in a fake-fur Cossack hat—complete with earflaps—I was a walking fashion nightmare but impossible to identify.

At quarter to three, cars began pulling in and out of the lot, as if everyone in Pronghorn had just realized the time. At the last minute a pale green sedan parked in the lone spot stating Reserved Parking, with the familiar outline of a wheelchair beneath. That alone wasn't unusual since the locals seemed to think that the reserved spot was for anyone suffering from split ends to an ingrown toenail.

The windows of my SUV were darkly tinted. That and new tires had sealed the rental deal. Now I took binoculars from the seat beside me and peered at the car, noting an Arizona license plate.

License plates meant little. My SUV had Idaho plates, even though I'd rented it in Nevada. Still, my heart beat a little faster, because supposedly Wendy had been in Arizona around the time of Calvo's murder.

The woman who emerged was tall, like Wendy, but from what I could see she had short red hair mostly covered by a cute wool cap with a narrow brim. If her lavender ski jacket was real down, it was newer and more expensive than mine, sleek and tapered at the waist. Of course I'd bought everything I was wearing at a thrift shop in St. George. She had shopped at the other end of the winter duds spectrum, but certainly not any store my sister would normally frequent.

Although it was hard to guess accurately, I judged the woman was about Wendy's build and weight. She carried herself like a model, walking with arms hanging freely, breasts jutting forward. Then, as I stared, she threw the post office door wide and marched in without paying attention to what or who might be behind her.

I opened my car door and started across the road.

Wendy handled doors the same way. Once when I was a teenager, a door she released nearly broke my nose. As blood trickled to my lip, I'd demanded to know if she ever looked behind her. Wendy found the question hilarious. She'd turned, hands on hips. "You think other people will watch out for you, Ryan Rosie? You're still a little girl, aren't you?"

Now, in the parking lot, I considered my choices. I could let the air out of the sedan tires, but not only would that take time, I might be creating trouble for a stranger. My second choice was to open the passenger door, which was probably unlocked, get in and wait for her. If the owner turned out to be someone else, I could explain that I thought the car had belonged to a friend and exit immediately.

But if the woman was Wendy, who knew where we might end up? She would literally be in the driver's seat, which sounded as bad as letting John Quayle follow me home four years ago.

In the end I just leaned against the hood, arms folded, and waited.

The door opened. Two other people exited, got into their cars and roared away.

The third was the red-haired fashion plate.

My sister, Wendy Gracey Wainwright.

"Fancy meeting you here," I said, when she looked up and saw me.

She had either learned to act as the high school Daisy Mae, or she really wasn't surprised to see me.

"I thought you'd find me eventually," she said. "How'd you do it?"

"Trade secret."

"Well, since we're in the parking lot of a post office, I assume it has something to do with my mail."

"I'll tell you what. You answer about a million questions, and then I'll answer that one."

She shrugged. "I'm not that interested."

I pushed away from the hood. "Then do you want to hear about Milton Kearns? Or what he said to me when I saw him last week? Because I'm sure those details will interest you."

"Why didn't you just wait until I called?"

I studied her as she spoke. Wendy was still wearing the brimmed cap, which was a pretty shade of violet matching a feathery scarf. I couldn't tell how short her hair was, although long bangs curled over her eyebrows and wisps brushed her ears. The coppery color turned her pale skin sallow, so she had applied a rosy foundation to offset it. Unfortunately, the foundation highlighted the vertical lines carved deeply from nose to lips. She looked older, almost haggard, even after a world famous cosmetic surgeon had twice worked his miracles.

"I wasn't sure you'd call again," I said. "You didn't seem that anxious to straighten things out and come home."

Tears filled her eyes. "How can you say that?"

"With no difficulty."

"You think this is fun? You think I'm doing it as an adventure?"

"I think it's time we talked. You can take off again, and I can spend more weeks trying to locate you. But if that happens? I'll go to the police with everything I know, plus a description of the way you look and where I found you. You can keep running, and you can change your hair color and fashion choices, but eventually you'll probably be caught by somebody less interested in your welfare than I am."

The tears had dried. "Is somebody else watching from the bushes? Are you going to record me?"

"Neither, but feel free to check."

"I want your phone."

I reached in my pocket and pulled out the burner. "I only have this one with me, and you're the rightful owner."

She took it. "I'm sure you're angry. I asked a lot."

I looked across the street. "I'm going to meet you at Pizza Pleasures. Nobody will hear us over the country music they're so fond of there. You walk and I'll park your car in front." I held out my hand for the keys.

She almost smiled. "You don't trust me?"

"That's going to be the topic of conversation." I watched her silently debate, but at last she dug in the canvas purse that was slung across her body and handed them to me.

"Meet you there." I walked around to get in, and she started across the lot.

By the time I showed up at the restaurant with Wendy's keys in my pocket, she was in the booth where I most liked to sit, coat and hat gone, short red bob, cut much like Mom's, fluffed around her face. Weeks on the run had taught her to sit with her back to the wall. My usual server was bent over the table, and she and Wendy were chatting like old friends. When she saw me, the server smiled.

"Mrs. Miller tells me you're her cousin. I hope you can cheer her up. She's been through so much." I watched as she smiled sympathetically at Wendy before she strode away.

I slid into the booth. "Mrs. Miller? I must be the last to know. Exactly what have you done with the Mr.?"

"Maybe Frank's death in Afghanistan didn't mean that

much to you, Ryan, but it meant everything to me. He was the love of my life. I'm still trying to cope."

I had to admire how expertly she'd become the widow of a man who had never existed. I was sure the story had ingratiated her with everybody she'd met here. "I'm assuming Frank was your pretend husband."

She held up her left hand, which was adorned with the gold wedding ring that had once been part of the set Bryce had bought for her. "Fifteen years. Everyone here has been so kind while I try to put my life back together."

"Does Bryce know about Frank? That could be confusing."

"How is Bryce? He sounds angry in his voice mails."

"He's busy with his job."

"He would be. The job means everything to him. If he has his way he'll die in that sub and command his next one in heaven. He's fond of the girls, but he's not home enough to know them well. Not that there's much to know with children."

"I've actually found quite a bit."

"Really? Maybe you'll have your own someday. If that heart of yours keeps ticking."

I took a moment to absorb her blow. "At the moment I'm pretty busy with your children."

"They're okay?"

"They're understandably confused. Both their parents disappeared." I searched her face to see if my answer meant anything.

If it did, she gave no sign. "I'm sure you and Mom are keeping them entertained. How's Dad?"

"Worried about you."

Her expression softened. "I was always his favorite, wasn't I? The businesswoman willing to do whatever it takes to finish a deal. A chip off the old block."

"I don't think you're a chip off anybody's block. I think you're one of a kind."

I signaled our server, and when she came to the table, I asked for a mushroom calzone, since I no longer had to make my meal last for hours. Instead of ordering, Wendy asked the woman about her son, who had broken a leg while cross-country skiing. Wendy seemed riveted as the woman described everything the poor boy had endured. Not until she had finished did my sister finally order a house salad without dressing and a glass of red wine.

"Do you know you have to order food to get wine in this godforsaken place?" she said when we were alone again. "Give me your purse."

"Why?"

"So I can be sure you're not recording."

I handed her the purse, and when she'd finished searching it, I lifted up my shirt for a quick glimpse. "No wire."

"Coat, hat, scarf. Stand up and let me see your pockets."

I played along until she was satisfied. "And don't think I won't check my car for bugs," she said. "In case that's why you wanted to move it for me."

"A girl can't be too careful."

"So what turned you into James Bond? You say you found Milton Kearns? Want to tell me where?"

The last thing I was going to tell her was where to find Ex. She would be much happier and, in her mind, safer, if he turned up dead. "Let's play a game. You tell me how you really know him, and I'll tell you if you've scored a point."

"You're trying to catch me in a lie."

"You could be honest and win the big prize."

"I was afraid if I told you that I knew Milt, you wouldn't believe I didn't kill Vítor Calvo."

I nodded patiently. "And there's your excuse. But that's not the same as how you knew him."

"He was a bartender at Gracey Group's Autumn Mountain

Club. And yes, we had an affair. With Bryce gone so much, it was the only sex I got. I'm not proud of it, but that's how it happened."

"Poor old Frank wasn't delivering?" I held up my hand to stave off her reply. "Sorry. He was probably in Afghanistan by then."

"You think this is funny?"

"I'm going to laugh until I cry."

Her expression darkened. "You're a lot like Sean, your real father. You wouldn't know since you never met him, but he had a great sense of humor, even if he was stupid enough to get himself killed."

I absorbed that blow, too. "So, back to sex. You and Kearns had an affair. How did the three of you end up together at Golden Aspen? You, Calvo, Kearns. And please don't expect me to believe you just ran into Calvo."

"You've learned a few things from your podcast, haven't you?"

I leaned forward. "Whatever you have to say, Wendy, you should realize nobody has come looking for you. You're still off the radar. Just tell the truth and I'll see if I can help."

"After you leave I'm going to spread my wings and fly without a husband, without children—and that means all of you. I'll be able to survive just fine."

I knew exactly how she *had* planned to survive, but now she didn't have the flash drive. I wondered what she planned to do next.

"How do you know I haven't already alerted the police?" I asked.

She waved that away. "Because you need answers first. That's who you are, never satisfied until you have the whole picture. Besides, think how badly my little indiscretions would reflect on your podcast."

"You think that would stop me?"

"I know you, Ryan. You would never turn in your mother or your sister, whichever way you think of me. And the truth would absolutely gut Mom and Dad, plus there's Holly and Noelle. Do you want them to go through life knowing their mother was a murderer?"

"You'd rather just leave than try to fix this?"

"It can't be fixed unless the police have Milt's gun. And I don't think they do. Am I right?"

I nodded.

"Damn him." For a moment I thought she was going to slam her fist against the table. All this time Wendy had been hoping that the police had arrived at the casita, found the gun next to Calvo's body and the other evidence she'd left behind, and then later identified Ex's fingerprints in their system. My job? To find out for her, either way. Maybe hope had dwindled with time, but I thought my sister had, until this moment, continued to pin her future on this one thing.

"I know," I said. "Imagine the nerve of the guy. He should have left it beside the body after you killed Calvo."

She stared at me for a full minute before she spoke again. "Okay, I did kill Vítor. Not on purpose, but I pulled the trigger. And even though I know you're not going to tell anybody, I'm not taking chances on being found."

Wendy's order came, although mine was still in the oven, and she turned into the sweet young widow again, beaming her thanks. Then when the server left she turned back to me. "You don't seem surprised."

"I've already heard one version. Why don't you tell me yours? Start with why you went to Golden Aspen in the first place, and why you took Kearns along."

"Why should I?"

"Because I have things you want and need."

She assessed me. For so many years, when she'd looked at me that way, I'd thought she wanted to get closer, that she was trying to figure out how to be the best possible big sister. Now I knew she had always been plotting how best to use my obvious adoration.

She threw up her hands, as if I'd finally worn her down. "Vítor and I fell in love. Or, at least, I thought we did. After my first procedure the attraction was obvious. We spent time together whenever we could. And then, when I went to Rio for the second time, he asked me to divorce Bryce and marry him."

I'd considered multiple possibilities, including this one. But it still packed an emotional wallop. "That's a surprise."

"Why? I was fed up with being the wife of a sub commander. I was fed up with Connecticut, and the mommy track, and our sweet little house."

Their house was anything but little. Still, I nodded. "And life with Calvo would be very different."

"That life would have been so amazing." For a moment she looked genuinely sad. "I told him yes. I would move to Rio. He had houses in Europe, a plantation in the rain forest. I would have met so many famous people."

"So you asked Bryce for the divorce?"

"No. I *told* Bryce I was divorcing him, but not exactly why. I just told him I was unhappy and needed something different. Apparently, he followed up with some snooping and discovered I—"

"Hadn't always been faithful?" I supplied.

"You are so well informed. For the record I don't think he found out about Vítor, but yes, there was Milt, too. Bryce told me if I gave him full custody, he would keep what he discovered to himself. I could see the girls when I wanted, but he would have control."

"You agreed?"

"It suited me." She stopped, as if she realized she should say more. "And, of course, it was better for the girls. I wasn't sure how much time I would be able to devote to them once I was Vítor's wife."

"So, how did Calvo end up dead?"

She sipped half her wine before she began again. "He sent me a letter in October, calling off the marriage. Wasn't that a remarkably old-fashioned thing to do? Send me a Dear John letter? Pen, paper, the whole nine yards. He said he was sorry, but with time, he'd realized we weren't right for each other. He wished me well, and actually told me…" Her gaze was smoldering now. "He actually told me a part of him would always love me."

Calvo had hurt her. Then I realized how unlikely that was. Calvo had rejected her, and nobody rejected Wendy Wainwright.

I struggled to keep my tone even. "That must have come as a big surprise."

"I couldn't believe it! I hired somebody to look into it. Long story short? Vítor found a younger woman."

"Was that when you decided to murder him?"

"No!" She stopped while our server brought my calzone and asked if we wanted anything else. Then as I began to dissect it with my fork, Wendy leaned forward. "I knew I had to talk to him. Too much time had passed since we'd seen each other. I thought if we met in person again, I could rekindle what he'd felt before."

"So you arranged to meet him at Golden Aspen?"

"No! Of course not. Do you think I'm an idiot? Would he have come? I had to be sure. So I got his schedule from someone open to giving it to me." She rubbed the fingers of one hand over her palm. "Money speaks Portuguese, too. When

I saw he was going to do his promotional seminar in New Mexico, I decided to go myself and talk to him."

"But you showed up with a man."

"I had everything planned. The minute I was sure Calvo had checked into the resort, I was going to haul Milt into the spotlight. He's good-looking, and certainly younger than Vítor. I thought Vítor might sit up and take notice. You know, reassess."

I was surprised at the amount of detail in her story. Maybe she'd been lonely, but Wendy was enjoying the limelight, even if the only audience was me. "You really went to a lot of trouble."

"I had a goal. Unfortunately, the first morning I was there, Vítor saw me. The bar beside the lobby wasn't open yet, but I'd gone in to scope it out. He followed and asked what I was doing at the resort. I pretended to be surprised to see him, but he was angry. So I told him that I wanted to talk to him in person, that letters couldn't convey what we really felt. And I hoped that if we sat down and remembered the good times, maybe he'd feel differently."

"I'm guessing it didn't work."

"Do you know what he did?" Her voice shook with anger. "He had the gall, the nerve, to pull out a photograph of his new love. And he said—" she took a deep breath "—that she was prettier than I had ever been, even after he'd worked his magic on me. And now that I'd seen the winner, I should stop trying to run the race."

Calvo sounded as cruel as my sister. "And that's when he pushed you away and left. Is that the moment you decided to kill him?"

"I never decided to kill him. But that night I went to his room. I freely admit it, and I took Milt's gun—"

"After you drugged him."

"Is that what he told you?"

"I think you'd had practice." I didn't elaborate. "Besides,

you wouldn't have taken his gun unless you were sure Milt was asleep for the night."

"I only went to scare Vítor. That's all, I swear it. I wanted satisfaction after what he'd done to me. I was divorcing my husband for him, giving up my daughters, changing my whole life. And did he care? So I knocked on the door, pretending I was the maid there to turn down his sheets. He let me in, and I pointed the gun at him. He was terrified."

She actually smiled before she went on, as if Calvo's panic was the fondest of memories. "I'll never forget the way he backed up toward the bed. That was all I wanted, really. Just to see him act like the loser he was. Then after he cowered and pled for a while, I was finished. I lowered the barrel, but before I could leave, he leaped at me and made a grab for the gun. Unfortunately, it was loaded. It went off."

She turned up her palms. "The end. Not the one I'd planned, but exactly what that bastard deserved."

I let the story wash over me. "Not exactly the end. Because next, you tried to pin his death on Milt."

"Not very nice of me, I guess. But Ryan, Milt's not exactly a nice guy, either. And he has no life. I doubted he would be convicted, but if he was, the world would keep spinning. On the other hand, I had everything to lose."

"You killed a man."

"I was out of my mind. My world was falling apart. I'm not a murderer, just a woman who was treated badly. It's an old story."

"Without his gun, there's absolutely nothing to tie Milton Kearns to Calvo's death. He didn't even use his real name when he registered."

Her eyes widened. Obviously that surprised her.

I nodded. "You missed that, didn't you? So now there's no record Kearns was ever at Golden Aspen. He paid cash. He left with the gun, the bloody jeans, Calvo's watch and wallet. They're gone forever, and nobody's looking for him. But if I were the sheriff, I'd sure be looking for the pretty blonde who fought with Calvo in the bar that morning."

I was due one small lie after listening to so many. "Milt told me several people saw your fight. He certainly did. Another guest, an employee in uniform, both of them witnessed it. I'm not going to turn you in, but somebody else may. I guess you were right all along. You really aren't safe."

She tapped her fork against her salad bowl, but not in rhythm to Clint Black's "Killin' Time," the eerily ironic title of the selection playing over our heads. "You're not going to tell me where you found him, are you? You never were. You're not going to give me a chance to talk to him."

I shook my head. "I don't think a conversation with Milt is what you had in mind."

"You want me gone, don't you?" she said.

"First I wanted to be sure. But you know? Now, I really do." I leaned closer. "I want you gone for good. I don't want you to ever come near your daughters, including me. I want Bryce to have closure and the divorce he so richly deserves. I want Mom and Dad to mourn you and move on. Maybe you can find a good life for yourself, but I don't want to know, because if you ever come near anybody I love, I'll turn you in. Without a second thought. I'll write down every single detail of this meeting, and I'll willingly share it with the Santa Fe sheriff's department. That's how serious I am."

"Be sure you write down that Calvo's death was an accident. A dumb stunt, but an accident. If you're going to tell the truth, that's it."

I wondered if any of us would ever know. I found it doubtful, since Wendy had tried to frame Kearns, maybe even, as he'd guessed, by drugging him first. But could I prove what

I suspected? It was a safer bet to threaten her with exposure. Safer for everyone.

I picked up my coat and slipped an arm in one sleeve, then another. "You've probably figured out that I opened the safe and have everything in it."

"How did you get Jonah to make the call about that?"

I ignored the question. "I'm keeping the gun, but I brought your passport. I want you to use it." I wanted her as far from her daughters as possible.

"Aren't you kind?"

"You'll also find your flash drive. Only, just so you know, it's been erased. You'll never be able to blackmail those men."

"Ryan..." She shook her head. "Silly girl. You think that's the only copy of those photos that I had?"

I had hoped, but not with much optimism. "You're playing such a dangerous game."

"Yeah, I know. But it's not as bad as you think."

Wendy was living on the razor's edge and probably had been for a long time, maybe even before I was born. She was poised to balance there forever and liked the view. Until she slipped and fell.

"The stuff's in my car," I said, getting to my feet. "Say goodbye to your new best friend."

"I'm leaving Utah. If you've been lying to me, it doesn't matter. Nobody's going to find me. And I won't fall for your postal trick again."

"I'll wait outside."

When she joined me down the block from Pizza Pleasures, a light snow was beginning to fall, and the sky was dark with heavy clouds above us. I was sorry that this gorgeous countryside would forever be associated in my mind with this night.

I held out a canvas bag, then I pulled it back. "I have the

divorce papers for you to sign first. I can witness them. Do it, and I'll give you the stuff I brought."

"You're so organized. You got that from me, you know. We're more alike than you think."

"No." I'd attached the papers to a clipboard. I had a pen. She signed everywhere I indicated. I put the clipboard back in the car and locked the side door before I handed her the bag.

"There's some artwork of Holly's and Noelle's inside," I said as she pawed through it. "Since it's the last you'll see, I thought you might like to have it. I brought some of your jewelry, although I kept the most valuable pieces for your daughters."

Her tone was acid. "Aren't you sweet?"

"Some personal items, scarves, the beaded purse Mom bought for you at Christmas, some medications you left on the counter to tide you over, and refills until you can get new prescriptions. I want you to stay well so you can get the hell out of our lives." I didn't mention the medicine cabinet. She would deny drugging the girls, and I didn't want to hear more lies. "That's about it." I took out her car keys and handed them over. "You leave first."

Wendy took the keys and clutched the bag to her chest. "Believe it or not, I'm sorry everything turned out the way it did. I may not have wanted you, but I did try to be a good big sister."

"Appearances are everything, aren't they?" I started around the car, but then I turned back.

"Just one more thing? Are you going to miss Holly and Noelle? Because they'll miss you. As bad a mother as you were, they'll always miss you and wish you had loved them. Isn't that sad?"

I'll never be sure if her tears were real, but after she was gone and I drove back to the bed and breakfast, mine fell like rain.

CHAPTER THIRTY-SEVEN

I had booked the Utah trip with an open return, and after my confrontation with Wendy, I booked a flight home for the next day, rising just after dawn and driving through the mountains as the sun gradually peeked over them. My flight was delayed, and when I finally landed in Fort Lauderdale, I was too exhausted to make the drive to Seabank. Instead I spent the night at my duplex, and the next morning I jogged on the beach as I tried to recover.

That evening the sun was going down when at last I turned into the town house driveway. Teo's SUV blocked my way.

I had texted him from Utah to assure him I had survived, and again today once I was on my way back to the town house. Now I wondered if he was here to learn details or to persuade me to call the sheriff's office.

I parked behind him, and by the time I got out he was waiting for me.

"Hey." I didn't know what else to say.

"Have you eaten?"

That was not what I'd expected. "Just a snack on the road."

"I have dinner almost ready at my house."

My eyes filled with tears. "Teo, I'm too wiped out to be grilled tonight."

"I was thinking more along the lines of grilling grouper. Everything else is ready."

He moved closer and put his arms around me, and I leaned against him, tears spilling down my cheeks. "That bad?" he said.

"Oh, yeah."

"Let me take care of you." He kissed the top of my head and stepped back. "Unless you really need to be alone?"

"I'll meet you there."

By the time I pulled up to his house, lights were on inside and lanterns glowed on the porch. Outside the car I filled my lungs with the humid, pine-scented air. Tubs of petunias and marigolds bloomed along his steps, and I was so glad to be in Florida again. "I love this place."

"It's a good cure for a bad day." He held the door open and ushered me inside. Bismarck barked a happy welcome and did a little spin dance.

The house smelled wonderful, too, like onions and maybe bacon. I straightened after giving Bismarck his due. "Did you always cook? Because this feels new."

"I never had the time, but now I enjoy it. I made my mother's pigeon peas and rice to go with the grouper."

"I didn't expect this." I put my arms around him. "You weren't happy I left. I thought we might be over. And instead, here we are, and you even cooked for me."

He held me tight, and his voice rumbled in his chest. "While you were gone I realized the things that upset me most about you are the things I love. Your independence. Your spirit. Your desire to get to the bottom of everything. I have a feeling whatever you learned about your sister, and whatever you plan to do about it, will probably be things I don't like. But maybe we don't have to agree. We just have to trust our differences."

I looked up at him. "Somewhere in there you used the love word."

He kissed me. I melted against him, and my hands crept under the hem of his shirt to rest against his firm, warm skin.

His lips trailed a path to my ear. "Do you have to pick up the girls tonight?"

"Nobody knows I'm back yet, except you."

"Stay here."

"Oh, yeah."

"How hungry are you?"

"Starving." I kissed him again. "But not for dinner."

Before I left the next morning, I made coffee, and Teo prepared toast and eggs. Over breakfast I finally told him the upshot of my confrontation with Wendy.

He listened carefully and waited to respond. "It sounds like you're going to back off, unless she tries to come home."

I was glad we hadn't had this conversation the night before, because just being with Teo and not having to explain had helped me pull myself together. We'd pretended my sister wasn't in the room. We'd made love, grilled and eaten dinner, then slept together as if nothing, most notably our differences, would ever separate us again.

Biz had even given up his prime spot on Teo's bed and curled up on his new doggie sofa at the foot.

This morning I'd opened my eyes to find Teo propped up on one elbow smiling at me.

"Not at my best in the morning," I'd said, turning away from him.

He rolled me back. "Let's see if that's true."

It's possible I might have been wrong.

Now our lovemaking felt like something from a distant past. My sister was front and center once again.

"I haven't decided for sure what I'm going to do," I said. "I couldn't record what she told me. So I don't have proof she killed Calvo. Just Ex's story."

"And now, *hers*."

"She swore she didn't intend to kill him, that the gun went off when he threw himself at her."

He nodded, as if he'd heard that before. "So here's what you could do. You could tell the sheriff everything you know and let the law take it from there. Wouldn't it feel good to let go of responsibility once and for all? All these decisions should never have been yours in the first place."

"I told her to stay away. We won't see her again."

"Think. What's to stop her from showing up at Holly's wedding in twenty years, or Noelle's? Or worse, when they're teenagers and as impressionable as hell. Calvo's death will be old news by then, and your story will be suspect because you waited so long to tell it, and who knows? You might be suspect, too. Can you really trust her to stay away?" He shook his head. "Can you trust her not to kill somebody else?"

I felt that last question like a knife in my already wounded heart. "If the sheriff found her, Teo, do you know what an arrest would do to my parents? To Bryce's career? To Holly and Noelle?"

"On the other hand the truth might be the best way to protect the people you love. One blow now, but not a fatal one. Bryce knows who Wendy is, maybe not every lurid detail, but enough that he wanted her out of his life. Your mother has come to terms with what you've told her so far, and your father must suspect more is going on than he's been told. And the girls?"

I hadn't told Teo about Holly's nightmare or the revelations afterward. If Wendy was convicted of murder and imprisoned, the girls would have closure of a sort. If she remained at large, she would be a shadow over their lives. They would always wonder why she had abandoned them. They would always wonder if she might show up again.

I had questions, but no answers. "Is my decision going to affect us?"

Teo considered, and I respected him more for not answering immediately.

"She's your family," he said after a long moment. "I don't know what I would do if she were mine, so how can I fault you? But the fate of a murderer should be up to God and the law, nobody else. And those who love the victim or the murderer? They're least likely to make the right choices."

"The law's not always right. Nothing is black or white."

"You're trying to be judge, jury, sister and daughter. You can't be. You shouldn't be."

Teo rose to clear the table, but I put my hand on his arm. "Thank you. I listened."

He leaned over and kissed me. "Do what you need to."

On the trip home I considered swinging by my parents' house, but I wasn't up to telling my mother what I'd learned. I wished I could bask in the warm glow of my night with Teo, and in our budding respect for each other's differences. But even though I'd left Wendy with the impression I'd said goodbye forever, I still had doubts.

At the town house I took care of mail—just mine now. Wendy's mail would probably pile up at the Pronghorn post office indefinitely. Afterward I checked the phone and discovered the line was dead. Wendy had finally gotten around to canceling the phone service.

Without Holly and Noelle or Bismarck, the house seemed starkly empty. The refrigerator was almost empty, too, and I made a mental note to buy groceries before I picked up the girls that evening.

At some point I had to call Sophie and report what I'd

learned, but at the moment I wasn't ready to face another explanation. Upstairs I lay down to nap on the same bed where
Wendy had slept. Instead I stared at the ceiling.

When had my sister turned into a monster? My mother
thought the change had begun after Greta's death. As terrible
as that must have been, how had the drowning transformed
her from the perfect daughter, student, friend into someone
who, in the most positive scenario, had pulled a gun on a former lover as retaliation for abandoning her?

What was the connection? Greta had abandoned Wendy,
too, only not by choice, by drowning. Had that memory lingered in Wendy's subconscious to make her react in terrible
ways to every abandonment in her future? Had Bryce paid a
price, too, for abandoning her to his job?

I wasn't a psychologist, but children and adolescents routinely suffered abandonment. How many of them lost their
moral compass?

Too tightly wound to sleep I got up. Wendy's scrapbooks
were still in the bottom drawer of the bedroom dresser, and
I pulled out the one filled with photographs, paging through
them again and watching my sister-mother turn from an ador-
ably chubby infant into a toddler and then a girl.

Photos of Greta began to appear. The more I gazed at them,
the more I felt this was a girl I would have been friends with.
I remembered my mother's story about the bouquet with the
chocolate bar hidden among the flowers. When had she and
Wendy grown close? Had she cared that Wendy was prettier?
Had she been happy in Wendy's shadow?

Then Greta began to blossom, too. Since Wendy was in
most of the photos, I examined her, as well. Was she happy
her friend was turning into someone she might have to compete with? Did friendship override jealousy?

I came to the last photo of the two girls together. I hadn't paid attention to it before, but now I realized it might be the last one taken before Greta's death. They weren't arm in arm, as before, but then they were no longer children. They were adolescents, moving from middle school to high school. Hadn't my mother said that Greta died right before Wendy went into ninth grade?

They looked happy enough, but almost anything could be hidden behind a smile. I slid the photo out of its holder and carried it to the window where the light was best. I searched their faces, although I wasn't sure why. Wendy's hair was nearly white from hours in the sun, and her skin was tanned. Greta's dark hair was shorter, but beautifully cut in layers to frame her face. Her cheekbones were high, her eyebrows perfectly shaped, and her lashes were long and dark. My mother had said Greta would have been striking, but I saw real beauty here, the kind that would deepen with age.

I almost missed the necklace. I would have missed it entirely if it hadn't looked so familiar. I held the photo closer, and after a moment I took it with me to my nieces' room. Noelle's carved wooden box was still hidden under a stack of unworn sweaters, a testament to how much she loved her absent mother. I sat on her bed and lifted the top. Inside were the same familiar objects, but only one interested me. I lifted a necklace, half a heart on a tarnished chain, and held it next to the photo. For the first time I noticed that the heart had words engraved in it, but they were too worn and tarnished to read.

I stared at both photo and necklace for a long time, then I slipped them into my pocket.

After I waited on the high school line for a full ten minutes, Claire Durant finally came to the telephone. "Ryan," she said. "What can I do for you?"

"Claire, did you know my sister in middle school?"

She seemed surprised by the question, and possibly relieved, since we hadn't spoken since she'd given me the yearbook and I'd been plunged headfirst into family secrets.

"No," she said, "my family moved here at the beginning of our sophomore year."

I was disappointed. "Oh."

"Why?"

"Well, I was hoping to talk to somebody who knew Wendy and her friend Greta..." I searched for Greta's last name. "Harold, I think. Greta Harold. She died the summer before she was supposed to start high school, but you wouldn't have known her."

"No, but I knew about her. Adolescents take death especially hard. When I arrived, people were still talking about the way she drowned."

"Is there anybody you know who's still living in the area and might have known her? Anybody who went to school with her? With Wendy?"

"I'm going to assume you have a good reason for asking this?"

"Me, too."

"I gave you Diana Gordon's yearbook."

"You had your reasons. I'm still trying to absorb them."

I half expected her to ask me what I was absorbing, but she didn't. Claire had told me it was her job to keep secrets.

"Diana is a physical therapist at a clinic on the outskirts of town. I think her married name is Reynolds. I can't remember the name of the clinic, but somebody told me she's very skilled. Why don't you try her?"

"Thank you. And thanks for...the yearbook."

"I'm glad to help."

I went to my laptop. Maybe I was trying to avoid the moment when I told my mother what I'd learned. But I knew for certain I wanted to talk to Diana Gordon Reynolds before I talked to Mom that evening.

Before her death, Greta Harold wore half a heart on a chain around her neck. In the same photo, Wendy's neck was bare. Yet now, residing in my pocket, was a necklace like Greta's. And unless the necklace was flipped when the photo was taken, the half in my pocket was exactly like the half she had worn.

I hoped Diana, the same Diana who had badly defaced Wendy's yearbook photo all those years ago, could explain.

CHAPTER THIRTY-EIGHT

I considered multiple ways to persuade Diana to talk to me. In the end, at noon I made the trip to Mangrove Bay Physical Therapy, located at the end of a strip mall filled with exclusive shops. Once inside I asked the young receptionist who was juggling paperwork if Diana had time to see me.

The woman who came out to greet me looked nothing like her Seabank High senior photo. She was slender and attractive, with long brown hair that glowed with red highlights, and sassy black-framed glasses. She smiled warmly and held out her hand. We shook.

Diana launched right in. "Jenny said you'd like to make an appointment. What do you need help with?"

I moved to one side, hoping she would follow, and she did.

"I'm not here for an appointment. I'm sorry that was the impression I gave. But you went to school with Claire Durant, and she suggested I talk to you."

"I missed your name."

She hadn't missed it, I hadn't given it. Now I was afraid she wasn't going to like it.

"I'm Ryan Gracey. You went to school with my sister."

She didn't miss a beat. "You don't look like Wendy."

"No, I look like my father." I didn't elaborate, and if that clicked for her, she didn't show it. "Please don't let our relationship influence you."

She didn't smile. "Why do you think it might?"

"I have your yearbook. Claire gave it to me. I guess somebody picked it up at a garage sale. You probably don't remember, but you more or less destroyed Wendy's photo."

"It's a little late to say I'm sorry, isn't it?"

"This has nothing to do with the photo, honestly. Or the yearbook. But I need to talk to somebody who knew Wendy and her best friend in middle school, Greta Harold. I know it's not fair to just corner you this way but—"

"Are you the same Ryan Gracey who produces *Out in the Cold?*"

I was so surprised I didn't answer.

"Yeah, I'm a fan, so sue me." Diana smiled a little. "I listen to true crime podcasts when I run. Yours is one of the better ones. Your name made me think of Wendy, which is why I remember. I didn't know you were actually related."

"We're years apart."

"You aren't going to like anything I have to say about your sister. Are you sure you want to talk to me?"

"That probably makes you the person I most need to talk to."

She still looked skeptical. "Are you doing a story on Greta's death?"

I shook my head.

"Okay. I don't have anybody to see for the next two hours. I was going to catch up on charts, but I can spend a few minutes with you."

We walked to a café several doors down. At the counter I

asked for a bagel with cream cheese, but Diana only wanted coffee. Once we had our order, we tucked ourselves into a booth at the back. Suddenly the whole encounter struck me funny, and when Diana asked why I'd laughed, I turned up my palms.

"I've done this talk-over-coffee thing a lot. Nothing good ever comes of it."

"What do you mean?"

I gave her a brief description of my Starbucks encounter with John Quayle, and the aftermath. I didn't tell her about Ella.

She leaned forward, the stiffness in her spine melting away one vertebrae at a time. "That was you? At the time your name didn't register. An officer and his dog were shot?"

"They saved my life." I decided sharing something more might be helpful for our rapport. "He's my guy, and the dog is happily retired and living with him."

"Happy ending. Good for you."

"I'm guessing my sister wasn't kind to you in high school."

She played with her coffee spoon. "I was the gawky girl she always made fun of. And she did it so tactfully. She'd suggest I take up the hems on my skirts, or give me the address of a salon where I could get a better perm, or tell me new glasses would look so much nicer. She'd always do it in front of other girls, like she had my welfare in mind. Of course, I don't know what she said when I wasn't around. I shudder to think."

"That sounds so cruel."

She grimaced. "Those years were tough. My father had a stroke when I was ten, and my mother had to care for him until I came home in the afternoons. Then I took care of him while she went to work cleaning office buildings. I shopped at thrift stores, used the same frames for my glasses every time I got a new prescription, and the perm? My mother saved for a year to take me to the beauty school for my birthday. I hope the girl who did it went on to a different career."

"I bet your dad's condition spurred you to become a physical therapist."

"It did."

"So that's Wendy." I paused. "How about Greta? Did you know her well? Because my mother tells me that she and my sister were best friends until Greta drowned."

"They weren't friends as long as that."

"No?"

"They were close for years, true. Greta more or less basked in the glow of Wendy's friendship. But in middle school she started coming into her own. She realized people liked her for herself, not for her connection to Wendy. And she also saw the way Wendy manipulated things so Greta was always on the sidelines."

"Are you guessing, or did she maybe tell you this?"

"Both. But one of the reasons Wendy picked on me was because Greta and I became friends that last year before she died. She started sitting with me at lunch instead of at Wendy's table where the popular kids sat. She invited me to her house." She set the spoon away from her and folded her hands. Her coffee was untouched. "I still get Christmas cards from her mom."

I had my opening now. "I have a photo of Wendy and Greta. I think it may be the last one Wendy had of them together before Greta died." I took it from my pocket and held it out for her.

She held it up to see it better. "That's how she looked in the last photos I have of her, too. You're probably right. She died on the sixth of June, 1986. I put flowers on her grave every year."

I was touched. "From the photo it looks like she and Wendy were still friends."

"Greta tried not to make enemies. But by then, your sister wasn't happy with her. Not by a long shot. And Jeff was the main reason, I guess."

She returned the photo, and I set it on the table. "Jeff?"

"Jeff Fishler."

The name was familiar, and I mentally paged back through the yearbook. "Was he homecoming king in high school?"

"A shoo-in. He was also voted the most likely to make a hole in one. He's a pro golfer now."

"That's why the name sounds familiar." I didn't follow golf, but my father did, and once he'd mentioned that a guy playing in a tournament in Naples had graduated with my sister.

Diana continued. "In eighth grade Jeff started hanging out with Greta, and they got about as serious as anybody does in middle school. Wendy tried everything to get his attention, but when he made it clear he preferred Greta, Wendy told her she was disloyal. Greta didn't buy it."

"I went to a girls' school. I think I'm grateful."

"Lucky you. It was a big deal between Wendy and Greta. In middle school, of course, everything is a big deal, but Wendy wouldn't give up. She flirted with Jeff, belittled Greta. Finally Greta just stayed as far away from her as she could."

I lifted the photo again. "I noticed the necklace Greta's wearing here. I wondered if it's a friendship necklace of some kind. I thought maybe Wendy had the other half and just wasn't wearing it in this photo."

Diana didn't have to look. "No, Jeff wore the other half."

"The photo's not clear. I can't read the writing." Nor could I read it on the half in my pocket.

"It's what they call a mizpah necklace. A silver one, very pretty. Jeff was Jewish, and the words are a quote from the Old Testament. When the two parts come together, the quote says something like 'The Lord watch over us while we are apart.'

That's not exact, but it's something like that. Jeff wore one half, and Greta the other. I remember because, at the time, all I wanted in the whole world was for some boy to like me that much."

I hadn't taken a bite of my bagel, and now I shoved the plate away, my appetite gone. "Were Jeff and Greta a couple the summer she died? Was she still wearing his necklace?"

"Yes, and he was, too."

I struggled to find a way to ask the next question, but I didn't have to. Diana went on.

"After she died, Jeff wore his half all the way through high school. He said it was a tribute to Greta, that her half was lying somewhere on the bottom of the gulf. When they found Greta's body—" she took a deep breath "—hers was missing. Either it came off when she was trying to get to shore, or it washed away in the waves that swept her down the beach."

I sat very still, trying to find a way to explain the half in my pocket. I finally met her gaze. "Diana, is there any chance that Jeff might have given his half to somebody else after he graduated? As a keepsake? Maybe even to my sister because she and Greta had once been so close?"

"No, he despised Wendy. I'm sorry if that's harsh, but he did. Jeff thought your sister was responsible for Greta's death. If she hadn't left Greta alone in the water that night, even if she did run back to find help like she said, then Greta wouldn't have drowned." Diana was frowning now. "Why are you asking?"

"Just a mystery I'm trying to solve." I managed a smile. "That's what I do."

She wasn't convinced. "There's more to it, isn't there?"

I had to use everything inside me not to fish the necklace out of my pocket and place it in her hand, fold her fingers over it and tell her to get in touch with Jeff. Instead, because nothing that I now believed could ever be proven, I stood. "You've been a real help, Diana. You're happy now? Your life smoothed out after high school?"

"Husband, kids, job. I'm happy."

"I'm so sorry my sister treated you the way she did. For what it's worth? I believe every word you said."

I walked out of the café without telling her how lucky she had been that Wendy had only bullied her.

Because now I knew my sister was capable of so much worse.

CHAPTER THIRTY-NINE

On my drive back to the town house, I went over every sentence of my conversation with Diana. I knew exactly where her story led, but one detail that hadn't resonated at the time haunted me now.

Diana had given the date of Greta's death as the sixth of June, 1986. I wanted that to be wrong. I didn't want to be led even farther into the darkness of my sister's heart, but once I was home and on my computer, I found an archived article about the drowning. And Diana had been right.

June 6, 1986.

6-6-8-6, the combination that had opened the laundry room safe.

The day we'd worked so hard to find those numbers, Glenn had suggested birthdays and anniversaries. None had worked, only I hadn't known about this one.

Had Wendy chosen the date of Greta's death as a macabre memorial to her friend? Or was the truth so much worse? Was 6/6/86 the date that Wendy had struck out against perceived abandonment and rejection and drowned her childhood friend? Did she view the day triumphantly, as the day she had retaliated for all her grievances?

The way she undoubtedly viewed shooting Vítor Calvo?

Horror stole the breath from my lungs. I had chosen exile instead of prison for my sister. I hadn't been completely fooled. Had I believed that Wendy had never intended to murder Calvo? Or had I believed she'd only set up Ex as the real murderer at the last minute? No, but because of the slight possibility those things were true, because of how calamitous an arrest would be for our family, I had turned a sociopath loose.

How many other people would die because I hadn't been brave enough to do what was required?

I was in the car and halfway to my parents' house before I realized where I was going. I wasn't sure I had closed the garage door. I didn't know if one or both my parents were home. I had simply gotten into my car and begun the drive to Gulf Sands.

I wanted to tell my mother first. Telling her would be bad enough, but what would happen when we told Dad? Dale Gracey was a man who took charge, yet throughout the weeks of Wendy's absence, he had stepped back. Part of his reaction could be explained by surgery, and the depression that sometimes followed. Dad had suffered from fatigue and anxiety, as well, but none of those things could explain why he hadn't immediately demanded we find Wendy or let a professional do it.

Had my father really wanted to know where his older daughter was? Or had he, who had worked hand in hand with her, sensed the truth and been too sick or loyal to confront it?

The news that Wendy had murdered a man and was now on the run would be cataclysmic. But would it be a surprise? I was no longer sure.

I buzzed past the security gatehouse, just missing the arm as it rose to allow me through. Even so, once I'd parked in front of my parents' house, I stayed in my car, wondering if this would be the last time I visited here. When I drove away this afternoon, I wasn't sure if I would ever be welcomed back into our family again.

When I finally walked up to the porch, the cleaning woman was just leaving. She held open the door so I could enter without knocking, and I thanked her, but not by name. She was another in my mother's endless chain of women who would never clean as well as she did.

I found Mom by the pool, staring at the gulf. Dad was nowhere in sight.

She turned when she heard my footsteps and got to her feet. "I didn't know you were back yet. You didn't call."

"There was nothing I could say on the phone."

She took in my expression, my posture, and her hand flew to her mouth. "Is Wendy...dead?"

I shook my head and found myself wishing it were that easy. In contrast to what we faced now, how wonderful would it be to mourn the woman we'd thought we knew, the perfect daughter, the sister who had given me thoughtful gifts, the young mother and career woman raising girls and expertly handling all the pressures of a life with a husband so often at sea.

Now, we would never be able to mourn that woman, because she had never existed.

I rested my hand on her shoulder. "Mom, this is really bad news."

She stared out at the water. Then she turned. "Tell me while we walk."

I slipped my arm through hers, and once we were on the beach, I did.

Almost an hour later we sat staring at mugs of tea that had grown cold without either of us taking a sip.

"I didn't tell you everything." I looked up. "You still have doubts she's guilty, don't you?"

"She's my daughter."

"I know." I stirred my tea, even though there was no sugar, lemon or milk in it.

"There's more, isn't there?"

She sounded like someone waiting for the next blow to fall. From her tone, I knew she more than halfway believed everything I'd told her was true. I had debated this, saved it until I was sure I needed it. But now I pulled the necklace out of my pocket and laid it on the table.

"Noelle keeps a stash of things Wendy throws away. She's only six. It makes her feel closer to her mother."

"She started doing that after Wendy left?"

"No, I found it under her sweaters when I first got to the town house." I tried to find a way to continue. "She wanted to be close to her mother. This was the only way she knew."

Mom didn't protest or defend. She picked up the necklace. "You just want to show me that Wendy isn't close to her daughters?"

"No. That's just how I happened to find it. I didn't think anything about it until today."

"So what is it? It doesn't look familiar. I don't remember Wendy having anything like this."

"In eighth grade Jeff Fishler gave Greta Harold a necklace with two parts."

"Fishler, the golfer?"

I nodded. "They were boyfriend-girlfriend. Maybe you knew that. Anyway, this is called a mizpah necklace. When the two parts fit together, you can read a quote." Now I knew exactly what it should say, because I had looked it up on my phone while parked in front of the house. I recited it. "'The

Lord watch between me and thee, while we are absent one from another.'"

"I'm not sure what this has to do with anything."

"The night she drowned, Greta was wearing her half of the necklace at the beach party. When they found her body, the necklace was gone. Jeff kept his half and wore it all through high school as a memorial."

"Wendy had one, too?"

Of course that was a possibility. Maybe later in her life somebody had given Wendy a similar necklace, but I didn't think so. If we ever wanted to know for sure, or if anyone in authority did, Jeff Fishler might have kept his out of sentiment, and a match might be made.

Now though, I told her what I believed. "I don't think Wendy ever had one of these, Mom. Not until the night she grabbed Greta's from her neck while she was drowning."

She stared at me, but she didn't say anything. I couldn't tell what she was thinking. I had no idea what she was feeling, either, or what she would say when she could speak again.

Could my mother ever believe that Wendy had done something so horrifying? That when she was barely fourteen, her perfect daughter had killed her own best friend, held her under the water in the dark as retaliation for attracting a boy Wendy had wanted? Or even the kinder version? That Wendy had allowed her friend to drown and still retained the presence of mind to snatch the necklace as she went under?

I pushed my chair from the table. "After Wendy told me her side of what happened in Santa Fe, I thought exile was good enough. I thought if I made sure she never came back, not to Seabank, not to this family and most clearly not to her daughters, we could struggle through this together. We would be okay. But we aren't, Mom, we aren't going to be okay. Not as long as she's out there. Wendy is a murderer. And we can't protect her one second longer."

She stood up, towering over the table. "What are you going to do?"

I stood, too, my eyes filling with tears. "I'm going to call the sheriff in Santa Fe, and I'm going to tell him everything I know. Then I'm going to help him find Wendy. We can't be the ones who decide who pays and how high a price." I felt the tears running down my cheeks, but for the first time since this whole sad saga had begun, I knew that what I was doing was right.

I touched her arm. "I'm so sorry. I know you and Dad are going to hate me for this, but I have to stop her."

As I watched, she tried to speak and couldn't. I had never seen Arlie Gracey at a loss for words, but I understood. I had been at a loss for the right words, the right action, for weeks.

Finally she shook her head. "No, Ryan, you don't."

She held up her hand when I started to speak. "No, you don't have to call and you don't have to stop her." Then she reached for me. I flinched, not knowing what to expect, but instead of a slap or a push, she folded me into her arms.

"You don't have to make the call," she said softly, "because I will."

EPILOGUE

In the two months since I'd returned from Utah, all the furniture in the town house master bedroom had been replaced. I had not wanted to spend another night on the bed where Wendy had brought admirers, and without asking for an explanation, my mother had agreed that the room needed updating.

Gracey Group could easily have afforded a painter, but together Mom and I painted the walls a soft blue-green and furnished the room with bright, coastal pieces, finding comfort in working on the project together. Afterward I moved everything I still wanted from Delray Beach to the town house and gave everything else away. I was back in Seabank for good now, and new renters were already moving into my old digs.

The one thing I'd loved most in my duplex, I gave to Sophie's oldest daughter. I could no longer bear looking at the painting of the two little girls on the beach at sunset. Was I reminded of Wendy and me? Wendy and Greta? It didn't matter. Someday I would find and hang more of the same artist's work, but I already had too many reminders of Wendy and always would.

The alligator clock had gone out with the trash.

My mother had done what she said she would. While I sat beside her, she phoned the authorities in Santa Fe and told them everything I'd discovered. A few days later I flew out to be interviewed. But before I even boarded the plane, the investigators knew Wendy's latest location. I told them that she'd slipped up and mentioned where she planned to go next without realizing it.

I hoped it was the last lie I ever told, but it served its purpose. Authorities in Los Angeles detained my sister just hours before she was scheduled to board a flight to Montenegro, a charming Balkan country without an extradition treaty. It's possible Wendy might have been happy there in a cute little villa by the sea, but I wasn't sure she was capable of happiness.

Now, with the case against her gathering momentum, she would probably find whatever happiness she could in prison.

Ex had been persuaded to tell his story to detectives from the Santa Fe sheriff's department. His family had arranged the meeting in Costa Rica, and at this time there was no talk of arrest or extradition. Several people really had seen Wendy fighting with Calvo in the bar on the morning of his death, and after her arrest, each of them had identified her.

If everything, including a set of fingerprints Wendy left on Calvo's light switch, didn't lead to a conviction, she had also been arrested with a flash drive of photos in her possession. When contacted, several sheepish men had admitted she was blackmailing them. Most likely she would be tried for that crime, as well.

Since there was no death penalty in New Mexico, and with the mounting evidence against her, Wendy was weighing her options. My father and Bryce had agreed to pay for her attorney, but only if she plead guilty. Good legal representation might get her the best sentence, but Vítor Calvo had been internationally acclaimed, and even the best attorney couldn't sneak the legal proceedings under media radar. For everyone's sake, I hoped the judge felt enough pressure that Wendy went to prison for a very long time.

As expected, our local authorities said that Greta's necklace was not enough evidence to have Wendy tried for her best friend's murder. None of us would ever know exactly what had happened that terrible evening so many years ago, but some of us would suspect the worst.

Today I was upstairs with my nieces, helping them pack. Each girl had one small suitcase to take back to Connecticut, where they would spend spring break with their father. Bryce was on the way from the airport now, to scoop them up and take them home.

We had all decided that he should be the one to explain to Holly and Noelle that their mommy was never coming home again. I thought he would probably tackle it once they were in familiar surroundings.

I didn't know what else he would tell them, because we'd hardly spoken. I'd seen Bryce twice since returning from Utah, both times when he was able to get emergency shore leave. The visits were short, and I had moved out of the town house to let him stay with the girls. Of course now he knew everything that had transpired with Wendy, and he had thanked me for doing the right thing. I'd assured him I wanted the girls to finish the school year in Seabank, and he had promised he didn't hold Wendy's actions against our family.

It was all so wonderfully civil. It was also frustrating.

Holly and Noelle needed me. I was more convinced of it every day. And I wanted them. I visualized being with them when they started middle school, started their periods, fell in love for the first time and got rejected. I would know how to dole out consequences if they got caught smoking or drinking, cheated on a test or even turned into straight A students. I would always love them, no matter what. The girls felt like my own.

How did I tell Bryce I wanted to keep his daughters with me? Of course, he would always be their father. I told myself they could spend time with him whenever he was on shore, as long as it coincided with school schedules. I would never stand between them in any way. And if Teo and I ended up together? I would make sure he didn't replace Bryce in their hearts. Wasn't there enough room for all of us? Bryce could continue doing the job he loved, knowing that his daughters were under the loving care of their aunt and grandparents.

Didn't my mother and father need the girls now? When Mom and Dad were still trying to deal with the ugly truth about their older daughter?

"I want to bring my fairy night-light." Noelle pulled it from the socket closest to the door and crossed to put it in her suitcase.

"I'm bringing the Paddington books," Holly said. She was almost giddy with joy that she was spending a whole week with her father.

"Clothes?" I asked. "I know you have some in Connecticut, but anything you want from here?"

I watched them select a few shirts, Holly more carefully than her younger sister. Noelle added a stuffed toy, Holly a string art kit my parents had given her. Once Bryce picked them up, he had promised to take them to Gulf Sands to say goodbye to Mom and Dad.

I told myself all was well. They would be back in a week.

Bismarck announced we had a visitor by barking sharply at the front door. Teo had brought him over to spend one last night with the girls before they left for the week. They'd been overjoyed.

I'd been happy to see Biz and even happier to see his owner. I was seeing a lot of Teo these days, and while the girls were gone, I would be seeing more. Sophie and Ike were already planning to come for a visit over the weekend and another dinner at Seabank Seafood. She'd warned me that before long I might not be the only producer of *Out in the Cold* living on Florida's west coast. And wouldn't it be convenient to have Sophie living just an hour north? In-person meetings were always best. Now, when needed, we could drive to Delray together to meet with the rest of the crew, too.

The girls beat me down the stairs and flung open the door. Then they were both in their father's arms.

I stayed back and watched the reunion. And as I watched... I knew.

Bryce finally came inside, a little girl held tightly under each arm. "Have these girls been good?"

"These girls are the absolute best."

"Their aunt's pretty wonderful, I think." He smiled. "I can't find the words to thank you for all you've done."

I knew goodbye when I heard it. "Girls, can you take Biz out for a short walk so I can talk to your dad?"

As expected, the request was met with groans, but eventually Bismarck was on his leash and they headed out the front door.

"Just for a few minutes!" Holly glared at me.

"I love you, too, sweetheart."

She closed the door with a bang.

"She's a character." Bryce looked exhausted. I could see lines of fatigue that had never been there before. His dark eyes seemed to take in everything and nothing. I could relate.

"They are so excited," I said.

"We'll have a whole week together. I can't wait."

"You're still bringing them back?"

"You're still willing to stay here with them until school's over?"

"And later, Bryce. I'll keep them till they're grown. I adore them."

His expression softened. "I've been reassigned, Ryan."

I had assumed his security clearance would be at risk. I felt a sharp stab of sympathy. "Because of Wendy?"

"That was a factor, but I asked for this. I've been reassigned to Naval Support in Orlando. I'll be on land most of the time, but I asked to get as close to you and your parents as I could. I'm surprised it all worked out, but it did. I was lucky."

"You didn't have to do that—"

"Of course I did. Did you really believe I loved my job more than I loved my daughters? Holly and Noelle need me now in a way they never did before." His expression darkened. "Obviously that's not true. They needed me in the worst way, and I left them with a murderer."

"Don't blame yourself. None of us knew."

"I ignored every warning bell. Every day I ask myself if I'd just been more focused on them and less on my position, would I have seen the truth?"

"You loved their mother. We never see the people we love clearly."

"I promise you and your parents can see the girls as often as you want. You can drive up and stay with us when you have time. We won't be that far, and I'll still need to travel. You'll be the first I ask to babysit, and, of course, they can come here to see you on school holidays. But I'll hire a live-in house-keeper to stay with them when that's not possible. And I'll make sure I'm free to spend every second I can with them."

I tried to absorb the blow, although I'd known it was probably coming. I met his gaze and the truth was clear, although I hadn't wanted to see it. Bryce Wainwright would not be single for long. He was exactly the kind of man women dreamed of having in their lives. And when he remarried, he would choose a good woman who loved children, most especially his.

I would always be Holly and Noelle's beloved aunt, but I would never be the woman they thought of as their mother.

"I'm going to miss them so much." I swallowed tears.

"You kind of got used to having them around?"

"I kind of did. It's been tough, and it's been great." Then I pulled my courage out of storage. "But they need to be with you more. I wish they didn't, but they do. They deserve that, and you deserve it, too."

He hugged me. "Have a few kids of your own, Ryan. The girls will need cousins."

I stepped away to search his face. "One of the few things Wendy did right? She married you. Maybe she hoped she could be the wife you wanted and needed. Maybe she thought she could pretend, and eventually, it would be real."

"While we're away, I'm going to explain whatever I can to the girls about their mother. But someday they'll need to know the whole story. We won't be able to keep the truth a secret."

"No more secrets. They were forced to keep too many. When she's comfortable with you again, Holly will tell you hers. But bring everything into the light whenever you can. That's how they'll heal."

"You'll really be okay keeping them until school's out? I need to sell the house in Connecticut, buy one in Orlando in a good school district near the base—"

"Would you let Mom and Dad help with that? Nobody's more qualified, and being involved will ease the ache in their hearts. Mom will be up there scouting school districts before the words are out of your mouth."

He nodded. "How are they taking this?"

"Dad had a setback and went into the hospital to have meds adjusted, but he's improving again. Mom spends as much time with the girls as she can. That helps her the most. You'll see a lot of her in Orlando if you want her."

"It was never your parents' fault."

"Someday, maybe they'll believe that."

The door flew open and girls and dog charged back in.

"You ready to go?" he asked.

Holly did a little dance.

I helped drag suitcases down the stairs, gave them snack bags I'd packed for the flight, straightened Noelle's skirt and tightened the elastic band on Holly's braid.

And then, just like that, they were gone.

"Just for a week," I told Bismarck, but for a moment he looked as desolate as I felt. Then he gave a happy little bark. The door opened again, and Teo walked in.

"I said goodbye to the girls out by the road. Bryce looks thrilled to have them."

I went into his arms and let him hold me as tears trickled down my cheeks. By my own count, I had cried more since Wendy's disappearance than I'd cried in my entire life up to that point.

"You're not crying because they're leaving for a week?" he said. "You were looking forward to the time away."

"Teo, they're leaving for good. Not right away, but Bryce has a new job in Orlando. I'm guessing it's a demotion, but he loves the girls more than his sub. He wants to be with them." I sniffed. "And I know before too many years go by he'll be calling to say he met a woman, and she'll be their new mother. I'll just be their aunt."

"You're already their aunt *and* their sister. Being their mother, too, would put you in the Guinness Book of Records."

I slapped his back. "Not funny!"

He wiped my face with the hem of his T-shirt. "Ryan, you told me once you probably don't want kids."

"Well, I wanted those two!"

"Since you can't have them, you might consider other options."

I snorted. "Like?"

"Like, oh, I don't know. Maybe getting married someday and having children the way other people do it? Or adopting kids if the other way doesn't work out? Just saying you could be open to possibilities."

"Is that a back-assed proposal?"

"Far be it from me to ever approach a proposal from the front, if the woman happens to be you."

I smiled a watery smile. "We haven't even lived together. You've only hinted you love me."

"We could live together this week. I have a house, you have a suitcase. That might even give you enough time to come up with something else we disagree about. If you put your mind to it."

"Like what?"

"Like the fact you lied to the authorities about how you happened to know where your sister could be found."

"Really, Teo? What makes you think so?"

He slowly shook his head.

"Not saying this has anything to do with your question, but for the record, I have the kind of job where I'm never quite sure what's legal. The law's a little murky since I don't work for the police. And sometimes other people are involved."

"Sophie?"

"Couldn't say."

"Your friend Glenn, the spy guy?"

"Couldn't say, but he does have some wonderful gadgets at his store."

"Like?"

"Like trackers so small you can slip them under car mats. Only, of course, Wendy was driving a rental, which I knew she'd trade in the moment she left Pronghorn, so even if I'd been tempted to do such a thing, that wouldn't have made sense."

"What else tempted you?"

"There are so many sophisticated possibilities. GPS units so tiny they fit into prescription bottles. Pharmacies put them on shelves with their schedule I and II drugs, so if somebody breaks in, the bottles can be tracked and the perps can be caught. It's very cool."

"I've heard of that."

"All the tracking's done by computer. Wouldn't it be interesting if one of those GPS bottles had been labeled by someone with a certain expertise and filled with one of Wendy's prescriptions?"

"And the tracking?"

I shook my head. "It's all hypothetical. Who has that kind of know-how, really? Like I said, Wendy just happened to tell me where she was going. She slipped up."

"You're something, you know that?"

"You still want me?"

"I still want you. So does Bismarck."

"Well, if Biz is involved."

There was no doubt after the kiss that followed, that he meant exactly what he said.

He and Bismarck left a few minutes later, and I went upstairs to pack what I would need for a week.

I decided to swing by my parents' house before I drove to Teo's. I wanted to check on them again. They were strong, but they had been through too much not to be marked by it. I hadn't moved back to Seabank just for the girls and Teo. I'd moved back to be close to them and to provide all the comfort I could.

I had other family here, too. One of Sean Riley's brothers lived in town, and I was working up my courage to go and see him. Once the shock died down, if he thought it was a good idea, I would ask him to break the news to his parents about me. They might even be glad to have me nearby.

I had cleared Wendy's clothes out of the closet, and Mom had carried them away. I didn't know if everything was in storage or a landfill. She had to deal with losing Wendy one step at a time, in her own way.

I realized now that we'd forgotten something important. When the moving crew had carried out the old furniture from the bedroom, I'd rescued Wendy's scrapbooks from the bottom of her dresser. With the furniture gone, I'd set them on a closet shelf.

Now I reached up and pulled down the photo scrapbook. I wasn't sure what to do with either, but eventually this should be another decision for my mother to make. There was one thing I had to do, though.

On my new bed I paged through the scrapbook. Baby Wendy, toddler Wendy, preteen Wendy, high school Wendy.

I came to the photo of Wendy holding me as an infant. I slipped it out of the scrapbook and methodically folded and tore it until there was nothing left but dust.

Who was the woman who'd reluctantly given birth to me? Had she been born with evil in her heart? Or at the beginning, had she been eager to please, eager to do the right thing? Had my parents loved her so much that one day, she started to believe she deserved anything she wanted? Had her beauty and talent made manipulation too easy? Had she always been acting when she was kind to others?

If she'd ever felt love, was it still buried deep inside, or had it been extinguished years ago?

There were so many questions that would never be answered, a sister's questions, a journalist's questions. But the one answer I did know? I had done exactly what I needed to. Whoever Wendy was, my sister, my mother, my enemy, with any luck, she would never hurt anybody again.

The man I loved was waiting across town. Someday maybe we would find a way to create our own family. I was ready to try.

★ ★ ★ ★ ★

ACKNOWLEDGMENTS

Every June I look forward to spending five days with my energetic brainstorming friends. Thanks as always to Serena B. Miller, Casey Daniels/Kylie Logan, and Shelley Costa Bloomfield, whose enthusiasm and vision make every book we work on together that much better.

Thanks, too, to our free press, whose accurate and truthful reporting of the news is fodder for every book I write. The idea for this novel came from a story in the Cleveland *Plain Dealer* more than a decade ago. Sometimes it takes that long.

Thanks to my insightful editor, Emily Ohanjanians, and my equally insightful agent Steve Axelrod for their encouragement and input. Thanks to the art department at MIRA Books for this cover, which I loved the moment I saw it— words they never expected to hear.

Special thanks to fabulous authors Jayne Ann Krentz and Diane Chamberlain, who volunteered to read the manuscript and then gave me wonderful quotes for my cover.

Every author knows that when doing research, the questions we forget to ask are the ones that get us in trouble. So, as always, any mistakes in this novel are my own. That said, the staff of Central Florida K-9 in Orlando enthusiastically allowed a stranger to spend most of a day at their sides learning what they do and how they do it. My thanks to Rock Galloway, the director of training and operations, Rina, Sarah and JT, instructors, and Paul, the kennel tech. I have such admiration for all of them. They successfully work with many kinds of dogs, often aggressive and difficult. Their love and respect for their work and the dogs under their care is obvious.

Imagine my surprise when after plotting this book, we added a K9 officer to our own family. My thanks to Eric Smith, of the St. Petersburg, Florida police department, who gave me colorful insights into the life of a K9 officer, including some real life encounters he and others have experienced.

My thanks, too, to the creators of my favorite true crime podcasts: *Accused, Breakdown, In the Dark, Serial* and *Criminal.* Each one features professional, in depth reporting, and helped me create Ryan's fictional podcast, *Out in the Cold.*

Finally thanks to my husband, Michael McGee, who fixed delicious meals and brought me countless cups of tea as I finished this novel. I'm sure that without his love and support, suggestions and critiques, I would never have written more than seventy novels, nor wanted to.

A
FAMILY
OF
STRANGERS

EMILIE RICHARDS

Reader's Guide

mira

1. As the novel begins, Wendy asks her younger sister, Ryan, for a surprising favor. While the two sisters aren't particularly close, Ryan feels obligated because of her ties to Wendy and their parents. In Ryan's situation, would you have agreed to move back home and take care of Wendy's young daughters? Have you ever been in a situation where you've had to drop everything and put the needs of your family first?

2. Ryan hardly knows her nieces and isn't particularly fond of them. How well do you think she managed as their caretaker? Did you like or dislike her parenting style? Did Ryan develop a new relationship with Holly and Noelle as the book progressed?

3. Four years before the book begins, Ryan fell in love with K9 officer Teo Santiago, until her stubborn miscalculation nearly ended both their lives. Did you believe they could surmount the trauma of their past and gradually find their way back to each other? Was time the healer? Did both of them grow enough in the interim to try again?

4. As a loyal younger sister with investigative skills, Ryan tries to help Wendy prove she's innocent of murder. At what point in the novel did you begin to believe Ryan's loyalty was going to be seriously tested? Did you think she accepted too many things about Wendy at face value? Could you understand why?

5. Imagine that a member of your own family came to you and asked for your help because they believed the police might soon suspect them of murder. Where would you draw the line? Would you be able to see that person clearly, despite a lifelong history of love and acceptance? Would you be able to question your mutual past and form new, logical conclusions?

6. All families keep secrets, some large, some small. Arlie, Dale and Wendy chose to keep the whole story of Ryan's birth a secret. Could you empathize with their choice? Are lies always wrong, or are they sometimes appropriate? Once revealed, did Wendy use this particular secret to try to form an even stronger bond with Ryan? What did that say about her?

7. Do you believe it's possible for anyone to hide their true nature from the people they love? Have you experienced this in your own life? Have you discovered that someone you thought you knew was really someone entirely different? Do we ever see the people we love clearly? Do we choose not to see what we don't want to face?

8. Ryan is torn by nearly impossible choices in this novel and chooses her love of family over her love of the law. Teo counsels her otherwise. Could you understand both their points of view? Did you believe they could find a way to still respect and love each other, despite their differences?

9. Did you believe that Holly and Noelle ended up exactly where they should be at the novel's end?

10. After everything her family endures, do you think Ryan's new episodes for *Out in the Cold* will be even more insightful, and more compassionate? Has she learned as much about herself as she's learned about her family?